BOOK OF LOVE

ERIN SATIE

LITTLE PHRASE PUBLISHING

CHAPTER 1

A listair Chandos, Duke of Stroud, welcomed the drum major into his office with a hearty handshake and a cheery, "Can I offer you some tea? It's dreadfully cold out."

Pale morning light bathed the large and perpetually cluttered room perched several stories over the quiet streets of Mayfair. A thick carpet muffled their steps, and steam curled from the teapot.

"Thank you, Your Grace." The drum major, a tall, wiry man with a dusting of gray in his hair, inched toward Alistair's desk as though it might bite him. He watched Alistair pour with nearly tangible dread.

"Sugar?" Alistair asked. "Cream?"

"Oh, no. No. Thank you, Your Grace." The drum major pinched the narrow, arabesqued handle of his cup between thumb and forefinger and took a single, tentative sip. He savored the flavor—it was excellent tea—and quickly returned the cup to its saucer.

"I'm not sure when *exactly* I'll be needing a marching band," Alistair began.

The drum major's shoulders slumped fractionally. Unlike other marching bands in the region, most of them boasting a wider repertoire or better synchronized steps, the drum major's

1

band had no engagements booked over the coming months, the coldest and bleakest stretch of winter.

He rallied. "I'm sure we'd be able accommodate your schedule…"

"Which is why I'd like to hire you for the rest of the season," Alistair finished.

"The… season?" the drum major's hand, which had crept close to the teacup, vanished into his lap.

Hope hit some people hard.

"So that you can assemble on very short notice," Alistair explained. "You'll need to be in uniform, instruments at the ready, all day and for some of each evening. I may only be able provide an hour's warning before you begin to play."

Now the drum major sounded confused. "You need a *marching band* on short notice?"

"You'll perform for acquaintances of mine." Alistair leaned forward, excited to put his plan in motion. "You'll form up in front of their house and then, when they venture forth—*only* when they're headed to a specific location, and *every* time they're headed to this specific location—you'll follow behind."

"It sounds like a…" The drum major glanced across the desk, took in the gold pen perched beside a ceramic inkwell shaped like a snail shell, flitted behind Alistair to heavy velvet drapes tied back from the wide window with ropes of braided silk, and hesitated.

"Prank?" Alistair nodded. "Exactly. It's a prank. You'll have full-time work through March at least, a comfortable and convenient place to assemble and rehearse, and of course we'll provide incidentals like food and coal." Alistair spread his hands, smiling sweetly. "My secretary, Mr. Wallace Fisk, will organize everything. I'll instruct him to accommodate all reasonable requests and he is a marvel of promptness and efficiency."

The drum major's expression sagged with a mixture of disappointment and relief—a combination Alistair encountered rather often. To be precise: a combination he *provoked* rather often. But what was he supposed to do? *Not* make a generous offer that the drum major couldn't refuse?

∼

THE BAND'S first outing took place less than a week later. Alistair carried word himself, incognito in an ill-fitting brown suit, so he could spectate afterward. The band had settled into a flat he'd leased for the occasion, empty but for the tables clustered around piping-hot stoves and the small garden that they'd converted into a rehearsal space.

"If any journalists show up, I'd appreciate it if you not mention who hired you," Alistair warned the drum major. His secretary, Fisk, had reminded him several times to emphasize the point.

"It is a secret?" the drum major wondered.

"That's a strong word," Alistair hedged.

"Of course I'll respect your wishes," he hastened to add.

"It's not an *important* secret."

The drum major startled. He seemed awfully surprised for someone who'd just asked a pointed question.

"It's a *little* secret," Alistair soothed. "A *friendly* secret."

"As you say."

"Nothing to worry about."

"I will endeavor not to worry, Your Grace."

"You needn't make it sound so difficult," Alistair complained, which made him feel peevish. He changed the subject. "Enough fretting! Lead on."

The drum major called his flock to order with a sharp, "Ten-*hut*!" and within minutes the musicians had assembled in the square where the Hemsworth family, well-heeled and well-connected members of the landed gentry, kept a townhouse.

Alistair had hired the band to follow the Hemsworths whenever they set out to visit the Olds, also well-heeled and well-connected members of the landed gentry. One of the Olds—specif-

ERIN SATIE

ically the eldest son and heir Christopher Old, nickname Chilly—was an old school chum turned bosom companion, confidant and accomplice in Alistair's many schemes.

When a friend needed a favor, Alistair spared no effort. In this case, Chilly was struggling to redirect the attentions of a matchmaking mama. Mrs. Hemsworth's attempts to secure Chilly as a son-in-law were getting in the way of Chilly's efforts to reconcile his parents to the girl of his choice, Nell Dowell. Chilly had been in love with Nell for years, and his parents had been begging him to look elsewhere for just as long.

Mrs. Hemsworth wanted Chilly to marry her daughter, Laura. Chilly's lack of interest in Laura hadn't deterred Mrs. Hemsworth; she'd been campaigning primarily with Chilly's mother, Mrs. Old.

Enter the marching band. They formed into crisp lines, hefting their instruments. Momentarily a fine, unmarked carriage rolled out from the mews and slowed to a halt at the Hemsworths' front door.

Laura Hemsworth emerged from the townhouse, followed by her mother. Laura was young, pretty, and well-dowered. A fine choice for any young man who hadn't already pledged himself elsewhere. Mrs. Hemsworth was older, still handsome, the sort of woman who paired dull gowns with bright patterned shawls and thought herself very fashionable for it.

The drum major cast an inquiring glance at Alistair, who nodded.

The two Hemsworths vanished into the carriage. Their driver shook his reins, urging the horses into motion. The drum major raised his baton and drums began to roll, trumpets to blare. A flautist waved traffic to halt as the group flowed into the street, keeping close to their accelerating quarry.

Alistair laughed so hard he stumbled into the balustrade of a nearby stairwell, clutching his sides to contain his mirth.

The next day, the drum major visited to meet with Fisk. Alistair couldn't resist the urge to join them; he suggested another round of tea.

"We lost the carriage after only a few minutes," the drum major apologized, ignoring the tea. "On busy streets, even when traffic is light, it would be dangerous to move any faster but we are anxious not to disappoint—"

"Please stay safe. I'd be miserable if anyone were hurt," Alistair interrupted. "To be perfectly honest, it would be a disaster if you followed them all the way to their destination. Just keep doing what you're doing. I'm very happy."

The second outing went swimmingly, as did the third and fourth. Passersby collected around the band as it formed into rows, excited for an impromptu parade. A few journalists loitered by the shopfront where the musicians spent most of their days rehearsing, always hungry for light, funny stories with which to leaven their grimmer news. (Alistair kept well clear of them—he was, fortunately or unfortunately, easy to pick out of a crowd.) The Hemsworth ladies pointedly refused to acknowledge their musical accompaniment, while their driver marshaled all his skill to outpace them.

The fifth time that the Hemsworth ladies exited their home to find a marching band crisply arrayed opposite, forty members strong in matching uniforms with polished brass tubas shining in the sun and drumsticks at the ready, clarinets lifted and lips pursed, Laura Hemsworth paused on the stoop.

Mrs. Hemsworth tried to hustle her daughter into the waiting carriage but Laura wouldn't budge. She turned around and went right back inside. Mrs. Hemsworth stiffened, arms rigid as a pair of pokers with her gloved hands curling into angry fists, and followed suit.

For Chilly's sake, he hoped she'd give up. For his own, he hoped she wouldn't. He was having too much fun.

CORDELIA KELLY HAD BEEN RAISED in a fashion that folk in her small town described as "unconventional." Her father, a judge of some repute, had educated his only child in traditionally masculine subjects like history and philosophy, cutting back on the usual instruction in dance and deportment.

He regretted it now.

If she'd never learned history or philosophy, she would not have rebelled against him—she wouldn't have been able to see his hypocrisy so clearly, could never have articulated her objections to it so well. If he hadn't instilled her with strong principles, she couldn't have clung to them long after a properly raised daughter would have surrendered to obedience.

If he'd treated her like he was supposed to treat a daughter, she'd still be at home. She'd be comfortable, all of her material needs taken care of completely, invisibly, almost without her noticing. She certainly *wouldn't* be living unmarried and unattached in London, sharing a flat with a friend and struggling to transform a hobby into a career.

She felt a bit young to be observing, with wry humor, that life did not always go according to plan. Neither her mother, her father, nor least of all herself would have planned this. Yet here she was, a tradeswoman knocking at the townhouse where her best client resided, desperate for a new commission.

A footman answered. "Mrs. Dowell is expecting you, Miss Kelly," he informed her, taking her outdoor things. "Go on up."

While the shell of the rented townhouse had no personality at all—rooms painted white, identical curtains of faded green velour framing every window—the Dowells had made it their own. Colorful pictures hung from the walls, most of them capturing members of the family at leisure: in a rowboat on a silvery lake, curled up before a fireplace with a silky-haired hound, strolling along an arbor path. Cordelia found the paintings sloppy but charming, an opinion she had *just* tact enough to keep private. The furniture was eclectic, a mix of new and old, cheap and dear. One couldn't quite tell if the Dowells had just fallen on hard times or just climbed out of them.

Cordelia ascended one flight of stairs and turned left, toward the parlor. She knew the route well by now—she'd completed three substantial commissions for Mrs. Dowell and had high hopes for a fourth.

Mrs. Dowell, like many members of the leisured class, hosted friends at her country estate for visits that lasted for days or even weeks. She fostered a literary, artistic environment at these gatherings and had come upon the idea of "setting the tone" by presenting each guest with a welcome gift: a specially bound volume of their favorite book.

Several successive strokes of luck had brought Cordelia to Mrs. Dowell for that first commission. She'd purchased a box of fabric scraps from a theater, which included a number of gorgeous patterned silks that had been used in the making of costumes. The manager of Hatchards had, after much coaxing, featured several of the books she'd made with this silk in the display windows of his shop. And finally, Mrs. Dowell had *noticed* the display at just the right time.

Cordelia had lavished every detail of that first commission with care, ensuring that she hadn't needed luck to secure a second commission, or the third. By now, they had a process. Once Mrs. Dowell had finalized her guest list, she invited Cordelia to tea. She spent the better part of an afternoon sketching out the character of each guest—their tastes, their occupations, their quirks. She wanted Cordelia to feel like she knew these strangers, allowing her to customize the volumes in a way that made each guest feel seen, understood, and welcomed by their gift.

The copious notes Cordelia took during these teas guided her in the selection of materials. She returned to Mrs. Dowell periodically with questions and samples, since the books couldn't easily be changed once they were finished.

She'd learned to bind books as a hobby, freely experimenting with new materials and techniques instead of conforming to any established tradition. She'd read every single book that she bound. She thought of her bindings as a response to the text, a cross between a review and a tribute.

But now she bound books for money. The books she made for Mrs. Dowell were beautiful, but she didn't love them the way she loved the ones that she used to make for herself, or for the circulating library she'd founded with her best friend, Bonny.

Bright, overlapping chatter spilled into the corridor. Cordelia paused at the threshold and peeked inside, where the Dowells— Mr. and Mrs. Dowell along with their three children, Charles, Nell, and Winny—fairly vibrated with excitement.

"I'm telling you," said Winny. At nineteen, she was the youngest and least sophisticated of the Dowell children. Nevertheless, she considered herself a much-needed voice of wisdom in the family. This was particularly funny since she, like all the Dowell women, had a wide, round-cheeked, baby face. "The Duke of Stroud hired that band."

"You don't know that," put in Charles, the eldest at twenty-three. He took after his father, rather more dull in both appearance and personality than the ladies.

"I don't." Winny pointed a finger at her elder sister. "But Nell does."

"I don't know anything," protested Nell, middle child and eldest daughter. Slim and tawny and ever so slightly fey, she had a sly, feline air that (unjustly or not) undermined her claims of innocence. "I haven't the least clue about—"

"Don't overdo it, dear," murmured Mrs. Dowell, their mother. With her wide jaw and high, broad cheekbones, her moon-round face remained—at times sweetly, at times poignantly—girlish, despite the threads of gray blending gracefully into her light brown hair.

Nell subsided into silence.

Winny cackled. "Do you see? Nell is trying to keep a secret, and that's all I need to know to piece the rest together. The band only shows up when Laura Hemsworth is going out. What's so special about Laura? Maybe, possibly, the fact that she wants to marry the dearest friend of a known prankster?"

"It's Mrs. Hemsworth that wants the match," Nell countered. "I doubt Laura has any say at all."

"I wonder what it's like to have such an obedient daughter," Mrs. Dowell mused aloud.

"Dull," Nell deadpanned. "Very dull."

Right at that moment, Mrs. Dowell caught sight of Cordelia. "Miss Kelly!" she called cheerfully, drawing the gossip session to an end. "Right on time, as always. Let's find a quiet place to talk, shall we?"

Cordelia followed Mrs. Dowell to a little sewing room on the other side of the house, which was warm and cozy with a view of the winter-barren back garden and the mews.

"I ought to have cancelled this appointment but things have been changing so quickly I didn't have the chance." Mrs. Dowell gestured Cordelia into a low cushioned chair. "I've had to reconsider the commission I had planned."

Cordelia hid her disappointment, though it was bitter. She needed to sell a book a week just to make ends meet. Every commission she lost meant more time spent searching for new ones, squeezing the time she had for crafting. "I understand. If you should decide, in the future, that you have need—"

"Oh, try not to be discouraged! In fact, there's a possibility—I shouldn't talk about it, I really shouldn't—but there's a possibility that I'll have a substantial commission for you in the near future... only everything is up in the air."

Cordelia didn't get her hopes up. She'd known people who softened bad news with a cushion of false hope—a coward's tactic, but the world was full of cowards.

"Once things are more settled, I'll have you back for a proper sit-down."

"I am at your disposal," Cordelia assured Mrs. Dowell.

"Thank you for understanding." Mrs. Dowell beamed in a bright, final sort of way. "You'll hear from me in a week, one way or another."

They said their goodbyes, all the little pleasantries

surrounding a leave-taking only slightly hurried by Mrs. Dowell's desire to return to the family huddle in the salon.

Cordelia wondered what had thrown the Dowells into such a state, while simultaneously chiding herself for nosiness. Mrs. Dowell was a client, not a friend. They were not equals, and the various travails of her life were of no concern to Cordelia.

She nearly collided with a stranger as she gained the pavement. A very *large* stranger. He stood at least a head taller than she, with shoulders a prize bull would envy and arms the circumference of cured hams.

"Beg your pardon," she said sharply, and tried to swerve around the obstacle.

"My fault, of course," the man replied in a bright, cheery, and decidedly upper-crust tone. "Say, what's the mood like inside?"

The giant was handsome, in addition to being large. Biscuit colored from top to toe, with skin the color of fresh dough and hair the warm golden brown of bread crust baked to perfection, all capped off by a blinding smile. Very white teeth.

Some women would have been charmed, but not Cordelia. By coincidence—or, perhaps, not such a coincidence—the man who'd sparked her flight to London, Charles Gavin, had also been large, well-bred, and handsome.

To be fair, Charles Gavin had never had much interest in Cordelia. He'd courted her best friend, Bonny Reed. When Bonny chose someone else, he'd punished her. Cordelia had taken Bonny's side in the resulting scandal, and that had been enough to alienate her from the community she'd been born to, the family she'd trusted so blindly.

Charles Gavin was the sort of man who took what he wanted, gave nothing in return, and considered it the natural order of things. Events proved him right often enough to make Cordelia sick.

But it would be wrong to jump to conclusions about this stranger. They were different people. For one thing, the stranger was quite a bit taller.

"None of your concern," she answered.

Instead of being offended, the giant regarded her like a toddler presented with a new toy. Rapt and curious and much too easily distracted. "How do you know it isn't?"

"If it *is* your concern, go inside and find out for yourself," Cordelia told him, still trying to scoot around his massive bulk. He took up the whole pavement and, unless he shifted himself sidewise, she'd only get past by swerving into the street.

"But I'd rather ask you."

"You did ask," said Cordelia. "I refused to answer. The exchange is over."

"All right, all right." The giant raised his hands in surrender, though his hazel eyes continued to sparkle mischievously. "I understand."

"What a tremendous relief. Would you please step aside?"

"Of course!" He grinned. "But before I do… you can tell me if the family seemed happy, can't you? Blink once for yes."

Cordelia summoned her fiercest glare.

The man blinked rapidly, apparently dazzled. "What's your name?"

He'd understood her request to step aside as an invitation to ask more intrusive questions. Cordelia had no intention of humoring him. She feinted right and, when he tried to block, quickstepped around him to the left.

He gave chase. "Do you want to know mine?"

"Not in the least." Cordelia noted, with a cynicism that still felt new to her, that though he wore a plain suit of indifferent quality, both his boots and gloves were new and very fine. Something not quite right about that.

"That's too bad," murmured the man. "Well, have a nice day. Perhaps we'll meet again? If you're interested—"

Cordelia continued on her way without looking back.

CHAPTER 2

With Mrs. Dowell's commission in limbo, Cordelia no longer had enough paying work to keep busy. A new client, Mrs. Hillier, had commissioned a set of journals. A devoted diarist, she wrote on a schedule, filling exactly five pages every day and finishing exactly four volumes in a year. She'd ordered a single volume late in the previous year, and now she wanted a complete set, with uniform leather binding but unique, seasonal endpapers painted in watercolor.

Cordelia hunted through her records for notes she'd made about the earlier project. A book was stitched and pressed together from its component parts: covers, spine, endpapers, and book block. These parts could be further disassembled: a cover divided into recto and verso, a book block separated into signatures, the signatures into individual sheets of paper.

In general, books were categorized by size. Size was defined by the number of times the original sheet of paper used to make the signatures had been folded. Fold it once to make a folio, twice to make a quarto, thrice for an octavo, and so on. The fold aligning with the spine would be sewn, the other three cut with a razor to create four, eight, or sixteen pages. The resulting pamphlet was called a signature. Book blocks were made by stacking a series of signatures side by side, in the right order, and binding them together.

Ordinarily she bought finished book blocks from a publisher, printed but unbound. Books were expensive and most collectors used them as decoration, once (or if) they'd been read. Publishers accommodated them. She'd never made a journal before, so her first task would be the creation of blank book blocks.

The fundamentals of bookbinding resulted in finished volumes whose total number of pages divided cleanly by four. Always, every time. The average year had three hundred and sixty-five days. 1856, being a leap year, had three hundred sixty-six. She had to divide those days into portions that felt seasonally appropriate, formed a matching set, and, as a matter of professional pride, avoid left over blank pages along the way.

According to her notes, Cordelia had supplied the first volume with enough pages to last Mrs. Hillier through March 24, the day after Easter. With a calendar and a sheet of paper near to hand, she calculated how many pages the remaining volumes would require. The period from March 25 to the June solstice on the 20th added up to 88 days, also dividing cleanly by four.

The September equinox formed a natural endpoint on September 22 for the third volume, adding up to 94 days but leaving two pages left over. September 23 through the end of the year totaled 100 days or 500 pages, which fell badly out of balance with the first volume, much slimmer at only 420 pages.

After some thought, she cut four days out of the final volume, leaving it to cover a 96 day period, and added them to the second, bringing it up to 92. Nothing to be done about the two wasted pages in the third volume, but the others would be exactly right. And they all began and ended at important seasonal turning points.

If she were fortunate enough to receive a second commission, she'd make the first volume a bit longer next time. Easter had seemed like a fitting end to the first quarter of the year, but a few days more would have given the whole better balance. But she couldn't think of any other improvements.

She'd spent a full day selecting the paper she used for the first volume, first collecting samples and then testing them for ink absorption and bleed through. With the additional commission in hand, that effort had paid off. She sent in an order for the sheets she'd need. Inevitably, the notice that she could pick them up came on a day as grim and gray as the season had seen, with a bank of low clouds blotting out the sun and spitting icy sleet onto anyone forced to venture out.

Cordelia bundled up in her warmest clothes and tucked a folded length of oilskin cloth inside her coat to keep the paper dry. After making her purchase, which the shopkeep wrapped in waxed paper, she swathed it in the oilskin. One layer of protection might suffice, but she felt safer with two. Then she hurried home with the bundle in her arms, terrified of every ice patch on the pavement. A single stumble could ruin the paper and with it, her profits.

She climbed three flights of stairs to reach the flat she shared with Ruby Twisby and let herself in, removing her hat and gloves with a weary sigh. The door to the left was shut, Ruby most likely inside and hard at work. Cordelia turned right, toward her own room, pausing at the threshold.

She was a tidy, methodical person. She and Ruby split the cost to hire a girl to cook and clean, but she could only do so much. Over the last year, Cordelia had taught herself to sweep and dust, scrub and polish. She kept her personal space clean and organized.

When she departed the flat that morning, she'd left behind bookbinding tools sorted neatly into cases, scraps into the trash, and the trash emptied. She'd cleared her desk and rubbed it down with oil, so that the wood would be smooth and dry when next she sat down to work.

This evening the clean, uncluttered surface of her desk had an occupant. A porcelain dog.

A porcelain *dog*.

She took a single step into her room, glancing left and right, the hair at the back of her neck prickling. The modest space didn't contain any hiding places large enough for a human. She looked anyhow.

Had the mail come? Had a friend left it for her? If Bonny had sent her a present, it would have arrived in a box. But perhaps Olympia or Tess had dropped by with it. If so, Ruby would have had to let them in. Ruby would remember their visit.

Cordelia retraced her steps down the corridor and knocked. After a bit of shuffling and knocking about, Ruby opened the door. Thanks to her half-Indian ancestry, she had long black hair of astonishing thickness which she wore combed smooth against her skull and twisted into a tight bun at her nape. She would have looked mannish if it weren't for the glorious abundance of lashes that framed her large, dark eyes and the ripe fullness of her lips.

Ruby wrote mystery novels under the name R.E. Timothy. They'd met through a lucky coincidence: her mother hailed from the same small seaside town as Cordelia. When Mrs. Twisby discovered that Cordelia and Bonny were enthusiastic readers of her daughter's books, she'd arranged an introduction.

Upon meeting, they'd gotten along so well that Ruby had offered to rent Cordelia the spare room in her flat. What's more, she'd guided Cordelia through the difficult early stages of independence. How to open a bank account, how to carry her coin in a city rife with pickpockets, how to boil water on the hob.

Cordelia admired Ruby. She made her own way in the world. She lived wholly on income that she earned from writing books and articles. Her remarkable success had afforded her this beautiful, spacious flat in Soho.

Today she wore a man's silk smoking jacket over an Indian ensemble of loose trousers and a tunic made of fine thin cotton.

"What's the matter?" she asked crisply.

"Did you leave a porcelain dog on my desk?"

"A what?"

"A porcelain dog."

Ruby blinked. After a brief pause, she asked, "There's a porcelain dog on your desk?"

"Come see."

Ruby followed Cordelia back down the corridor. She surveyed the scene, then took Cordelia's hand. Cordelia squeezed, comforted, and they approached the desk together.

"You didn't put it there?" Cordelia asked.

"I've never seen it before."

The dog stood about eight inches tall and half as wide, exquisitely detailed, with shiny black eyes and a little pink tongue lolling out from its open mouth, painted toenails peeking out from a fringe of fur.

Cordelia picked it up and, finding the statuette fairly light, turned it upside down. A scroll of paper poked out from the hole in the base.

Ruby swore under her breath.

"Have we fallen into one of your novels?" Cordelia asked, not entirely in jest. She plucked the paper from the dog's belly and returned the sculpture to its spot—slowly, giving herself time to gather her courage—before carefully unrolling the note.

Rules of the Game

1. You have one week to deliver Homer the Roamer to a new owner.

2. You may employ any and all means at your disposal.

3. Do not get caught!!!

4. If you are caught, you must try again.

5. Each attempt must be unique. Once a delivery attempt has failed, you must devise a new scheme.

5. Once you are successful, you may enter his new address into the Official Register at Stroud House.

A picture of two hounds rampant stamped in red wax marked the end of the letter, in lieu of a signature.

"Well, well. You weren't far off—I've read about Homer the

Roamer in the gossip rags, and I *had* thought about putting something similar in one of my novels." Ruby ran her finger along the raised rim of wax. "Where did you meet the Duke of Stroud?"

"I haven't."

"You'd remember him if you had," said Ruby. "He's a giant—it's rather comical to see him in any sort of assembly or procession, because he towers over everyone like Gulliver among the Lilliputians."

A description that fit the giant in front of the Dowell's home perfectly. The giant who'd worn a gold pinky ring, with the setting turned to face his palm. Could it be…?

"You have met him!" Ruby exclaimed.

"Not exactly," countered Cordelia. "Someone matching his description made a nuisance of himself in front of Mrs. Dowell's yesterday."

"Mrs. Dowell's?" Ruby tapped her index finger to her lips. "I wonder if we can figure out what he was up to? Let's check the papers."

Cordelia followed Ruby down to the street level, where she gave one of the sweepers on the corner a coin to fetch copies of the most recent scandal sheets. The child returned fifteen minutes later, bearing her stack aloft with both arms. Ruby handed half of the papers to Cordelia, and together they returned to the flat.

"I'm going to put on a kettle. You start reading—see if you can find anything mentioning the Dowells." Ruby headed for the hearth. "Failing that, anything especially ridiculous or absurd."

After a few minutes, the water began to boil. Ruby poured from the kettle into the pot as Cordelia asked, "Is this ridiculous enough?" and read aloud an article describing how, for several weeks now, a marching band had periodically met Lady Hemsworth and her daughter Miss Laura Hemsworth when they left their home. "Yesterday, apparently, the Hemsworth ladies abandoned their venture and the marching band appeased disappointed spectators with a lively polka."

"That's his handiwork, no doubt about it." Ruby planted a hand on her hip. "But how are the Dowells involved?"

"I didn't understand it at the time, but I overheard the Dowells discussing who'd hired the band as I arrived for my appointment," Cordelia mused. "Stroud was loitering outside. He didn't identify himself, but he tried to quiz me about their mood."

"A clue! How would you describe their mood?"

"They were enjoying their gossip. Then Mrs. Dowell told me that she'd changed her mind about a new commission, before hinting that their plans might be changing in a major way."

"Have you done anything to displease her?"

"I hope not." Cordelia winced. "But I have to consider the possibility."

"And the even greater likelihood that Stroud's prank led directly to the excitement you witnessed." Ruby handed Cordelia a cup of tea and took the paper for herself, squinting as she scanned the brief article. "The author of this article speculates the mysterious figure behind the display is a suitor. Stroud *is* a bachelor. Though one assumes he'd aim higher than Miss Laura Hemsworth."

"I don't think so." Cordelia recollected that the Dowells had spoken of the Hemsworths in a tone of distaste, even animosity. "Why would Stroud care how the Dowells feel about a woman he's courting?"

"Don't ask *me*. I know less than you do." Ruby rolled the top sheet into a cylinder and bopped Cordelia on the head with it. "If you want the good gossip, you need to ask Tess."

CORDELIA SPENT most of the next morning with a leatherworker, talking about custom-dying a calfskin hide for Mrs. Hillier. Once the negotiations had been completed and a date set for Cordelia to return and collect the finished product, she continued on to Olympia Swain's house.

Olympia's parents had died very young. Perhaps for that reason, they'd done little to prepare for their own deaths. All their enormous wealth passed to their only child, Olympia, unencumbered by trusts or entails. Olympia herself ended up in the care of a widowed aunt, Mrs. Peet, whose child-rearing could most kindly be described as negligent. Negligence suited Olympia, and the two now enjoyed a symbiotic relationship: Mrs. Peet allowed Olympia to do as she pleased, and in return, Olympia supported Mrs. Peet in lavish style.

Their mutual friend Tess—Theresa Hurley—spent most afternoons at Olympia's. She'd been born in Africa but never spoke of her childhood, though the broad outlines of her life were well-known: she'd been violently orphaned as a child, captured, and then taken as a prize by the English captain who'd given her an English name before presenting her to Queen Victoria as a *gift*.

Queen Victoria had called Tess "clever" and "pretty" and adopted her as a goddaughter, catapulting her into the upper echelons of English society. More than ten years later, Tess had progressed from clever to subtle and from pretty to beautiful. She had skin like burnished bronze, face a perfect oval, and eyes as deep and dark as a great, quiet lake.

Cordelia showed Tess the porcelain dog and the note, explaining what had happened. "I'm hoping you can help me understand, because I find this whole sequence of events baffling. What is going on? Is the Duke of Stroud *threatening* me?"

Tess, swaddled in blankets by a cosy fire with an open book upside down on her knee, reviewed the letter with cursory interest. "Not at all—though I can see how you might wonder, not knowing his reputation. He's harmless, poor man. No one takes him seriously and, what's more, serious people avoid him."

"Avoid him." Cordelia blinked. "A *duke*?"

"Oh, yes. He could be one of the most powerful men in the country, but you see how he occupies his time: by making a fool of himself pulling pranks."

"You're not fond of him."

19

"If I'd had one quarter the opportunities presented to him, you may believe I'd have made different use of them." Tess grimaced, just a discreet tug of her lips. "You've caught me in a terrible mood, I'm afraid—have you met the gentleman Olympia seems to be favoring?"

"Mr. Grant, isn't it?"

"Yes, and he is selfish, oily, and… oh, too good at what he does."

"What does he do?"

"He is a seducer—a cad, a flatterer. And obvious enough that I'm surprised Olympia has been fooled, but…"

"Can I help?"

"Speaking honestly and directly hasn't worked, so far," said Tess. "I'm open to other ideas."

Cordelia tapped the porcelain dog. "One fool at a time."

"Get rid of that dog, and point Stroud at some new distraction," Tess advised. "He'll be easier to dispose of than this leech who's attached himself to our friend."

Cordelia walked directly from Olympia's to Stroud House, ready to be finished with this game. She didn't expect the Duke of Stroud to be at home, even less to be promptly admitted into his presence—she had, in fact, counted on *neither* of those events occurring—but that was what happened.

High ceilings kept the interior airy, despite furniture predominantly of heavy dark wood. Embroidered pillows brightened the antique armchairs, fresh flowers clustered in priceless vases, statues peeked playfully from every alcove. Everything everywhere was beautiful and unique and somehow *friendly*.

Cordelia steeled herself. She had a right to be angry. Even here, where the very walls sought to disarm her.

The footman guiding her through the house swung open a pair of double doors and revealed the Duke of Stroud kneeling on a Persian carpet, rubbing a puppy's belly. The duke was big and golden and exuded good cheer like cologne applied with a heavy hand. The puppy was small and golden and thrilled by every scritch and pat.

"Who's a good boy?" Stroud crooned. The puppy's eyes rolled in delirious ecstasy. "Is this a good spot? Do you like that?"

His broad shoulders strained the cloth of his jacket, his thighs flexed against his trousers, locks of light hair hung loose over his forehead. And his broad, toothy smile *twitched* as the puppy squirmed in his huge hands, vibrating with joy.

Good grief.

A young woman sat on a sofa by the window, a book in her lap. She had Stroud's beak of a nose set in a long, narrow face— the effect was equine but elegantly so. She smiled warmly but didn't rise from her seat.

"Oh, hullo." Stroud jumped to his feet, awfully springy for a man his size. "Miss Kelly, isn't it? Did you have a question about the game?"

"No." Cordelia extracted the porcelain dog from her valise and set it on a table. "No questions."

Stroud blinked at the porcelain dog. The puppy pawed at the hems of his pristine trousers, begging for more attention. "Did you read the rules? It doesn't count if you just bring it over."

"I read them. Of course I did." The memory of fear and shock welled up fresh. "A strange object appeared in my room and I had no idea how it had gotten there. I examined it carefully."

"I didn't mean to scare you," Stroud said, immediately contrite. "Your maid offered to take Homer up for me—there was nothing inappropriate about it!"

"Nothing inappropriate about it in *your* opinion," Cordelia corrected him. "I disagree."

Stroud grinned at her, delighted. The exact same grin he'd directed at the puppy, huge and wholehearted and infuriating.

She'd refused to disclose her name, let alone her address, yet he'd discovered both by means she could only guess at, pursued her, and introduced a foreign object into her bedroom. He might be a duke, and he might live in a beautiful house where every little thing seemed charming and fun, but *she* didn't. She didn't have time for nonsense.

Nor, for that matter, did she have much patience for it.

"Perhaps it is not enough to tell you how it felt to come home last night and find out that a stranger had invaded my private space, without my knowledge or consent." Cordelia picked the dog up from the table and turned it over in her hands, admiring once again the lively eyes, the pink lolling tongue. Such fine craftsmanship. "Perhaps I should show you."

"How would you do that?" Stroud wondered.

The young woman on the sofa, not even pretending to read, scooped the puppy up from where it still gamboled about Stroud's legs and tucked the adorable little creature into her lap.

Cordelia threw the porcelain dog at the wall. It cracked at the neck, splitting into two pieces, one of which shattered when it hit the floor. Stroud shouted, as did the young woman, clapping her hand to her mouth. The puppy yipped.

"Homer the Roamer has been in my family for eighty years," cried Stroud, sounding heartbroken.

"Then you ought to be more careful with him," snapped Cordelia. "You had no right. You knew you were not welcome. I am astonished that you could ever have imagined such a threatening, invasive act to be a friendly gesture."

He didn't flinch from her gaze or from her tone. Quite the opposite. He seemed to find it invigorating.

"I rebuffed your attempts to make conversation." Cordelia seethed. "I declined to answer your inappropriate questions. I refused to tell you my *name*."

"You did," he breathed, eyes wide.

"I will not play your game," Cordelia finished. "I've no room in my life for presumptuous men who trample over my wishes for their own amusement."

CHAPTER 3

C ordelia spent the next day out of doors. She met with a
potential client who, she could tell, decided not to hire her
the moment he saw her and realized she was a woman. After
nearly half an hour of polite chitchat, he declared that he wasn't
ready to make a decision, and promised to be in touch at a later
date.

Her next appointment took her to a lovely flat in Marylebone.
A matron Cordelia had liked very much at their first meeting had
commissioned a complete set of Mary Wollstonecraft. Cordelia,
who adored Wollstonecraft, had spent more time than was
perhaps wise painting the endpapers and tooling the spines.

The matron accepted these volumes, marveled over every
detail, and then said, "I'm afraid we're a bit short right now. I'll
pay as soon as I can. It'll only be a few weeks." She sounded
apologetic but held the books deep in her lap with one arm
draped casually over the stack, which made Cordelia wonder if
she'd done this—or something like it—before.

"It will be no trouble at all for me to return with the books
when you're ready." Cordelia held out her arms in a beckoning
gesture. "Just send a note and I'll bring them right over."

"I think you can trust me."

"I made these books because I trust you," Cordelia returned, calm but unmoved. "It will be my pleasure to hand them into your possession, just as soon as you're ready to pay."

"You're insulting me," the woman snapped. "How very rude. Inexcusably rude. If you take these away now, when I've already gone to so much trouble finding you and scheduling appointments and all this ridiculous back and forth, I'll never buy from you again."

"I'm sorry to hear that," said Cordelia. Her arms remained where they were, outstretched and expectant.

"Take them, then." The woman shoved the books off her lap and onto the floor. "Pick them up and go. I didn't want them anyhow."

Cordelia dropped to one knee and collected the scattered volumes, smoothing any bent pages before stacking them neatly.

"Go on, then." The woman shouted, working herself into a fury. "Get out of here. It was shoddy work anyhow. You should be ashamed of yourself."

Cradling the books in her arms, Cordelia rose to her full height. She let herself feel her own anger, vibrating in her chest and hot on her tongue.

"Thank you for making it so easy to leave," she said, and not a single word followed her out the door.

Anger couldn't buoy her for long, though. She'd lost a whole month of work, along with the cost of materials. And she'd feel honor bound to hold onto the whole collection for at least another month, before trying to sell it elsewhere.

A disaster of a day. She would have said it couldn't get any worse but when she turned the corner onto her own street, a familiar mountain of a man waited beside the door to her building.

Oh no.

She fished her keys out of the pocket she wore underneath her skirts, which was accessible through a slit in the fabric. Once she'd gripped her fingers firmly around the right one, she steeled herself, hefted her sack, and marched firmly toward her door.

"Good afternoon, Miss Kelly," chirped the Duke of Stroud. He had a smooth, mellow voice. Higher than one might expect, given the acoustics of his lungs, and innately sweet.

"Your Grace," she murmured.

"I have a proposition for you."

"Thank you, but I'm not interested." She fit her key into the lock. She made herself move at a normal pace, neither curious nor disturbed.

Stroud snapped his fingers, and one of the sweepers—the same girl they'd sent to search for scandal sheets the week before —scurried close and piped out an eager, "M'lord?"

Stroud flipped the girl a coin. "Take Miss Kelly's things upstairs for her."

The girl beamed and held her arms out to Cordelia, ready to accept the stack of books.

"There's no need," protested Cordelia.

"Who said anything about need?" Stroud grinned. "You can play beast of burden tomorrow, or the next day. No one grows old and wishes they'd had just one more opportunity to carry heavy books up a narrow staircase."

"But—"

Stroud nudged the sweeper. "Go on and nick them."

The girl promptly snatched the books out of Cordelia's arms and darted up the stairs.

Cordelia crossed her arms over her chest. "It appears I am listening."

"Excellent!" Stroud brandished an envelope. "This is for you. Maybe."

"Oh my," Cordelia drawled in mock anticipation. "Please do tell me what wonderful surprise awaits inside, Your Grace."

"It's an invitation!" Stroud exclaimed, completely unfazed by her sarcasm. He was so disarming. "There's a discussion group for ladies. It's got a lady doctor, and a lady who owns a magazine that's all about lady things, and another lady who owns boarding houses... for ladies..." Stroud made a sour face. "I guess they all get together and discuss ladies."

Cordelia blinked. "The Soho Discussion Group?"

"You've heard of it?"

"Of course I have."

"Do you want to join?"

She hadn't thought they accepted new members. It was a select group—as Stroud had suggested, it consisted entirely of women who had achieved notable successes in their efforts to gain rights and privileges for themselves and others of their sex.

"How did you get an invitation?" she demanded. "Why should I believe it's authentic?"

"I'm a duke." His bored tone indicated he'd delivered the same answer in the same tone to a wide range of questions. "The more interesting question is: how will you convince me to give it to you?"

"Ah," Cordelia said, and nothing else.

He waited, and waited, that broad, toothy grin spreading slowly across his face. "You're not going to ask?"

"I'd like to go upstairs."

He savored this answer. Like she'd offered him a sip of fine wine. She'd clearly made a tactical error: He *enjoyed* her stubbornness. It was probably the only reason he'd taken an interest in her at all.

She ought to have embraced his plans and schemes, then bored him with poor execution. He would have drifted away of his own accord.

"I'll give you the invitation if you successfully pull off a prank."

"A prank." Cordelia ought to refuse. She didn't have time. She needed new commissions—she needed to work on the commissions she already had—one more piece of bad luck and she'd be in dire straits.

But she wanted that invitation. She wanted to meet these

women she admired. She wanted to contribute to a cause greater than her own sustenance. Most of all, she wanted to do something out of conviction rather than necessity.

The offer tempted her, as it was meant to.

It scared her, equally.

She took another look at the Duke of Stroud, so sunny and kind. After they'd met on the pavement in front of the Dowells', he'd dispatched someone to discover her name and address. After their encounter in his home, he'd found someone to ferret out her deepest hopes and desires. And then he'd manifested them in the form of an envelope that he could wave in front of her nose, like a carrot on a stick.

Seizing control of her own life had cost her. She believed she'd made the right choice, but she couldn't prove it. She had nothing to show for herself, nothing to place on the balance against the loss of her family, her home, the daily company of her dearest friend. She experienced freedom mostly as the daily struggle to make ends meet. Chasing this carrot would forfeit some of that hard-won freedom, the only thing of true value she possessed, and she wanted to accept.

She considered herself a strong person. Either she was wrong about herself, or Stroud was a very dangerous man.

"What kind of prank?" she asked.

"A good one," he answered. "Up to my exacting standards."

"That's it?"

"That's enough, I promise," he assured her, in all seriousness. "It's hard to pull off a good prank."

"I won't break any laws."

He shrugged. "That will increase the challenge, but whatever makes you happy…"

"I won't do anything unkind or mean-spirited, either," she added.

"I should hope not!"

"Do I have to execute the prank before you'll decide if it's good enough, or can I ask you beforehand?"

"It's more fun if you don't tell me."

"I did not ask what you would find fun."

"You can bring it to me for approval first," he allowed. "If you insist."

"Is there a time limit?"

"I believe in giving people all the time they need to devise something extraordinary," said Stroud. "But since I suspect you're mostly interested in the invitation, I'd take that into account. They only meet four times a year, and the next meeting is in a month."

"And if I play a prank for you, you'll give me the invitation and leave me alone?"

He grimaced, tipping his head from side to side. "Maybe?"

ALL THROUGH THE NEXT DAY, Cordelia kept her hands busy while her mind wandered. She labored over the stove in her flat to transform a sack of dried Irish moss into a tub of high-quality size, for custom marbling. Many clients didn't want—or couldn't afford—the painted inside covers she made, and marbling made a unique and beautiful alternative.

Ruby emerged several times from her writing room to put on the kettle for tea. Cordelia didn't mention Stroud until the evening, when they sat down to supper. She told the story while they ate.

"What are you going to do?" Ruby asked.

"The offer is humiliating. It makes me feel like a trained bear, lumbering onto my hind legs to dance a jig because the mighty Duke of Stroud commanded it." Cordelia scowled. A *prank*. As though she had no better use for her time. "But I can't stomach the idea of turning him down, either. If I set aside my feelings and ask myself what I'd give for an invitation to join the Soho Discussion Club, the answer is—well, a great deal. More effort than the duke is asking of me, however outrageous."

"So you'll think of a prank," said Ruby.

"Yes," Cordelia agreed, and then, "No."

Ruby fixed her with an unsympathetic look. "Make up your mind."

"It would have to be a very *particular* prank," Cordelia mused. "Complicated enough to meet his oh-so-high standards but dull enough to make him lose all interest in me."

"You've never pulled a prank before," said Ruby. "I doubt you need to worry about making an indelible impression with your first attempt. Treat it like any other disagreeable chore. Make a plan, carry it out, don't think more about it than you have to. Get it over with."

"That's good advice."

"Will you take it?"

Cordelia shrugged. "Ask me again tomorrow."

She took a cup of tea to her desk and settled in to make a list. She wrote *Pranks* at the top of the paper and underlined it twice. Then, beneath it, the number one. She stared at the blank sheet until, after a great deal of thought, she added her first item.

1. Place a lady's hat atop the statue of Nelson in Trafalgar Square.

She had no idea how she'd accomplish such a thing—the statue sat atop a tall column. What's more, she'd only come up with the idea because she'd visited Olympia recently, and Olympia had an odd, puckish habit of dressing her statues. She'd copied Olympia's idea, adding a dash of impossible absurdity.

Cordelia tapped her pen against her lips. She could come up with a better idea than that, certainly? Something a *little* more original?

2. Sneak a flock of geese into the Duke of Stroud's house without anyone noticing.

That was satisfying to contemplate (her recalcitrant imagination produced the most marvelous image of Stroud flailing to protect his hind parts from a goose's snapping bill) but she had no idea how she'd execute it. Stroud House fronted a busy street and boasted an ample staff. She couldn't have snuck a single goose through the front door without being noticed, let alone a flock of them.

It seemed to her that anyone with the capacity to execute a good prank also had a responsibility to put their abilities to some better use.

But she wanted that invitation. She desperately missed the feeling she'd had, back in New Quay, that she could make a difference. See what needed changing and come up with a plan. Here, in one of the premiere cities of the world, she hadn't the time or the *means* to accomplish much. The challenges were greater and she, fallen to the trades, smaller. But if she could join the Soho Discussion Group, that would change. She'd once again have work that truly satisfied, in the service of a worthy cause.

So, a prank. What expertise did she have that might serve in this endeavor? She was an intelligent woman but, as she'd discovered upon her arrival in London, with a limited repertoire of useful skills. Neither bookbinding nor pure stubbornness lent themselves to pranking.

Or did they? She narrowed her eyes, an idea sparking in her mind.

CHAPTER 4

Alistair perched on a windowsill and snickered while his neighbor, Lady Trickett, explained to her ten-year-old son that while, yes, a bizarre portrait of a man made entirely out of vegetables hung in their hallway, no, the strange green liquid that had begun to appear overnight in the nearest chamberpot had no relation to the portrait. The portrait was not alive, she insisted, it did not manifest as a ghost at night, and it had not exited its canvas to make use of the commode. Even if the green liquid *did* smell strongly of the spinach from which the portrait-man's hair had been made.

It smelled of spinach because it was a broth made of spinach. Alistair's cook had begrudgingly concocted it in his kitchen.

The Tricketts knew Alistair was responsible and had even tried explaining this to young George Trickett, who did not believe them. He, like the Tricketts' chambermaids, preferred to believe in a haunted painting rather than a trickster duke.

From the start, the chambermaids had been Alistair's greatest ally in this endeavor: they screamed every morning when they found the chamberpot.

Eventually, Lord Trickett would pay Alistair a visit and ask him to stop, but it hadn't happened yet. Maybe he'd decided to let his son enjoy being fooled. It was a fun, harmless sort of prank, the sort of thing little George would remember fondly as an adult. From that perspective, Alistair was doing the whole family a favor.

Or at least, so he told himself. He took the question seriously. He'd begun playing pranks because he hated for people to be afraid of him.

He'd been big from the start. He'd been so massive as a toddler he'd been forbidden from playing with other children his own age—for their safety. He'd slept in the nursery right up until the day he was sent away to school because he couldn't so much as *breathe* in any of the public rooms without breaking something. He'd sent lamps and vases to the dustbin by the dozen.

He'd arrived at Eton a lumbering, sweaty, pimply adolescent. Half the boys had flinched at the very sight of him. Of course they had. He could have ruled them with his fists and gotten away with it because of his name—a perfect, deadly combination.

He understood how it all worked. He wasn't an *idiot*.

New arrivals at Eton played servant to the senior boys, in general and in specific. A senior boy picked among the first years, choosing one to make his breakfast, polish his boots and cater to any other whim that caught his fancy. The senior boys considered it well within their rights to beat their junior charges for failures, mistakes, or laziness.

Alistair had been chosen by a lantern-jawed baronet who'd ordered Alistair to poke one of his classmates with a toasting fork. A cruel command both for the proposed victim—a short, scrawny, terrified boy—and for Alistair, who would have made a lasting first impression as a bully.

Alistair had been scared to defy the senior boy, but equally scared to obey him. The conflict raged inside him so strongly that he had not been as excruciatingly aware of his surroundings as usual. He'd knocked over a table and scattered the remains of an al fresco lunch, sending plates and scraps flying. A horde of pigeons promptly descended on the feast, all flapping wings and reckless courage, and the lantern-jawed baronet ended up with droppings in his hair.

The baronet fled the scene without waiting to make sure his orders were carried out. Alistair had turned to the boy he'd been meant to poke, stuck out his hand, and said, "Hullo."

The boy, Christopher Old, had taken it. They'd been friends ever since.

Eventually his sister had signed him up for dancing lessons, and while he hated dancing—matching his steps to those of a partner half his size felt like trying to build a ship in a bottle—he'd kept at it doggedly, for hours every week, because slowly but surely dancing taught him to be nimble. He'd found the confidence to try rugby and other sports, where his teammates appreciated his newfound agility and celebrated his size.

Fisk poked his head through the door. "Miss Kelly is asking to see you."

"Already?" He hadn't expected to hear back from her for days, if at all.

Her stubbornness had caught his attention when they crossed paths in front of the Dowells' house. She'd spied the signet ring on his hand then looked him right in the eye. No fear, no hesitation. No attempt to soften her rejection or make it more palatable. His first thought had been: *I wonder what she'd say to a man who disappointed her in bed.* The second, following quick behind: *I wonder what she'd say to a man who* didn't *disappoint her.*

Chances were, he'd never learn the answer to either of those questions (and were they mutually exclusive? A real puzzle, there), but it didn't hurt to find out her name. And address. And invite her to join in a game that he'd been playing with his friends for nearly a decade.

"Where's Flea?" Alistair asked Fisk.

"Lady Florence is reading in the salon."

"Send Miss Kelly there, would you?"

In the salon, Flea greeted him with a long-suffering sigh. "Can't you just leave this poor woman alone?"

33

"Why would I do that?"

"Because she asked you to?"

"Some people don't know what's good for them," he told her. "Besides, do you want all of Fisk's hard work to go to waste?"

It had been Fisk, of course, who sleuthed out Miss Kelly's name and address, and Fisk who'd had Miss Kelly followed until she visited someone Alistair knew—which luckily hadn't taken very long at all, as it turned out Olympia Swain was a mutual acquaintance.

"It already does," Flea retorted, picking up a book she could pretend to read as Miss Kelly walked through the door.

Miss Kelly arrived ready to do battle, which made his stomach flip in a combination of anticipation and... well... arousal. It wasn't that he enjoyed rudeness or anger or reluctance—he didn't—or took pleasure in harassing strangers, let alone women. But he liked cleverness, a quick tongue attached to a quicker mind. He liked a challenge, and real challenges were rare for a man who'd been, er, shunned by most of his peer group.

Most of all, he liked people who weren't afraid of him.

Not for nothing, he was also violently attracted to Cordelia Kelly. She was so tall and slim and fierce. Like a spear made flesh. He'd always wondered what it would be like to make love to a spear.

"Hullo, good morning. It's so good to see you." He stood and bowed, because he had manners. "How do you do?"

"I'm well." And then, grudgingly, "And yourself?"

"I'm excellent." He beamed. "Have I introduced you to my sister Florence? Would you like to meet her? She's right here."

Flea looked up from her book. "I'm sorry about Homer the Roamer but it was bound to break eventually, considering the way Rip treated it, and I don't blame you for hurrying along the inevitable."

"Oh." Miss Kelly gave Flea an appraising look. "Thank you."

"It needed to be said." Flea looked back down at her book. "Nice to meet you."

"So." Alistair rubbed his palms together. "Have you thought of a prank? I'm excited to find out what."

"As a matter of fact, I have." Miss Kelly's lips curved in a small, private smile. "Can I run it by you? I want to make sure what I've planned meets your expectations."

"Of course, of course!" He waved her to a sofa. "Why don't you take a seat?"

She sat and opened a notebook, turning the pages to show him a beautiful sketch of Trafalgar Square and the statue of Lord Nelson. She'd annotated it in an elegant, legible script, with arrows pointing to a flock of pigeons flying overhead.

"Trafalgar Square?" He felt his eyebrows climbing up his forehead. "Are you sure you want to start with something so public?"

"Quite sure," Miss Kelly replied calmly. "I have a friend who owns a hutch of carrier pigeons. He will aid me in flying a band of them across the square, with a trajectory that takes them over the top of the statue of Lord Nelson. At the right moment, we'll pull a string tied to the pigeons' feet, releasing a knot that will drop their cargo—a lady's hat—right onto the statue's head."

It was a gorgeous plan, but he felt conscience-bound to warn her against it. "I'm not sure this is a good idea."

"Why not?"

"Well, if you miss with your first attempt, you'll have to try again but find a new method. You can't just do the same thing over and over again. It's one of my rules. And there won't be many easy or legal ways to get a hat onto Lord Nelson's head."

"Then we'll have to do it right this first time," said Miss Kelly, unperturbed. "I'll be practicing with my friend in the days leading up to the release, to make sure we've perfected the maneuver."

"Practicing with his pigeons?"

"That's right."

"How exciting." Alistair grinned. "I can't wait to see you try."

"It will certainly be an event," Miss Kelly agreed.

Alistair hoped she wouldn't take it too badly when she failed. It seemed a long shot at best, especially for a novice, but perhaps she'd manage it. Stranger things had happened. Maybe he'd let her pick a different prank if it failed. She was too green to realize how difficult this one would be... and too stubborn to admit it before she'd tried once or twice.

"I take it you approve?"

"It has to succeed to count, remember."

"I would expect so." Miss Kelly smiled. "And you'll attend?"

"I look forward to it."

"Excellent. Will you be available next week?"

"I'm sure I will. Just send a note, Fisk keeps my schedule in good order."

Miss Kelly left, looking quite satisfied with herself.

"She is scheming at something," murmured Flea from her spot on the sofa.

"Like maybe she'll tie a ribbon around the lady's hat, and the ribbon will say something mean about me?"

"That sounds more like something you'd do, dear brother."

"Of course it does, it was my idea. My point is that anything she does to make the prank more interesting just makes the prank more interesting. What's wrong with that?"

"I'd wager that her notion of interesting and yours differ in material ways."

"It sounds like she's awfully dedicated to causes." He'd quizzed Olympia about Miss Kelly, so that he could obtain a good lure for her. "She set up a circulating library in her hometown. And then she came to London because of... Actually I didn't follow the whole story, but it wasn't any scandal she'd caused. She's taking a stand about something."

Flea blinked. "You're telling me Miss Kelly left her home and her family by choice? She *chooses* to live alone, in London, as an unmarried woman, and to work for her living, for principle?"

"That's what I was told."

"And you think you can persuade a woman like that to do... absolutely anything? At all?"

"Why not? The invitation was a really good idea, by the way—she's desperate to have it."

Flea continued to regard him incredulously.

"Either she's a humorless sourpuss, in which case she walks away with this invitation and we have a fair trade… or, who knows, maybe she has fun. Even strong principled women who take stands need to have fun."

"Indeed." Flea paused. "I can't wait to find out what happens next. Truly."

THE APPOINTED day arrived bright and sunny, without much wind —ideal for Miss Kelly's prank. He still doubted it would succeed, but he was glad she'd get a fair shot.

To his surprise, Flea decided to come along. She usually had no interest in his pranks. And then, during lunch, Christopher Old arrived out of the blue. Chilly—the nickname arose inevitably from his given name, initial C and surname Old—was smart and savvy in ways Alistair had always envied.

"Morning, Rip." Chilly drew up a chair at the breakfast table and perched on the edge of it. He was short, slim, sprightly. The term elfin could have been coined just for him. "You're looking well."

Alistair had earned his nickname by getting a truly staggering number of "rips" at Eton—the name for what happened when a student failed an assignment and had to bring his bad work to his house master and tutor to be signed. Now everyone called him Rip. The papers, the prime minister, the paupers who begged him for coin. Everyone.

"I wish I could say the same." Alistair noted the anxious way Chilly's foot wagged just out of sight, the seemingly-idle flicking of his fingers against lapel and cuff. "Any news from home?"

"My mother isn't speaking to me," said Chilly. "Which could mean anything."

"Not *anything*," Alistair countered. "She'd press the advantage if she thought she had it."

"Indeed she would." Chilly flashed a brief, pained grin. "But silence doesn't mean she's given up. I have no doubt she's devising a new plan of attack as we speak."

"What about the Hemsworths? Any reaction from their camp?"

"Miss Hemsworth has put her foot down. I'm told she finds the marching band *very* embarrassing and won't accept any further invitations to any domicile where I am resident." Chilly poured himself a cup of tea and raised it in a mock toast. "Not bad, Rip. Not bad at all."

Alistair rose to his feet briefly, to take a self-congratulatory bow. "So when's the wedding?"

"I wonder." Chilly spooned sugar into his tea and stirred meditatively. "How long do you think it will take to convince my parents that the companionship of a wonderful wife is worth more than an extra five thousand a year from Miss Hemsworth?"

Alistair pretended to do sums on his fingers. "So it'll be a while, then."

Chilly shrugged and sipped.

"Your mother can't *force* you to marry one of her choices," Alistair said. "Bide your time, let her wear herself out…"

Chilly shook his head. "Nell won't wait forever."

"How long will Nell wait?"

"If I can figure that out, so can my mother."

Alistair finished the thought. "And all she'd need is to hold out for a single day longer."

Chilly nodded.

"So what can you do?"

"I've talked myself hoarse pleading with her and it doesn't change a thing. My mother's mind is set." Chilly stretched out in the chair, outwardly loose and relaxed, though he continued to toy anxiously with the handle of his teacup. "Nell refuses to marry without my parents' blessing. Can't say I blame her. She won't bring a lot of money—not that I mind!—but that makes it hard for me to risk my inheritance."

"What about your father?"

"Doesn't want to get involved. Hates conflict."

"We need to push him off that fence before it gets too comfortable." Alistair grunted. "I have news about the marching band, by the way. They didn't have a single performance scheduled when I hired them but Fisk tells me they've filled out their spring program since they started chasing after the Hemsworths."

"Well, that's nice."

"Isn't it?" Alistair beamed. "I think it's because they've had so much time to rehearse."

Chilly paused with his cup halfway to his mouth, eyes narrowing. "What are you after?"

"After?" Alistair crossed his hands over his heart. "I'm here to help, Chilly. As a friend."

"And then, additionally…"

"I had an idea for a prank," Alistair admitted cheerfully. "A fun one."

"I like the fun ones," Chilly said brightly, then winced. "Let me have a word with my father first. He did like the marching band. Sends his compliments."

"I'll keep that in mind for his next birthday."

Chilly snorted. "I'll warn him."

"I'm on my way to Trafalgar Square. That woman I told you about, Miss Kelly, she's arranged to pull the most *outrageous* prank. It's sure to fail, but it'll be grand."

"Outrageous how?"

"She says she's going to have trained pigeons drop a lady's hat onto Lord Nelson's head."

Chilly whistled low. "Imagine if she pulls it off, though!"

"How could she? Just to start: where in England will she find a rope long enough to pull the release?" Alistair shrugged. He enjoyed a glorious failure more than a dull success. "Still, come see. I'm sure she'll be glad to have someone else rooting for her."

"Oh, do," added Flea from the doorway. She'd dressed for the excursion in dull brown and the strings of a horrifically frumpy hat dangled from her fingers. Flea liked to disappear into crowds, something Alistair had never been able to do. "I think it's going to be an exciting afternoon."

"You're coming, Flea?" Chilly sounded surprised. "You hate pranks."

"I suspect Miss Kelly has something interesting planned."

"More interesting than pigeons dropping a lady's hat onto Lord Nelson's head?" Alistair asked, astonished.

"That's my hope." Flea cupped one hand beside her mouth and stage-whispered, "Miss Kelly doesn't like Rip very much."

"She doesn't?" Chilly turned a speculative glance on Alistair. "That's not what you told me."

"I said she's fun," Alistair countered. "I didn't say she's fond of me."

"Why isn't she fond of you?"

"Because he keeps trying to rope her into his pranks," Flea answered. "She's not interested."

"So who came up with this one?" Chilly asked. "The trained pigeons dropping a hat...?"

"She did!" Alistair exclaimed.

Chilly turned to Flea, brow comically furrowed.

"So you'll come, won't you?" Flea prompted.

"Oh, yes, absolutely."

CHAPTER 5

For all its grandeur, with the granite-fronted facade of the National Gallery looming grandly to the north and the tiered steeple of St. Martin-in-the-Fields piercing the sky from its corner to the northeast, Trafalgar Square always reminded Alistair ever so slightly of hell. Carriages hurtled through the streets, and woe betide any two- or four-footed creature who should get in their way—the drivers had no place to swerve and no room to slow. For all that, people regularly darted through the moving gaps between the back of one carriage and the noses of the horses pulling the one following close behind, curses flying in both directions.

This deep into winter, both of the monumental fountains that anchored the plaza had frozen. Sooty ice crusted over the pale stone and dirtied the basin. Scaffolding clung to the plinth of Nelson's Column, which soared more than one hundred and fifty feet into the sky, thick and fluted, surmounted by a florid Corinthian capital made of bronze. The bulky capital did an excellent job of rendering the statue sitting atop it invisible to passersby.

At least the pigeons would enjoy an unobstructed view.

Miss Kelly waited by the scaffolding, calm and still and

straight. Her pale beauty didn't do the cheap gray fabric of her dress any favors. According to Olympia, Miss Kelly had been gently raised and much indulged by her parents, who were gentry in a small town on the coast. But she'd entered the working classes and made no attempt to disguise her circumstances.

He wouldn't have expected her to. Not Cordelia Kelly. If she doubted herself, he'd never seen it. Her confidence affected people in much the same way as his size did—others instinctively steered clear, fearing a collision with an immovable object.

She greeted him coolly, a faint smile playing about her lips that made him positively *itch* with anticipation.

"May I introduce you to my friends?" he asked.

"Please do."

"You remember my sister, Lady Florence? Normally she can't stand my pranks, but for some reason she can't wait to see yours. You should call her Flea, like all her friends."

Miss Kelly curtseyed. "It's a pleasure to see you again, Lady Florence."

Flea covered her mouth to hide a giggle. "Likewise, Miss Kelly. A very great pleasure."

Alistair mock-scowled at his sister before he directed Miss Kelly's attention to Chilly. "And this is Mr. Christopher Old. An old friend from Eton—one of the best men I've ever known."

Chilly bowed. "Miss Kelly. I've heard so much about you."

Miss Kelly paused with her gloved hand extended. "You have?"

"All good things," he assured her. "Though I'm mostly here on Flea's recommendation. She piqued my curiosity."

Alistair rubbed his palms together. "Are you nervous?"

Miss Kelly stared blandly into his eyes. Hers were the color of blued steel, inherently intimidating. "No."

He beamed. This woman was a *delight*. "Glad to hear it. What's the plan?"

"Right now we're waiting for a friend of mine."

"You're really going to do it?" Flea asked, astonished.

Miss Kelly smiled mysteriously.

"Don't be a skeptic," Alistair chided. His sister might doubt, but he'd known from the start that Miss Kelly would be bold and daring and interesting and wonderful. "She's here, isn't she? Wish her good luck."

"Thank you, Your Grace, I do appreciate your encouragement," murmured Miss Kelly. "Oh, look, I think I see her…"

Miss Kelly waved at a stoutly curvaceous redheaded woman. Square jaw, weak chin… She looked familiar, actually. They must have been introduced, though he couldn't remember exactly *where*.

"There you are." The woman leaned in to kiss Miss Kelly on the cheek before offering Alistair a curtsey. "Your Grace. What an honor to meet you again. It's a fine day, is it not? Clear skies, not too windy for a stroll."

Her low, rich voice surfaced his memory. "Miss Smith? Didn't we speak recently? About the club for ladies?"

"So we did." She blushed when he kissed the air above her gloved hands. "And you described Miss Kelly here in glowing terms. I'm delighted to tell you that my own encounters with her have absolutely borne out your high opinion."

Alistair blinked. "*Your* encounters?"

"Indeed." Miss Smith smiled warmly. "She contacted me last week with what seemed a wild story—she said that you'd offered her the invitation, which of course we'd discussed, but only if she were able to maneuver a clutch of carrier pigeons into dropping a lady's hat onto the statue of Lord Nelson."

"Um." Alistair turned a narrow gaze on Miss Kelly. "That's not exactly how it went."

"Oh? Indeed? That's concerning. What parts of her tale are untrue?" pressed Miss Smith.

Alistair scratched his nape.

"Because that hadn't been our agreement at all." Warmth leaked from her tone in little drips and drops until it had frozen harder than the ice crusted around the fountains' spouts. "Indeed,

I was shocked to learn you used an invitation to our discussion group—where we work diligently to improve women's lot in society—as the means by which you'd subject a woman to what I can only describe as an indignity."

"I'd have done the same with a man, though," Alistair protested. "I mean, fair treatment for all, that sort of thing. I'm sure Chilly here remembers a few times I encouraged him to pull a good-natured prank…"

"Oh, more than one!" Chilly bounced up on his toes and back to his heels, brimming with glee.

"Such as?" prompted Miss Kelly.

"I shouldn't describe them in mixed company."

"I'm not sure we should take His Grace's word on the subject," said Miss Kelly.

Well that was uncalled for. Alistair would never lie about his pranks. "What about the time I convinced him to hang a pair of lady's drawers from Lupton's Tower?"

"I wasn't going to mention that." Chilly winced. "In my defense, I was five and ten at the time."

"How charming," murmured Miss Smith, clearly not at all charmed. "I wouldn't want to keep you from your entertainments —or prevent Miss Kelly from joining you in disrespecting our city's monuments, should that be her pleasure—but I won't have the Soho Discussion Club used to compel her."

Miss Smith extracted an envelope from a threadbare valise. "Which is why I've come to extend the invitation to her directly. It's an unusual step, but if today's events are any indication, she'll fit right in."

"Thank you." Cordelia took the envelope and offered Miss Smith another kiss to the cheek. "I will endeavor to deserve the honor."

"I was happy to have an opportunity to rectify my earlier mistake." Miss Smith nodded to the others. "Wonderful to meet you all. Do enjoy the rest of your day!"

As Miss Smith sauntered off, Flea bit her knuckles.

"Stop that!" Alistair protested, to no avail. Flea bent double, peals of uncontrollable laughter spilling from between her fingers.

That set Chilly off. He'd acquired a distinguished chuckle over the years, but something really funny brought back the wheezy, high-pitched cackle of his youth, which split the air at a volume sufficient to attract a few gawkers.

"So there are no pigeons?" Alistair ventured.

"Not a one."

"And you haven't spent the past week practicing, like you claimed?"

"I couldn't have, even if I'd wanted to," answered Miss Kelly, her tone bone dry. "I haven't the leisure. I work while there's daylight."

Alistair had been outfoxed, shown up, beaten at his own game —and it was glorious. A grin spread across his face, wide enough to make his cheeks ache. He couldn't help it. He didn't play to win. He couldn't, really. It wouldn't be sporting. He played to *play*. He loved a good game. Loved a good player. And he loved to be surprised.

"Well done, Miss Kelly." He extended his hand for a shake. "Well done."

Miss Kelly stared at the proffered hand as though she didn't know what it was for.

Maybe she didn't. A handshake was a masculine gesture, after all, exchanged between equals. He was a slow study about most things, but he had good instincts about people. He'd wagered that she'd take the offer of a handshake as a compliment, but he hadn't considered that it might be her very first.

"Thank you." She inched her fingers closer to his without making contact.

He closed the gap, pressing her palm against his, folding his fingers over in a gentle clasp. A standard handshake, just like any other. Her grip started out limp but tightened until, when he let go, her fingers traced lines across the side of his hand.

He didn't entirely understand her reaction, but he knew by the way she stared wide-eyed at her own hand and carefully firmed her slim shoulders before meeting his eyes again, that he'd done something right. In the process, he'd caught her attention—all of it—for the first time since they'd met.

"I do not choose to spend my time in frivolous pursuits," she said finally. "I hope you can respect that."

Beside him, Flea winced. Alistair's smile never faltered. "You have my utmost respect."

Her fine eyes narrowed infinitesimally. "If you respect me, then you must, as a consequence, respect my wishes."

"I understand."

He did understand. And he'd respect her wishes. Sort of. In pranks, as in life, if at first he didn't succeed, he'd try and try again... but by a new route every time.

THE HANDSHAKE RUINED HER.

If anyone had asked, she would have insisted—as she had throughout, deceiving the friends who had such faith in her honesty—that the Duke of Stroud was a nuisance, that she cared only for the invitation he'd obtained to the Soho Discussion Club, and that she'd defied him on principle, not for fun.

This last was critical. She could not, under any circumstances, admit how she'd enjoyed thwarting him. It would be tantamount to confessing that she enjoyed his games. Which she didn't.

But he'd been so sincerely happy for her success. Like she'd given him a present. Not just any present, either. A perfect present —exactly the thing he'd most wanted—and his joy was contagious.

So she spoiled it. Deliberately and thoroughly.

"I do not choose to spend my time in frivolous pursuits." Her voice held all its usual firmness, even as her heart dropped right to her stomach. "I hope you can respect that."

The duke's expression warmed. "You have my utmost respect."

No other words could have devastated her so completely.

"If you respect me, then you must, as a consequence, respect my wishes," she pressed on miserably.

"I understand."

She believed he did. Everything she'd said and most of what she'd been careful not to say. He was a silly man but not a stupid one.

And she was very much in danger.

That was a first. A baffling, enraging, laughable first. Cordelia had spent her final years at her parents' home meeting a succession of potential husbands. They'd tempted her with scholarly men, with prosperous men, with distinguished men. She came from a good family, well-connected on both sides, and her father had risen high in his profession. Her mother had not struggled to drum up interest.

She had turned them all down. She'd identified their flaws, justifying her rejections so thoroughly that her mother threw up her hands and conceded defeat, time after time.

All along Cordelia had been painfully aware that none of her suitors liked her very much.

They didn't like the way she looked at them—too direct, too confident. They didn't like the way she spoke, always so aggressive. They didn't like being contradicted, and they *especially* didn't like being proven wrong. But it was in Cordelia's nature to speak her mind. She couldn't change it any more than she could have changed her height or the color of her eyes.

Her parents had promised not to force Cordelia into marriage. Her father had held firm, over her mother's frequent objections. Their relationship had begun to deteriorate. It had been damaged beyond repair long before Bonny's misadventure.

Cordelia believed her parents had intended to keep their promise. If it weren't for Bonny, the Kellys might have carried on as they had been for years, a family strained to the breaking point because Cordelia refused to resign herself to an unhappy marriage.

Bonny had changed everything when she'd betrayed her fiancé, Charles Gavin, with the man she eventually married, Lord Loel. She'd unleashed a scandal that had shaken their small town to its core. New Quay turned on Bonny, and when Cordelia supported her, it turned on Cordelia too. She'd been shunned, tainted by her friend's ruin.

The critical moment had taken place on a sunny afternoon only a few steps away from the church where she'd attended services since she was a girl. The townsfolk had gathered to see Bonny punished, and Cordelia had stood at her friend's side, hand in hand, come what may. Because she loved her friend but not *just* because she loved her friend. It had been the right thing to do.

A boy threw clods of mud at Bonny. A brawny man with a stone in each hand had raised his arm, ready to let fly. The rest had watched, content to accept his decision.

In the end, Cordelia and Bonny had stared the man down. He'd dropped his missiles and they'd escaped serious physical harm.

Afterwards, Bonny had returned to her husband. She'd immersed herself in her new marriage, in hard work and true love, and her view of the world had not substantially changed. She still saw the best in people, treated them kindly, wished them well.

Cordelia had gone home, where her father demanded she abandon her dearest friend. She had refused. She had explained that while Bonny had made a mistake, she didn't think it warranted complete ostracism. She understood the situation better than most of the angry townspeople, and the man Bonny had jilted, Charles Gavin, deserved the greater share of blame. Was her father aware that Charles Gavin had fathered an illegitimate child?

Yes, he'd answered. He'd known since Mrs. Gavin had

dismissed the housemaid her son had impregnated without a reference.

Would he ostracize Charles Gavin for *his* sins?

No, he'd answered. He wouldn't.

Why not?

He might not approve of Mr. Gavin's behavior, but the world judged men and women by different standards. Charles Gavin knew the rules and manipulated them to his own advantage, a fine quality in a man. Bonny and the pregnant housemaid knew the rules but refused to abide by them, behavior few appreciated in women.

Cordelia had asked her father when he started caring more about the way of the world than he cared about right and wrong. Hadn't he raised her to think for herself, to stand on principle, and hold the mob in contempt? How many times had he quoted Thomas Moore to her? Or Socrates? How often had he extolled the greatness of Galileo, whose integrity had ushered in the age of reason?

Her father, the man she'd once admired above all others, had looked her right in the eye and said, "When you tell me you'd die to defend your friend's right to be a whore, all I can think is that I have educated you very poorly indeed."

Fights had grown more frequent after that. Soon her parents had given up on persuasion and turned to threats. Her father had always taught that only the feeble-minded used force to make a point when reason could win the day, and yet when she accused him of employing just such feeble-minded tactics, he'd slapped her.

That was when she'd decided to leave. She'd explained her decision dozens of times to dozens of people, but she'd never told *anyone* about the slap. She'd never feel the same way about her father again, but she'd worshipped him for too long to shame him by speaking the truth aloud.

Before that fateful summer afternoon, Cordelia had believed that people were basically good. No one could be perfect, but the magical combination of religion, law, and education allowed creatures who'd once scrabbled in the dirt with stone tools to build cities, cross oceans, paint masterworks.

And then her own community mobilized in support of an evil cause. People she'd thought good turned on a woman who deserved mercy. She'd witnessed the full ugliness of humanity on display, and her own *family* had expected her to participate.

She no longer believed that people were basically good. Not even herself. How could she? Cordelia had been selfish at every step along the way. Selfish to subject her mother to years of fruitless searching, selfish when she stood with Bonny, selfish when she ran away.

She wasn't sure if she was an especially bad person or if selfishness and self-determination were fundamentally inseparable.

She understood, too, that choices had consequences. For example: she'd probably be a spinster for the rest of her life. A difficult woman, living without the protection of her family, without the lure of a dowry, wouldn't tempt many gentlemen into offering matrimony. They'd only be interested in *other* things.

She'd accepted that spinsterhood would be the price of independence. It had seemed a good bargain. She hadn't liked any of her suitors. They hadn't liked her. What was she sacrificing, really?

Now here was the Duke of Stroud, a man so far above her station her mother wouldn't have dared to *dream* of a match. Young and handsome, to boot. He possessed every quality that usually indicated a proud man with a tender ego, the sort she could never get along with. Yet the more she defied him the more he liked her.

And she had to wonder, a full year after she'd burned her bridges, if she'd actually made a very *bad* bargain. Because if the Duke of Stroud existed, maybe he wasn't the only one of his kind. Maybe there were other men like him, men closer to her rank, who might have been similar. She might have found a husband who liked her exactly as she was, who treated her as an equal, and forged a true partnership.

She hadn't known what to do at first. He had a loose, easy grip and enough confidence to smooth over her own awkwardness. She'd mimicked him until, right before letting go, Stroud had given her hand a little squeeze. A tiny signal of intent, gentle and invisible but oddly reassuring.

It had been the most painful moment of her life. Any memory that compared—holding Bonny's hand while the people of New Quay threw dung, her father's slap—had been different in one crucial respect: she'd been sure of herself and her choices.

Not this time. She now faced the possibility—no, the *probability,* the *drearily high likelihood*—that she had made a grave mistake. But it was too late to do anything but carry on with her life, newly conscious of all she'd given up.

So, yes. She'd been rude to the Duke of Stroud. Ruder than he deserved. But she needed to keep steady. She had to be able to rely on herself, and that required focus and discipline. She had no room in her life for a man who made her ache with regret.

CHAPTER 6

Cordelia soothed herself with a visit to Olympia. Olympia flitted through high society like a bee gathering nectar, efficient and tireless, but her door was always open to her intimates. Sometimes Cordelia arrived and had the whole vast townhouse to herself. Sometimes she'd find Tess taking tea alone or bent over a writing desk. Eventually, Olympia returned, and she was always glad to see them.

She called out her destination on her way out of the flat, so Ruby wouldn't worry, and Ruby answered, "Wait, I'll join you!" so they left together and split the cab fare.

They found Olympia lounging about in a frilly dressing gown, sipping chocolate with her golden hair gathered into a loose chignon at the nape of her swanlike neck. She invited Cordelia and Ruby into the parlor attached to her bedroom, a sort of gilded pastry-puff decorated in shades of pink and cream.

"I've been very lazy today," Olympia admitted, pouring cups of chocolate for Ruby and Cordelia. "Scold me if you must."

"Tell me about this strange word, 'lazy.'" Ruby kicked out one leg, toe pointed, and extended both arms overhead in a luxuriant stretch as she relaxed into the pillows. "I'm not familiar with the concept."

"Yes, just like that." Olympia grinned. "You're wonderfully obliging."

Ruby winked—she was one of those rare people who could wink convincingly. Cordelia lifted her cup to her lips to hide a smile and closed her eyes as the rich flavor hit her tongue—perfectly balanced between sweet and bitter, thick with cream. If there was one thing Olympia understood perfectly, it was self-indulgence.

"This is exactly what I needed," said Cordelia, settling in gratefully. "Tell me about being lazy, Olympia. Every single detail—especially the boring ones."

"If that's what you want..." Olympia trilled a little laugh, sweet and musical. "You do look a bit frazzled. Let's see. I woke up around noon and had breakfast in bed. Fruit, mostly, with little fried oatcakes and fresh jam and soft whipped cheese."

A knock at the door preceded Tess's arrival. She murmured her thanks to the footman as she entered, wearing a gown of acid green silk that set the rich brown of her skin aglow. The dress, along with the citrines glittering at her ears and throat, suggested she'd spent the morning out and about.

"Tess!" Olympia cried. "Where have you been? It's been *ages*."

"We saw each other yesterday." Tess poured herself a cup of chocolate and made herself comfortable. Her whole demeanor changed at the first sip: her expression opened and warmed, the stiff set of her shoulders softened.

"Every minute without you feels like a year," Olympia exclaimed.

Tess rolled her eyes. "Cordelia, Ruby. What brings you here?"

"I've spent so long at my desk this week that I lost the ability to read my own handwriting," Ruby answered brightly.

Olympia shuddered.

"What about you, Cordelia?"

"I just wanted to see my friends," Cordelia admitted.

"She was asking me to tell her about my day," Olympia cut in.

"But I've thought of something more interesting to tell you all: I'm planning a little party. Doesn't that sound fun?"

"Oh, a party?" Tess tapped her lower lip with one finger, mock-confused. "I wonder what the occasion could be…"

"I want everyone to meet Mr. Grant, of course!" Olympia clapped excitedly. "It's not a secret."

Ruby hummed. "Mr. Grant, is it? Has he proposed?"

"I told him not to."

Tess's good humor vanished in an instant. "You did *what*?"

"I told him not to," Olympia repeated. "I enjoy courting too much! The endless scheming is a delight—finding ways to meet, to enjoy a little private conversation, maybe exchange a kiss or two…"

"You're playing a dangerous game," Ruby warned.

"I *know*." Olympia sighed happily. "Eventually I'll have to decide, one way or the other. But for now…"

"Since your plans are still so tentative, I'd be grateful if you chose a date that falls after the next meeting of the Soho Discussion Club," said Cordelia.

"The Soho Discussion Club?" Olympia repeated. "What's that?"

"It's a group of women that meets periodically to discuss how to improve conditions for our sex," Cordelia answered.

Olympia wrinkled her delicately sloped nose. "What a bore."

"No doubt you'd hate it, Olympia." Ruby shrugged one shoulder philosophically. "But it sounds perfect for Cordelia. To each his—or her—own taste, isn't that right?"

"It sounds like a great deal of work," observed Tess. "I hope it's worth the effort."

"Progress is always worth the effort," said Cordelia. "It's my understanding they've spent the past year circulating a petition to grant married women many of the rights they lose the moment they arrive at the altar—the right to sign contracts, to sue and be sued, to control their own income."

"It sounds wonderful when we say that marriage makes man

and woman into a single flesh," murmured Ruby. "Somewhat less charming when the reality is that, legally, for all intents and purposes, the woman ceases to exist as a result of the union."

"So many women I meet seem to envy my freedom." Olympia canted her head and began to speak in a high falsetto, fluttering her lashes. "'Oh, Olympia, with your vast fortune and your lax guardian, what a wonderful life you must lead.'" Returning to her usual tone of voice, she said, "Not that I disagree, mind you. My life is wonderful. But a married woman has so much freedom of *movement*."

"If her husband allows it," countered Tess. "Many don't."

"But she has no *innocence* to protect," Olympia insisted. "She can go about her business. Have frank conversations without always looking over her shoulder or naming her pets Aunt Emily and Mrs. Potts."

"I beg your pardon," objected Tess. "I named your pets."

"And I love their names!" Olympia cried. "No one else's pets are so cleverly named."

"The fact that a married woman's life has a wider scope, *socially*, than an unmarried woman's doesn't mean she should be constrained *legally* to compensate," Cordelia snapped, frustrated. "We aren't trying to balance a scale. A man's freedoms and rights increase continuously throughout his life, as he grows into adulthood and takes on more responsibilities. The same ought to be true of women."

"Admit it, Olympia," Tess chided. "You're arguing for the sake of it."

"Of course I am." Olympia smiled innocently. "It's Cordelia's favorite activity. I just want to be hospitable."

"A spirited debate does make me feel more at home," Cordelia admitted.

"You see? This is why I'm so well-regarded as a hostess, Tess. I make my guests feel *at home*."

Tess opened her mouth to retort but then subsided with a faint, warm smile. "It does appear to be your gift, Olympia."

Cordelia and Ruby stayed for dinner and returned home together, on foot to save the cost of the hackney, pleasantly refreshed and ready to work again.

The daily grind of sewing loose pages into signatures, gluing covers to cardboard, and painting endpapers dominated the next few days. When her palms stiffened and her fingers cramped, Cordelia went looking for new clients. She found a few, too: the owner of a small bookstore wanted a copy of *Gargantua and Pantagruel* and hinted that if it sold quickly, he'd be interested in further commissions. Selling through a bookstore squeezed her already meager profits, but she had that Mary Wollstonecraft set to sell, and the newfound fear of similar incidents in the future. An arrangement with a bookstore could provide a safety net.

One morning, after reading an article in the newspaper by Caroline Norton that denounced the idea of equality between the sexes, Cordelia had to add an extra spoonful of sugar to her tea, to get the sour taste out of her mouth. While she stirred, another headline caught her eye. "Statue Takes a Turn." According to the article, a statue had been turned 180 degrees overnight, as though by magic.

Acting on impulse, she took note of the address—a private garden square in Knightsbridge—and layered on her coat, scarf, and gloves. She could think of two shops she'd been wanting to visit in the neighborhood; a short detour wouldn't cost her much time at all.

She arrived, midmorning and midweek, at a small park showing the first signs of spring: sodden trees beginning to leaf, tender shoots of grass hemmed in by pavement, scattered mud puddles unlikely to dry out before the next rain. This unremarkable tableau formed a perfect backdrop to the statue given pride of place: a larger-than-life bronze horseman on a poured concrete plinth. The horseman sat upright and proud, wore a military uniform, rested one hand lightly on his sword. Doubtless the name on the plaque identifying him would be illustrious, but the monument as a whole could not have been more forgettable.

For all that, a fairly large crowd had gathered to admire it.

While the gawkers asked one another how the prank had been accomplished, Cordelia took note of the churned earth and wagon-wheel tracks, the scrapes on the concrete. Clearly the bronze statue had been lifted from above and rotated, the plinth left undisturbed. Still a monumental task requiring specialized equipment, apparently transported to and from the scene on a wagon bed.

From a purely technical perspective, moving a statue weighing —what? A ton? More?—was a true accomplishment. Taking into account its height, the very public location, add the fact that in order to escape detection the prankster had to execute the scheme quickly, quietly, and in the dark?

Of course, this only made the stunt worse, in all the ways that counted. What a waste, to see a good mind bent on trifles, valuable resources frittered away for a joke. Why would a man with so much potential dedicate himself to—

"I didn't think I'd run into *you* here," murmured Mrs. Dowell. "Out for a stroll, or did you come to see the statue?"

"I came to see the statue," Cordelia admitted, certain now that her suspicions had been correct. Stroud had rotated the statue and, somehow, the Dowells were involved. They wouldn't be here otherwise. "And you?"

"I admit to being curious." Mrs. Dowell gestured to her eldest daughter, standing at her side. "Nell couldn't resist."

Nell grinned impishly. "I couldn't!"

"Turning a statue so large is quite a feat," Cordelia observed.

"It *is* rather impressive," Mrs. Dowell acknowledged.

One corner of Nell's mouth sharpened to a sly point. "You'd never imagine a man like—"

Mrs. Dowell cut in. "We can only speculate about who's behind this, just like everyone else here."

"If the Duke of Stroud isn't responsible, I'll eat my hat," said Cordelia. "The mystery isn't *who*. It's *why*."

"You don't know that," Mrs. Dowell chided. "It's not like you to be so rash, Miss Kelly."

Cordelia weighed her reply. Explaining that she knew Stroud could backfire catastrophically, but it rankled to let anyone, especially a client, believe her mentally lazy.

Thankfully, Nell piped up. "If you want a clue as to *why*—"

"*Nell*," Mrs. Dowell interrupted.

"—you need only ask who currently resides in the square."

Cordelia raised her eyebrows. "Is that so?"

"I'm just guessing!" Nell chirped, hazel eyes twinkling. "That's what Mama wants me to say, anyhow. And I am her loving, obedient daughter."

"Are you?" Mrs. Dowell murmured.

"Luckily, Miss Kelly, you've a wickedly sharp mind." Nell grinned. "I doubt you need any more clues from us."

"Us?" Mrs. Dowell echoed in mild disbelief. And then, with a rueful shake of her head, "We have plans for the afternoon and not much time to spare. Forgive us for being on our way so quickly?"

"Of course," Cordelia agreed. "Enjoy the afternoon."

"And if your speculations do progress toward a conclusion"— Mrs. Dowell's girlish face twisted into a pained grimace—"do be discreet?"

"Miss Kelly's no gossip, Mama," said Nell. "You worry too much."

"We are gossiping right now," Cordelia pointed out. "*I* am gossiping."

Mrs. Dowell gave her daughter a significant look.

"Whose side are you on?" Nell demanded.

"Side?" Cordelia repeated.

"You're teasing me," Nell complained. "And after I was so helpful!"

"Enjoy the clear skies." Mrs. Dowell ushered her daughter away. With a wry backward glance she added, "And the gossip."

The two women wove their way through the gathered crowd.

Cordelia waited until they'd turned the corner before asking the loiterers if they knew who, exactly, lived in this square? The Jamesons, the Nesbitts, the Frushars, the Leskovs... the Hemsworths. The second Cordelia heard that name she knew she'd found the clue Nell had been hinting at. The horseman, she discovered, had once faced the Hemsworths' home. Now the horse's ass faced the Hemsworths' home.

She'd first met the Duke of Stroud loitering about the Dowells' home, inquiring about the family's mood. Inside, they'd been excitedly discussing the prank he'd just pulled. Now that Cordelia had taken on the role of loiterer, two of the Dowells had not-so-coincidentally strolled by.

Both pranks targeted the Hemsworths. The first one, with the marching band, had been joyful and charming. This one, while subtler, expressed pure contempt.

She could see the vague outlines of a story here. She could guess at the particulars, but why speculate when she could go to the source? Stroud had the answers, if she wanted them.

Did she want them? She had no business prying into the private affairs of her clients. The Duke of Stroud might indulge her curiosity, but she could already estimate the cost: whole days spent picking apart the knot her heart would twist itself into, after being confronted with something it wanted and would never have.

Reaching out to Stroud would expose her to risk. Most stories about aristocrats taking an interest in young ladies undefended by their families ended badly. Innocent girls started down the primrose path and soon found themselves lost, alone, ruined.

Cordelia caught herself.

Lost? Alone? *Ruined?* Contempt for women lay at the heart of all those cautionary tales. The fairer sex, the weaker sex, soft-willed and easily deceived. Nonsense, as anyone who'd met a woman ought to know, and Cordelia refused to treat nonsense as wisdom.

Perhaps seeing Stroud again *would* fill her with regret. If so, then she had yet to make peace with her own choices. The Duke of Stroud would have been just as unattainable in her old life as he was in the new; nothing had changed on that count. She had not lost anything—excepting, of course, the comforting lie she had told herself: *You're not losing much.* That lie had given her comfort at a trying time, but now she had to give it up. Face the truth.

She had to see herself clearly, see her choices clearly, and accept the consequences with grace. By leaving her family, she'd closed all the many doors they could have opened for her. Some of those doors *would* have led to a happy marriage, a bright and joyful future. Others—most, by her reckoning—would have locked her into a life of grim, unending struggle.

But she couldn't know which it would have been. She had not trusted her parents to spin the roulette wheel that decided her fate. Instead she'd left the gambling hall.

What kind of person did she wish to be? The answer was so easy: she wished to be brave and strong and good. Having seized control of her life, she could only blame herself if she failed. So. If she avoided Stroud because she feared temptation, would that make her brave—or a coward? If she avoided Stroud to lift the weight of regret from her heart, would that make her strong—or weak? If she avoided a man who had shown her kindness, who'd given a gift and asked for precious little in return, would that make her good—or selfish?

Stroud had earned better treatment than she'd offered. All her reasons for keeping him at bay made her lesser, by all the standards she had set for herself.

ALISTAIR WAS NOT ashamed to admit that he needed several days of rest after the statue prank. He slept until the sunlight spilling through the window began to dim with afternoon and then he ate until his stomach hurt.

He loved hot chocolate. And cheese. He especially loved them together, as a meal. So he broke his fast with six cheeses on toast and two pots of chocolate, and he'd looked at the garnish of parsley, so that was almost a vegetable. An hour to digest and a fresh set of clothes and he felt like himself again.

He'd come up with the prank as a direct response to Mrs. Hemsworth's latest attempt at matchmaking. Though perhaps 'matchmaking' wasn't the word—she'd crossed a line when she locked Chilly and Laura alone in a room together at a party. Alistair pitied Laura, who deserved better, but he was furious on his friend's behalf.

He had, as usual, left most of the work to other people. He'd pressed the head gardener of his nearest estate, the Beehive, into making the hoist. By putting most of his grounds crew on the task, they'd constructed the thing in a little under a week and then hauled it to London on a wagon covered in a few sheets of canvas.

It was just the beginning of March, the start of the busiest months of the year for the gardeners. One of his aunts lived at the Beehive full-time, and she'd written him angry letters every day that the project went on, lambasting him for ruining the whole year's plantings. He'd had Fisk pen long, apologetic responses in Alistair's name, mostly because he knew this would make his aunt even angrier. She had a sour temper.

The hoist had been delivered. Chilly, almost vibrating with rage, had organized the lookouts. Alistair's only job had been to work the winch. When the head gardener had practiced on one of the marble statues in the Beehive gardens, he'd needed a team of six to work the winch. Unfortunately, he'd done his trial run before loading the hoist into the wagon, and there hadn't been *room* for a team of six in the wagon bed. So Alistair had managed it on his own.

The day after the prank, he woke with the muscles on his back and shoulders screaming with pain. Three days later, he was still sore. Fisk dragged him into the office to look at all the mail he'd been ignoring, which included at least one curiosity—a small, square painting only a little larger than his palm.

It depicted a graybeard standing by a man-made lake, surrounded by a well-tended park vibrant with flowers. The old man wore an eyepatch over one eye, a wide-brimmed hat that cast most of his features into shade, and a wispy beard long enough to trail over his loose robes. He held a tall spear firmly in one gnarled hand.

"Um." Alistair flipped the painting over to look at the back. Nothing. Not even a signature. "It's... nice?"

"I thought so," Fisk agreed. "Beautiful technique."

"Who sent it?" Alistair asked.

"I couldn't say. It arrived by post, in a blank envelope. No note, no return address, no clues as to the author or the provenance."

"What am I supposed to do with it?" Alistair wondered.

Fisk shrugged. "It's not for me to say."

"That's not a helpful answer, Fisk." Alistair pointed at a lozenge-shaped building in the background of the painted scene, long and curved where there ought to have been corners. "Is that Kew?"

"Oh, indeed. It could be the Palm House. I've not been, myself, but it certainly resembles the building as it appears in drawings and photographs."

"Who brings a spear to Kew Gardens? The more I look at it, the stranger this fellow becomes. He's not dressed like any gentleman I've ever met."

"His robes are rather ragged. Perhaps a university don, down on his luck?"

"But the spear." Alistair squinted. "He's too old to use it as anything but a walking stick."

"Hmm." Fisk tapped his chin. "Perhaps a meditation on the stages of life? A young man fights, an old man reflects in his garden..."

"In the riddle, life has three stages. Sometimes the poets and such stretch it out to four, to match the seasons. In which case an old man in a spring garden doesn't fit at all. Maybe it's the first of a series and there are more to come? Some trick to pique my curiosity?" Alistair scowled at the painting. "It's working, damn it."

"I wonder what happened to his eye. It seems significant." Fisk hummed. "Perhaps a war wound?"

"A wounded soldier fallen on hard times, maybe? Is this a request for a donation? A charitable fundraiser at Kew?" Alistair flipped the painting over, but the backside remained completely blank. "If so, they've forgotten to mention the date and the time and especially the *price*."

Fisk's expression cleared. "Ah!"

"What is it?"

"I've figured it out."

"And?"

"Keep looking, sir. The answer is within your reach."

"How would you know?" On second thought, Fisk *would* know. "How long will it take me to figure out?"

"Five minutes? Less?" Fisk tipped his head from side to side to indicate his answer allowed for a bit of wiggle room. "The key, for me, was realizing that the painter had not, in fact, neglected to mention the date. Or the time. Or, obviously, the place."

"Had not—but—" Alistair stared down at the painting in frustration. The place was unambiguous: Kew. The time proved easy enough, once he thought to look. The painter had depicted the sun just short of its peak, with eleven thin rays of gold ink radiating out from the lemon-yellow circle.

Finally, the date. Fisk had figured it out. He thought Alistair could figure it out. That meant the answer had to be obvious. The only element of the picture they hadn't deciphered yet was the strange man, so probably something to do with him. With his spear and his robes and his missing eye...

Oh.

Oh.

"Odin's day!" Alistair exclaimed triumphantly. "The man is

Odin, Odin's day is Wednesday. So the mysterious correspondent wants me to visit Kew at eleven o'clock on Wednesday."

"That was my conclusion. Though I'm not sure you should actually attend—"

"Of course I will."

Fisk ignored the interruption. "Since anyone who wishes to lure you into a public place while disguising their identity may mean you harm."

"Me?" Alistair looked down at himself doubtfully. "Good luck to them."

"You make a tempting target to anyone foolish enough to dare," Fisk added. "And the instigator of this plot, if he means you harm, certainly wouldn't assault you alone."

"You can accompany me," Alistair conceded. "And bring a pistol."

Fisk sighed. "Just... just what I'd hoped you would say, sir."

Alistair tacked the little painting to his wall, beside one of the huge mirrors he'd had custom made—his first real extravagance after inheriting—so that he glanced at it every time he paused to tidy his hair or check his cravat hadn't gone limp. Further examination mostly revealed that if the grande dames who pestered him with invitations knew how easily they could catch his interest, he'd be in real trouble.

Come to think of it, how *hadn't* they realized?

Anyway, he arrived at Kew early on Wednesday because all of Fisk's fretting had finally planted a seed of suspicion in his mind. Maybe he'd show up in front of the Palm House and a dozen men would be waiting with nets and handcuffs and a demand for ransom? No harm in foiling them with a bit of un-ducal promptness.

Spring had only touched the gardens, lightly and incompletely. The great oaks had begun to bud, and a whole field of daffodils bloomed bright and pure, like concentrated sunshine. Wispy clouds scudded across the sky, and the temperature hovered a degree or two away from sheer perfection. Cool enough to be comfortable with his cravat and gloves on, not so cold that he needed a scarf.

He aimed for the glass bulk of the Palm House, rehearsing a few disdainful yet defiant phrases suitable to the occasion ("You never stood a chance!" sounded good. "It was always going to end this way," had a certain ominous ring to it…), completely unprepared to encounter Cordelia Kelly in a state of repose.

The sight of her hit him like a locomotive in full steam.

He hadn't thought anything could excite him more than she had in Trafalgar Square, lips curled in triumph, eyes sparkling with delight. And probably, if it hadn't been for Trafalgar Square, he wouldn't have cared. He'd never before melted at the sight of a woman *reading*.

She sat with her back curved and slim shoulders sloping, smooth sweeps of blonde hair shining against her cheeks. Every time he'd encountered her in the past her demeanor had struck him as guarded, but that wasn't the case now. She smiled as she read, furrowed her brow, bit her lip. Emotion played freely over her face.

He'd never thought a woman's quiet might be private, a secret she hoarded for herself rather than putting it on display for others. Miss Kelly seemed to have acquired a man's need to hide her tender parts, and she'd done such a good job that he'd never guessed at their existence.

She glanced at her pocket watch. He mirrored the gesture reflexively: ten forty-five. He'd been loitering in the shade for fifteen minutes? It had felt like seconds.

Miss Kelly tucked the book into a small valise and straightened her slim shoulders, folding her hands in her lap. She took a deep breath, and her features settled into blank watchfulness as she exhaled. She looked expectant, now, alert and ready for battle.

For battle? But… that meant… Whatever cosmic thief had stolen the last fifteen minutes had taken his wits, as well, because he wasn't usually quite so slow. He hadn't encountered her here at Kew by accident. She'd sent him the coded picture. Had almost certainly painted it herself.

He was going to marry Cordelia Kelly.

It came to him as a foregone conclusion, as simple and sure as the sun rising in the east and setting in the west. He felt no fear—he'd long ago accepted that he'd have to marry and couldn't imagine being rejected. And Fate, always so generous with him, had not only sent the perfect woman, she'd done it well ahead of schedule.

CHAPTER 7

He twisted to catch Fisk's eye but his secretary had already retreated, apparently unaffected by the time-stealing madness that had seized Alistair. God, how embarrassing.

Alistair emerged from the concealing shadow of the tree and whistled cheerfully to catch Miss Kelly's attention. She twisted to face him, waving as she rose to her feet.

"Miss Kelly!" He bowed at the waist, holding the position until she offered her hands. He kissed the knuckles on each with an exaggerated flourish. "I have to say, you are the last person I would have expected to contact me in this way. Didn't you recently tell me that—oh, what were the words?—that you don't have time for frivolous pursuits?"

"Which is why I felt I owed you an olive branch." She patted the bench. "I'm glad you were able to decipher the invitation. Never having made anything like it before, I had no idea if I'd bungled the job."

"It was a good puzzle once we knew what to look for." He planted himself beside her. It was a good-size bench, but, as always, he took up quite a bit of space. Miss Kelly's eyes dropped to trace the length of their thighs, which pressed together from hip

ERIN SATIE

to knee. When she didn't object, he continued. "So I'd say you designed it exactly right. But you'll forgive me if I save my compliments for later. What brought this on? Do you need something?"

Considering her previous hostility, he feared this sudden desire to ingratiate herself owed more to some instability in her life than an honest desire to deepen their acquaintance. She shared an upper-story flat with a friend, and both worked to make ends meet. It had to be a precarious existence.

"Because it's all right if you do," he added. "I could help."

Instead of jumping at his offer, she jumped right off the bench. "I beg your pardon?"

"No—no—I didn't mean it like that!" Though he should have realized the implications. A man offering a woman a gift usually expected something in exchange. A kiss, a fondle... more.

"I wasn't thinking," he hurried to explain. "I only meant— you must understand it's the only truly good thing about my position. If a friend comes to me for help, I can give it. But they're usually men... or asking through my sister..." He spread his hands. "I forgot how the circumstances would affect the offer."

"The *only* good thing?" she repeated skeptically.

With anyone else, he'd have responded with a joke. With Miss Kelly, he resisted the urge. Best be honest with his future wife, right?

"I'm not a very good duke." He tried not to mind when she snickered. "You must think I haven't noticed—you and everyone else—because people are always trying to tell me, as though I had no idea. Well, I know. I'm not a good duke. But when a friend needs something and I can provide it, for a little while I feel like I'm exactly where I ought to be."

She stared at him in narrow-eyed silence. It stretched and stretched, well past the point where he felt a desperate need to fill it with babble. He had a ridiculous urge to explain his family to her, how they'd broken like a bone and set in the wrong shape.

68

But he didn't even talk with *Flea* about that, and she'd lived through it.

"I believe you," Miss Kelly said finally.

"You do?" He sounded surprised even to his own ears.

"I do." She returned to her seat. He flexed the muscles in his thigh and watched her eyes dart down to where she'd felt the slight movement before sliding suspiciously in his direction. "I haven't summoned you to ask for a favor—I would *never*..." She paused. "I shouldn't say never. I can imagine it. As a last resort, perhaps. A *very* last, after I'd lost all hope and shame."

He waggled his eyebrows. "Ooh, tell me more."

She tried to whack him with her stare again—which didn't bother him the way she wanted it to, but he couldn't blame her for trying. She had an impressive stare. Like a battering ram, if battering rams could look inside a person very judgmentally and then target the soft spots.

That stare probably turned most men to jelly. But he wasn't most men. He was a lot bigger, for one. He could take it.

"You're asking me to describe a future where I am destitute, friendless, and so desperate that I seek out a man I hardly know in order to exchange sexual favors for temporary relief?"

"Oh. Hmm." He scratched his chin. "Sorry."

"I suppose it would all be great fun for *you*," she added. "Which brings me, in a roundabout way, to my invitation. I had hoped you might answer a few questions."

"That's... ominous. What sort of questions?"

"I read an item in the papers about a statue that had been turned one hundred eighty degrees overnight. I wondered if it was your work."

Alistair tried to look innocent. "Oh, who's to say?"

"You," she answered. "That's why I asked."

"I thought you weren't interested in frivolous things and wasting your time and..." *Me*, he didn't add, even though he'd been the one doing all the things she couldn't be bothered with and probably belonged on the list.

"I went to see it myself." Miss Kelly's expression went a bit vague as her attention turned inward. "The statue had attracted a tremendous crowd, everyone gossiping and speculating. The prank had been accomplished so neatly that no one saw the culprits at work. Not the nightwatchman, not the lamplighter, not a single passerby."

"Is that a… compliment?" Alistair wondered.

Miss Kelly nodded.

Alistair beamed. "Almost everyone employed at Stroud House helped. We blocked all the roads and—"

"So it *was* your work!"

"Oh." Stroud scratched at his chin. That hadn't been very clever of him. "Hard to deny it now, I suppose."

"Do you know what else I learned from the gossips?" Miss Kelly asked.

"Gossip can be unreliable."

"I imagine they'd correctly identified which house belonged to whom," Cordelia countered. "The statue had rotated away from the Hemsworths, showing them its backside where once it had faced them."

"Hmm, interesting." Alistair rubbed his cheek, surreptitiously tugging at his lips to stop himself from smirking. "I wonder what that could mean?"

"And do you know who happened to walk by while I was there?"

"I think you're about to tell me."

"Mrs. Dowell and her eldest daughter—you must know the Dowells, since we first met in front of their home."

"We're acquainted."

"How?"

"Through my friend Chilly." Alistair added, in case she'd forgotten, "Mr. Christopher Old. He was at Trafalgar for your prank."

"You and he are close, are you not?" Miss Kelly hummed

meditatively. "What about the Hemsworths? Why were you targeting them?"

Alistair shifted uncomfortably. It wasn't a secret, exactly. The pranks had to be understood in order to be effective. But the primary advantage of making a point indirectly was that not many people looked past the joke.

"What did you intend to accomplish?" Miss Kelly pressed.

"I'll tell you if you agree to keep the answer in strict confidence. We're not looking for a scandal."

"I can keep a secret." She spoke with such cool certainty that, if Miss Kelly been any less righteous, he'd wonder if she'd spent her youth burying bodies out in the moors.

"Chilly is in love with Nell Dowell, has been for ages. He's never looked at another girl, never will. But his mother doesn't approve. She was a Soubry before she married Franklin Old. Chilly's grandfather on that side is Baron Soubry, his aunt—mother's sister—is the Countess of Redesdale. Mrs. Old wants her son to marry well, and she knows that he could do better than the Dowells." Alistair tipped his head to the side, squinted. "She's not *wrong*. He could set his sights much higher if he cared to. He doesn't. He's in love with Nell."

"Where do the Hemsworths come in?" Miss Kelly asked.

"Earlier this year, rumors started circulating about Nell. A few truths mixed in with a few lies, nasty but believable enough to be convincing. Nell was devastated. She and Chilly tracked the rumors to their source and discovered that Mrs. Hemsworth had been behind it all. Mrs. Hemsworth wants Chilly to marry one of *her* daughters, Laura, and she thought she'd improve her chances of success by damaging Miss Dowell's reputation."

Miss Kelly hummed her understanding. "Mothers can be very determined."

"What's worse," Alistair continued, "is that Chilly's mother *encouraged* Mrs. Hemsworth. Chilly had started to talk about proposing. Mrs. Old must have hoped the rumors would convince Mr. Old to intervene with his son, or run Nell out of the city, or even sour Chilly's interest. That last will never happen—Chilly doesn't care what people say about Nell—but the rest of it? Entirely possible."

"So you hoped to put a stop to these rumors with your prank?"

"Chilly didn't want to confront Mrs. Hemsworth directly. He thought that would add to the gossip, start a new round of chatter and cement the scandal in people's minds. This way, Mrs. Hemsworth gets the message without anyone having to make a scene."

Cordelia folded her hands in her lap, brow furrowing with concentration. "What exactly is the message?"

"That they should leave Chilly and Nell alone."

"And you also hired the marching band?"

"That's right. It played every time Laura was scheduled to visit Chilly."

"But that didn't dissuade them?"

"It seemed to. We thought we'd succeeded when Laura put her foot down and refused to visit Chilly." Because Miss Kelly seemed interested, Alistair added, "And, to be perfectly honest, I'd only hired the marching band for so long. All those public performances—plus the extra rehearsal time!—drew quite a bit of public attention, so now they're booked solid."

"What prompted this new prank?"

"Last week, Mrs. Old and Mrs. Hemsworth conspired to lock Chilly and Laura alone in a room together at a party. As you may guess, Mrs. Old didn't warn Chilly that Laura would be in attendance. As far as Chilly can tell, Laura had no knowledge of the scheme either. She helped him to escape out a window before they were discovered."

"Imagine being pushed to marry a man who'd pledged his heart elsewhere—who rejected you again and again—" Miss Kelly shuddered. "That poor girl."

"Poor Chilly, you mean!" Alistair exclaimed, incensed on

behalf of his friend. "He's found the girl of his dreams, and his family keeps asking him to marry someone else!"

Miss Kelly's steel-gray eyes met his, sharp and searching. "But they won't succeed, will they?"

"What do you mean?"

"You'll remove the obstacles in your friend's way," said Miss Kelly. "I'd wager he'll marry Miss Dowell before the end of the year."

"Sooner than that, I hope," he admitted. Why did he feel like he was being interrogated? In a bad way? "It's not a hardship, you know. I help a friend, we all have fun, and nobody gets hurt."

"How will you persuade Mrs. Old?"

"We'll think of something."

"Yes, I'm sure you will."

Alistair frowned. For some reason, Miss Kelly did not sound admiring.

"And even though your pranks make the papers, and thousands of Londoners gossip about them over their dinner tables at night, hardly anyone will ever guess at their true purpose."

"No, of course not." The words came slower and slower as he felt more and more lost. "That's the whole idea. We want to avoid a scandal."

"Do you know…" Her gaze swept slowly over him, from top to toe, as though she were seeing him for the first time. "I think you might be the most dangerous man I've ever met."

Alistair laughed. "Don't be ridiculous."

"It's true." Not the faintest trace of humor leavened her tone or expression. "I doubt the people who stand in your way last for very long."

"I don't know what you're talking about."

"My objections, fierce as they were, hardly inconvenienced you. A pair of matchmaking mamas, both ambitious on behalf of their children, don't stand a chance." Miss Kelly nodded, quick and firm. "We chart a path towards our goals, and you lead us into a maze. It's diabolical."

"Diabolical?" Alistair's voice jumped at least an octave. "You've got this all wrong."

"No, I don't think so." She met his eyes, her gaze still searching, still curious. "Possibly, however, *you* have it all wrong. Do you really believe these are just silly pranks?"

"I'm not a bully."

"No, you're nothing like the bullies I've met," Miss Kelly agreed. "What you do is more creative, and more clever, and far more frightening."

"More *frightening*? Can you hear yourself? Do you have any idea how easy it would be, how hard I have to work"—everything he'd done, everything he'd changed about himself, how careful he had to be *all the time*—"I am not *worse* than a bully."

She stood, too, reaching out as though to offer comfort. "I didn't say 'worse.' That's not what I meant."

Alistair jerked away. "I've had enough of this conversation." He fumbled for his pocket watch and flicked it open but didn't actually look at the dial. "My, it's gotten so late. What a shame."

"You're a great strapping fellow, Your Grace," murmured Miss Kelly. "But you do bruise easily."

He bit back a snarl. *Bruise easily.* Rather a euphemistic way to describe sticking a finger into an open wound and rummaging around for a while. His heart was not a dusty old desk drawer. Not that she had any idea what she was doing, or any way of guessing how he'd react, but still.

He remembered how confident he'd been earlier, thinking that he—Alistair Chandos, so big and strong—could withstand Cordelia Kelly's scrutiny better than other men. Ten minutes later and he wanted to leave. He probably never wanted to see her again.

"On the contrary, Miss Kelly." He bowed shallowly. "It would be more correct to say that you hit especially hard."

PACING UP and down in the drawing room of Chilly's house a few hours later, Alistair recounted his conversation. Not for the first time. He'd come straight here and hadn't let his friend get a word in edgewise.

"She doesn't know what she's talking about," he concluded. "She's making serious accusations—and what am I supposed to do, anyhow? Nothing? She'd probably call me a bully even if I did nothing!"

"I think she's right," said Chilly.

Alistair turned on his heel. *"What?"*

"If you want my advice…" Chilly smiled wryly. "Actually, I don't think you do. You need to hear it, though. I think you should let your temper cool, and then give everything she said serious consideration."

"I can't believe you're taking her side," Alistair exclaimed.

"I can't believe she saw it before I did," Chilly replied. "That's the curse of a long friendship, I suppose. I remember when they *were* just silly pranks."

"All right, explain to me how Homer the Roamer is—is—" Alistair flailed his arms. *"Diabolical?"*

"Homer the Roamer is no more," said Chilly. "And, forgive me if this seems like a change of subject, I assure you it's not: I have interesting news to share."

"What kind of news?"

"I'm engaged to be married."

"Married." Alistair hesitated, afraid of being wrong. "To Nell?"

"To Nell."

"How?"

"Turns out my father found that statue prank hilarious. He asked me about it, so I explained why I agreed to your plan. He didn't want to believe that Mother would go so far as to trap me in a compromising situation. I told him to ask her about it directly, and she admitted it. My father said she'd gone too far. And then he told me that if I wanted to marry Nell Dowell so badly, I might as well get on with it."

"Chilly!" Alistair seized his friend by the shoulders, dragged him to his feet, and engulfed him in a hug so enthusiastic that Chilly began to cough and splutter. Oops, too much. Alistair set him down and settled for clapping him hard on the back. "Congratulations!"

"Yes, well." Chilly gave his own chest a thwack and coughed again. "I proposed before he could have second thoughts. The Dowells are hosting the wedding party in about a month. I hope you'll attend?"

"What's that? You're asking me to make a toast at the wedding breakfast? I humbly accept."

"Oh, no, Rip. Absolutely not. You know my family—"

"I'm so glad you appreciate all my tireless support!"

"They'll all be coming," Chilly protested. "My mother is already hanging by a thread—"

"I'll only say nice things, I promise."

The teasing continued all afternoon. Alistair couldn't think of a better way to let his friend know that he cared.

JUST WHEN CORDELIA was ready to move Mrs. Dowell from the "current client" category into the "former client" category, Mrs. Dowell sent a letter urgently requesting Cordelia's attendance—that very afternoon, if she could come.

Cordelia returned a brief acceptance: she'd be delighted, waited on Mrs. Dowell's convenience, etc., etc. She set aside the bespoke dictionary she'd been binding for an eccentric professor, changed out of her much-stained work clothes and into a day dress, combed her hair smooth, and presented herself at the appointed time.

Mrs. Dowell received her in a state of nervous excitement only a hair's-breadth short of panic. She couldn't hold still. She clapped giddily and exclaimed, "We're hosting a wedding party!" as she waved Cordelia toward her usual chair, then hopped right back onto her feet so she could fetch the little calendar she'd commissioned at the beginning of the year.

Once found, she flicked rapidly through the pages. "As small as we can manage, just family." She looked up to add, "Though that's already a long enough list! Nearly a hundred people!" and promptly lost her place.

Cordelia took a sip of tea every time she was tempted to voice her impatience.

"I'm not explaining well, am I?" Mrs. Dowell apologized. "Yesterday Nell accepted a proposal of marriage from Mr. Christopher Old. They're, well"—Mrs. Dowell chuckled—"an *old* family, impeccable reputation, *very* wealthy. Dear Chilly has been as warm and attentive as any prospective mother-in-law could wish, but his family isn't thrilled."

Mrs. Dowell closed the calendar over her index finger and sighed. "A gift can only do so much, but it's a start, isn't it? A way to show them that, while we're grateful for the connection, we're people of good taste and good breeding ourselves."

Cordelia had never mastered the kind of subtle social maneuvering Mrs. Dowell was describing. She had no way of knowing if Mrs. Dowell was smartly ambitious, a victim of false hopes, or foolishly justifying a lavish expenditure on an inadequate pretext.

Luckily, Mrs. Dowell hadn't asked her for advice. "What sort of book are you thinking of?"

"*Two* books, one for each of Chilly's parents. Of course we'll be hosting—and not just us, I've written to every one of our neighbors to see if they'll open up their spare rooms—but it's bound to be chaotic, so I want to do something *special*." A quick lift of the eyebrows emphasized the final word. "So. Mr. Old's favorite book is Marcus Aurelius's *Meditations* in the original Latin, I presume because he had to memorize the highlights as a boy and hasn't read a single book since—" Mrs. Dowell caught herself and paled. "Oh dear."

"Marcus Aurelius's *Meditations* in the original Latin," Cordelia repeated in a calm, neutral tone. "That won't be difficult to obtain. What sort of binding?"

"Mr. Old has a sense of humor—Chilly must get it from him because it's certainly not from his mother—so do something very staid and dignified on the outside with a nice bit of humor on the interior. I'm thinking brown calfskin, gold tooling, then add some color to the endpapers, let your imagination run free."

Cordelia hummed her understanding as she made note of the instructions. "And Mrs. Old?"

"Voltaire's *Candide*." Mrs. Dowell leaned in conspiratorially, one soft cheek a pillow for her fist. "She is exactly the sort of person who would like *Candide*, you know. She thinks herself very sophisticated because she spends a great deal of her leisure time mocking the naive."

Cordelia blinked.

"Don't look surprised," Mrs. Dowell chided. "One thing I like about you, Miss Kelly, is that you're smart about people without being a cynic. It's a rare quality."

"Given enough time..." Cordelia demurred.

"No, you're not the type," Mrs. Dowell said firmly. "I've been around long enough to know. Now, Mrs. Old will like something fashionable that stands out at a glance. Make the cover white, or a nice French blue—something unique, a color she won't see anywhere else."

"And the endpapers?"

"Attention grabbing, modern. She likes things that make her feel clever."

Cordelia smothered a burst of laughter. "You don't think much of her."

"I hope one day we're very good friends." The sparkle in Mrs. Dowell's eyes undermined her prim delivery. "The wedding will be in a month, is that enough time?"

"They'll be in your hands in three weeks."

"At the usual rate?"

Cordelia nodded.

"I love that I can count on you, Miss Kelly. I know you'll make something marvelous."

She'd certainly do her best. She had to—she desperately needed the income.

CHAPTER 8

O n the morning of the Soho Discussion Group's quarterly meeting, Cordelia woke with a strange, twisting, hollow ache in her stomach. She fortified herself with a substantial breakfast, which simply exchanged the ache for persistent roiling nausea. Around midafternoon, when her stomach ought to have settled back into hunger, she instead felt like she'd drunk an entire punch bowl of carbonated water.

I'm nervous, she realized. *When was I last nervous?*

She honestly couldn't remember.

She dressed carefully and left for the meeting with plenty of time to spare—better to arrive early than late for a meeting of busy women, where everyone's time mattered.

After Cordelia had written to Miss Smith about Alistair's attempt to use the invitation as a bribe, the club president had responded with an invitation to meet. So Cordelia knew her way through the maze of Soho streets and recognized the brick-fronted facade of Miss Smith's home.

A woman in uniform answered her knock, stern and stout with her gray hair in a plain bun at her nape. "Miss Kelly. Right on time. Miss Smith is inside. I'll show you in, if that's acceptable?"

Cordelia, who'd brought her invitation and held it in her hand, tucked it away. "Of course."

The interior reminded Cordelia of the home she'd grown up in, everything good quality but nothing so new or so fine as to grab the attention. Knickknacks cluttered nearly every flat surface, an endless series of porcelain figurines and heirloom china and vases full of silk flowers preventing the tables and counters from serving any useful purpose.

Upstairs, a sunny salon had been prepared. Three rows of seats faced a simple podium. Around half were already occupied with clusters of women, heads bent toward one another in quiet conversation.

Miss Smith, flitting from group to group, snatched a piece of paper from a waiting stack and brought it to Cordelia.

"Take a seat, take a seat!" She shooed Cordelia into an empty chair. "I'm afraid you'll mostly be observing today—Lord Brougham will be presenting our petition to the Lords shortly. It's a critical moment, and we've a great deal of last-minute business. Why don't you read it while we sort ourselves out?"

Cordelia took the sheets and started at the top. *To the Honourable House of Peers*, it began. *The Petition of the undersigned Women of Great Britain, Married and Single, Humbly Sheweth—That the manifold evils occasioned by the present law, by which the property and earnings of the wife are thrown into the absolute power of the husband, become daily more apparent.*

Cordelia paused, a thrill of anticipation skittering up from where fingertips touched the paper to the very base of her skull. Here, indeed, lay a matter close to her heart. She'd never marry, but most women would face this dilemma. And they deserved better.

The petition discussed the increasing presence of women in the labor force, the tendency among families of means to set up trusts that protected a wife's wealth from her husband's depredations. *Few parents are willing entirely to entrust the welfare of their offspring to the irresponsible power of the husband, to the chances of his character, his wisdom, and his succession a profession.*

Exactly!

How much more unequivocal is the injury sustained by women in the lower classes, for whom no such provision can be made by their parents, who possess no means of appeal to expensive legal protection? Cordelia could only imagine. Certainly, she would rather remain single for the remainder of her life than float her own fate on such waters.

The petition advocated for women who made a living in the arts and women who worked as laundresses, particularly concerning itself with married women who earned wages—any income a woman earned after speaking her vows legally belonged to her husband, and he could seize it at will, spend it as he liked.

Since modern civilization, in indefinitely expending the sphere of occupation for women, has in some measure broken down their pecuniary dependence upon men, it is time that legal protection be thrown over the produce of their labour.

Every word of this petition spoke to Cordelia profoundly. She itched for a pen and a place to put her name; she would have happily carried these words into the street and read them aloud from a soapbox, like a mad preacher.

Miss Smith detached from the trio of women she'd been chatting with and approached the podium. The remaining members quieted, straightened, found their seats. When Miss Smith finally spoke, not two minutes after taking her place, she addressed herself at a normal volume to a completely silent room.

"Good afternoon, ladies. I hereby call to order the Spring 1856 meeting of the Soho Discussion Club. Today, instead of our usual discussion, we'll finalize our plan of attack during these last days before our Petition for the Reform of the Married Women's Property Law is presented to Parliament. The presentation, by the way, is now firmly scheduled for March 14. As always, Miss Leanne Hadley will be taking minutes. Before we open discussion, I'd like to welcome our newest member, Miss Cordelia Kelly. Before coming to London, she independently organized a circulating library intended to promote literacy among the women of her hometown. I know she's eager to contribute, and I believe she has the skills to help our group thrive."

A small round of applause followed this introduction, many of the members turning to smile and nod at Cordelia in acknowledgment.

"Mrs. Hodgeson, have you any news for us?" asked Miss Smith.

A bespectacled matron answered this query. "I have collected notarized testimony from a woman who founded a successful millinery with the aid of her friends. Her husband, all of whose attempts to start his own business failed, survived for many years on his wife's support. He died recently and bequeathed all *her* property to the children of *his mistress*."

Gasps and angry mutterings spread through the room. The laws that recognized a husband and wife as a single person effectively meant that, legally, a wife was a nonentity. Everything she owned belonged to her husband. This fact led to a whole host of small, petty crimes—but it took a special sort of villain to reveal how *extreme* the injustice could be.

Mrs. Hodgeson finished with a vicious edge to her tone. "Leaving her penniless."

"Appalling," Miss Smith murmured. "Miss Cornwallis?"

"I can think of several papers that would publish this story," said a young woman.

"I have more," caroled Mrs. Hodgeson.

"There are more such stories than we'll ever know," whispered the woman sitting right in front of Cordelia.

"What woman would sign her name to such a tale, if she had a choice?" answered another woman, seated beside the first. "Would you?"

The first shook her head.

"Imagine the humiliation," the second said knowingly.

"I will soon publish an opinion piece on husbands who drink

away income their wives have earned, stealing bread from the mouths of his own children," said Miss Cornwallis, "a situation that requires no specific examples, as cases are so numerous that every reader will be familiar with one. And I will balance it with tales of wives who contract debts for which their husbands are liable."

"It will help our cause to show that the laws currently in place sometimes allow wives to take advantage of husbands," Miss Smith admitted.

"Try not to paint all women as frivolous featherheads who can't keep track of accounts," put in another woman.

"But some of them are," returned Miss Cornwallis. "When words are precious, I'd rather spend them on the important points."

"An interesting subject for *later* debate," Miss Smith said firmly. "I've spoken with the Law Amendment Society and Sir Erskine Perry plans to take these proposals to the Commons, but that won't happen immediately. I'll keep in touch so we can coordinate our schedules."

The meeting adjourned shortly thereafter. Cordelia returned the petition, which was carefully scripted on fine thick paper whose value she could tot up in her head automatically now, by reflex.

"What do you think?" asked Miss Smith. "Are you with us?"

"I did not know it, but I had been waiting to read these words. They are so true they felt familiar even as I read them for the first time."

"Then you'll sign it?" Miss Smith asked.

Cordelia's eyes widened.

"It's not an invitation I extend to just anyone," Miss Smith continued. "We need the signatories to paint a picture, if you will. By their very existence, by placing their names on the paper and calling themselves to mind, the women who sign must further our argument. I think you qualify."

"You flatter me," Cordelia admitted. "Right now I am just…"

"A gently raised woman, from the country, making her way in the capital in a career that is by and large populated by men," Miss Smith finished. "I see the steely glint in your eye, and I know what it means, Miss Kelly. You are a woman to be reckoned with."

"Let me prove it," Cordelia said passionately. "If there's anything I can do to contribute—anything at all—I am at your disposal."

"You may have cause to regret that offer, Miss Kelly," returned Miss Smith. "We have a great deal of work to do."

ALISTAIR REFUSED the invitation from Mrs. Peet. He saw right through the fiction. Anything done in Mrs. Peet's name had been initiated by Olympia Swain—an arrangement that satisfied both women and horrified any outsider who understood it.

Alistair didn't know exactly how many invitations he received. Fisk handled most of his correspondence and, therefore, most of the rejections. Then Alistair looked at the rest and turned them down too. Mostly. But Fisk had been quite correct to suggest "Mrs. Peet's" party because Alistair had recently asked Olympia for a favor and accepting would have been the polite thing to do.

Except the favor he'd cajoled out of Olympia had been a means to contact Cordelia Kelly. He wasn't angry at her anymore, but he wasn't ready to see her again, either. And since Miss Kelly would almost certainly attend her close friend's party, Alistair had declined "Mrs. Peet's" invitation.

But it didn't end there. Olympia called on Flea a few days later. He could hear them chatting from his office and listened with half an ear as the conversation ranged from gossip to politics to fashion to household economy. Afterwards, she hopped across the corridor and knocked at his open door.

"Rip! There you are! What are you doing in here all alone?"

"I'm trying to figure out how to lift a live cow onto a roof without being caught." Alistair gestured to the pile of sketches on the table. "It's not going well."

"Probably because live cows do not belong on roofs," said Olympia.

"What's that got to do with it?"

"Nothing, apparently." Olympia laughed. "I came to prod you about my invitation. It's going to be a lovely party—is there anything I can do to convince you to attend?"

He grimaced. If Olympia didn't know about the meteoric rise and fall of his infatuation with Cordelia Kelly, he wasn't going to explain. She'd take Miss Kelly's side, and he got enough of that from Flea.

"Because I know it's very gauche of me to admit this, Rip, or to think this way at all, but there's someone I'm desperate to impress. It would be *such* a feather in my cap if you showed up. Not everyone knows a duke."

"Someone? You can't give me a name?"

"Mr. Martin Grant," answered Olympia.

"Never heard of him." Alistair frowned. "What's this about?"

"You've already guessed it, I think." Olympia fluttered her lashes. "He's courting me."

"Who told him he could— Oh, all right, I'll come." Alistair flicked a pencil across his desk. "Can't let you marry a twit."

"You'll *love* him. He's handsome and charming, and best of all he *adores* me."

"You deserve nothing less," he said dutifully.

"Exactly. So I'll see you there?"

"I'll, um. I'll look forward to it."

He told Fisk to add the party to his calendar, and then roped Chilly into coming along. Most people wouldn't insult their hostess by adding a stranger to her guest list, but if Olympia wanted a duke, he'd oblige her by acting like one: high-handed and self-indulgent.

For all that, he knew he'd made a mistake the moment he stepped through her door. Cordelia Kelly had already arrived and taken up position by a window, where she had her head bent in conversation with an elegant black woman. The queen's ward, wasn't she? They'd been introduced at some point.

Most women, when confronted with a man they had no desire to see, would beat a quick retreat and commence gossiping. Not Miss Kelly. *She* walked right up to him and said, "What are you doing here?"

He mimicked her affronted tone. "Where else would I be? Knebworth is one of my dearest friends."

"Knebworth?" Miss Kelly echoed.

"That's right. Charles Knebworth." Alistair kept a straight face. "Maybe I should ask what *you're* doing here."

"A man named Charles Knebworth invited you to this party?" Miss Kelly pressed. She was beginning to sound confused, and confusion was an inherently funny emotion on a woman whose temperament resided at the intersection of "grave" and "fierce."

"He invited me to his *own* party, silly." Alistair looked around, feigning bafflement. "He's lived here for as long as I can remember—and I visit all the time."

"Oh. I see." Her expression smoothed. "You're having me on."

"What do you mean? Knebworth is probably in the next room, let me fetch him—"

"I should have known the second you said 'Knebworth.' It's a ridiculous name."

"He's a real person who'd be offended by your mockery."

"You enjoy nothing better than mockery."

"I can think of a few things."

"Oh? Like what?"

Nothing he could discuss in polite company, actually. He changed the subject. "Anyhow, Miss Swain invited me. Or Mrs. Peet, if you prefer the polite fiction."

"*Olympia?*" Miss Kelly's brows slanted into an angry divot. "You know one another?"

"Since we were children. Our fathers were close." Their fathers were also *dead* and had been for a long time. So Alistair didn't know Olympia very well, though he did feel profoundly protective of her. "How do you think I discovered your address?"

"Olympia gave you my address?"

He nodded, and Miss Kelly stormed off—presumably to pick a fight with Olympia.

Hmm. Perhaps he ought to find Mr. Martin Grant, feel him out with a bit of conversation, and beat a quick retreat.

He turned to Victoria's ward—Hurley, her surname was. There, he had half of it. She surprised him by offering her hand. She was very petite and very pretty and very composed, a perfect lady in every way, but her eyes were watchful. This one, he thought, sees too much.

He bowed over her hand. "Please forgive my teasing, Miss Hurley."

Her bland expression did not warm in the slightest. "Olympia said you were hoping to meet Mr. Martin Grant."

"I am."

"Shall I take you to him?"

"Please."

She gestured for him to follow. He trotted at her heels as she guided him through the house, boggling at the decor. It couldn't be much more than a year since he'd last visited but every single room looked different than he remembered. Why go to the trouble when, as far as he could tell, her taste hadn't changed much?

"You're a friend of Olympia's?" he asked.

"I am."

"And also of Miss Kelly?"

"That's right."

He groped about in the cavernous vacuum of his mind for some other tidbit of polite conversation. He wondered how she'd react if he asked how Olympia had ever befriended a rigid, uncompromising moralist like Miss Kelly.

Miss Hurley paused, turned, and placed a finger across her lips. After he mirrored the gesture to show he understood, she plastered herself to a wall, peeked through a doorway, and then stepped back, waving for him to take her place.

Alistair crept forward silently, grateful again for his endless dance lessons. Through the doorway lay a grand ballroom decorated in Olympia's uniquely eye-searing fashion. The fresco on the ceiling displayed hundreds of people dancing, pictured as if seen from above. If a ball were in full swing, dancers whirling about the room, they might look up and mistake the ceiling for a mirror. The real mirrors hanging from the walls enhanced the effect.

The room was nearly empty—two servants bustled urgently around a buffet table at one end and, closer to the middle, a young man watched himself in the mirror while practicing the steps of a waltz.

Alistair backed away from the door and turned an inquiring expression on Miss Hurley.

"That's Martin Grant."

He was supposed to notice something, but he didn't know what. "He likes to dance?"

"I doubt it," said Miss Hurley, before dipping him a brief curtsey and walking away.

Odd.

Alistair glanced back in the ballroom. The young man had paused his dancing so he could admire himself undisturbed. So he was vain. Everyone had flaws.

Alistair knew from personal experience how satisfying an encounter with a large mirror could be. He'd commissioned a custom set, one for each of his homes, so he'd have access to a reflective surface where his shoulders weren't cut out of the frame, he didn't have to duck to see the top of his head, and he could still check the line of his trousers. They had cost him a small fortune. He didn't think of it as vanity, but it came close enough that he wouldn't be throwing any stones at Martin Grant.

Yet.

He saw Chilly in the foyer and made a beeline for his friend,

ERIN SATIE

hailing him by name. Chilly rocked back on his heels and smirked, which spoiled whatever surprise he was preparing— poor Chilly, he was an awful liar.

Out of pity, Alistair pretended not to notice. When he raised his arm to clap Chilly on the shoulder, his friend reached into his pocket and threw a handful of small, black, spider-shaped things at Alistair's face.

Alistair snatched one out of the air. Before he could examine it, someone to his right screamed, jumped, and whacked Alistair in the solar plexus with his elbow.

Alistair grunted and turned on the stranger, irritated. But the offender was a boy, or almost—in his teens, tall and skinny and pink-cheeked.

"At least your prank worked on *someone*," Alistair murmured to Chilly, offering his hand to the boy. "Hullo."

"Who did that?" cried the young man, his voice cracking. "What were those?"

"Um." Alistair squinted at the black, spider-shaped object in his hand. "These look like stems to me. Tomato stems? Strawberry, maybe? Nothing to worry about."

"What? But—I saw—the legs moved!" The boy cleared his throat, lowering his voice a little further than was natural. "I believe you owe me an apology."

Chilly appeared ready to offer one, but Alistair silenced him with a raised finger.

"You first," he said.

"Me?" The boy's voice cracked. "Apologize? For what?"

Alistair tapped his chest. "You hit me."

"I was—yes, but—" The boy cut himself short. Now that he knew the "spiders" had been kitchen refuse, he didn't want to admit he'd been afraid. He straightened and threw his shoulders back. "So what if I did?"

"If you don't want to apologize, I don't see why Chilly should."

"He started it!"

"And you made 'it' into a crisis." Alistair sighed. "I guess we'll have to settle this the old-fashioned way."

The boy's eyes went wide. "What?"

"You know, the old-fashioned way," Alistair repeated. "We'll duel."

"I don't—" The boy looked around, realizing that a crowd had begun to gather. He tried to bluster again. "You can't be serious."

"Of course I'm serious." Alistair smiled lazily. "Don't tell me you're a *coward*."

The poor, fuzz-lipped boy's face turned the color of sour milk. "Fine. Have it your way. We'll—"

"Arm wrestle," Alistair interrupted.

The boy blinked, caught by surprise. Again.

"Do you have a second?" Alistair asked. "Chilly will be mine."

Chilly clasped his hands behind his back, adopting an expression of sympathetic commiseration. "Indeed. Your second and I will arrange the field of play with great care. Who will you nominate?"

Someone in Alistair's peripheral vision snickered, but looking away would have ruined the moment. He kept his eyes on the boy.

A young man raised his hand and, glancing at the boy for reassurance, volunteered. "I'll be his second."

"Excellent." Chilly gestured him toward the door. "Let's find a quiet room and make the arrangements."

The crowd parted for the two seconds.

Alistair asked, "What's your name?"

"Firth," the boy answered. "Harold Firth."

Alistair offered Harold Firth his hand. "May the best man win."

The boy took one look at Alistair's hand—big enough to span most dinner plates with his fingers spread—and lost his nerve.

"Well?" Alistair prompted. "Everyone's watching."

The boy could only raise his hand halfway. Alistair had to

91

cover the rest of the distance, swallowing his opponent's hand in his own and shaking vigorously.

Before he left the room, he surveyed the crowd. Miss Kelly stood among the onlookers, right beside their hostess, looking smug. Probably already trying to turn this into something it wasn't, more proof that he was a terrifying, diabolical bully.

Firth had hit Alistair hard enough to wind a smaller man, refused to apologize, and let pride trap him in an obviously unequal contest of strength. But all Cordelia Kelly saw was a poor, innocent boy.

Alistair shot her a toothy grin. He was not sorry at all. He hadn't done anything wrong, and even Miss Kelly would admit it before the end—he'd bet on it.

CHAPTER 9

The young man who volunteered to second Mr. Firth, a friend by the name of Peter Unsworth, drove a hard bargain. Or—just as likely—Chilly hadn't bargained at all, because he thought it would be funny to see Alistair in a short chair at a short table, facing a window and late-afternoon sun.

Probably the latter. No, scratch that. Unquestionably the latter.

But Harold Firth didn't know that. He seemed to have no sense of humor at all. He couldn't laugh at Chilly's joke, he couldn't laugh at himself, and instead of laughing at the sight of an overgrown duke scrunched into a chair made for a toddler, he settled into his own seat with a smug smile.

Alistair repressed a sigh.

Martin Grant had joined the crowd of spectators. He hovered at Olympia's side, staring dreamily at her with his lips slightly parted, as though struck dumb by her many exemplary qualities. Alistair wondered uncharitably if he'd really gone to the ballroom to practice looking besotted.

The rest of the onlookers sipped punch, nibbled on petits fours, and made friendly wagers. One very daring matron promised a kiss to the winner.

"I don't know about you, but I'm getting nervous," Alistair

murmured to Harold Firth, propping his elbow on the table. "This is quite an audience."

Harold Firth mirrored Alistair's pose, fit his palm to Alistair's. "You should be ashamed of yourself."

"I should?" Alistair asked.

"If you had any decency, you'd forfeit the match."

Alistair clucked his tongue. "Looking for the easy way out, are we?"

Firth's face reddened. "You're not going to prove anything by beating me, you know."

"Well, it's been a nice chat, but perhaps we should move this along." Alistair looked up at Chilly. "What do you think?"

"Mr. Unsworth will be counting down to the start of the match," said Chilly.

"Of course he will." Alistair turned to the young man in question. "Will you do the honors then?"

"You may begin on the count of three," said Unsworth. "One… two… three!"

To young Mr. Firth's credit, he threw himself into the struggle. His lips went white, and tendons strained in his neck as he channeled the whole strength of his body into his arm. He was stronger than Alistair had expected, probably strong enough to put up a real fight against a competitor closer to his own size.

That did not mean, however, that he had any chance against Alistair. Alistair held his hand steady at the starting position, humming and looking idly about the room, while Mr. Firth twisted in his seat, eyes bulging from their sockets.

"So, here's my thought," said Alistair, calm and conversational. "My friend here found some stems that look like spiders. He hoped to fool me but instead he fooled you, and that's embarrassing."

Mr. Firth released a furious, hissing exhalation. He probably would have spat if his mother weren't present.

"I sympathize. Nobody likes being embarrassed," Alistair continued. "But what's more likely to make people think less of you? Squealing at a tomato stem, or soothing your dented pride by shouting at a stranger?"

Mr. Firth gasped out, "Go to—"

"My point is," Alistair said sharply, cutting him off. "Learn to be a good sport. It'll serve you better in the long run."

"Learn to take your own advice," snarled Harold Firth.

"I intend to." Alistair smiled sweetly and relaxed his arm. Harold Firth promptly smashed Alistair's knuckles into the wooden tabletop, winning the match.

"The match goes to Mr. Firth," intoned Mr. Unsworth. "Congratulations to Mr. Harold Firth!"

Firth stood, expression uncertain. A few of the guests stepped out of the crowd to shake his hand and clap him on the back. A matron—his mother?—kissed Firth on the cheek before winking at Alistair and leading her son out of the room.

The crowd had thinned substantially by the time Martin Grant strolled over, leaned his cocked hip against the table, and observed, "You didn't do that boy any favors by letting him win."

Alistair looked up at him. "What?"

"We hold contests to sort the strong from the weak, the able from the incompetent," Grant continued. "When you hand a young man an undeserved victory, you're deceiving him about his own strength *and* about the world—thus setting him up for very real failures down the line."

"So what should I have done?" Alistair asked.

"Why, you should have pinned the boy's arm right to the table and held it there until he understood that he'd picked a fight with the wrong man."

"If you insist." Alistair gestured to the now-empty chair. "Sit down and we'll try it your way."

Grant blinked. "What?"

"You're challenging me, aren't you?" Alistair asked.

"I'm offering a bit of sage advice—"

"Oh." Alistair blinked innocently. "What's the difference?"

95

Grant sneered. "I wouldn't expect a great hulking brute like yourself to understand."

"I admit, I'm having a hard time. You're saying that 'sage advice' is when you tell me I'm wrong and then insult me?" Alistair gave his head a little scratch, to see if that clarified anything. "And that's different than a challenge how…?"

"This conversation is fatiguing me," Grant announced, marching out of the room. "Some people can't be helped."

"Does anyone want to explain how someone who starts by insisting all contests must be won fair and square ends by walking away to avoid losing an argument?" Alistair asked the room.

That won him a few laughs, easing the tension enough for the crowd to disperse. Olympia followed Grant, shooting Alistair an angry look over her shoulder as she went.

He wondered if he ought to feel guilty. It was Olympia's special day, she wanted to impress Mr. Grant, and Alistair had antagonized him. A real friend would have set him up to look smart or impressive.

He was still mulling this question when Cordelia Kelly circled the table and sat down in the chair opposite.

CORDELIA CONSIDERED Stroud as she made herself comfortable. He looked ridiculous crammed into a tiny chair. His narrow (and shapely) hindquarters sank between the wooden arms of the chair, but the rest of his body appeared comically outsize. Like a bear riding a toy train.

At first she'd been embarrassed for him. But only at first. He'd acquitted himself well.

She didn't speak immediately. Stroud mirrored her regard, chin lifting pugnaciously. He didn't understand her nearly as well as he thought, but he was right to expect a verbal punch.

"Why do you pretend to be stupid?" she asked.

Stroud answered with practiced ease. "I'm not pretending."

Cordelia pursed her lips and waited.

"I'm not!" Stroud wriggled in his too-small chair. "You've heard my nickname, haven't you? It's Rip. I got it because my work at Eton was so bad. I had to take it to the tutors and masters to be signed, and then sometimes they'd rip it into shreds in front of everyone."

"So you can't speak Latin or Greek. Neither can I. Am I stupid?"

"I'm sorry to tell you this, but running circles around me with your clever arguments only proves my point."

"And when you neatly counter my 'clever' arguments with your own, *you* prove *mine*."

Stroud leaned forward. "Why do you hate me?"

Cordelia recoiled. "I don't."

"I know we started off on the wrong foot, but I thought I'd find a way past that. If I showed you that I meant well, you'd stop being so hostile. And every time we met, some little glimmer of fun led me on…" A shadow flickered in his tawny eyes. "But nothing I do makes a difference."

"What is your idea of friendship?"

"Um…" Stroud's eyebrows slanted, one lifting and one lowering. "You get along with someone, spend time together, share interests. That sort of thing."

"That's it?"

"Isn't that enough?"

"Not for me."

"Someone you look to for help when you're low," he added. "Who you're happy to help in your turn."

"I agree, but…" Cordelia shrugged one shoulder. "It's possible, your grace, that we are simply too different to get along."

"That's a little dramatic." Stroud rolled his eyes. "Why don't you tell me what you were hoping I'd say?"

"I wasn't—"

"Oh, trust me. I know this trick. Someone asks a question that

ERIN SATIE

sounds like it could have a thousand answers but actually, only one of them is right and I can *never* guess. Rip, remember?"

"Point taken. I apologize." Cordelia considered. "You've just demonstrated exactly the quality *I* most value in a friend: you spoke frankly. And in doing so you helped me to see myself more clearly. Now I can modify my behavior, ask questions differently in the future."

"And will you?" He sounded skeptical.

"Of course." Cordelia hesitated. "It's hard to change a habit you've never noticed you have. It won't happen overnight, but I can be strict with myself. It will happen."

"That's... nice."

Stroud looked like he wanted to say more. Cordelia waited, willing to listen, but the words never came. So she moved on. "You obviously want something else from your friends."

"I like people who bring out the best in me, I suppose." Stroud scratched his chin. "Which is almost the same as what you said, except that it's nice instead of mean."

"I beg your pardon?"

"*Your* perfect friend cuts you down to make you better. Mine makes me feel like a better version of myself. So I'd say my friends are better than your friends because they do the same thing only I have fun along the way."

"And yet here you are, sitting in a tiny chair that makes you look ridiculous and baiting fools with a pretense of stupidity." Cordelia paused. "Perhaps *my* friends are better than yours, after all? They get better results."

"That's a low blow," said Stroud.

Cordelia shrugged. "What kind of person would I be if I didn't defend my friends?"

"A *nicer* one," Stroud insisted. "Instead of telling me I pretend to be stupid, you could say, 'Why, by Jove, you're a smart fellow,' and it would amount to the same thing."

"*Half* of the same thing," Cordelia countered. "First half: you're a smart person. Second half: who pretends to be stupid."

"Third half: except that I'm really bad at it, considering how easily you saw through my disguise."

"Third *half*?"

"Third third," Stroud corrected.

"Perhaps I'm wrong about your intelligence," said Cordelia. "What would you have me believe instead?"

"I didn't say you were *wrong*."

"Highly debatable."

"Look." Stroud spread his hands in a conciliatory gesture. "A great many people, all of them smarter than me, have made their opinions on the subject clear. What sort of person would I be if I decided they were all wrong?"

Cordelia gave the expected answer. "A stupid one?"

Stroud lifted one shoulder, mouth slanting into a half-smile of acknowledgment.

And then she pressed on with, "But since you *believe* these people, you're… also stupid?"

Stroud groaned. "Do we really have to keep talking about this?"

"Your Grace, a properly designed test allows for more than one possible answer."

"I know you mean well, Miss Kelly, but… enough. Please."

Cordelia bit the inside of her cheek. She had an almost irresistible urge to dig deeper—he was wrong about himself and it explained so much. Everything, really. How else would a wealthy, titled man come to believe that the best outlet for his capacities was an endless series of ingenious pranks?

But she wouldn't convince him with words. If he could be convinced at all—and that was by no means a certainty—it would take something more. Something special.

A spark of an idea flared in her mind… and then died. He'd made his wishes clear.

She stood. "I won't distress you further."

"Wait." He reached out and took her hand, brow furrowing as he searched her expression. "What were you just thinking?"

His hand fairly swallowed hers, like swaddling clothes or a boa constrictor. Warm and firm and... She couldn't remember the last time she'd felt delicate, if she ever had. It wasn't a quality she prized or an experience she'd craved and yet, to her surprise, she didn't hate it.

"It's not important." She flexed her fingers, and he squeezed tighter, shifting his grip to draw her knuckles into the meat of his palm. She ought to protest but didn't want to. How strange.

"Then there's no harm in answering."

What was he asking about? Sharing her private thoughts? Under no circumstances. "And no benefit, either."

"Your face lit up," he protested. "It was... Humor me."

Cordelia tugged her hand free of his. Instantly her body temperature cooled by several degrees and her mind cleared. "I thought it might be interesting to prove you wrong, and myself right. But—"

Stroud interrupted. "Go ahead."

"What?"

"Don't tell me what you planned, just... go ahead with it." His smile was sweet as honey fresh from the comb. He had a kind face. Anyone who bothered to look past the big nose and the manly jaw could see it. "I'm curious to see what you'll do."

Cordelia blinked. "I don't understand you at all."

"Why, Miss Kelly, that's the nicest compliment I've heard in a while."

She went looking for Tess but found her way blocked by a short, elfin man with a mobile mouth and twinkling eyes.

"Miss Kelly?" he asked. "We've been introduced. It's—"

"Mr. Old," Cordelia finished. "I remember. How do you do?"

"I've been better." He smiled apologetically. "Feeling rather embarrassed, as you might imagine."

"At least you needn't fear distressing the hostess," said Cordelia. "Olympia considered the duel very fine entertainment."

Mr. Old burst out laughing. "She did?"

"Oh, yes." Cordelia smiled. "And why not? The guests will

repeat the story to all their friends and acquaintances. Anyone who didn't merit an invitation will be jealous, but those who got one and turned it down? Oh, they'll be sick with regret. And yet no one was hurt in the making of this spectacle. Stroud didn't embarrass Mr. Firth too badly—if he'd won that match, I think it would have spoilt the mood—and nothing about it will reflect poorly on Olympia herself."

"What about you, Miss Kelly?" Mr. Old raised his eyebrows. His eyes still twinkled, but she saw a cool calculation there she'd never glimpsed in Stroud. "Given how you reacted when Rip tried to drag *you* into one of his pranks, I would have expected another dose of stern disapproval."

"My opinion isn't relevant."

"I'd still like to hear it," Mr. Old replied.

"If you insist. Your prank frightened Mr. Firth, and nobody likes being afraid. It's such an awful sensation. I'm scared all the time. Scared of crossing the street, scared of being robbed—it's happened twice already—scared that I'll run out of work."

"I can't imagine that will ever happen," Mr. Old protested glibly. "I've heard so many good things about—"

"And yet the thought haunts me every day," Cordelia continued, uninterested in flattery. "Now, Mr. Firth channeled his fear into anger. I understand that too. Anger can be such a relief. And yet I firmly believe, Mr. Old, that any man who reacts to fear by lashing out at the nearest living creature deserves a bit of humiliation. Or worse."

Mr. Old rocked back on his heels. "You aren't going easy on poor Mr. Firth, are you?"

"Women, children, and laborers suffer at the hands of such men every day. And why? Because they are ashamed of their fear and rely on cruelty to soothe the ache," Cordelia finished. "I doubt Mr. Firth will derive any useful lesson from Stroud's prank, but perhaps one of the onlookers will."

"Have you shared these thoughts with Rip?"

"No, and I doubt he'd be interested to hear them. But I suspect he was motivated, in his unreflecting way, by a similar conviction."

"You're right of course." Mr. Old's expression turned speculative. "You surprise me. I can name more than one person who's known Rip for years without understanding him half as well as you do."

"They ought to pay closer attention."

"Maybe so, Miss Kelly. Maybe so." Mr. Old chortled, and the twinkle reignited in his eyes. His good humor wasn't as natural or as deep-seated as Stroud's. He could set it aside if he liked, return to it when he wished. "We'll speak again soon, yes?"

Cordelia spent the next few hours mingling. She'd never enjoyed parties until she met Olympia, and she'd probably been spoiled for events hosted by anyone else. Olympia collected people the same way that she collected antiques and jewelry, and gatherings at her house were uniquely fascinating.

In the space of an hour, Cordelia met a man who'd been in France during the revolution and smilingly told stories that made Cordelia's blood run cold, a woman who wrote stories for the *Boys' Own* magazines under a male pseudonym, and a baron whose passion for yacht racing had led him to circumnavigate the globe three times.

As the sky darkened, the dancing started. Cordelia kept to the edges of the room, enjoying the spectacle as the artist had imagined it: couples whirling across the smooth wood, lamplight glancing off of mirrors lining the walls, and the painted figures on the ceiling, who almost seemed to whirl with the dancers.

Olympia could be frivolous and maddening and yet... sometimes... sometimes Cordelia really believed she worked magic.

Cordelia sighed and collected her outdoor things. She couldn't stay late. She'd have to work in the morning. She had to earn enough to pay for food and shelter and... the list of necessities could get depressingly long, but it certainly included sleep.

CHAPTER 10

That week a young woman pregnant with her first child asked Cordelia to rebind a handful of her favorite childhood books, volumes so often reread that the covers were disintegrating. The work would make up most of the ground Cordelia had lost with the Wollstonecraft set, even though the mother-to-be's budget didn't allow for elaborately painted inside covers. Cordelia suggested custom marbling, and since she'd already made the size, she could congratulate herself for having used the lean time to good advantage.

She celebrated with a long lunch at Olympia's, where she could finally ask, "Why did you give the Duke of Stroud my address?"

"I assumed he wanted to send you flowers or something along those lines." She blinked. "Did you get any flowers?"

"No."

"What a shame. It's always nice to have fresh flowers about the house. Perhaps I'll send you some, to make up for his rudeness."

"He wanted to rope me into playing pranks, which are a terrible waste of time," Cordelia continued, undeterred. "Honestly, Olympia. He asked me for my name and I refused his request. He came to you in order to circumvent my wishes, and I wasn't happy to learn that you answered his questions without consulting me first."

"You've nothing to worry about." Olympia smiled in relief. "He's harmless, I promise. A lovely man—and a duke!"

"He's a lovely man who found some untraceable means by which to introduce objects into my bedroom," Cordelia protested. "He gave me a fright, Olympia. *You* facilitated it."

"I'm so thrilled he's taken a liking to you!" Olympia tapped the tips of her fingers against the palm of her opposite hand, her version of a clap. "Shall I invite him around a bit more?"

A reasonable person would have drawn a very different conclusion from what she'd just said. Luckily for Olympia, Cordelia didn't expect her to be reasonable. "I was hoping to ask you to do exactly that. Maybe while Bonny is visiting?"

"The orchid auctions are coming right up, aren't they? Time does fly." Olympia's expression softened. "You must be counting the days."

"I miss her more than I can express," Cordelia admitted. "I was wondering if you'd host a small, fairly intimate gathering while she's here, and invite Stroud and Mr. Old to join us."

"What do you want with Rip and Chilly?"

"A… prank, of sorts," Cordelia kept her answer vague. Of all her friends, Olympia was most likely to slip and spill a secret. "The duke is fond of pranks, you know."

"He is," Olympia affirmed. "*You*, however. I seem to recall you saying something about how pranks are a waste of time. You mentioned it, oh, when was it? I'm searching my memory and… Ah, yes. It was just now, actually. Not even a minute ago."

"I am trying to prove a point."

"Well at least we're starting on familiar territory."

"I believe I will be more persuasive if I speak his language, as it were."

"Oh, I'm going to tell Rip that you called pranks a *language*."

Olympia giggled. "He'd finally be able to say he speaks more than one!"

Cordelia sighed. "Will you help?"

"Of course!" Olympia beamed. "Plus, it will provide a perfect opportunity to introduce Bonny to Mr. Grant."

Cordelia made a face.

"Mr. Grant is a delight," snapped Olympia. "And you are heartless."

"Even if you are right on both counts—and you're wrong on at least one—a man who is superficially delightful may yet be vile at the core."

"You've grown cynical, and I feel sorry for you." Olympia gestured for the next course to be served. "Imagine being suspicious of *Rip*."

"He's earned it."

"Are we going to talk about what he earns? Because I'll tell you." Olympia leaned over the table and lowered her voice to a conspiratorial whisper. "Oodles and oodles of money. Really, Cordelia. I'd imagine you'd be thrilled to make a connection like that."

"He has so much power that if he's reckless with it—as I suspect he is—he must hurt people thoughtlessly, without even noticing." Cordelia shrugged. "I'm fond of him, but not nearly so fond as I am frightened."

Olympia scowled. "You sound like Tess."

"I should be so lucky." Tess navigated tripwires of high society with the grace of a ballet dancer. "Where is she, by the way?"

"Off in a snit," Olympia said breezily, and Cordelia didn't have to ask the cause. It could only be the headache of the moment, Mr. Martin Grant. Olympia waved and changed the subject. "You've a prank in mind?"

"I do."

"You may leave the rest to me."

105

CORDELIA WAS STARTLED to receive a note from Miss Smith wondering if she had the evening free to do work on the petition that might last "until possibly quite late." When Cordelia returned an immediate "Yes," the note which Miss Smith sent in reply included an address and asked her to arrive at three in the afternoon.

Cordelia dressed and set out early, since she didn't know the neighborhood. As a result, she had to idle nervously on the corner of a quiet street, keeping an eye on everyone who passed while studiously not making eye contact—a skill she'd been forced to develop upon arriving in London and which she had not mastered—until Miss Smith stepped out of a hired cab and greeted her with an apologetic, "Poor dear, how long have you been here?"

"Hardly a moment—"

Miss Smith *tsked*. "Now, now. No polite lies. That's not what we're about. I've got a terribly tedious task for you tonight—necessary but dull, dull, dull—and I thought I'd take you along on a very *interesting* errand in order to compensate."

"You've piqued my curiosity," said Cordelia.

"Then let us assuage it." Miss Smith gestured Cordelia toward the stoop of a well-maintained cottage. She knocked, and a bleak-faced servant answered, ushering the pair of them inside when Miss Smith announced that they'd come to visit Mrs. Mitchell.

A woman about the age of Cordelia's mother, comfortably middle-aged and energetic as any adult in her prime, intercepted them in the middle of a corridor.

"Miss Smith." The woman took both of Miss Smith's hands in her own and squeezed hard. "And not too soon. It'll mean so much to her that you've come."

"It is my very great honor to be here," Miss Smith returned. "Thank you for the invitation."

"I think it's all that's kept her going." The woman blinked, her eyes sheened with moisture, and added in a slightly wobbling tone, "Perhaps I shouldn't let you in!"

Miss Smith folded the woman into a hug. As they separated, the stranger's eyes fell on Cordelia. "And who is this?"

"Miss Cordelia Kelly." Miss Smith gave Cordelia a friendly pat on the arm. "She's agreed to help us prepare the petition. I thought your mother might appreciate a—well, a witness. A member of the younger generation, waiting to take up the work we've begun."

"A beautiful thought." The woman clasped both of Cordelia's hands in her own and squeezed. The brief pressure felt intimate, less a greeting than a shock to the nerves. A startling and direct connection to the stranger's heightened emotional state. "Welcome, Miss Kelly. I'll take you to my mother. She's been in good spirits; speak slowly and clearly and she'll understand well enough."

"Miss Kelly," added Miss Smith, "this is Mrs. Mitchell's eldest daughter, Mrs. Heloise Green. She read about our petition in the papers and wrote to me about her mother's interest in signing."

This was all the warning Cordelia had before she was escorted into a sickroom. While the walls carried a long, long lifetime's worth of mementoes—paintings, mounted butterflies, mirrors, embroidered landscapes, clocks—all furniture beside the large bed in the center of the room had been cleared away. The room was scrupulously clean, every nook and cranny dusted, but a faint antiseptic scent mixed with something sour in the air.

Mrs. Mitchell sat upright in the bed through the assistance of at least a dozen pillows. The thick velvet bed curtains had been tied back to let in light, and a book lay open and upside down on her knee. She idly fingered the worn spine while staring at the door with unseeing eyes.

"Mama?" called Mrs. Green. "Mama, we have guests. Miss Smith has come to see you."

"Barbara." Mrs. Mitchell pronounced Miss Smith's Christian name correctly, with obvious effort. "Sit. Let me see you."

Miss Smith obediently settled into the comfortable armchair positioned at Mrs. Mitchell's side. The old woman craned her neck and squinted, but Cordelia did not have the impression that she saw very much. When Miss Smith took Mrs. Mitchell's hand, however, she smiled with real joy.

"You'll read it to me first," Mrs. Mitchell said. "I can't sign... if I don't know what it says."

"Of course," Miss Smith agreed.

"Heloise, make sure the words are right," Mrs. Mitchell added, gesturing her daughter closer. "Every word."

"Of course, Mama," agreed Mrs. Green, positioning herself at Miss Smith's shoulder.

Miss Smith extracted a leather folder from her valise. She withdrew a copy of the petition and another sheet which bore at least a dozen different signatures.

"To the Honourable House of Peers," Miss Smith began. "The Petition of the undersigned Women of Great Britain, Married and Single, Humbly Sheweth that the manifold evils occasioned by the present law, by which the property and earnings of the wife are thrown into the absolute power of the husband, become daily more apparent..."

It took quite a while read the whole petition aloud. Mrs. Mitchell had not asked for appearance's sake alone—she frequently interrupted Miss Smith's recitation, asked for phrases to be repeated or explained.

She was sharp and listened well, but her focus couldn't hold through to the end. The effort alone seemed to exhaust her; her breaths grew quicker, shallower, her expression pained. When Mrs. Green at last fetched a pen, Mrs. Mitchell added her name to the rows of signatures with a shaking hand.

"There," said the old woman. "Do some good with it."

"That is my aim, Mrs. Mitchell," Miss Smith agreed. "That is exactly my aim."

Mrs. Green escorted them out and Miss Smith breathed a tremendous sigh as the door closed behind them.

"We'll share a cab." Miss Smith hailed one as she spoke. "You probably haven't heard of Mrs. Mitchell, but she's a woman after your own heart. After her husband died, she found herself at a loss. She gravitated to women's causes and took it upon herself to recruit other widows to aid her efforts. She had quite a brigade by the end, mostly fundraising around the goal of ensuring that girls be allowed to finish primary school."

"You're right," said Cordelia, humbled. "I'd never heard her name before."

"So much good work never receives the recognition it deserves." Miss Smith cocked an eyebrow. "Perhaps that's not news to you?"

"It is, in a way. It surprises me to discover that life lessons I acquired in my little hometown can apply to the wider world."

"Is it a good surprise or a bad surprise?"

Cordelia didn't answer, which made Miss Smith laugh. "While I'm busy disappointing you: our work tonight will be a very menial task, I'm afraid."

The hackney rolled to a stop, and Miss Smith was quick to reach for her coin purse. One of her servants opened the door, and by an effort of will, Cordelia managed to bite her tongue on any questions until they'd arrived in a small workroom.

After a bit of bustling about, Miss Smith presented Cordelia with a stack of papers. The top one, and the one beneath, and all the rest Cordelia managed to flip through were full of signatures. "Here we go. This might not be all of them—I'll check while you get started. But first..." A bit more scrambling and Cordelia received a pot of glue and a coarse-bristled brush. "Your task is to glue the pages together."

"Glue?" Cordelia wondered.

Miss Smith took the top page, laid it flat on the table. She placed the next directly below the first, so that the bottom of one just overlapped with the top of the other. Running her index finger across that overlap, Miss Smith explained, "Right here. Lay down a thin line of glue and attach each page to the next. Be careful to keep the sheets even! Once it's all dry, we'll roll them up into a scroll for Lord Brougham to unfurl when he presents the petition to the Lords."

"This is well within my realm of expertise," Cordelia assured her.

"You'll do a fine job," Miss Smith said confidently. "Go ahead and start while I make sure that I've gathered all the pages... and we should count the signatures while we're at it. So first we'll fetch you a pencil and paper. You can make a tally as you go."

Within a few minutes, Miss Smith's servants had converted a bare table into a simple workstation. A bit of foolscap and a pencil for the tally, the stack of signed pages, the glue, and a towel to wipe up spills were all placed within reach.

Cordelia set to. It proved, as Miss Smith had warned, dull work. Her skill in papercraft ensured that she swiped a thin, even layer of glue across each page and always lined them up perfectly, without any wrinkles or errors.

It was the sort of task she could have accomplished in her sleep. As her tally marks extended across several rows and the lengthening scroll began to creep across the floor, she eyed the remaining stack of pages and realized that only someone who could glue in her sleep would be able to complete this task, as she'd surely be at it all night.

Miss Smith kept her company and, at first, tried to help. But her gluing was neither as neat nor as efficient as Cordelia's, and after only a few minutes of observation, she simply couldn't stand it anymore.

"Let me." Cordelia swatted the air. "It will go faster."

"It's not right to let you—" Miss Smith began.

"It's not *right* to make me watch you glue wrinkles into the paper," Cordelia returned crisply. "Please, Miss Smith. I can't bear it. Truly."

Miss Smith gave her a thorough once-over and replied, wonderingly, "I believe you are serious. Well. How shall I make myself useful?"

Cordelia didn't hesitate. "Tell me about the pamphlet you wrote. The ladies' guide to English law."

"You know about that?"

"That was how I first learned your name. My father is a judge, and the guide came to his attention, so he passed it along to me. He had a few words about whether such a thing ought to exist, but he couldn't criticize its accuracy. I thought it an amazingly useful document."

"I worked with several renowned lawyers—that's how I came into contact with the Law Amendment Society." Miss Smith paused. "Well, I'll tell you about it while you work, shall I?"

Cordelia smiled. "Please."

"TWENTY-FIVE THOUSAND." Cordelia rubbed her eyes, tired and gritty and aching from the strain of working by candlelight all night long. "You've collected nearly twenty-five *thousand* signatures for this petition."

"And we could have had more, if that were our aim. But we had to avoid the impression that this sort of progress is disruptive, so we focused on women of good reputation—especially married ones." Miss Smith reached for a drawer and extracted another sheet of paper. "Here. Last but not least: those of us who organized the petition, along with our more renowned supporters, all signed on a separate page. We'll attach it to the top, along with the text itself, and then… at last… we'll be done."

Cordelia couldn't help but run her fingers lovingly over the signatures on this leading page of signatures. "Elizabeth Barrett Browning," she murmured. "And Mrs. Gaskell! Oh, I do adore her novels."

"She was reluctant to sign," Miss Smith noted. "But lent us her name, in the end."

"Why reluctant?" Cordelia wondered.

"Her own husband pockets the money she earns from her

writing, and she's vocally content with the arrangement." Miss Smith shrugged. "But she understands that not all of us are lucky in our marriages."

Carefully, Cordelia glued the signatures to the top of the petition while Miss Smith rolled it from the bottom. At last, they tied the cylinder with a red silk ribbon. Cordelia, who'd avoided looking at the clock out of sheer dread, steeled herself: nearly four in the morning.

"My goodness," she murmured.

"Let me put you up in my spare room for what's left of the night," Miss Smith offered. "I can't let you go home alone at this hour."

Cordelia, seeing the wisdom in this caution, could only agree. In the morning, when she woke, Miss Smith told her she'd had a letter from Mrs. Green. Mrs. Mitchell had died during the night.

CHAPTER 11

A few days later, Cordelia read an account in the papers of Lord Brougham's presentation of the petition before the House of Lords. While the article only briefly described the *contents* of the petition, it mentioned that the scroll unrolled across the whole length of the hall—a dramatic display of the widespread public support mobilized in favor of married women's property rights.

It was thrilling to see her own, tiny role in the making of the petition reach the papers. She'd helped to craft that bit of pageantry, the flourish that drew the eye to a critically important issue.

Next time, she vowed, she would have more to contribute than paper craft. Next time, she would be in the thick of things.

But first, she had to finish Mrs. Dowell's commission. She wouldn't be able to enjoy Bonny's company with important work left undone.

As Bonny and her husband, Baron Loel, were disembarking from the train and scrambling to transport an enormous quantity of orchids safely to the auction house through the spring chill, Cordelia presented the finished volumes to Mrs. Dowell. She watched nervously while her client flipped through each one—

she was always confident of her work right up until the moment when her client passed judgment, which never failed to make her sick with fear—but Mrs. Dowell pronounced her a genius and paid her in full.

Cordelia tucked the coins into a pocket fastened to a ribbon inside her skirts and continued on to Olympia's townhouse. Chatter and laughter filtered down the stairs into the foyer.

Waving away the strapping Swiss footman who offered to guide her to his mistress, Cordelia followed the sounds of merriment to their source. Everyone had gathered in one of the few rooms where Olympia prioritized comfort over eye-searing extravagance. She called it the Causerie and changed the furnishings almost every season. She'd begun to clear away the cozy winter throws in favor of potted plants and bright bouquets that didn't quite fit the dreary March weather.

Lord Loel leaned against the wall, content to remain on the sidelines. A year of marriage had softened his grim countenance, rendering him somehow—impossibly—even more handsome than before. Still tall and rangy and intense but with a new looseness to his posture, an air of being at ease with the world.

Olympia sat on an oversized rocking chair with her legs folded crosswise, her house slippers discarded. Tess had installed herself at a small desk and appeared to be writing letters. Cordelia had the impression that Tess's "family" would read and comment on any letters that circulated through her "home." Perhaps make copies for the Queen. So all her private correspondence went to Olympia.

Bonny leapt from her seat on the sofa with a gleeful cry. She was the sort of person who lit up any room she entered, gentle and good-hearted and achingly beautiful. Perhaps it was the shock of seeing her after a long absence, but she positively glowed.

Bonny stumbled, and Loel was at her side instantly, an arm hooked beneath her breast to hold her steady.

"Thank you." Bonny patted her rounded belly. "I ought to know better by now, shouldn't I?"

Loel said nothing, which nevertheless made his opinion on the subject clear.

Cordelia's heart squeezed at the byplay. She never would have pictured Bonny, so bright and effervescent, with a man who bordered on the taciturn... and yet they were a perfect match, each made whole by the other.

Growing up in a small town felt like navigating the world with blinders on. But Cordelia had been part of a community, she'd made friends and met their families. Experience more than education had made her cynical about marriage. So few married couples seemed happy with one another. More often, they wore one another down, grew numb to one another, ended up impoverished rather than improved by their years of intimacy.

The rare exceptions, like Bonny and Loel, complicated matters. How could she condemn an institution that, every once and a while, got everything right?

But all these complicated thoughts could wait. She swept Bonny into a full-body hug. "Why didn't you tell me you were pregnant?"

"Are you furious?" Bonny asked, returning the embrace. "I thought I ought to but I wanted to deliver the news in person. You can't hug me in a letter."

"I am overjoyed, Bonny." Cordelia linked her hands with her friend's and pulled back to arm's length, so she could fix this moment in her memory. "This little baby is the luckiest child in England to have you for a mother."

"Don't exaggerate."

"I always say exactly what I think, you know that."

Loel, slinking back to his position at the wall, smothered a smile with his hand.

"*I'm* the lucky one." Bonny had a unique ability to make the most well-trodden, saccharine sentiments seem spontaneous and sincere—because, from her, they were. She hadn't an unkind bone in her body. "You're looking so well. Tell me about your business and your books—I can already tell you've been working too hard."

"It's the only way to survive." Cordelia touched the thin skin beneath her eyes, wondering exactly how she'd changed over the past year. If Bonny's diplomacy had failed, she must look worn indeed. "But I've finally found something to fill the hole in my heart where our circulating library used to be. I've joined forces with a group of women who are advocating to give married women increased legal rights."

"Oh, that's right. You met with that women's group you were so excited about." Tess looked up from her writing, propped her cheek on her fist. "How did it go?"

"I was invited to sign the petition." Cordelia still felt a thrill every time she remembered seeing her name in stark black ink next to the signatures of women she'd admired for so long. "Did you read about it in the papers? How Lord Brougham unrolled it across the floor of Westminster?"

Tess nodded. "I thought of you."

"Well, *I* glued all the pages together," Cordelia told them—bragged. It turned out she was proud of herself. "The night before. It was four in the morning before I finished."

"Exactly how many signatures were there?" Bonny wondered, returning to the sofa.

"Twenty-five thousand."

"So many?" Tess whistled. "I wonder if anything will come of it. Have you heard anything since?"

"I haven't." Cordelia sat beside Bonny and linked their arms. "But these things take time."

"The conservatives hold a great deal of sway right now," Tess cautioned. "No news isn't good news."

"But Lord Brougham has shepherded a number of important laws to a successful conclusion," Cordelia countered. "If our petition has his support, it has a chance."

"We are not going to become bores who while away our afternoons prognosticating Parliament." Olympia slapped the arms of her rocking chair, mock-petulant, but she wasn't joking. "We can discuss causes and certainly we can exchange gossip—if you have it always share—but I don't invite fortune tellers of any kind. Including the sort who disguise themselves by putting on grave faces and talking politics."

Tess laughed. "My favorite of your rules, Olympia."

"Mine too." Olympia relaxed, which set the chair to rocking. She looked very cozy. "Here's something a bit more fun. I'm going to host a dinner tomorrow. All of you will attend and together we're going to trick the king of trickery."

Tess snorted. "A grandiose title for a six-foot toddler."

"Who's this?" Bonny smacked Tess lightly on the arm. "I live in the country. You need to *explain* things."

"They're referring to the Duke of Stroud," Cordelia answered.

"The *Duke of Stroud*?" Bonny's eyes went wide as saucers. "Cordelia, what on Earth? I thought you were hand-binding books?"

"I am. The duke and I are acquaintances—though Olympia— and there's nothing untoward about it."

"He wheeled Cordelia's name and address out of Olympia," Tess added, apparently unimpressed by Cordelia's attempt to trim the story of its unsavory elements. "And he's been pursuing her ever since."

Bonny covered her mouth with her hand. A sheen of moisture glossed her fine blue eyes. "Do you need help? Just say the word. You can come live with us. I know it's not ideal but surely it's better to be safe—"

"Stroud is a *lovely* man," Olympia interrupted. "I've known him for*ever*, so I know him best, and I assure you he's a gentleman. Once you meet him, you'll see."

"Cordelia?" Loel prompted, green eyes glinting as he folded his arms across his chest.

"I believe he has a good heart." Cordelia struggled to form a dispassionate opinion. All her thoughts about Stroud were

117

complicated and *personal*. "And that he has been misled into thinking he is not very bright."

"Because he's *not*. He's a dear old friend and great fun at a party but..." Olympia spread her hands helplessly.

Cordelia disagreed. Strongly. "If you think so, then you aren't paying enough attention."

"I've known him much longer than you," Olympia exclaimed.

"Perhaps," murmured Tess, "we can all agree that this test Cordelia has concocted has the potential to be illuminating?"

"Why is everyone against me?" Olympia complained.

"Oh, darling." Bonny heaved herself out of the sofa and crossed the room to hug Olympia. "No one's against you. I've noticed that sometimes people say surprising things around Cordelia because they want to impress her. Maybe she's seen a side of this duke that you haven't?"

"We haven't seen much of one another lately." Olympia leaned into Bonny's embrace. "Not for the past few years really."

"So what's this about a test?" Bonny asked.

"I'll need your help in particular," said Cordelia.

"Anything," Bonny answered immediately. "You can count on me."

"I know I can." She knew with the bone-deep certainty that could only come from experience. "Luckily, this should be a fairly easy task. I'd like for you to playact an allergy."

Bonny looked adorably confused. "An... allergy?"

"You'll sniffle and tear up strategically, and none of the men in attendance will be able to resist the desire to fuss over you," Cordelia explained. "They'll all try to figure out what's causing your sniffles. I think Stroud will be the first to make a correct deduction."

Loel snorted.

"You don't mind?" Cordelia asked.

"I'd find life very difficult if I did," he drawled.

"Must we really..." Bonny flailed her hands about, blushing.

"Which isn't to say that I won't try! I'll start practicing my sniffles this very afternoon."

"Should I postpone the dinner?" Olympia wondered, mock-innocent. "So you have enough time to get them just right?"

Bonny snatched one of the pillows propping up Olympia's back and smacked her with it. "Silly!"

Olympia tore it from Bonny's hands and threw it to Tess, who tossed it in her hands before, with an impish little smile, heaving it right at Cordelia. The evening devolved from there.

CORDELIA AND RUBY arrived at Olympia's while the hostess and her house guests were still dressing for the evening. Since neither dared venture near the room Bonny and Loel shared—Cordelia had spent several days with the couple while making her escape to London and she'd learned her lesson—they invaded Olympia's gold-and-pink boudoir instead, perching on footstools while her lady's maid finished styling her hair.

While Cordelia had dressed simply, because she had no choice in the matter, Ruby wore a fabulous gown with a bodice fashioned after a military uniform, a navy jacket complete with rows of brass buttons and epaulettes at the shoulders, but the skirts split down the front to reveal layers of frothy white lace petticoat. With her hair in its usual sleek bun, she looked fierce and fiercely beautiful.

Olympia happily filled the silence with chatter. "Stroud said he wouldn't come if I didn't invite Chilly and Flea and that girl Chilly's in love with, Nell Dowell. They've all sent word that they'll attend." The lady's maid stepped back, and Olympia tipped her head from side to side as she admired herself in the mirror. She murmured a quick word of approval and the maid retreated. "The only other guest will be Mr. Grant."

"A fairly intimate gathering," Ruby noted.

"I'm glad, because I'll be able to spend more time with

Bonny." Cordelia shuffled close enough to give Olympia a hug. "I could never have arranged a gathering like this on my own, and I know you're doing it mostly for my benefit. Thank you, Olympia. I'm grateful."

"You can't be grateful! I'm grateful!" Olympia returned the hug, neck craned to protect her hair but arms tight around Cordelia's middle. "You've given me an excuse to indulge myself."

"It's kind of you to—" *say so*, Cordelia would have finished, but Olympia pressed her index finger across Cordelia's lips before she could.

"Not one more word on the subject," Olympia ordered. "Show your appreciation by having a wonderful time. I've spent the past few days arranging everything, all the food and the entertainments and *especially* the decorations. I can't wait for you to see."

"Not only am I looking forward to dinner"—Ruby leaned down to give Olympia a kiss on the cheek—"now I have the pleasure of disobeying a direct order by telling you how thrilled I am to be here. Such excellent hostessing!"

"Oh, tut tut, how very rebellious." Olympia stood and smoothed her skirts, hiding her pleased smile. She looked like a fashion plate brought to life, somehow effortless in her elegance— though Cordelia had seen how much work went into crafting that effect. "Shall we go downstairs?"

Cordelia could hardly believe her eyes when she saw the ballroom. Papier-mâché trees surrounded a long, low table draped with a scarlet cloth and laid with fine crystal. A carpet of green velvet covered the floor, and an abundance of potted flowers trailed real blooms across the fabricated tree roots. Lanterns hanging from the spreading branches cast a gentle golden glow over the scene. Their light reflected on the mirrors that still lined the walls, creating the impression of a vast and mysterious forest.

Even Olympia's pets, a miniature pig named Mrs. Potts and a cat named Aunt Emily, had been dressed for the occasion. Mrs. Potts wore a tiara, a tulle skirt, and a bell on her curlicue tail. Aunt

Emily—more dexterous and thus more likely to destroy an elaborate costume—wore a jeweled collar.

"Oh, Olympia, this is lovely," Ruby enthused.

"I'm rather pleased with how it all turned out," Olympia conceded.

"You've completely transformed the room," Cordelia agreed, stunned as always by Olympia's commitment to excess.

"I bought the sets from a theater that had just finished a run of *Midsummer Night's Dream* and used most of the props to create this tableau, just for this evening."

"You never do anything by halves," said Cordelia. "As much as it upsets me, I must admit it's somehow, simultaneously, one of my favorite things about you."

Ruby laughed. "You have a hard time with mixed emotions, don't you, Cordelia?"

"Doesn't everyone?" Cordelia wondered.

"I think the rest of us experience them more often," said Ruby. "Often enough to make peace with the experience, in any case."

Bonny and Loel descended from the room they were sharing. Like Cordelia, circumstances forced Bonny to dress plainly—the Loels poured every spare coin into their orchid-growing business. Unlike Cordelia, Bonny looked phenomenal, pillow-soft and curvaceous and eternally clear-skinned. Simplicity highlighted her beauty while it made Cordelia look like the headmistress of a school for recalcitrant girls.

Cordelia greeted her friend with a hug. "Seeing you twice in as many days feels like the most decadent luxury."

Bonny hugged back. "I miss being able to walk across the street to knock at your door. It almost makes me wish we could go back to those days."

"Almost?" Cordelia prompted.

"I want find out what happens next." Bonny beamed, brimming with hope. "Surprise me?"

Mr. Grant arrived, slim and stylish and well-coiffed and so repulsive that Cordelia felt a little guilty for her profound dislike of him. Something about his full lips and limpid blue eyes and the precise way his hair crowned his head in a luxuriant wave of wheaten gold. He ought to have been handsome—Olympia obviously found him attractive—but he made Cordelia's skin crawl.

He gasped at his first sight of Bonny and made a beeline to her as though mesmerized, not looking left or right, and Cordelia remembered that her poor opinion of the man was entirely justified. When Bonny inched closer to Loel, Mr. Grant realized his mistake and froze.

Olympia gave him a pinch but didn't react, otherwise. At first Cordelia wondered at her tolerance but the second thoughts came quickly. Bonny had that kind of beauty; men often misbehaved around her. If one wanted to be friends with her, one had to make peace with it.

Mr. Grant—obviously embarrassed by his reaction—greeted the Loels coldly and with a very shallow bow. Cordelia's opinion of the man, already low, dropped a little further.

Stroud arrived looking, as always, like a god who'd snuck away from Olympus to make trouble for mortals. The way his wool coat hugged his broad shoulders and tapered around his waist was less flattering than *admiring*, a love letter from the tailor to his heroic proportions.

Cordelia suppressed a wistful sigh at the sight of him, then another (less wistful this time) as she mentally prepared herself to watch yet another man make a fool of himself over her oldest friend. To her astonishment, Stroud paid no mind to Bonny. He took in the transformed ballroom with a wary eye, suffered Olympia's introductions with obvious impatience, and then sidled close to Cordelia.

The sharp, smoky scent of his cologne filled her nose as he stooped to whisper, "What are you up to?" in her ear, his usually light voice lowered to a mellow rumble that vibrated right through her.

Cordelia licked suddenly dry lips. "Olympia planned the party. If you have any questions, take them to her."

"You're answering a different question than the one I asked."

"Am I?"

"You are."

"Funny that you should notice." Cordelia tapped her index finger against her pursed lips. "What is this challenge meant to prove, again?"

Stroud's tone turned wheedling. "Give me a hint, at least?"

"Don't be a pest." Lady Florence wore dull brown silk with a few matching feathers pinned into her hair. She hooked an arm around Stroud's elbow and began tugging him away. "Is he bothering you, Miss Kelly?"

"He's wasting his breath. But if he doesn't have anything better to do with it…"

Stroud bit his knuckle to hide a grin—she caught the shape of it in the spread of his fingers, the dimples in his cheeks. Before he could reply, Tess arrived. She wore a pair of costume fairy wings made from wire and covered in pink netting, a perfect match to her petal pink dress, and greeted Olympia with a hug.

"You've really outdone yourself," Tess marveled. "I don't recognize the ballroom at all."

"Look at your wings." Olympia gasped in delight. "Now my fairy garden is complete."

And they might have gone on like that, exchanging compliments by turns, if Christopher Old and Nell Dowell hadn't arrived, completing the company for the evening.

"I thought we might start with a game!" Olympia declared, while a pair of handsome servants introduced a selection of punches and petits fours onto the table.

Cordelia reached for a platter lined with green velvet, upon which a fairy ring of mushroom-shaped… somethings… had been arranged. They were charming, all different shapes and sizes, the meat of varying shades of taupe with spots and shading made, presumably, from a brown sauce of some sort.

"You have a very *imaginative* cook," Stroud observed warily.

"You needn't fear she sacrifices flavor for appearance, Rip.

Everything that emerges from her kitchen is delicious." Olympia pointed to the fairy ring and smiled beatifically. "Why don't you give one of those a try? I'd love to have your opinion."

Cordelia winced in sympathy. Olympia obviously had something up her sleeve, but it would be rude to refuse such a direct request. With a self-pitying sigh, he selected one from the ring and took a bite.

Olympia's blue eyes sparkled in the candlelight. "Be honest."

Stroud chewed glumly and shuddered as he swallowed. "I honestly think you are a cruel woman who delights in the suffering of others."

Mr. Grant leapt from his chair, trembling with rage. "I beg your pardon!"

Olympia restrained her suitor with a pat to his forearm. "It's so sweet that you're defending me, but we all say things in the heat of the moment, don't we?" She cast a sly smile at Stroud. "And I'm sure Rip can admit that, every once and a while, he deserves a taste of his own medicine."

"Perhaps not so literally." Stroud scowled at the tray of mushrooms. "I really hate pâté."

"Is it still pâté if it looks like a mushroom?" Olympia fluttered her eyelashes.

"Yes." Stroud gestured to the fairy ring, announcing to the rest of the table, "The mushrooms are made of goose liver. Please enjoy the delicious meat mushrooms."

Mr. Old immediately popped one in his mouth. "They really are delicious." He tipped his head toward Nell. "Why don't you try? You love pâté."

"Make it stop," Stroud mock-despaired, falling back in his chair. He glared at Cordelia. "Is this your doing?"

"Your Grace, it would not have occurred to me to torment you with exquisitely prepared *petits fours*."

"Put it that way and it's really much more Olympia's style." He took a nugget of something that appeared to be made of beets, jewel red and shining with glaze, and set it on his plate. Low enough that only Cordelia could hear, he added, "You'd never strike at a man's stomach when you could aim at his heart."

"What?" Cordelia asked.

Stroud glanced sidewise at her and then placed a second bite-sized delicacy, this one glistening with translucent, golden-orange caviar, right beside the first. He nudged both to the center of the plate, which was porcelain painted with a lush pattern of leaves and vines, and stared at the arrangement critically.

"Are you—" *nervous*, she almost asked, but caught herself in time. What a rude question. Though she thought the answer might be *yes*. It was hard to tell with a man like Stroud. "—not hungry?"

Stroud frowned. "You're asking about my appetite?"

"Just being polite."

"Too polite."

"Now that we've all had a bite to eat, let's get on with the game!" Olympia clapped, and her handsome manservants reappeared, this time distributing little slips of paper and stubby lead pencils. "I'll ask a question, you'll write down your answer, and then I'll collect all the slips. Simple, isn't it?"

"What will you do with our answers?" asked Lady Florence.

"For the next five minutes that will remain a mystery," Olympia replied. "Here's the question: If you happened to acquire —it doesn't matter how, we'll leave that discussion for a later time —but should you happen to acquire a pet tiger, what would you name it?"

"I don't want a pet tiger," Cordelia objected.

"It seems a poor choice of pet," agreed Bonny.

"Thank you for illustrating why we won't be discussing how or why these pet tigers came into our possession," said Olympia.

"But—" Cordelia began.

"No," Olympia interrupted. "You have a tiger. Name it."

At her side, Stroud began to snicker.

"I bet you'd love a pet tiger," Cordelia muttered, angrily seizing her pencil and paper.

"Of course I would."

"You'd let it sleep on your bed, and you'd be surprised when it mauled you."

Stroud widened his eyes. "It would never!"

"And you'd name it—"

Olympia clucked her tongue. "Keep your answers private and don't try to manipulate the results. That means you, Cordelia."

Cordelia rolled her eyes and wrote DANGER BEWARE on her slip of paper before folding it into quarters and passing it to Olympia. While she waited for everyone else to come up with answers, she scooped Aunt Emily off the floor as the cat slunk past her feet and cuddled the animal in her lap.

Bonny began to sniffle.

"Are you all right, Lady Loel?" asked Mr. Grant. "Please—take my handkerchief—it is yours. Soothe yourself. It pains me to think that our loose talk has offended your delicate sensibilities."

"Thank you, Mr. Grant." Bonny took the handkerchief and dabbed at the corners of her eyes. "I'm enjoying the conversation, actually. Please"—she sniffled again—"let's just play Olympia's game? I hate to be a bother."

"If you need anything, I am at your disposal," Olympia assured Bonny. "For now, I'll collect the slips. Is everyone ready?"

Everyone at the table passed their slips to Olympia.

"Now I'll choose one of the slips at random, read the name aloud, and we all have to guess who wrote it." Olympia tipped the slips into a jar and shook it. "I think it will be great fun."

"So… before we get to the slips…" Mr. Old leaned over his forearms, folded on the table, and waggled his eyebrows. "It's safe to ask Miss Kelly what she thought Stroud would name his tiger."

"I suppose." Olympia hummed her discontent. "If you must."

"Well?" prompted Mr. Old.

"Pudding," said Cordelia.

"Pudding?" Stroud spluttered. "I would not name a tiger *Pudding*."

"We'll see."

"We'll—but I just told you. It's not Pudding."

"Let's not spoil any more surprises, Rip." Olympia pulled a slip from the jar with a flourish. "The first slip says… Rossi."

"Oh, that's too easy," said Bonny. "It's Loel."

"Easy?" Stroud wondered aloud.

"You know what they say about marriage," said Lady Florence. "Two persons, one flesh. One mind, in this case?"

"It's no great mystery," Bonny explained. "Tiger orchids belong to the family *Rossioglossum,* that's all. Loel doesn't want a tiger. All he cares about are hothouse orchids."

Everyone looked to Lord Loel, who shrugged one shoulder. "She's right."

"Congratulations to my dear friend Bonny, who cheated." Olympia blew a kiss across the table and picked up another piece of paper.

"How is that cheating?" Tess reached for one of the caviar treats. "She knows her husband well enough to guess correctly. Isn't that the game? Knowing one another well enough to guess?"

"So in order to be fair, we'd have to pause the game, live together for a year as a group, and then reconvene?" Mr. Old appeared to consider his suggestion. "All right. If that's what it takes."

"Don't listen to him." Miss Dowell's lips pursed in an oddly affectionate smirk. "Chilly wouldn't last a week. He hates house parties."

"That depends on the company," Chilly protested.

"Not in my experience," Stroud said.

"Rip would know." Miss Dowell pointed at Stroud and nodded sharply. "So we might as well finish the game on unequal footing."

"Thank you, Miss Dowell." Olympia brandished a slip of paper. "The next name is Poodle."

Cordelia looked pointedly at Stroud. "I have a guess."

Across the table, Mr. Old burst out laughing. "Oh, Poodle. That's marvelous."

"You'd tell all your friends you want them to meet your Poodle." Miss Dowell snickered. "And then, oh, *look*. It's a tiger."

Olympia dissolved into giggles. "Surprise!"

"So we're all in agreement that Poodle was the duke's choice?" Tess asked.

A chorus of nods followed this question.

"Admit it," said Cordelia. "I was awfully close with Pudding."

"Pudding, poodle, pudding, poodle..." Lady Florence sing-songed. "They sound so alike. Rather impressive for a blind guess."

"I disagree," Stroud replied. "Poodle is a much better name."

"A poodle is a *dog*," said Cordelia.

"So?"

"A tiger is a *cat*."

"And?"

Cordelia made an exasperated noise.

"Next name—"

Bonny interrupted Olympia's hostessing with a violent sneeze. Aunt Emily, startled, skittered away to hide amongst the potted plants. All the humans at the table offered napkins and handkerchiefs, murmuring, "Bless you."

"Are you sure you're all right, Lady Loel?" Mr. Old asked. "Perhaps you're having a violent reaction to all this greenery that Miss Swain has imported for the evening? So many flowering plants in an enclosed space can spark an allergic reaction."

"I doubt it." Bonny smiled kindly. "I live in the country and spend most of my days in a greenhouse. If I had an allergy to pollen, I'm sure I'd know by now."

"I'll have dinner served outdoors, just in case." Olympia stood. "Excuse me while I have a word with my butler." She returned shortly to announce, "The next name is Grace."

Everyone looked blankly at one another except for Mr. Old,

who stared blandly into the middle distance, and Miss Dowell, who smiled into her petits fours.

Tess guessed. "Miss Dowell."

"How did you know?" asked Miss Dowell.

"I suspected a woman had chosen the name," said Tess. "And since I know most of the ladies in attendance fairly well, I was able to eliminate them as contenders."

"I believe Mr. Old had guessed as well," Cordelia observed.

Mr. Old smiled genially. "I didn't want the hostess to accuse me of cheating."

Bonny reached impulsively for Mr. Old, squeezing his hand. "You've nothing to fear, Mr. Old. Olympia is a dear friend, and I took her teasing in good spirit, as she meant it. Please set your mind at ease."

Mr. Old blinked owlishly, unprepared for the full impact of Bonny's goodwill. Cordelia had seen it happen over and over again in New Quay. Even people who'd known Bonny from childhood could be thrown by her.

Miss Dowell stiffened at the byplay. She threw a quick glance at Lord Loel, who'd compressed his lips to hide a smirk, and relaxed.

The next two names were Softie—courtesy of Mr. Old and easily guessed by Stroud—and Cousin John, at which half the table immediately pointed to Olympia. She already had a pig named Mrs. Potts and a cat named Aunt Emily, in accordance with Tess's theory that naming pets after imaginary relatives would confuse eavesdroppers. Ruby chose Azizam, apparently a term of endearment in her mother's native language, and Bonny Gallant—she insisted that the tiger would be compelled to live up to its name, and thus behave itself.

Olympia read the words *Danger Beware* in a carefully neutral voice. Immediately, Stroud burst out laughing.

Tess clucked her tongue. "What's the word for someone who's unintentionally funny? Like Polonius in *Hamlet*."

Cordelia straightened. "What did you call me?"

129

"I think he's just a fool," Mr. Old said apologetically. "Which would mean…"

Tess fluttered her lashes, pretending innocence.

"Polonius thought himself a wise man speaking to a naive one," Cordelia said. "I think anyone with a modicum of good sense knows it would be an awful idea to keep a pet tiger and—that being the case—the few who remain would benefit from some warning."

"The *few*?" Flea interjected. "I wouldn't have pegged you for an optimist, Miss Kelly."

Cordelia groaned. "Please don't tell me I've been *optimistic*."

Mr. Old, Miss Dowell, and Tess all chorused, "You've been optimistic."

"But that's lovely!" Bonny beamed. "Perhaps I've had an influence on you after all?"

"We can't help but influence—and be influenced *by*—our friends." Cordelia cast a sidelong glance at Stroud. "A frightful thought, considering the present company."

"A delightful thought," Stroud corrected.

"Frightful," Cordelia insisted.

"Delightful," Stroud repeated.

Cordelia sucked in a breath, ready to stand her ground, but she'd only embarrass herself by letting Stroud draw her into a childish game. She looked to Olympia and nodded minutely, holding her tongue.

"Only two names remain." Olympia brandished the nearly empty jar. "Which means one of them belongs to Tess and one to Mr. Grant. How shall we proceed?"

Stroud leaned close and murmured, "Delightful," in the barest whisper.

"The more you insist, the less I agree," Cordelia returned, at the same low volume.

Stroud subsided into his seat.

Cordelia had a truly infantile desire to say more, to clarify that

Stroud definitely had not won the exchange, and by the small, pleased smile tucking in the corners of his mouth he could tell.

"Read them both at once," Tess suggested. "That way no one has to go last."

"An elegant solution," responded Mr. Grant. "I second it."

"Very well. The last two names are… Zulu and Hubris."

"Tess's tiger is Hubris, which means Zulu must be Mr. Grant's," said Ruby.

Cordelia nodded to Ruby. "I am confident that you've guessed correctly."

"How do you know?" Miss Dowell wondered.

"How?" Ruby's lip curled, but she took a long look at Olympia and wiped the sneer away before offering a diplomatic answer. "Tess has a distinctive sense of humor."

"And I suspect she is aware that tigers are not native to Africa," Cordelia added.

"Of course they are!" Mr. Grant objected. "Those great beasts roam the primordial forests—"

"Of Asia," Ruby interrupted.

"Have you studied the subject?" Mr. Grant scoffed. "Please, what is the source of your great knowledge—"

"There are no tigers in Africa," Tess said flatly.

Bonny sneezed loudly.

"Are you all right, Lady Loel?" Miss Dowell's gaze skittered to Mr. Grant and then back to Bonny. "I'm afraid you're coming down with a cold—it is the season for it."

"Oh dear." Bonny wrung her hands. "I hope not, our time here is short and we have so much to do."

"Dinner is ready," Olympia announced. "Perhaps you'll feel a bit better once we've moved? I've had a table set up outside. The fresh air should help."

"Before we go…" Stroud plucked the slip of paper reading DANGER BEWARE from the pile and tucked it into his pocket. "Who won?"

"I wasn't keeping score," Olympia answered. "It wasn't that kind of game."

Stroud looked heartbroken.

The company left behind the ballroom that had been transformed to resemble a fairy forest for the outdoor garden, which had been transformed to resemble a ballroom. Tall wooden panels finished with beautiful wallpapers sheltered the tables from wind while a half-dozen braziers provided heat. Anyone who paid attention would notice that such an elaborate setting couldn't be the result of twenty minutes' hasty effort.

"A toast to our hostess?" Mr. Grant raised his glass of wine. "Who else could have assembled such a divine setting and peopled it with such glorious company? Only the inimitable Miss Olympia Swain. Her good taste and infinite charm, her genuine warmth and unfailing ebullience allow her to orchestrate the finest events in all of London—perhaps the world. Miss Swain, your presence is a gift that we all treasure."

Tess caught Cordelia's attention and rolled her eyes, but they all drank. Mr. Grant wasn't *wrong* exactly, but somehow even when he said things Cordelia agreed with she found him repellant.

The conversation flowed naturally until Lady Florence, who'd taken a seat next to Bonny, unearthed Aunt Emily from her perambulations underneath the table and gave her an affectionate cuddle.

Bonny promptly began to sneeze.

"Oh dear!" Lady Florence dropped Aunt Emily. "Lady Loel, are you allergic to cats?"

"I am, yes!" Bonny sniffled. "I hadn't seen one about, but I should have guessed."

Everyone fussed over Bonny for a bit. A strapping Swedish manservant was called to carry Aunt Emily away for the rest of the evening before conversation drifted onto other topics. Cordelia let it flow around her, simultaneously soothed by the presence of her friends and too discouraged to participate.

CHAPTER 12

Her test had been a failure. Everyone *but* Stroud had tried to puzzle out the source of Bonny's sniffles. Every single man present had been helpless against the urge to dote on Bonny—except, of course, for the one she'd assumed to be most vulnerable.

Stroud had defied her expectations. In a way, she admired him all the more. As he'd explained at Kew, it required no small amount of ingenuity to design a prank. Cordelia had worried over the possibilities, asked favors of two friends, and yet she couldn't even be sure a test had been *administered*. Had he passed? Had he failed? She didn't actually know.

As Olympia's handsome footmen reemerged carrying trays heavy with glazed berry tarts, Cordelia excused herself from the table. She needed a minute to herself. She'd wanted too badly for her scheme to succeed, and now her disappointment was out of proportion with anything that had actually occurred.

She'd wanted—no, no. It didn't matter what she'd wanted. *Wanting* didn't accomplish anything. Preparation did. And discipline, and diligence. And despite all that, without sufficient expertise, she'd failed.

She returned to Olympia's ballroom and dropped into an

empty stool. The fairy forest looked eerie now, silent and empty. Light from scattered wall sconces flickered through the papier-mâché trees but left the long, low table in near darkness.

Stroud seemed content to be *Rip*, the court jester wearing a coronet of strawberry leaves. Why not let him be?

Because of that handshake at Trafalgar Square. Because of the way he'd looked at Kew, sitting on the cold stone bench with his fingers laced in his lap like a schoolboy while he explained that the only good thing about his position were the times when he could help a friend. He had given her something she craved—desperately, more than she'd known—and she could return the favor.

All true. Completely true. And yet, at the same time, enough a lie that she felt embarrassed for trying to believe it.

"Why are you sitting alone in the dark?" asked Stroud, emerging from the gloom to take the seat at her side.

Cordelia squeaked. She hadn't heard a scuff or a shuffle, nothing to announce the arrival of such a big man.

"Inviting you to sneak up on me, apparently," Cordelia snapped.

"I was worried." He sat with his back to the table, thick thighs slightly spread, elbow propped against the wood so he could rest his cheek on his fist. "You got quiet. I counted at least five times you could have corrected someone—"

"That's not all I do," Cordelia interrupted. "These are my friends. I love them, I care for them... I don't just cut people down."

"You don't *just* cut people down," Stroud agreed amiably. "But you're prone to seizing the opportunity."

Cordelia deflated. "Not tonight."

"So what happened, Coco?"

Cordelia scowled. "I didn't invite you to give me a pet name."

"I invited myself." He sounded incredibly pleased about it too.

Being addressed as *Coco*, of all things, released her temper.

Instead of dodging his question, as she should have, she gave him an honest answer. "You failed my test."

"Your test?" Stroud's eyebrows climbed right up his forehead. "What kind of—wait, wait, don't tell me. Does this have something to do with the fact that your friend Lady Loel was pretending to have an allergy?"

Cordelia froze. "Pretending?"

"She only sneezed when the cat was in her line of sight. At one point it spent a few minutes on that papier-mâché branch"—Stroud pointed—"that one, about a foot away from her, but she couldn't see it so she didn't fake a reaction."

Cordelia blinked. "When did you realize she was pretending to be allergic to the cat?"

"Almost immediately?" Stroud shrugged his heavy shoulders. "I thought it was odd, but in my experience, most beautiful women have an odd habit or two. Makes sense, when you think about it. Watching a beautiful woman do almost anything is enjoyable, so who's going to tell them to stop? So she does something odd, enjoys the applause, does it again, and all of a sudden it's a habit. A few years later she's bonkers."

"She wasn't pretending to have an allergy because she's been driven to madness by her own good looks," Cordelia said flatly. "I *asked* her to pretend."

"Oh, the test." Stroud sighed. "It wasn't a good test, Coco."

"Stop calling me *Coco*."

"Guessing someone's fake allergy is nice—I guess you're impressed?—but it's not conclusive the way that failing a Latin exam is. Or a history exam, or a chemistry exam. I failed all of those, by the way." He paused. "Many times."

"I had to start somewhere," Cordelia countered. "I don't know why you failed at school—how could I? I've never been allowed inside a classroom where advanced subjects are taught. But my father is an educated man. And while he never went so far as to teach me calculus or chemistry, he taught me that the building blocks of intelligence are patience, persisting through discourage-

ERIN SATIE

ment, attention to detail, the elements of logic... That's what I set out to test. And you possess those qualities, Your Grace. In abundance."

"Why don't you call me Rip?"

"I refuse."

"What about Stroud?"

"No."

"Why are you so stubborn?"

Cordelia pursed her lips. "I could ask you the same."

"I'm very agreeable."

"Agree that you passed the test."

"It was a faulty test."

Cordelia laughed. She couldn't help it. "Very agreeable indeed."

"I don't think agreeing would impress you very much."

"Clever of you." The smile that had appeared unbidden on her lips dimmed. "So is it your opinion that a valid test of intelligence must be administered in a classroom and executed in writing?"

Stroud frowned.

"And if that's not enough, then—" *What would be?* But she only finished the question in her mind because Stroud silenced her with a kiss.

She had a vague impression of softness before all her faculties ground to a halt, like a smashed clock. First shock overwhelmed sensation, then sweetness rushed in to fill the cracks.

He fastened her lips closed with his own, silky and firm. The tip of his nose nudged her cheek, cold from being outdoors. When she didn't react, he leaned in. Pressed a dozen small kisses into the seam of her lips, each one gentle as a butterfly sipping nectar from a flower.

She felt like someone had flicked a feather duster around the inside of her ribcage. Jumpy and breathless and overwhelmed from the lightest of touches. Stroud brushed his lips along her cheek, puffed his breath warm against her ear. He nipped at her earlobe and the strange, ticklish panic built and built.

"Coco…" Stroud thumbed her chin, a furrow appearing between his brows. "You really didn't expect that, did you?"

"What?" Cordelia sounded strange to her own ears. Scared. Was she scared? She didn't think so, but she couldn't tell exactly. "How?"

A strange, sad expression flitted across his face. "Do you *like* it?"

"Yes." The word came first and the certainty second. Yes, she had liked it. So much affection distilled into a touch, washing over her. She hadn't understood that if words could expand a thought until it made clear sense, then touch could do the opposite, condense it all down into a moment of fugitive, bafflingly powerful sensation.

He kissed her again. Soft again, so soft. No pressure, only patience. He was big and close, radiating heat like a furnace. He smelled of starch and dog and, ever so slightly, apples.

If that scent came in a perfume, she'd have paupered herself for a bottle of it.

Her first kiss, and it was a revelation. Why risk it, she'd wondered. She'd never been tempted. If any of her former suitors had wanted to—which she doubted—they'd restrained themselves. The stakes were too high. Even a whisper of a kiss, like this one, meant so much. A gentleman would never tease the pleasures of his bedchamber to a lady who might never occupy it.

For a moment, she let that sink in. This big, silly man had decided to court her. He infuriated her, yes, but he also smiled when she argued and shook her hand when she thwarted him. He presented himself as an easygoing oaf, but the truth was so different. He gave as good as he got. Would it really be so bad if… if…

…*the Duke of Stroud* wanted to marry her? Because the idea was absurd. *Laughable.* Dukes rarely married daughters of the gentry, as she had once been. They aimed higher, as was their right and privilege. They certainly did not engage honorably with disgraced, estranged, no-longer-entirely-respectable young women like herself.

Cordelia leapt from her chair. She found herself breathing hard, tear ducts stinging. Shame burned through her, braided with heartache. "I won't let you toy with me!"

Stroud blinked, looking dazed.

"I knew you could be careless." Cordelia couldn't strain the emotion out of her voice and cringed at the sound of it, low and throbbing and revealing so much more than she wanted to share. "I didn't think you were cruel."

"Cruel?" Stroud stood. His expression was wide open, painfully vulnerable. "Coco, I think I'm in lo—"

It took effort, but she sucked all the warmth out of her tone. Her next words were icy cold. "Don't you *dare*."

She'd accused him of being cruel, but watching hurt flash across his face before he could hide it made her feel like a monster. She did not apologize. Let alone admit that she, too, had been hurt.

Cordelia turned on her heel and left. Unlike Stroud, she could not afford to show weakness.

ALISTAIR WANDERED BACK out to the dinner party. Still lost in a daze, he dropped into the empty seat Coco had vacated with a thud. What a kiss, he thought. She'd fallen right into it. *He'd* fallen right into it. He'd never thought all that claptrap was real, about two souls touching. Nonsense, he would have said. Sex was fun, it felt good, nothing else to it. Fine, fine, a little else. Not much else. Nakedness was always unnerving at first but anything could be intimate, really, a game of croquet or a game of cards. All the same, right?

God, he had been completely wrong. His lips touched her lips, and all of a sudden his brain caught fire and all his feelings melted right into his mouth. She'd kissed him back, and for a moment he really felt like he was dissolving. Into mist, or spirit stuff, or those invisible waves of heat that undulated over very hot flames. Maybe some combination of all that, half-erotic and half-ascended.

He'd been so sure she was *with* him. Sure down to his bones, ecstatic because her spirit had spoken to his in a language more clear and unmistakable than words had ever been, and then the moment shattered. Coco had pulled away. Faster than he could follow, she'd turned cold and closed.

"Would you say that your friend Miss Kelly has a temper?" he asked Olympia, seated now to his right.

"Not in my experience." Olympia gestured toward Lady Loel, snagging her attention. "Bonny, would you say that Cordelia has a temper?"

"No," Lady Loel answered immediately. "She's incredibly cool-headed. I think it can be disconcerting to some people, but that's who she is and"—Lady Loel held his gaze, her cornflower-blue eyes both kind and painfully direct—"if you don't mind my saying so, it's one of her finer qualities. She has been a rock for me at very difficult times."

"I see," said Alistair. "Interesting."

Miss Hurley quietly excused herself from the table, disappearing inside—in search of her friend, no doubt. Alistair winced. Perhaps he shouldn't have asked. Coco's friends were all so clever.

The meal had nearly ended by the time it dawned on him—whatever Coco imagined, he really wasn't the sharpest knife in the drawer—that she believed he'd been trying to *seduce* her.

He hadn't been. He hadn't been thinking much at all. He'd been flattered and frustrated, in almost equal measure. It was nice to be told he was smart, even if he didn't think she was right. But it also frustrated him, inordinately, that Coco talked circles around him. He'd wanted to silence her.

And his mouth was good for *something*. Not talking, obviously, but he had a firm grasp on other skills. And his intentions *were* honorable.

So far, at least.

Maybe he shouldn't have kissed her? No wonder she'd taken it so badly. He pulled Olympia aside on his way out the door to tell her, as kindly as he could, that she ought to throw Martin Grant out with the trash before returning to his own woes.

He brought it up with Flea on the way home. "If you were Miss Kelly, and I kissed you, how would you react?"

Flea grimaced. "This isn't the sort of conversation you should be having with your sister."

"You'll give a better answer than Chilly, though."

"I don't know her well enough to answer. And even if I did..." Flea sighed. "Some parts of your life are not for me to judge, Rip. But I would be disappointed to learn that you'd treat a woman like Miss Kelly shabbily. Her situation is precarious."

"Precarious? That woman cuts like an arrow through life. I feel sorry for anyone who gets in her way."

"It's a lovely image, Rip, but she's a woman who works for her bread. She'll find that work drying up if rumors start circulating about her involvement with you. At which point all her lovely friends will have to decide between joining her in infamy and cutting her from their lives."

Alistair scowled. "So you're saying she was right to be angry with me?"

"Miss Kelly?"

Alistair nodded.

"I'm glad to hear she had sense enough." Flea straightened in her seat, apparently fortified by Cordelia's show of backbone. "Brave of her too."

Alistair grunted. "What if I told you my intentions were honorable?"

"Are you asking whether I want her in the family? Because I'm not sure I could put myself in her place. Or predict her answer."

"The first question."

Flea's gaze flitted away, and she fidgeted with the gold bracelet at her wrist. "You realize Cordelia Kelly is not an easy woman to get along with."

Alistair grinned. "It's come to my attention."

"So long as you understand that I won't be roped into mediating your disagreements, you have my blessing," said Flea. "I honestly expected you to pick someone much worse."

"Worse?" Alistair frowned. "Why would you think that?"

"You're a young, unmarried duke. Women want to catch you more than you want *not* to be caught. And the worst of them are often the most determined."

"Miss Kelly thinks *I'm* clever," Alistair blurted, and then felt his neck burn with embarrassment. He didn't want his sister's pity.

"Does she, now?"

"She pesters me about it."

Flea hummed. "Try not to bungle the proposal, Rip. I know you'll be tempted."

"I don't know what you're talking about."

"I think you do, though."

CORDELIA RETREATED to the Causerie after her conversation with Stroud. She could have put on a brave face, but why make the effort? She'd do more good for herself, and for Olympia and her guests, by stepping aside to gather her wits.

She liked Stroud so much. His easy good grace, his quiet walk, his light tenor voice, his laugh, his *smell*. He admitted when he was wrong, he found the fun in every moment, he was generous with his compliments and listened when she spoke.

But he was not for her. And if he was the sort of man who would take advantage—who would use a woman lightly—then he was not a man she could respect, or befriend. At all.

"What in heaven's name did that man do while we weren't looking?" Tess demanded, storming into the room. "We all thought we were doing you a favor by giving you two a minute alone, but then he came back and asked Olympia if you have a *temper*?"

Cordelia shrugged. "It doesn't matter. I will avoid him in the future—that will settle matters."

Softening, Tess threw herself onto a pile of crocheted blankets. Her wire fairy wings, somewhat mangled already, distorted further. With a grimace, she unfastened the straps that held them in place. "That bad?"

"Must you quiz me about it?"

"I'm afraid so." Tess tweaked Cordelia's ear. "It's better than exchanging dire hints until both of us are thoroughly confused."

"When you put it that way." Cordelia steeled herself. "He kissed me."

"Ah."

"You're not surprised?" Cordelia asked. "Is there more to his reputation than I'm aware of?"

"I haven't heard a word of gossip, either to his credit or against it. Either he's a monk or he's discreet, and I wouldn't place any wagers on monk." Tess brushed this question aside. "But it's not hard to see that he's smitten with you. He's not trying to hide it."

"I wish he were."

"Do you?" Tess wondered, one eyebrow cocked. "Do you *really*?"

"Oh, Tess." Cordelia smiled, and while it was a true smile, it was also as close as she thought she'd come to actually crying about all of this. What a bittersweet moment. "I think I really *do* wish. If only because I'll miss him."

"What a shame." Tess sighed. "I am sorry. Though he's not the sort of man I'd have expected to catch your interest."

"He really is cleverer than he lets on. You know why he didn't have any guesses about Bonny's sneezing?"

"Why?" Tess laughed. "Did he tell you a tale?"

"He'd figured out that she was faking," Cordelia answered. "He didn't say anything because he didn't want to be rude."

"*Really.*" Tess narrowed her eyes. "You're beginning to persuade me. But if he's clever, why does everyone think he's stupid?"

"Think about the effort, both mental and physical, that must have gone into rotating that statue. It's *staggering*. A feat of engineering and organization and… well, I can only guess what else. But do you know any respectable adults who'd sing his praises for it?"

Tess snorted.

"Exactly," Cordelia said. "I think he's brilliant and demonstrates it often, but primarily in ways that escape notice, or even attract censure."

"Seems a waste."

"It is," Cordelia agreed. "Though there's hope for him, which is more than I can say for Martin Grant."

Tess sneered. "That worm."

"There's something truly repulsive about him."

"He's like a snake—"

"—and a peacock—"

"—and a little lapdog—"

"All in one," Cordelia exclaimed. "How has he fooled Olympia?"

"It's chilling, isn't it?" Tess agreed. "I've watched more talented charlatans try her and fail. And yet *he* slips through?"

"It's like the myth of Achilles," Cordelia agreed. "All the best training and equipment a warrior could have and yet a single, seemingly insignificant weakness spells his doom."

Tess shuddered.

"There you are," cried Bonny from the threshold, Ruby at her heels. "You disappeared! What happened?"

"I'd had enough socializing."

"Is that the truth?" Bonny cuddled into Cordelia on the sofa. She took one of Cordelia's arms and draped it across her own round and firm belly. "Or were you disappointed that your little experiment failed?"

"It didn't." While Cordelia explained how Stroud had solved the puzzle, Ruby made herself comfortable. Olympia swanned in, drooped dramatically, and began plucking the pins from her hair, dropping them into a crystal dish.

"So he admitted that you'd won the bet!" Bonny exclaimed.

Tess clucked her tongue, a hint of a smile playing about her lips. "Don't leap to conclusions."

"He wouldn't concede the point at all," Cordelia said.

Ruby smiled cynically. "Women are always told not to upstage men, and now we know why. So that men don't embarrass themselves with their poor sportsmanship when they lose."

"Our Ruby is wise in the ways of the world." Olympia combed her fingers through her hair, now hanging loose, picked up a pin that dropped to the floor, and tossed it into the dish with a satisfying *plink*. "Now. What did everyone think of Mr. Grant? Isn't he marvelous?"

"He plays you false," said Tess flatly. "And you won't see it."

Hurt flashed in Olympia's summer-sky eyes. "I already know what *you* think."

"I don't like him." Ruby never sugarcoated her opinions. "But you don't need my approval, and I have no more to say on the subject."

Cordelia agreed with Tess and Ruby, but since Olympia didn't seem receptive to their opinions, she tried for a diplomatic approach. Not one of her strong suits, but she'd spent enough years in Bonny's company to make the attempt. "He isn't good enough for you, Olympia."

"I thought he seemed wonderful," Bonny enthused. "He's handsome and attentive and he adores you."

Cordelia groaned. She loved Bonny, she really did, but... "Olympia, I think you know as well as I do that if you only have Bonny's support, you might as well not have any at all."

"I beg your pardon!" cried Bonny.

"You like *everyone*," Cordelia explained. "It's a wonderful quality but not very useful at times like these."

"I'm not trying to convince anyone that Mr. Grant is perfect." Olympia paced circles around them as she spoke, gestured with her arms. "But who is? Whatever his flaws, he worships the ground I walk on. Do you know what he told me this evening, as he left? He said, 'What beautiful memories you made for your guests this evening.' That's exactly what I agonize over, what I hope to achieve—"

Tess interrupted. "Have you ever mentioned this to him in the past?"

"We talked about it a little, while I was planning the party this evening."

"So it's possible he's just repeating your own words right back to you?" Tess pressed.

Olympia tossed her head. "I think you're jealous, Tess. You know you won't have a happy marriage, so you don't want one for me, either."

When Tess tensed and fell silent, Cordelia decided she'd had enough of diplomacy. "Your Mr. Grant is frivolous, pompous, and —I am convinced—cowardly, as well. You'd be happier with a better man who loved you less."

"You've only just met him," Olympia protested.

"I think it sounds like they have a very special connection," said Bonny, ever the peacemaker. Even, as now, when it helped no one. "It's true that I tend to like people, Cordelia, I can't deny it. I think most people *are* likable, if you give them a chance. And they are—we *all* are—so happy to be seen and appreciated. But more than anything, I know how it feels when the people I care about most hate the man I love. I can't bear the thought that we'd subject Olympia to that sort of pain…"

Olympia sat on Bonny's other side and gave her a hug. "It's hard, isn't it?"

"Sometimes," Bonny confessed. "But I had you, at least… all of you… I don't know how I'd manage if I didn't."

"We have a different sort of responsibility to our family than to our friends," Cordelia protested. "Our families make demands and burden us with expectations in order to thrive. I know you're not proud of the fact that you turned your back on that duty; I did the same, and while I can't regret it… I am ashamed. But our friends are free to care for us as individuals."

"Not as free as all that," Tess objected.

Cordelia sighed. "Perhaps not. We all have to look out for ourselves."

"Do you love Martin Grant?" Bonny took Olympia's hands in her own, gaze soft and earnest as a doe's. "Do you really, truly love him? Would you tend him when he is sick, comfort him when he's hurt, listen patiently when he drones on and on about something you don't find particularly interesting—"

"Like orchids?" Cordelia quipped.

Bonny grimaced. She'd never been interested in horticulture but was slowly becoming an expert, whether or not she liked it. "I'm not complaining, mind you…"

A chorus of laughter interrupted her.

"And stop distracting me!" Bonny exclaimed. "If Olympia loves him, that's all that matters. That's the only question I have— and Olympia, if the answer is yes, then of course you have my blessing."

A brief silence followed this declaration. It was so passionate, so heartfelt, and so obviously rooted in an experience foreign to the rest of them. Cordelia felt a twang of jealousy; Bonny had found something special, something rare.

Olympia looked into Bonny's eyes, bright and brimming with conviction, and slumped. "Can I tell you all something in confidence? Can I trust you with a secret?"

"Of course," Cordelia promised. "Your secrets are safe with us."

"I've met him secretly a couple of times now, alone, without a chaperone…"

"*Oh no*," Tess groaned.

"I won't pretend they were chaste encounters. In all honesty, I can hardly stop myself from… well…" Olympia sighed. "He makes me feel things I've never felt before. And when he embraces me, I feel a kind of happiness I've never known. It's so pure and intense."

Bonny sighed dreamily, a faraway look in her eyes. "Yes, that's exactly it."

"No, it's *not*," said Cordelia. "Lord Loel is a good man, Bonny, but this is exactly how bad ones lure young ladies to ruination."

"How do you know?" Olympia demanded. "Have *you* ever kissed a man?"

Cordelia froze. She couldn't *lie*, neither deliberately nor to her dearest friends, but neither did she want to admit the truth. She caught a sympathetic look from Tess and considered that, perhaps, she ought to offer them the trust they so often extended to her. Ask for their advice.

"Don't be silly." Bonny pinched Cordelia's cheek. "Cordelia would never make the same mistake *I* did. She's stronger than the rest of us combined."

Cordelia shook her head. Not true.

"She is," Tess agreed solemnly. "But even the strong stumble... and fall."

Cordelia shuddered.

"Well, *Bonny* has kissed a man," Olympia jumped in, blessedly uninterested in Cordelia's silence. "In fact, she's kissed two—and one of them was a terrible rake. What was *that* like?"

"I only kissed Charles Gavin once, but it made me feel sick to my stomach," Bonny admitted. "*His* kiss frightened me. I wanted to cry by the time it was over. I couldn't believe how different I felt when Loel kissed me. His kisses make me happy—just like you said, Olympia. They inspire the most marvelous emotions, things I'd never felt before."

"So it really is different when you love someone." Olympia took a deep breath. "I think that means I'm in love."

Tess's mouth tightened to a thin line as she visibly swallowed another objection. Her reaction gave Cordelia a chill because she knew Tess had read the situation correctly. Right now, Olympia would only hear what she wanted to hear. She'd listen to Bonny but any other advice, no matter how wise, would be ignored.

"There's no need to be hasty," Cordelia cautioned.

"I'm not in any hurry." Olympia smiled, joy transforming her cool beauty into something warmer and softer. "I like courting! It's fun."

Fun, thought Cordelia. She couldn't say the same—but then, Stroud wasn't courting her, was he? He wanted something far less proper.

CHAPTER 13

Stroud spent the next two weeks chasing Cordelia Kelly. He tried letters, he tried gifts, and both were returned unopened. Maybe he'd overstepped—he didn't think so, actually, he felt like he'd been doing exactly the right thing—but he couldn't believe Coco had cut him off completely as a result.

Without any explanation. She owed him that much, didn't she?

He pestered Olympia for news, but she wasn't talking to him either. He waited outside Coco's flat for hours at a time, even arranged an elaborate treasure hunt that Coco completely ignored. She evaded him so thoroughly that he never glimpsed so much as her elbow from a window high above or the feather bobbing on her hat as she slipped away.

He reached, and—he hated to admit—strolled right on past the limits of polite behavior. It was past time to accept the rejection her silence communicated so clearly. But just the thought made him feel cold and queasy.

He snuck into Chilly's house early one morning, jimmying a window and climbing into the still-empty breakfast room. He quickly replaced the berry jam at the breakfast table with a hot red pepper variety with the same vivid red hue. Whistling happily, he toasted a few slices of bread at the fire, turning the bread on a pair of tongs like in his Eton days. By the time Chilly entered, sandy-eyed and wearing a dressing gown, Alistair was halfway through a cup of coffee with an unread newspaper on his knee.

"What are you doing here so early?"

"I need a favor."

Chilly groaned and poured himself a cup of tea, which he liberally diluted with milk before reaching for the bread Alistair had toasted. "I'm afraid to ask."

"You owe me," Alistair reminded him.

"It's too early for me to be gracious about it, though." Chilly slathered his toast in butter and jam, then took a bite. His elfin features contorted with pain. Too polite to spit it out, he chewed and swallowed as tears leaked out of his eyes.

"Sometimes I don't know why we're friends," Chilly wheezed, shifting his plate to an empty setting.

"You're just upset that my pranks are so much better than yours."

"They are not."

"The last trap you set for me hit the wrong target entirely."

"I play the long game, Rip. Remember the tiny chair?"

"If I believed you'd planned it from the start, I'd be very impressed," Alistair admitted. "I need you to invite Miss Kelly to your wedding."

Chilly grimaced. "Why?"

"Or have Nell do it. It doesn't matter how it happens, so long as she attends," Alistair said. "And without letting her know I've interfered. She's upset with me right now."

"You want me to help you corner her?"

"Exactly."

Chilly leveled a flat, skeptical look on Alistair.

"In a nice way," Alistair added. "Nothing that would weigh on your conscience."

"I have your word?"

"Of course!" Alistair spluttered. "Why must everyone think the worst? First Flea, now you."

"Because it's hard to see where else this ends, Rip," Chilly said, completely serious for once.

"Then look harder." Alistair stood, suddenly angry. "I *like* her. You really think I want to ruin her?"

Chilly raised his hands, palms facing out. "Not intentionally, no. But life is challenging for fallen women, no matter how grand the patron—"

"I'm going to *marry* her," Alistair shouted. "At least, I'm going to try. My chances would be better if you'd stop insulting me and help."

Chilly's eyes went wide. "*Marry* her?"

"That's right."

"Last we spoke, you weren't sure—"

"Don't exaggerate."

"You were extremely angry. Is that better?" Chilly rolled his eyes. "Maybe you should give this a bit more thought?"

"I'll give it all the thought you want, once you bring her to the wedding," Alistair growled.

"I'll see that she attends the wedding party." Chilly raised his hand, index finger raised in caution. "But we're going to talk, do you understand?"

CORDELIA AND BONNY had one last lunch together before the orchid auction concluded and her friend departed London. The very same day that she saw her friend off at the train station, Miss Smith invited her to tour the school she'd founded, followed by an intimate dinner with several other ladies in the discussion club.

Cordelia asked after the petition, but Miss Smith would only say, "We are keeping hope alive," before changing the subject. An unsatisfying answer, but Cordelia didn't know the woman well enough to press for more. At least any truly important developments would reach the papers.

Aside from these small diversions, Cordelia devoted most of her time to work. She finished rebinding the young mother's childhood favorites and received an invitation to tea from Mrs. Dowell. A new commission already?

To her surprise, Christopher Old waited in the small salon with Mrs. Dowell, with Miss Dowell nowhere in sight.

"Lovely to see you again," Cordelia greeted him. "How do you do?"

Mr. Old puffed out his chest. "Happiest man in the world."

"He has a special request," interceded Mrs. Dowell. "It's rather unusual, so I'll let him explain."

Cordelia folded her hands in her lap and directed her full attention to Mr. Old.

"I had an idea for a wedding gift," said Christopher Old. "I'd like to make a book to commemorate the wedding, to capture this moment in time and show Nell how loved she is—and not just by me. So many people care for her. I'd like for everyone who attends the wedding to contribute. Perhaps they have a special memory to share, perhaps a few words about her character—the qualities they most appreciate."

"A Book of Love," Cordelia supplied, warmed by the thought. "What a wonderful idea."

"I want her to understand how I adore her," continued Mr. Old. "Only one copy, of course, so it'd have to be handwritten. Similar to an illuminated manuscript. Beautiful script, colorful illustrations, and later on we can keep mementoes between the leaves, letters and pressed flowers and the like."

The idea had considerable appeal, not least because it limited the scope of a potentially sprawling endeavor.

"The only difficulty is that in order for you to make the book, you'd have to attend the wedding," said Christopher Old. "What would it take to convince you?"

Cordelia hesitated. "It would be better if—"

"I'd like to present it to Nell on our wedding day," he hurried on. "And without you there—well, it's my wedding too. I won't have time to assemble all the contents. If money is an obstacle—"

"It is, but—"

"I'm prepared to be generous," Mr. Old continued doggedly. "Mrs. Dowell says she's paying fifty pounds for the custom-bound books she's already ordered. I'll add another fifty, for your time and effort, if you'll upend your schedule in order to attend."

An absolutely exorbitant fee. Cordelia knew a trap when she saw one, and while the bait was not particularly *original*, it tempted her. What worker wanted to turn away a job plum enough to smooth out months of life's inevitable ups and downs? Not she.

Her reputation was worth more to her than fifty pounds. Not just for pride, either. Once she lost her reputation, she'd struggle to find work of any kind—let alone the kind that offered some outlet for her creativity, like bookbinding.

But if she could walk the tightrope... Was she strong enough to spend days in close proximity to Stroud? No. He had tested her resolve and she found it wanting. Every second she spent in his presence simply increased the likelihood of a fall.

Fifty pounds, though. *Fifty.*

"I want to keep the gift secret until it's done," Mr. Old added. "Mrs. Dowell has agreed that we'll invite you to attend as a guest. She's already suggested it to Nell."

"She was delighted by the idea," said Mrs. Dowell.

With a seriousness inappropriate to the situation, Mr. Old added, "You'll be among friends, Miss Kelly. I promise."

She held his gaze, mild but unflinching. "Do you?"

"You have my word."

Cordelia sighed. "Then I accept your generous offer."

"Thank you," said Mr. Old. "We won't let you down."

"I'll need to make arrangements," Mrs. Dowell promised. "Let's discuss what facilities or supplies you'll need to work."

A DINNER later that week with Olympia, Tess and Ruby began pleasantly and ended in another bitter disagreement on the subject of Martin Grant. Tess once again tried to persuade Olympia to reconsider her affection for the man and Olympia, once again, answered cruelly. Tess stormed out halfway through the meal. Ruby followed. Cordelia decided to stay, though unease roiled in her gut.

It lingered days later as she traveled north. Mrs. Dowell had offered to find Cordelia a seat in a carriage with one of the other guests who'd be traveling directly from London to the event, but Cordelia opted for the train. A few shillings would spare her an afternoon spent struggling to make pleasant conversation with strangers, in the obsequious and grateful mode appropriate to a tradeswoman.

In her former life, she had moved in circles not too distant from Nell Dowell's. She didn't look forward to spending several days on a tour of the life she might have had.

She wasn't ready to see Stroud again. The anger she'd felt on the night of Olympia's dinner had boiled away, leaving behind a residue of sadness. He'd treated her with so much respect. And then he'd snatched it all away.

Her father, the hypocrite, had always taught her that the true test of a man's worth came when his principles fell into conflict with his personal interest, especially the pursuit of profit or acclaim. Great men chose principle at the expense of personal gain.

Bonny had provided a curious counterpoint to Cordelia's father's philosophy. Bonny would rather be loved than be right. Like a little sun, she warmed everyone she touched. But how could she have any goals of her own when she derived satisfaction from the successes of others? A softness at her core, a malleability, made the rest possible.

And yet when Bonny's goodness had been tested, she'd

passed with flying colors. It was Cordelia's father, the man of principle, who'd failed. One's vision of oneself didn't always match the reality.

Mrs. Dowell sent a private coach to fetch Cordelia from the train station and sallied forth to greet her in person. The Dowells estate sprawled gracefully across several acres of land, elegant and cohesive in design—that, and the whiteness of the stone facade, suggested all-new construction.

"Let me show you the way." Mrs. Dowell gestured for Cordelia to follow. "Our best rooms are taken, the smaller bedrooms didn't have enough space to fit a worktable, the nursery is *already* overflowing and we have more children arriving this afternoon... The house has never been so full. I did the best I could, Miss Kelly, but I can guarantee I've forgotten something important, so please do speak to me if you have any requests or complaints, particularly anything that might impact your ability to work."

She wasn't exaggerating. Despite the home's generous size, almost every room was occupied to capacity. Mrs. Dowell made introductions as she guided Cordelia through the crowd, offering little asides as they went. "Let me introduce you to my sister, Iva. She's here alone, like you, and absolutely one of a kind. You'll get along," or, "I apologize in advance for Lady Redesdale. All of Chilly's people are a bit, how do I put it? Let's say they like to tell me how very, very lucky my Nell is. I agree, of course, but... anyhow, Lady Redesdale married an earl, and now she's the worst of them. Chilly's aunt, on his mother's side."

Cordelia wondered where, exactly, she'd end up as the mistress of the estate guided her toward the family quarters. Eventually, Mrs. Dowell opened the door to a small room with lovely red and yellow wallpaper, gauzy curtains framing an excellent view of the manicured grounds, and almost completely empty of furniture. It had been outfitted with exactly two items: a simple cot on wheels against the far wall and, beneath the window, a chipped desk with several squares of felt tucked under one uneven leg.

"This was Nell's sitting room," Mrs. Dowell explained. "Her bedroom is right through that door"—Mrs. Dowell pointed to a connecting door—"and she's had all the furniture removed to Chilly's new house. It's the best we can do, I'm afraid. I hope you'll be comfortable?"

"Of course." Cordelia squeezed Mrs. Dowell's hand in gratitude. "You've been very accommodating. I'll have everything I need."

"I'm next door on the other side," Mrs. Dowell added. "Take some time to rest and refresh yourself. Travel is so tiring!"

Left to settle in, Cordelia unpacked first her clothes and then a separate trunk full of bookbinding materials. She couldn't start work until she'd collected at least a few stories, so once she'd refreshed herself, she ventured out into the public rooms.

Or tried to, anyhow. She got turned around and, without any other guidance, ended up following a jumble of male voices to their source. They drew her to a courtyard where a gaggle of men of varying ages—the youngest a child no more than six, the oldest a gentleman whose scalp showed pink through the oily tracks his comb had carved into his wispy silver hair—formed a circle around a pair of boys slashing at one another with sticks.

Cordelia eased closer, speechless.

Stroud stood head and shoulders above the rest, cheering enthusiastically. He shouldn't have noticed her at all, with his back turned and his attention on the ritual violence he clearly relished, but some sixth sense must have alerted him.

He turned, his light-brown eyes collided with hers, and his wolfish smile broadened. "Miss Kelly. What brings you here?"

"I ought to ask the same question of you," Cordelia returned in a furious whisper. "What is this savagery? How can you approve of it?"

"It's just a game."

"Those are *children*. Beating one another with *sticks*," Cordelia hissed. "You call that a game?"

"I call it back-sword, because it has a name. The first one to draw blood—on the head and enough to drip for an inch—wins." Stroud shrugged. "It's harmless. Dueling for schoolboys."

Cordelia pinched the bridge of her nose. What did the word *harmless* mean, if deliberately drawing blood in an act of violence didn't count? "I gather it's a favorite of yours?"

"I've only played a couple of times." Stroud gestured vaguely at himself and shrugged. "Not sporting, you know. These two are well matched. Same size, same age."

"It's barbaric."

"That's what makes it fun." Stroud's grin faded. "You never answered my question. What brings you here?"

Cordelia stuck to the story that would keep Mr. Old's involvement a secret and said, "Mrs. Dowell invited me."

"That's it?" Stroud asked. "She invited, you accepted?"

"She was quite insistent."

"And? You're stubborn as a whole team of mules."

"If the only way to say 'yes' to what I want is to say 'no' to everything else, then of course that's what I do. I won't apologize for mastering basic self-discipline."

Guilt shadowed Stroud's sunny features. He touched her wrist gently. "But I should apologize for failing to."

The kiss. He couldn't be referring to anything else. Cordelia nodded—she'd accept his apology, but not without conditions. "Don't do it again."

She believed Stroud to be a decent man and expected him to respond as a decent man would: by instantly and sincerely promising he would never again dishonor her with his inappropriate advances.

He did not.

In fact, she got no reply at all. She met his eyes, but she couldn't read what she saw in his. Greed? Hunger?

Lust?

A shiver traced down her spine and settled low in her belly.

She dismissed the sensation. If he wouldn't promise, she couldn't have anything to do with him. At all. "I'm not teasing."

Before he could answer, one of the other spectators peeled away from the fight to join them.

"Who's this enchanting stranger?" The speaker was slim and fair, haughty. "Stroud, can I impose upon you for an introduction?"

"Of course. Freddy, meet Miss Cordelia Kelly," Alistair answered. "Miss Kelly, this is Mr. Frederick Bolton. Chilly's cousin on his father's side."

Mr. Bolton bowed. "You must be one of the Dowells? Or the Sobels? Which of my lucky relatives should I congratulate?"

"I'm a friend of Miss Dowell's."

"Friend?" The young man's eyebrows arched. "I thought this was a small, intimate gathering? Just family, wider acquaintance excluded?"

"Chilly invited me," Alistair said smoothly. "So naturally Nell took the opportunity to invite one of her friends, as well."

Mr. Bolton rocked back on his heels, considering. "Fair enough."

In the ring, one of the boys wailed—his opponent had gotten a good whack in, and blood began to trickle down his forehead. Many of the spectators groaned, others clapped. A man well into his middle years began to taunt another half his age about the wager they'd made on the fight.

"They've gambled on this game?" Cordelia recalled something that Mr. Bolton had just said. "On their own family?"

"Not *money*," said Mr. Bolton peevishly. "Friendly wagers. Favors and the like—I think Joseph won a week at Soubry's Scottish hunting lodge."

Cordelia bit her tongue on the first response that came to mind and on all the subsequent ones. Her hostess was a client whose patronage she valued. She had to try not to provoke the guests.

"With all these missish nerves, I'm surprised you're a friend of *Nell's*," Bolton added.

"I'll tell Miss Dowell you said so." Cordelia smiled thinly. "I'm sure she'll appreciate the compliment as much as I do. Good afternoon, gentlemen."

CHAPTER 14

Alistair watched Coco sashay away, biting his lip to stop himself from whistling at the view. She had manners enough not to crow about her little victories, but a certain sway in her step convinced him that she did *enjoy* them.

"She's a sour one," muttered Freddy.

"She knows her own mind," Alistair corrected.

"Even worse."

Alistair declined to pursue the conversation. Not only would convincing Freddy of Coco's worth be difficult, it would be counterproductive. He had a hard enough time courting Coco without inviting any competition.

He congratulated the winner of the back-sword match—and then the loser, too, for putting up a good fight. Both boys pretended not to care. Then he continued the circuit of the property that he'd started before the game distracted him. Chilly was about to get married, and Alistair intended to commemorate this milestone in his friend's life with a truly spectacular prank. Considering the circumstances, he'd have to come up with something that Nell would appreciate. That limited his options.

As did the setting. Joseph Dowell, Nell's father, was the youngest of four brothers. Family resources stretched far enough to bestow an established estate upon the three eldest. Unfortunately, because the Dowells had run out of spare houses before their fourth son came along, the youngest boy had inherited a comparatively generous parcel of land with nothing on it. He'd had to build his own home, and reeling from the expense, he and his wife had raided the attics of their relatives for furniture.

The elegant new construction didn't at all match the eclectic decor, much of it shabby or damaged. Nor did it present as many possibilities for mayhem as Alistair might have hoped. Older houses had oddities he could exploit. New ones tended to be more straightforward.

He had a glimmer of an idea. Instead of chasing after it, he left it alone. Either it would develop flavor like a fine broth or go stale like unwashed drawers.

While the prank simmered, he returned to the front parlors where most of the guests had congregated. Knowing Chilly's family fairly well and only being moderately fond of them, mostly he was looking for Coco.

He found her listening attentively to a rambling story about taking Nell to the beach as a child. Quite… courteous of her. Not that he was *surprised*, exactly. Coco had excellent manners, sometimes. When she wanted to. Since Alistair didn't find the story interesting himself, he moved on to join Chilly.

"How are you holding up?" Alistair asked his best friend. "Nervous? Excited? The big day is almost upon us."

"As far as I'm concerned, the wedding is the prize at the end of all this"—Chilly cast a derisive glance across the crowded parlor—"*family time*."

"How can it be that so many people are delightful as individuals, and yet almost all families are appalling when assembled as a unit?" Alistair mused. "I think it's a paradox. Is that a paradox?"

"A riddle fit for the Sphinx," Chilly agreed dryly.

"Too good for the Sphinx. *Those* riddles have answers. Who'd really be stumped by the one about the creature having four legs and two legs and then three? It's so obvious."

"Only because you know the answer," Chilly countered. "The answer to a good riddle will always seem obvious—*in retrospect*."

Alistair wasn't convinced but he couldn't think of a clever rebuttal. "Maybe. Speaking of riddles: how'd you convince Coco to accept the invitation?"

"I hired her."

Alistair blinked. "To do what?"

Chilly smiled slightly. "Make a book."

"You mean make it *here*?"

Chilly nodded. "Had to be here, couldn't be anywhere else or any other time."

Alistair harrumphed. Chilly would explain if he asked, but if he hadn't already, that meant he thought it would be more fun to wait and see. Alistair did enjoy a good surprise.

"Paid through the nose for it, but that's what friends are for, eh?" Chilly's expression shifted into a gleeful smirk. "Plus—and we'll keep this thought to ourselves, shall we?—I think it will be fun to watch her stampede through the ranks."

Alistair gave a subtle jerk of his chin. "You call that a stampede?"

Coco had been circulating peaceably ever since he'd arrived. Listening, mostly, though even Coco's silence could be intimidating. The full weight of her attention could bring a man to his knees.

"Patience, Rip," Chilly drawled. "Just before you arrived she had a wee confrontation with Uncle Arnold. He was delivering his usual monologue in guise of a conversation and said something about the invention of the printing press. I don't know what, I ignore him on principle, but Miss Kelly corrected him. He objected, but she kept at it, going into more and more detail until I couldn't follow. Did you know Gutenberg was a metalsmith? I certainly didn't. Anyhow, Uncle Arnold stormed off in a huff and now Aunt Margaret is spoiling for a fight. Out for revenge and no idea she's fighting above her weight class."

Alistair beamed. "How did I get so lucky?"

Chilly snorted. "You haven't, yet."

"I will."

Chilly cast a despairing look at his bride-to-be, who promptly came to her fiancé's rescue. Nell had dressed demurely in a pale-green gown that complimented her eyes, lace fluttering at the neckline and twisted into her hair. Twin flags of color high on her cheeks betrayed her excitement.

"What mischief are you two plotting?" asked Nell.

"I'm not plotting anything," Chilly assured her.

"Lazy as ever." Alistair sighed mournfully. "You're much too good for him, you know."

Nell laughed, cheeks dimpling. "You couldn't be more wrong, but I won't complain if you convince Chilly to join you in your delusion."

"Do you hear that, Chilly?" Alistair grinned. "Join me."

"I'm already well and truly—" Chilly broke off and, lowering his voice to a murmur, said, "Here we go."

"And what could you, *Miss* Kelly, possibly know about marriage?" snapped Lady Margaret Pye, loudly enough to bring the surrounding conversations to a halt. Lady Pye, Chilly's aunt and the oldest of the three Old siblings, had aged comfortably into the role of matriarch. She commanded respect, expected deference, and considered it her right to make a scene.

When the rest of the family obediently fell silent, Lady Pye puffed up like a pigeon—bosom outthrust, hair a feathery halo around her square jaw.

"Personal experience informs our opinions, but is in no way sufficient for drawing conclusions that affect the whole of our sex," Coco replied, completely unruffled.

"And that's how you, an ignorant girl, justify lecturing your elders and your betters?" Lady Pye scoffed. "What does it mean to be united as one flesh but to share an interest, a common struggle, a—"

"You have two married daughters, do you not?" Miss Kelly

interrupted. "Did you provide them with trusts carefully fenced off from the common property controlled by their husbands?"

Mrs. Pye hesitated. "Of course I did, but—"

"So it is only women without easy access to lawyers—the lower classes—who must embody your vision of marriage? Rules for me but not for thee?"

"I beg your pardon," snapped Lady Pye. "You are a *child*—"

"I see you wish to end the discussion," Cordelia said calmly. "Please excuse me. I'll leave you to more pleasant conversation."

Coco tried to withdraw, but Lady Pye wasn't done. Apparently, she hadn't gotten the reaction she wanted from Coco (Alistair empathized; Coco never reacted the way *he* expected her to, either) and decided to give it another try.

"I *wish* to see a little humility from you, *girl*."

Coco didn't even flinch. *Alistair* would have flinched; Lady Pye had spent decades forging contempt into a viciously effective weapon. But not Coco. He shifted uncomfortably. Watching her in action made him a little… er… excited.

"And you have been disappointed." Coco curtseyed, clearly aware she'd become the center of attention, and withdrew.

Alistair let out a lusty sigh.

"Poor Aunt Margaret," murmured Chilly. "I almost feel sorry for her."

"Perhaps I ought to have warned her?" Nell wondered.

"She wouldn't have listened," said Chilly.

"Perhaps you can thank her, instead. For generously volunteering to demonstrate Coco's prowess to the other guests." Alistair frowned. "Except, if they're anything like me, they'll just want more."

Chilly snorted. "Don't worry, they're not."

"They might be."

"They're not," Chilly repeated, chuckling now.

"Their mistake," Alistair said lightly, before excusing himself.

If Coco wasn't here, he had business to attend to. Well, not so much business as a pleasure. To wit: a prank grand enough to suit the occasion of his best friend's wedding. He found Fisk in his room, at ease in an armchair with a book open in his lap.

"So." Alistair rubbed his palms together. "D'you think you could collect several hundred yards of white linens before tomorrow night?"

Fisk tucked a ribbon between the pages of his book. "I could try."

"And some colored bunting or swags? Preferably to match the ornaments on Chilly's cake?"

Fisk sighed. "Also before tomorrow?"

"Correct."

"I'll try my best."

"Excellent. Hop to it."

Fisk stood and gave the rump-shaped depression in the cushion he'd just vacated a longing look. "Consider me a rabbit, Your Grace."

Dinner dragged but somehow proved more tolerable than brandy afterward with the handful of men still awake enough to drink. Chilly, as the groom-to-be, had to spread his attention around, which left Alistair chatting with people he didn't like very much.

Of course Coco came up. Podge—that would be the name by which most of his acquaintance knew August Bewdley, Lord Leadsome, heir to the Earl of Redesdale and one of Chilly's cousins on the Soubry side—had heard Mrs. Dowell mention the circulating library that Coco founded in her hometown, which lent books exclusively to women, and which Alistair would have liked to hear about directly instead of thirdhand.

Podge, poor sod, identified this tasty tidbit of information as *ammunition*. Since he'd been watching Coco make mincemeat of every other dullard who'd tried to embarrass her, he ought to have learned a bit of caution. But he hadn't, a sure sign he wouldn't succeed where the others had failed.

Now he stood before the fireplace with one elbow propped on the mantle, waving about the brandy snifter held in the opposite hand as he rehearsed his arguments for a more receptive audience. Proper women, Podge insisted, didn't *want* to read. Those possessed of the perverse desire to surround themselves with *books* ought to resist it. Reading soured women's temperaments and transformed them into undesirable harpies.

The conversation hadn't gone so well when he had it with Coco. Alistair had the story from Violet Pye, wife to Margaret's son Louis. According to Violet, who'd repeated Coco's exact words with unnerving enthusiasm, she'd said, "Men who can only earn the admiration of ignorant women are right to fear a library." Whereupon Podge had huffed and puffed and beat a speedy retreat.

Podge forgot to consider the possibility that the tale of his confrontation had already made the rounds because he declared, while giving his toasty bum a surreptitious swat, "She insisted that men only admire ignorant women—can you imagine?" He waved the arm holding his sloshing glass back and forth. "I don't think that's true of anyone here."

"A woman ought to be *refined*," chipped in Freddie Bolton. "A creature of delicacy and taste."

"The problem with books is that most of 'em are boring," added Edwicker Esterbrook. "And what about the rest? Why, you've got books that are chock-full of lurid drama that fevers the brain—ladies love 'em but a smart man nips *that* in the bud before it gets out of hand—and then what's left? Books that are unfeminine, about wars and whatnot."

"Have you ever actually read a book, Edwicker?" asked Chilly.

Edwicker sputtered. "I went to university."

"That doesn't answer the question," Chilly retorted, which won a chuckle from the room.

"I haven't finished a single book since I started university," exclaimed Samuel Dowell's youngest, Kipper. Alistair didn't actually know the man's Christian name. He'd been Kipper since he was a boy in short pants with a tendency to fall asleep in his soup and, as an adult, retained a remarkable predilection for napping in public.

"Haven't sat any exams yet, either," countered Hugh, Chilly's younger brother.

As demonstrated by the present company, intelligence was not a prerequisite for admission to university. Men of good breeding but modest mental capacity took home diplomas every year.

Alistair had never considered the possibility for himself. He couldn't stand classrooms. He didn't fit in the chairs, and his knees pressed hard enough against the underside of most desks to leave him with bruises. The physical act of sitting through lectures had been agony. Beyond that, of course, there was all the fun of forgetting what lecturers had said the very second they stopped talking and giving wrong answers to absolutely every question and pretending not to notice all the sneers of contempt and etc., etc., which hadn't made the situation more pleasant.

Even if he had been a glutton for punishment, however, his father would never have allowed it. "Let's be honest, Alistair," he'd said, offhand. "Every day you've spent in school since you learned to sign your name has been a waste. Here's how dumb brutes get things done: they hire good people and stay out of their way."

He'd had similar words of wisdom for all the duties that had fallen to Alistair so much sooner than expected. The sum total of his father's advice about sitting in the House of Lords had been, "Keep your mouth shut, show up for votes, raise your children Tory, and no one will complain."

He hadn't been wrong.

Oh, good God. Was he really sitting about, nursing a drink and reminiscing about his *father*? Intolerable. He had better things to do—come to think of it, absolutely anything would be better—and he'd start by tracking down Fisk and making sure he'd be able to celebrate Chilly's wedding in the style his friend deserved.

≈

CORDELIA SPENT AS MUCH of the day as possible soliciting stories about Nell. She folded a few sheets of paper around a stub of a pencil and tucked them into her pocket so she could step aside and write them down while her memory remained fresh. She kept at it doggedly, withdrawing only to relieve herself or sharpen her pencil.

In the evening, Mr. Old and Mrs. Dowell joined her to share the tales they'd collected. Cordelia listened and wrote, fingers tired and cramping by the time she gratefully retired to her room.

Finally the real work could begin.

She'd brought a good quantity of fine paper from London, relying on the tests she'd conducted while working on Mrs. Hillier's journals to guide her. She opted for a thicker paper stock, knowing she'd be coloring most pages. While preparing for the journey, she'd cleaned her tools and refreshed her box of watercolors with new blocks of paint.

With the newlyweds scheduled to depart on their honeymoon in four days, she'd only allowed herself one day to collect material. She sorted the stories into chronological order, incorporating the mementoes Chilly had assembled. She sketched illustrations and embellishments on foolscap until her vision blurred and her fingers refused to cooperate.

Her cot waited, but it held no appeal. She'd been stiff and still for too long. Cordelia wrapped a shawl around her shoulders, slid her feet into a pair of slippers, and eased silently into the hallway. She'd take a brief walk around the grounds, let the fresh air and night noises soothe her.

At first, that's exactly what she got. Crickets, wind rustling through the leaves, indistinct murmurs filtering through the windows of the crowded house. Even a muffled moan or two.

She'd made a half-circuit of the house when a different sort of noise reached her: clacks, cracks, whispers. Thinking that only a very foolish burglar would choose to rob the Dowell house while it was crammed to the rafters with guests, she decided to take a peek.

She inched forward and crouched to hide behind a bush. She saw two figures silhouetted against the night: one extraordinarily tall, broad at the shoulder and slim at the hip, painfully familiar. Stroud. His companion was thin, with a long horsey face and a soft, floppy hat that didn't quite hide his balding pate.

These two were certainly up to something but almost certainly not a robbery.

She stood, brushed her skirts, and advanced on the scheming pair. The horse-faced man finished shifting a pile of folded linens from a wheelbarrow into a cart, leaning in to arrange them in neat stacks.

"Preparing a prank, I assume," said Cordelia.

The horse-faced man yelped and dropped the wheelbarrow. Stroud caught it with a huff, though one of the sheets still toppled onto the grass. The horse-faced man retrieved it, slapped away a bit of dirt, and added it to the cart.

"I'm sorry to have startled you, Mr...."

"Wallace Fisk," supplied Stroud. "My secretary. The most brilliant and long-suffering member of my staff. Fisk, you know Miss Cordelia Kelly, don't you?"—in a whispered aside—"He's been helping me with things, you know."

"Pleased to meet you, Mr. Fisk," Cordelia said.

"It is my very great honor, ma'am."

"What's the prank?" Cordelia asked. "I hope you aren't going to spoil your friend's wedding."

"After I worked so hard to make it possible?" Stroud clucked his tongue. "Have some faith, Coco. I'm not going to spoil it, I'm going to *celebrate* it."

"What are you going to do with all these linens, then?" Cordelia pressed. "Start a hospital?"

"You'll find out soon enough. Enjoy the surprise."

"I hate surprises."

"Appropriately enough, that doesn't surprise me at all." Stroud brightened. "I could give you a hint."

The possibility of a prank didn't really alarm her. Stroud's sincere affection for his friend had been obvious from the start. But she'd come outside to shake off the long hours bent over her desk. She'd take whatever diversion presented itself.

"All right. What's the hint?"

"Follow me." He turned, waved encouragingly. "I'll show you."

Cordelia narrowed her eyes. "Have you ever considered that your penchant for pranking renders you untrustworthy? What if I follow and you…?" She couldn't think of anything off the top of her head.

"Get you thoroughly lost, say 'Look over there!', and then sneak away while you're distracted?" Stroud suggested. "Plant one of my loyal servants in the bushes with instructions to jump out and shout 'Boo!' as you pass? Have all the furniture in your room rearranged while you're gone?"

"That's enough, thank you," Cordelia said. "You've adequately proven my point."

"I did, didn't I?"

"Don't sound so proud of yourself."

"Why not?"

"I was casting aspersions on your character."

"So? I'm used to it, and you're enjoying yourself."

Cordelia snorted. "Are you trying to make me feel guilty?"

"No." Stroud paused, his expression surprisingly earnest. "I'd never hurt you on purpose, Coco."

"Most wounds, I find, aren't inflicted on purpose. They're more often the accidental byproducts of some other intention. A man sprinting after the pickpocket who filched his watch may not *intend* to knock a bystander into the street. But if the bystander falls into the path of an oncoming four-in-hand…"

"That's a bit extreme, isn't it?"

"I'm sure it happens regularly."

"How often, do you think?" Stroud pressed. "Once a week, once a month, once a year…?"

"I could only guess."

"What's that? You're admitting you don't know? Mark the day, Miss Cordelia Kelly is at a loss—"

Cordelia silenced Stroud with a light smack to his arm. "Don't be ridiculous."

"I like to be ridiculous." Stroud, having led the way into the basements, opened the door to a cold storage room. It was empty but for a massive cake on a butcher's block, four tiers of decreasing size swathed in pounds and pounds of white icing.

"The wedding cake?" Cordelia wondered. "This is your hint?"

"That's right."

"I don't understand."

Stroud shrugged. "I'm not giving you another."

"I guess I'll remain in suspense. Until when exactly…?"

"That would be another hint."

"You're surprisingly strict about this."

"I take pranks very seriously."

They left the cold storage room behind and began to retrace their steps.

"And *you*," he added. "What happened to make you so suspicious of marriage?"

"An issue needn't affect me personally for me to take an interest."

"That's what you said earlier today. I was listening—nicely done, by the way. Lady Pye will still be holding a grudge on her deathbed, but I understand the rest of Chilly's family have already sent bouquets and thank you notes to your flat."

"Surely not."

"No, that was a joke. They're not nearly so organized." Stroud grinned. "Still, you must have a reason. There are hundreds of causes. Why pick this one?"

"The Soho Discussion Club is spearheading the effort. I wanted to contribute."

"So if they decided to circulate a petition about letting women take two husbands…?"

"I might abstain," Cordelia admitted. "But I was more interested in participating than in setting the agenda."

"So it's not…" He fumbled the end of the sentence. A first, as far as she could recall. It made her appreciate how often he'd maintained his sang-froid against all odds: when she'd smashed his porcelain dog, when she'd blindsided him at Trafalgar Square, when a stranger had picked a fight at Olympia's party.

The Duke of Stroud had an extraordinarily cool temper.

"There has to be more to it," he said finally. "You speak so passionately. Not at all like someone who's participating just for the sake of it."

Cordelia tried to explain. "Imagine, if you will, that you've entered a gaming hell. There's only one game to play, roulette, and you can only play it once. You must wager everything you own. All your savings, all your properties, all the income you'll ever make in the future. You might end up more or less where you are now. You might win wealth beyond your wildest dreams. But you might lose everything. Would you be eager to spin that wheel?"

"Oh, is this a metaphor? And the roulette wheel is marriage?" Stroud asked. "Because I take your point, but we don't marry at random. We—or our families, acting on our behalf—choose a compatible partner. A spouse with similar habits and ideals and acquaintance. We tip the odds in our favor."

"That's what we're supposed to believe. I used to." The story of Bonny's courtship with Charles Gavin was so personal and so knotted. How to boil down the lessons she'd learned into a few sentences? "I've seen it happen that a man's misdeeds are known to everyone but the young woman he is courting. Keeping us in ignorance preserves our innocence but prevents us from advocating for ourselves."

"You can't expect grown men to have spotless pasts," Stroud protested. "And most of the young women I've met are… er… very easy to shock."

"Spotless would be a gross exaggeration." Cordelia narrowed her eyes at Stroud. "What's the worst thing *you've* ever done?"

"What?"

"I'd like to gauge the scale by which you judge such matters."

"You can't expect me to answer that."

"I don't, actually." Cordelia sniffed. "But I'd think better of you if you did."

"That's—" Stroud spluttered. "That's very tricky of you, Coco."

"Then you ought to approve."

"Well *of course* I do, but…" Stroud scowled. "This just gets worse and worse."

Cordelia laughed. She didn't mean to—this was a serious matter to her, literally life and death, and she ought to approach it with the gravity it deserved. But something about Stroud flipped her upside down. A little snort forced its way out of her nose and, as though a dam had cracked, laughter burst free.

She turned her face away in a fruitless attempt to hide it.

"What's that sound?" Stroud peered at her, mock-concerned. "Are you choking?"

"Nn—nn—" She couldn't manage a single syllable answer, and for some reason that made her laugh even harder. Why, though? Incoherence wasn't funny.

"Crying? Was it something I said?" Stroud's huge hand landed on her back between her shoulder blades, delivering a gentle pat. "I'm sorry, Coco. I didn't mean to hurt you." Pat, pat. "Just let it all out, and I promise you'll feel better."

Cordelia reeled backward, clutching her stomach. "Stop!"

"Not a chance. I'm a duke, not a saint," Stroud protested. "This is the most fun I've had all day."

"I'm asking you"—Cordelia gasped for breath—"about the worst thing that you've ever done"—she tried to stand upright, bit her lips to contain her smile—"and you make jokes?"

"It's all I know how to do," Stroud said sorrowfully. Then he brightened, eyes widening in anticipation. "Pity me?"

"What?"

"You know, cradle me in your arms, weep gentle tears upon my brow..." He grinned. "Mostly it's the cradling I'm interested in."

"I will not."

"Please?"

Cordelia rallied. "What is the worst thing you've ever done, Your Grace? Because I have a guess."

"At least call me Rip."

"I detest your nickname, and I will never, ever use it."

"My Christian name is Alistair."

"So?"

"Stroud, then. Since you're such a spoilsport."

"How many young women have you seduced, *Stroud*?"

"Me?" He looked startled. "None."

"Not one." Cordelia scoffed. "I don't believe you."

"I've done bad things, Coco, but mostly to other boys." Stroud hesitated. "And, I'd like to think, mostly when I was much younger."

"I'd like an example, please."

"I broke a boy's arm by accident. We were wrestling." Stroud couldn't meet her eyes, rubbing his thumb across his mouth. "His right arm, and it didn't heal right. He lost some use of it, had to learn to write with his left hand, and he developed a stutter." The words came faster and faster, low and clipped. "I teased another—a whole group of us at did, at Eton—until he had to be sent away to live with family abroad. He's fine now. Came back good-looking and fashionable and fluent in Spanish. I threw a rock at my mother's dog, Angel. The leg healed crooked, and Angel's hated me ever since. My mother took her to Italy, and I felt like someone had lifted a boulder off my chest, not having to face that da"—brief stutter—"ratted dog every day."

"That's enough." Cordelia took Stroud's hand, used both of hers to enfold his one, squeezing hard to calm him. She hadn't expected this deep well of guilt to come pouring out, so fresh and raw when years ought to have dulled it. "That's enough."

Stroud fell silent. Nodded.

"Your mother is in Italy?" Cordelia asked.

"She left after my father died," said Stroud. "Off to have affairs and sunbathe."

"When was that?"

"Six, almost seven years ago." Stroud shot her a grim, sidewise glance. "It sounds awful, but before you express any condolences you should know my father's death was the best thing that ever happened to us."

"I see."

Stroud nodded. Anger transformed his features. His brows bunched into a heavy line that shadowed eyes gone dark, his majestic nose stood out like a hawk's beak, jaw sharp and severe above a thick, corded neck.

Subtle changes, but on a man his size? She'd started to think of him as puppyish, but he looked like he could crush rock into gravel with his bare fists. It didn't take much to render him terrifying.

A few more pieces of the puzzle fell into place. This anger was *old*, burning *low*, and it wasn't directed at her, yet her animal instincts tried desperately to seize the reins, flooding her legs with prickling energy and urging her to flee.

She could imagine that a man whose mildest foul mood terrified his acquaintance might dedicate himself to appearing friendly, approachable... harmless. He'd probably discovered far too late that success had its downsides.

Cordelia's heart ached for him. If it had been at all appropriate, she really might have drawn him into her arms and wept gentle tears on his brow.

"Let's get back to your secretary," Cordelia suggested. "He must be worried by now."

"We were already short on time," Stroud agreed, his mind still elsewhere. Called back to the present, his expression cleared. The light returned to his eyes. He was Stroud again, the anointed duke no one took seriously.

That no one was afraid of.

"Coco," he crooned.

She released his hand. "Don't call me that."

The moment she let go, he flicked his wrists and captured hers instead. She took a step back, he followed.

"Let me kiss you."

"No."

He gave her hands a yank, sharp enough to send her toppling into his body. Her breasts crushed against his broad chest. Her whole body flashed white-hot, but her mind remained strangely, startlingly clear. *This can't happen*, it informed the rest of her. *Don't you dare let this happen.*

Stroud dipped his head. His forehead came to rest against hers, a point of warmth and connection. His breath fanned across her lips, gentle and sweet.

"Let me kiss you," he crooned.

"No," she repeated, stronger than before.

He sighed and let go, stepping away, and her first impulse was to beg for him to come back. To finish what he'd started. Stroud looked miserable, sad-eyed and deflated, but she kept staring at his mouth, remembering how soft it had felt against hers.

Wondering how different their second kiss would be from their first.

"I have to go," she said, as a seed of fear took root deep inside her. She could not be alone with this man. Not ever, not even for a minute. Not because he'd try something but because she didn't trust herself to rebuff him.

She could not trust herself. What a shattering, utterly *humiliating* revelation. Without waiting for a reply, she fled.

CHAPTER 15

A listair didn't see much of Coco the next day. According to Chilly, she was hard at work on his commission. He did *hear* about her. Often. Given the sheer volume of chatter about Coco, one would imagine she'd been circling the house like a shark from sunup to sundown, shouting radical slogans from a blowhorn.

In reality, Cordelia had very little interaction with the guests. He thought he'd have the luxury of time. Whole days spent in her company, waiting for her to settle in, grow comfortable, let down her guard. She was always tense in his presence, chin up and ready for battle, and while he'd never complain about seeing Coco in all her glory, that wasn't why he'd convinced Chilly to extend the invitation.

He wanted to see her sleepy and relaxed at the end of a day, lulled by good food and easy company. He wanted to lift the burdens from her shoulders, all those higher causes piled on top of intense material anxieties, and let her breathe freely. Not forever—she was one of those people who needed struggle, sort of like how rodents needed something to chew on in order to stop their teeth from growing right through their brains—but for a few days.

He'd finally made her laugh, but once wasn't nearly enough. He could learn the secret of her smile if he only had enough time. If he were honest with himself—he tried not to be, but it was becoming increasingly difficult to pretend—he wanted other things too. He wanted to see the expression on her face after he took off all her clothes and she stood before him naked for the first time. He couldn't even begin to imagine Coco *shy* but if ever there were a time… He'd probably only get one glimpse and then it'd be gone forever.

He wanted to show her pleasure and wondered how long it would take before she learned to seize it for herself, forever unashamed of her own boldness. He wanted to hear her gasp when he entered her, whine when he withdrew… He wanted her helpless and needy and desperate. He'd spend the rest of his days toddling along in her wake like a moth after a flame, without resenting it in the least, if he could have her at his mercy in the dark of night.

He wouldn't get any of that here, surrounded by Chilly and Nell's obnoxious families. As concerned certain desires—the sexual ones—that was for the best. But he ought to have had more time, more leisure, more… *help*. He'd expected the convivial atmosphere of the wedding party to do some of his work *for* him. Grease the wheels, pave the way, etc. A whole array of metaphors described the genre of aid he'd been denied.

He reckoned wrong more often than not. But this had proven to be an embarrassing miscalculation, even by his standards. The Dowells hated Cordelia. The Soubrys hated Cordelia. The Olds hated Cordelia. Only the Sobels liked Cordelia, and there were hardly any Sobels. Just Mrs. Dowell and her sister, Iva. And Iva, a devotee of Sappho who'd lived abroad for most of her life, faced her own challenges with this crowd.

At least he had his prank to keep him busy. The bulk of the work would have to be accomplished *during* the wedding ceremony, a tight schedule that made it especially important to prepare.

He was on edge when the men retired for brandy, waiting for an excuse to leave, when Hugh Old said, "Look now, Rip, we've got to do something about Miss Kelly, and no one's as good as you."

"What are you talking about?" Alistair asked.

"A prank." Hugh'd installed himself at the center of a group including Podge and Freddy and Pye, the sort of motley crew that could be relied upon for a helping of dull conversation spiced with malicious jokes. "Take her down a peg or two."

Everyone insulted Alistair until they tried to imitate him. Once they discovered they couldn't replicate the scale and magnificence of his pranks, they told him he had a *knack*. They couldn't even give him his due when asking for favors.

But he didn't care who insulted *him*. He'd earned his reputation fair and square. Coco, on the other hand, deserved better.

"Why would I do that?" He doubted she wanted the attention that a more straightforward defense would attract. "She's done nothing to offend me."

"She's a tradeswoman, for God's sake," Hugh answered. "Nell can call her a friend if she likes, and invite her as a guest, but if *I* can't talk back to Aunt Margaret neither can *she*."

Chilly tsked at his younger brother. "Now, now, Hugh. All of us *can* talk back to Aunt Margaret. You can! Though, let's see, what happened the last time you tried...?"

"Think she made you cry, Hugh," taunted Podge.

"Nothing wrong with that," soothed Alistair. "I was always told that being publicly humiliated by my intellectual superiors was a precious opportunity to learn and grow and—"

"The last person to try that line on you was an old beak at Eton who ended up naked in Rowing Lake the next morning," Chilly cut in.

Alistair smiled beatifically.

"Back to the prank," said Podge. "Wouldn't it be lovely to outsmart Miss Kelly, Rip? Just think of the spectacle."

"To tell you the truth, I've tried. She turned it right round on me—didn't she, Chilly?"

"Flea nearly laughed her head off," Chilly agreed.

"So there you have it." A slow smile, spurred by sudden bright anticipation, spread across his face. Defending Coco the way he wanted to would cause more problems than it solved, but she could make these jackals eat their words without any help at all. "Why don't you give it a try? You'll fail too."

~

CORDELIA'S third day at the wedding party got off to an odd start. She sat down to an early breakfast, gritty-eyed and sour-tempered from lack of sleep, when Hugh Old took the seat across from hers. He shared Chilly's slim build and fine-boned features but lacked the air of contentment, of friendly self-satisfaction, that made his older brother so appealing.

Curious how a few subtle changes transformed Chilly's amiable demeanor into Hugh's insufferably smug one.

In an effort to spare them both, Cordelia addressed him first. "Let us not speak. It is early, and I am in a foul humor."

Hugh Old's mouth opened and then... froze in that position.

Cordelia sighed and returned to her toast. She had little patience for fools at the best of times, none at this hour.

"I am *certain* you'll want to hear what I have to say," Hugh Old ventured.

Cordelia couldn't help the mocking edge to her tone, the hint of disbelief. "You're certain, are you?"

"I was under the impression that you took pride in your work." He sounded affronted now. Cordelia couldn't blame him. "I would have thought you'd be grateful to learn about a new client."

For a new client? Yes, she could be grateful. It required effort, but Cordelia schooled her expression to polite interest and her voice to sweet inquiry. "You're quite right. My apologies, Mr. Old. Please tell me more."

Hugh Old inflated like a rooster, which made no sense at all. Even *Bonny* wouldn't be quite so thrilled at the prospect of doing Cordelia a favor.

"You see, I have a dear, dear friend who is a great eccentric." Hugh Old cleared his throat. "A great *lover of the arts*, that is. The sort with his head always in the clouds, or in Europe—amounts to the same thing, if you ask me. He has a particular passion for fine books and I think he'd appreciate your talent nearly as much as you'd appreciate his *generous* patronage."

"I would be honored to present my work to such a distinguished person."

"Nothing would make me happier than to facilitate the introduction—and deliver an enthusiastic recommendation—but I'd be much obliged if you performed a small *favor* for me first."

A favor? This did not bode well. "If it's in my power, of course. I am at your disposal."

"I've noticed, over the past few days, that you have quite a way with words," he began.

"That's one way of putting it," Cordelia said dryly.

"You've done an absolutely *masterful* job at cutting several of my least favorite family members down to size."

"I should think there's a great difference between briefly stating my opinion and cutting someone down to size," Cordelia countered, mostly for her own benefit. Hugh Old wasn't actually listening to a word she said.

"And if you'd be willing to direct the sharp edge of your wit toward a particular target, I would be so gratified I'd dash off a letter to my friend immediately."

He wanted her to pick a fight? If he chose a deserving target… But no. It would be bad business to offend the client she already had, who'd shown her such kindness, for the mere possibility of acquiring one she hadn't yet met. Better a bird in the hand than two in the bush, as the saying went.

ERIN SATIE

Besides, a deeper issue was at play here. Cordelia had often been reproached for her plain speech and hadn't yet been moved to change. But neither did she gloat. She sought truth, not shallow victories. She understood instinctively that taking pleasure in the humiliation of others would degrade her in some essential manner.

Hugh Old had set a trap. It would lead her toward the pursuit of fool's gold, away from the true.

"I'm afraid I can't oblige you," said Cordelia. "But thank you for the generous offer."

"You can't?" Hugh Old scoffed. "But surely—what if I told you to aim your sights at the Duke of Stroud? As aggravating and deserving a target as can be imagined."

"Then I would have something very unflattering to say about the scope of your imagination." Cordelia stood. "Now, if you'll excuse me, I believe it's time to dress for the wedding."

The ceremony itself was lovely. Nell and Chilly only had eyes for one another. They fairly glowed as they stood at the head of the aisle with hands clasped, radiating joy like a pair of suns. The warmth of it reached her and moved her. What a marvel that in a country where circumspection was a virtue to be cultivated and confession the dubious practice of heathens, any two people would be asked to put such intimacy on public display.

They all returned to the Dowells' home for the wedding breakfast, but Cordelia's carriage came to an abrupt halt on the drive at least a quarter mile away from the house itself. One peek out the window sufficed for an explanation.

White sheets swathed the house from roof to baseboard. Bunting swirled and swooped in horizontal lines across the cloth-swathed building, punctuated with fanciful whorls. Cordelia remembered Stroud's hint, and the spectacle made sense: he'd dressed the whole house as a wedding cake.

She unlatched the carriage door and hopped onto the gravel, approaching on foot. Lifting her skirts to keep dust off the hems, she found herself smiling as the other guests circled the house,

182

pointing out how the paper bunting had been bunched and pinned to match the frosting on the cake and rubber balloons substituted for clusters of pearls. She heard plenty of tut-tutting, especially older family members who complained about the nuisance and the delays, but Nell and Chilly stood by the front entrance, arms linked, laughing uproariously.

Cordelia held back, basking in the reflected warmth of their joy, when Mrs. Jane Esterbrook—if Cordelia remembered correctly, she was Nell's aunt and had related a lovely story of taking Nell to bathe in the sea as a girl—observed waspishly, "All these pranks are so *childish*. This is a *wedding*. Not a children's *birthday party*."

"Certainly if it were any other couple, I'd feel very put out on their behalf," Cordelia admitted. "But if Mr. Old hadn't wanted the Duke of Stroud to arrange something like this, he could have said so. I believe his friend would have respected his wishes."

"Then he ought to have, if only for his new bride's sake!" Mrs. Esterbrook clucked. "She can't be happy right now."

At that exact moment Nell had one arm hooked around her husband's, leaning on him for support as she doubled over with laughter.

"It appears the new bride has a compatible sense of humor," Cordelia tipped her head in that direction.

"What about her poor *mother*?" Mrs. Esterbrook sighed, defeated. "It's all very well to enjoy yourself and have fun, but it's in such poor taste. That lovely, elegant woman must be distraught."

A quick glance at Mrs. Dowell confirmed that in this respect, Mrs. Esterbrook had guessed correctly. If only because Mrs. Dowell was currently fielding complaints from other irritated matrons, including Mrs. Old.

Cordelia shrugged philosophically. "At least the duke timed his prank to take place after the ceremony—it was lovely, wasn't it?"

"I'm Jane Esterbrook, by the way," she said. "I was a Dowell before I married. Nell's aunt."

"Yes, I remember. You told me a lovely story about taking your niece to sunbathe when she was a child."

"That's right—you've a sharp memory, to call that up so quickly. I struggle when I'm launched into a crowd of strangers, expected to learn dozens of names and faces all at once."

Cordelia was ready to end the conversation with an easy platitude—*You're too kind*, or *The story you told was simply so memorable*, something along those lines—when Lord Pye approached.

He was Christopher Old's uncle, if she recalled correctly. His father's older sister, the ever-unpleasant Margaret, had brought him into the family through marriage. Together they'd had four children, most of whom were present at the wedding, and a small brood of seven grandchildren.

Ever since she'd corrected Mr. Pye about the Gutenberg press, he'd sought her out in an effort to—as far as she could tell—start arguments.

"What are we discussing?" Lord Pye began, looking down his nose in anticipation.

Mrs. Esterbrook did Cordelia the favor of answering. Or trying to. "I was just observing that—"

"Going on about *women's issues* again," Lord Pye interrupted. "A bit tedious, isn't it? Always harping on about the same thing, day in and day out."

Cordelia smiled politely.

"Actually," said Mrs. Esterbrook, "we were discussing—"

"I wager you're not a fan of weddings," Lord Pye barreled on. "Celebrating this sacred union of man and woman into a single, united whole. Engaging in so much frivolity and fellowship. *You'd* rather we scuttle down to the courthouse dressed like clerks, wouldn't you? No need for a vow when you've got a *contract*, eh?"

"What are you on about, Podge?" Mrs. Esterbrook exclaimed.

"I'm merely *observing* that Miss Kelly sees every conversation as an opportunity to evangelize." Lord Pye shot Mrs. Esterbrook a knowing look. "Is that your idea of good conversation?"

"I think it's entirely inappropriate," Mrs. Esterbrook admitted. "*However*—"

"I wonder where the women who appreciate your crusading actually *are*, Miss Kelly?" Lord Pye lifted one hand to his brow, shading his eyes as he looked about. "Not here, obviously. Are they anywhere? Or do they exist in your imagination alone?"

"In my imagination we are a multitude. It would be more than a life's work to realize that dream, but I will certainly try." Cordelia paused. "And yet I suspect—I don't know whether this thought makes me want to laugh or cry—but I *suspect* that such speeches as you're giving right now will convert more women to my point of view than all my most earnest efforts."

Mrs. Esterbrook burst out laughing and clapped a hand over her mouth to stifle the sound.

"What's that?" demanded Lord Pye.

Cordelia sucked in a breath. She could explain.

"Oh, enough of this," cut in Mrs. Esterbrook. "Both of you. If you'll forgive me for speaking my mind, Miss Kelly, it often falls to us—we of the fairer sex—to keep the peace. Whether or not I agree with the substance of your arguments, you've demonstrated how *essential* a truly feminine sensibility is to certain delicate conversations—by your utter lack of it." Mrs. Esterbrook threw up her hands. "Surely someone has told you that you'll catch more flies with honey?"

"I believe King Lear addresses that argument. And, not for nothing, my Christian name *is* Cordelia." When Mrs. Esterbrook appeared baffled by this reference and Lord Pye affronted, Cordelia's patience ran out. "If you'll excuse me, I'm going to go congratulate the bride and groom."

At the conclusion of the wedding breakfast, just before the real cake was cut, Chilly presented Nell with the Book of Love that Cordelia had spent the past several days creating.

It was a beautiful piece of work, though she had manners

enough not to say so out loud. Nell burst into tears as she turned the pages, fingers reverent on the silk binding, flinching when a teardrop fell to mar the thick paper. She clutched Chilly, graceless in her emotion, and scurried from table to table as she read each new anecdote, reminiscing about the stories and sharing hugs and kisses of gratitude with everyone who'd contributed.

Cordelia watched, warm with pride and something else. A pinprick wound in her heart that bled far too freely.

CHAPTER 16

O n the day of his best friend's wedding, Alistair greeted the
dawn like a man awaiting an execution.

He'd been busy with preparations for his prank for most of the
night and managed less than three hours of sleep. He had to dress
himself—Fisk being occupied—stooping in front of a too-small
mirror and struggling with his cravat.

He felt like a heel leaving Fisk in charge, but seeing to the final
preparations himself would require missing his best friend's
wedding. That had never been an option, but he'd dropped a
truly Herculean task into the lap of a man who, if he had his
druthers, would never have pulled a single prank in his whole
life.

He accompanied Chilly to the church, skewered by his friend's
enthusiasm. Not even the slightest shadow of doubt clouded
Chilly's countenance, and Nell's usual impishness gave a sparkle
to her joy.

It was lovely and over almost as soon as it began. They
returned to the Dowell's home and there, for the first time, he felt
a flash of hope.

The whole facade of Old's house rippled white, grand, and

silly, obvious and surprising. Swags and rosettes fluttered gently in the sunshine, imitating the white frosting on the cake.

A perfect prank—he was certain when he saw Nell's reaction. She hopped down from her carriage, laughing and crying by turns, scurrying between Chilly and Alistair, shouting, "You rascals! You're incorrigible, both of you!" and "How did you manage? It's not possible!"

She even rose up on tiptoes to kiss his cheek, eyes sparkling. "What a brilliant present!"

Chilly said, "Quite a feat," without a trace of humor and Alistair caught a few very intense looks from him, almost teary with fondness, so it was best they kept the conversation short.

As evening descended, Alistair found himself in an odd mood. He hadn't thought it would throw him for a loop to watch his best friend get married—they were the right age for it, Chilly had picked the perfect girl, everything turned out for the best—but he felt sad? Mostly happy, of course. But just a tiny bit sad. Wistful, maybe? Had he ever felt wistful before? He needed something to compare it to, to be sure.

Anyway, Chilly was gone now, off discovering joys of married sex, and Alistair had no desire to join with the other men for after dinner drinks. Nor did he want to go on a walk or plan his next prank or tease Fisk or *oh look* here he was in the family rooms, fist raised to knock at the door to Nell's freshly vacated study. He'd just so happened to overhear that Coco had been put up in this room and made a little note of it, for later, with no ulterior motive at all.

It was still early enough for the Dowells to be occupied with their duties as hosts, leaving this section of the house deserted. He paused a few steps away from Coco's door just in case, idling about with his ears pricked. He didn't want anyone to catch him entering Coco's bedroom.

Well. A part of him did want that, since he could immediately solve the problem by offering to marry Coco. He could do that anyway, of course. Should he propose? Had the time come?

More importantly: were those sniffles he heard from inside her room?

He tapped his knuckles on the door, kept his voice at a whisper. "Coco? Coco, are you all right?"

She didn't answer, and he'd been loitering for too long already, so he eased the door open.

Coco sat on her narrow bed with her back against the headboard, head bent and shoulders drooping, a picture of misery. When she looked up, alert to his intrusion, her eyes—her terrifying, steely eyes—were soft as goose down, glistening with tears. Not just one or two, either. Her cheeks were drenched from eyelash to chin.

"Coco," he crooned, his heart twisting itself into a knot. This was his fault. All his fault. He'd brought her here and left her to suffer. So many people had been cruel, and instead of defending her, he'd stood back to watch. As though she were a dancing bear, performing for his pleasure.

He rushed to her side, folded her in his arms, rocked her on his lap. "I'm so sorry. I should have taken better care of you. Stood up for you and spoken for you and made Chilly's family treat you with the respect you deserve. I failed you, I—"

Coco tried to squirm out of his embrace. "What are you going on about?"

"You seem so strong." He was beside himself with guilt. She'd fooled him into thinking she was invincible, but he should have known. How many people had treated him as though his size meant he couldn't be hurt? "But of course you have feelings. You're not made of stone."

"I'm not an *infant*." She slapped his chest. "Put me down."

"You don't have to be embarrassed," he soothed. "I don't think anyone could have guessed—you hide your tender heart so well. But you don't have to! Not from me."

"You're not making any sense," she said, still squirming.

"I hope you know that *I* think you're wonderful. The most amazing woman I've ever met."

189

"You're not listening to a word I say, are you?"

"I'm listening," he promised. "Is there anything I can do? Anything at all? Because there's nothing in the world that—"

"I am crying because something terribly sad just happened in the book I'm reading." She spoke slowly, overenunciating each syllable. "Whatever you've imagined, you are mistaken."

He sighed, disappointed. "You don't have to talk about it if you don't want to."

"Indeed I *don't* want to talk about it, but since you're here and *greatly mistaken*, I will," she retorted. "I am reading a *book*. That is *all*."

He slowly ceased his rocking. "You're crying... about a book?"

"Yes."

"You aren't crying because the wedding guests have been unkind?"

"I'd pluck out my own eyes before I let a handful of bothersome strangers make me cry."

"Oh," said Alistair. "So..."

He'd misread this situation. Now he was inside Coco's bedroom, sitting on Coco's bed, with Coco in his lap, and absolutely no idea how to proceed. Should he set her aside? Or should he let go and wait for her to remove herself? Indecision paralyzed him.

As his panic receded, a different awareness rose to the fore: the body cradled in his arms. Unlike most of the women he'd embraced, she was all angles and sharp edges. Firm everywhere— her legs, her arms, even her hindquarters tensed up like a sack tightly packed with sand. He bounced her a little closer to his chest, trying to decide how he felt about that.

Her body suited her, he had to admit. She was quick and beautiful but not easy. There'd be no sinking into oblivion here, no soft curves molding seamlessly to his own unbending shape. Even close she'd remain separate, even held tight there'd be gaps between them. That made him sad, a little, but he was in too deep to regret his choice.

It dawned on him that he'd been holding her for a while now and she hadn't attempted to escape.

"Shall I put you down?"

"Yes," she answered.

She did not, however, move.

Alistair wanted to do the right thing but for all the wrong reasons. He wanted to impress Cordelia with his moral rectitude the same way a peacock displayed its feathers. Look here! Choose me! He'd have given her anything, really, but Coco would be more impressed by a show of respect than, say, a gift of jewelry.

If it were in his power to become a paragon of high-mindedness, he'd have done it. Instead, he dragged his thumb across her damp cheek. So smooth. "It must be an incredibly sad book to make you cry like this."

She shivered.

"Yes? No?"

"Most books make me cry. Happy ones, sad ones. If they're at all good, I cry at the end."

"I don't believe you."

She slumped, letting her head fall against his chest—he could feel the weight of it and it thrilled him. She'd relaxed. She'd trusted him to hold her. It was so much more than she'd ever given him before.

"That's why I only read when I'm alone. If I read with my friends or family nearby and I started to cry while they knitted or played the piano?" She shuddered. "I couldn't *bear* it."

"I would never have guessed."

"Don't tell anyone," she said. "Even Bonny doesn't know."

"You can give me all your secrets," he promised. "I'll take good care of them."

"It's humiliating."

"I'm glad I found out."

"If you think this means I'm secretly sweet and sentimental, you'd be wrong."

"We'll agree to disagree." He began to rock her again. To

comfort her, to put her at ease. To, yes, bypass the boundaries she defended so vigilantly. He hated them.

She nestled her head into the crook of his shoulder and stared at the wall, her expression growing bleaker even as her body relaxed.

"What's the matter?" he asked.

She shook her head, lips thinning.

But he knew. He was not—it was slowly dawning on him—an idiot. And so he whispered, low, "Coco, I want to marry you."

Her brows notched together. "No need to add insult to injury."

"Will you marry me?" he asked. "Say yes. I'd marry you tomorrow if I could. Yesterday. Next week. Whenever you'll have me."

"Less than a month ago you vowed to cut me out of your life entirely."

"And how long did that last?" he replied. "I can tell you: five days."

"That's"—her lips moved silently for a moment—"one tenth of our entire acquaintance."

"The other ninety percent have been very persuasive," he argued. "For me, at any rate. What must I do to convince *you*?"

"Nothing. I'll marry you." She didn't look away from the wall. She *sounded* as though she could see through that wall and into a dim future.

He paused. "You will?"

"I'd be a fool not to."

"Oh."

His heart cracked. He'd always known that any wife he chose would probably want his wealth and his title at least as much as they wanted him, Alistair Chandos, the man. No getting around that. He possessed almost incomprehensible wealth and a first-rate title, and it would take quite an extraordinary character to measure up.

He'd still expected… more. A pretense of affection, at least? A bit of polite theater to soothe his pride? Not that Coco was the sort to engage in either pretense or polite theater.

Neither had he expected her to acquiesce so coldly. Yes, she'd described marriage as a kind of transaction—a gamble, specifically—but this was a woman who'd struck out on her own, who'd rejected expedience. Hadn't she?

"I didn't, um." He swallowed a lump in his throat. Had he made a mistake? Did he secretly want his children to grow up with all the same fears he had? Anxious and confused, as he'd been?

He'd promised not to become his father, but he'd never really felt in much danger of it. Neither had he spent much time wondering how his father had become the man he'd been. Perhaps he should have.

"I didn't think you'd marry without, um..." he hesitated "... without affection."

She shifted in his arms, chin tilting up so she could examine him. Her steel-blue eyes always saw too much. "I wouldn't."

"You wouldn't?" he echoed, pathetically hopeful.

She wriggled, and he lifted her off his lap. To his shock, instead of retreating she knelt on the bed and took a firm grip on his shoulder, urging him to twist and face her, eye to eye.

"I've only ever met one man I'd agree to marry," she said, in that way only she had: as though she'd blasted through all the doubt and uncertainty in the world, arriving at a bedrock of unshakable truth. "You."

"Me?" That made no sense. Almost anyone else would be better.

Not that it mattered. He wanted to marry Coco. Thanks to his title and his money, she'd said yes. He'd have what he wanted and figure out the rest later.

She cupped his cheeks and peered closely at him. "Ask me again when you're certain."

"I'm certain," he insisted.

"You're not." She swept her thumbs back and forth on his

cheeks, a gentle reassurance that made his heart flutter. "I needed to know you weren't toying with my affections. You needed to know how I am disposed toward you. Next time—if there's a next time—you'll be certain."

"I'm certain," he repeated, startled to hear the difference in his voice. Lower, steadier. He really meant it.

"Perhaps." A trace of humor twitched at the corners of her lips. "If so, you'll ask again."

"A kiss." After their first kiss, and then his second *attempt* at a kiss, he feared the third time wouldn't be a charm. So he seized her wrists, expecting her to recoil. "To mark the occasion."

He needed to *see* her reaction. Those first two times, they'd been in the dark. Literally. And her reaction had left him in the dark *figuratively*. She'd run hot and cold, but in what order—it mattered—and to what degree?

He watched carefully. Her eyes dilated and her breath caught —yes!—before the tendons on her wrists sprang tight and she tried to pull away.

"One kiss," he coaxed, confident now. He recognized desire when he saw it. Whatever battle raged on inside her head, he knew which side he wanted to win. And if he could tip the scales...

Her gaze dropped right to his mouth. The pink tip of her tongue poked out as she licked her lips. He waited, and waited, every second excruciating. Why bother? He'd told her, in words, that he wanted to marry her. He'd offered her the grand prize, and still she quibbled and second-guessed.

"Don't you want to?" he wondered, more plaintive than he really intended to be, and she sighed right into him.

Her lips dipped close and then lifted, skimmed and then settled. He liked it so much that it took him a while to realize she was *copying* him, nipping and nuzzling the way he'd done at Olympia's. His own first kiss had been a disaster, and he vowed to make this good for her. Whatever Coco wanted, he'd learn to like. Whatever she liked, he'd learn to give.

He made a soft noise of encouragement, which broke the spell. Coco pulled away, looking half dazed and half ashamed.

"You're good at that," he told her, because he wanted her to like kissing. And him. And kissing him.

She straightened, and her expression realigned, eyebrow cocked and skeptical while her lips remained pink and wet and kissable. "Is that so?"

He nodded earnestly. "A natural talent."

"You're incorrigible." She flicked her fingers in a shooing motion. "Off with you, now. I don't recall giving you permission to enter in the first place."

"Fine, fine." He eased off the bed quietly, careful of the creaking floorboards as he crossed to the door. "Coco, will you—?"

"Not yet."

"How soon can I ask?"

"Tomorrow at the earliest."

"At breakfast?"

"Breakfast is too early."

"Luncheon?"

"I'm trying to do you a favor," she complained.

"That's how I'll introduce the subject tomorrow." He opened the door so she couldn't answer, guaranteeing himself the last word. With a final, gleeful smile, he left.

STROUD JOINED CORDELIA for breakfast so soon after she sat down that she felt fairly confident his long-suffering secretary had been deployed as a lookout. Stroud arrived in a state of near-glee, too, beaming sunnily over his eggs and toast, little laugh lines crinkling around his eyes as he asked, "How d'ye do?" and declared, "The weather is certainly shaping up to be fine."

He obviously had a prank of some kind planned. Cordelia

wondered whether he'd be more flummoxed if she ignored the obvious or asked him about it directly.

"Miss Kelly," he singsonged.

"Yes, your grace?"

"I'd like to do you a *favor*."

Cordelia froze. She hadn't lied the night before when she told Stroud he was the only man she'd ever seriously considered marrying. Possibly she had misjudged all the others. Possibly she'd only fantasized about Stroud because he seemed so far out of reach.

Certainly she'd intended to remain a spinster. All her excuses had been just that—excuses. When Stroud proposed, he'd called her bluff. The choice he offered was too stark, the correct answer too obvious. Dukes did not grow on trees.

Then she'd realized that he was nervous too. That he, too, had so much to lose. Her fears, once shared, became so much less dreadful. She'd always imagined herself alone with that roulette wheel, her heart in her throat as she faced a murky, unknown future.

She wasn't alone. Once she said yes, they'd face the future together. It might spin out in a hundred different directions, a thousand, all of them better with Stroud. Brighter and more joyful.

She wouldn't hesitate, next time he asked. She would be so, so happy to accept.

"Here." Stroud passed her a small, shell-shaped dish full of salt. "To season your eggs."

Cordelia took the dish. "This is your idea of a favor?"

Stroud nodded, his eyes twinkling merrily.

"I see." The dish came with a matching, toothpick-sized spoon for scooping minuscule portions. Cordelia made use of the spoon and the seasoning and then said, offhand, as though changing the subject, "Did you know that salt catalyzes a chemical reaction with certain foods that can generate heat?"

Stroud blinked. "It does what?"

"Adding salt to certain dishes keeps them warm," Cordelia answered. "An old cook's trick that modern scientists have been investigating recently."

"No." Stroud squinted. "That can't be right."

"Feel for yourself." Cordelia gestured to her eggs.

Stroud extended his hand, palm down, over her plate. He squinted, as though he might somehow be able to *see* the change in temperature.

Cordelia smacked his palm into the eggs.

Stroud yanked his eggy hand back with a shout.

"Oh, did you fall for that?" Cordelia smiled tranquilly. "Are you a bit slow in the mornings?"

Stroud sighed, "*Coco*," as he wiped the mess away with a napkin.

"Thank you for passing the salt." Coco took a bite of plain, unbuttered toast. "I'm excited to find out what other *favors* you have planned for today."

Stroud sat back in his chair, legs slightly spread, a lordly sprawl whose effect was somewhat undermined by the grin splitting his face. "Surprise grows more and more unreliable as a tactic, the better you know a person."

"I'm not worried."

"Don't underestimate me," Stroud warned.

"Your Grace, I would never."

"No. You don't, do you?" Stroud shifted and stared down at his hands, fingers laced together like a schoolboy. "Coco. There's something I need to understand. Are you reluctant to marry, or are you reluctant to marry—?"

Me.

He didn't say the word but she heard it loud and clear.

"Neither," said Cordelia.

"Don't..." His expression clouded. "Don't lie, Coco."

"Since last night," she clarified. "Neither."

"Oh." The doubt lifted, just like that.

Cordelia did not make a habit of asking people to have faith in her. She'd rather prove herself first and stand on firmer ground. But he was so ready to believe in her, and it took her breath away.

"And before yesterday?" Stroud pressed.

Before yesterday, she hadn't wanted to get married at all. But how to explain, when she'd had a hard enough time admitting it to herself? "Think of your acquaintance. Across the whole span of it, how many happily married couples do you know?"

"I couldn't name them all," Alistair protested. "There must be dozens."

"Try," Cordelia urged. "And don't count newlyweds. Only couples who have been married for five years or more."

Stroud began counting on his fingers, mouth moving silently. He reached six rapidly and then stalled.

Cordelia waited.

"Six," he answered finally. "But the vast majority of marriages are *tolerable*."

"Do you think so?" Cordelia cocked an eyebrow. "Why do so many men commit adultery?"

"I— What?" Stroud's hands flew up, palms out. "I'm not answering that."

"If most married men conclude that adultery is essential to their happiness and indulge freely while most married women are prevented from seeking the same relief, it stands to reason that the average married woman is unhappier than the average married man."

Stroud frowned. "Are you saying you plan to commit adultery?"

"No, of course not, but—"

"Well, neither will I," said Stroud. "So I don't see the problem."

"There isn't one," Cordelia admitted. "But marriage makes so many people unhappy. Most people, by my estimation. Until yesterday, I would have said: why take the risk?"

"This all goes back to that roulette metaphor of yours." He sat back in his seat, straightened decisively. "You disapprove of gambling, is that it?"

"Nothing in life is certain," said Cordelia. "In that sense, we're all gamblers. Whether we like it or not."

"But don't you think you've stretched the comparison a *bit* too far?"

"I find it clarifying."

"I suppose I should feel honored that you're willing to take the risk."

"You've got it backwards." She waited for him to meet her eyes. "With you, it doesn't feel like a risk."

He blushed crimson, from his cheeks all the way to the tips of his ears. "Well, um. You're returning to the city this afternoon, aren't you? By train?"

Cordelia nodded.

"I'll walk you to the station."

"Mrs. Dowell has offered to send me in her carriage."

"She'll be delighted to learn you've made alternate arrangements, making the very challenging day she has ahead a little easier," Stroud returned. "I'll send your luggage to the station with my own things, and she'll be able to worry about her other guests."

"If I can find a chaperone," Cordelia demurred.

"I've already found one."

"Already?"

"Two of them," Stroud continued. "Did you know that planning a pleasant afternoon stroll is much easier than planning to rotate a large statue in a busy city square?"

"When you put it that way…"

"Everything's arranged." Stroud stood and pointed at the eggy napkin. "You've opened the door, Coco. It's my favorite door."

"It's your least favorite door," Cordelia countered.

"No, it's my favorite."

"If you leave it open all the time and never want it shut, it's your *least* favorite door."

199

Stroud stared at her for a minute. "It's my favorite door," he insisted, and then beat a quick retreat before she could disagree again.

Stroud had convinced two members of the Dowell family to walk with them to the train station. The first was Iva Sobel, Mrs. Dowell's spinster sister, who'd traveled all the way from Italy for the wedding and would be staying with the family for an additional fortnight. The second was Nell's sister Winny, the youngest of the Dowell children at nineteen. The two planned to explore the town for a few hours before returning in Mrs. Dowell's carriage, which would be ferrying guests to and from the train station all day.

Mrs. Dowell had tried valiantly to hide her relief when Cordelia informed her that she wouldn't need a ride into town. And then, having failed, she laughed and said, "I know it's awful to admit, but I'm so glad the wedding is over! I haven't had a minute to myself in days. Just a moment... Chilly left it with me before they left..." and she'd slipped Cordelia a purse containing the rest of her fee before squeezing her palms with surprising fervency.

"That book you made will be cherished for generations," she said. "I am so glad Chilly insisted, it is a treasure."

"All credit goes to Mr. Old, who came up with the idea," Cordelia replied.

"It's kind of you to say so," murmured Mrs. Dowell. "We'll work together again soon?"

"Whenever you have need."

They set out across country as a foursome, Cordelia arm in arm with Stroud while Miss Sobel and Miss Winny trailed behind. Wind gusted between dips in the rolling hills, and an intermittent drizzle kept Cordelia's shawl damp.

As much as she'd grown to love London, Cordelia was glad to have a glimpse of spring in a place where it could show its full glory. Air unclogged by thousands of coal stoves carried the fragrance of budding fruit trees, rain sparkled on wild grasses instead of pooling around clogged drains.

As they crested a hill a vista unfurled before them, wildflowers speckled amongst the green, willow trees swaying in the breeze, and Stroud dropped to one knee.

He carried her hand to his lips and kissed her gloved knuckles. Passionately. "Miss Kelly, would you do me the honor of becoming my wife? If you agree, I promise I will spend the rest of my life endeavoring to make you as happy as your very presence makes me."

"Oh!" Even though she'd expected a proposal, it still surprised her. "I think my heart just skipped a beat."

The laugh lines at the corners of Stroud's eyes crinkled. "Mine's going double-time, so you can have the extra."

"Yes." It felt so good to say that she did it again. "Yes, *yes*, I am delighted to say yes."

He picked her up and spun her around in a circle, skirts flaring as her stomach flipped. "I'll have the banns posted—no, no. Three weeks is too long. Do you want an elaborate wedding? You don't, do you?"

"Not at all."

"Then I'll get a special license," Stroud said, satisfied. "We'll be married within the week."

Miss Sobel and Miss Winifred, who'd fallen behind, caught up in time to overhear Stroud's announcement. Miss Winifred gasped and feigned a swoon, collapsing gracefully into her aunt's side. Miss Sobel administered comforting pats to her niece's shoulder.

"Congratulations," said Mrs. Sobel. "It seems that one felicitous event—I mean my nephew's lovely wedding—has already given birth to another. What a good omen for the future."

"I feel very lucky." Cordelia wondered if she'd just unearthed the true source of her unease. It had been easier to imagine a disingenuous aristocrat preying upon her vulnerabilities than an adorable duke falling in love with her.

Fortune had positively *drenched* her in blessings. She could try for the rest of her life to deserve them and never come close. And all of it originated with Stroud, a man she'd underestimated again and again, whose patience she'd tested, who'd proven himself without asking for much in return.

She owed him more than any one person could give. And she loved him, so she wanted to try. That desire made her feel so light and so heavy all at once. A blessing and a burden, a gift and a doom.

CHAPTER 17

Stroud didn't speak to her directly on the train—instead, he regaled the entire cabin with extravagant, ridiculous stories about *his fiancée.*

"My fiancée," he began, addressing himself to the insurance salesman to his right, "oversees the most superb kitchen."

Cordelia could only stare in astonishment. Ruby's flat didn't have a kitchen and, though she'd find herself in charge of several substantial ones rather soon, she had no idea how to oversee them.

"You must like to eat." The insurance salesman, middle aged and comfortably plump with a bigger beard than he could carry off, seemed happy to engage. "A man your size."

"Oh, indeed." Stroud preened. "And whenever my fiancée's family invites me to dine, she has exotic dishes prepared from ingredients I've never heard of before. Why, just last week she served Swedish oranges!"

The woman sitting across from Stroud, a governess on her way to a new position, demurred. "I think— Are you sure—?" She shifted her weight, hands folded politely in her lap. "That is, Sweden doesn't have a favorable climate for citrus, does it?"

"That's what made these so special."

"What did they taste like?" asked the insurance salesman.

"Very much like regular oranges," Stroud answered. "Only Swedish."

"That's... erm." The insurance salesman traded a significant glance with the governess. "Quite a treat."

If Cordelia could have reached, she would have kicked Stroud in the shin. Her glare had *some* effect; she caught Stroud's eye and he flashed a devilish grin.

"My fiancée," Stroud said next, "is the most beautiful woman in the world."

"She's certainly captured your attention," the governess observed.

"From the moment she enters a room until the moment she leaves, I cannot look away."

Cordelia leaned against the window to hide her blush. After the previous piece of nonsense she could guess where this anecdote would lead, but couldn't help the butterflies that tickled her stomach.

"She's exceedingly modest, which is a fine quality in a woman, so I must satisfy myself with tantalizing glimpses of her chin. But her mother assures me she has a marvelous figure."

"Her mother?" the governess sounded quite skeptical now. "Is that appropriate?"

"Discreetly," Stroud clarified. "In the most delicate language."

"How exactly does she obscure her face?" the insurance salesman wondered.

"I don't think we should be discussing this in mixed company," the governess pointed out.

"Aren't you curious?" asked the insurance salesman.

The governess hesitated and then, grudgingly, "I can't say I'm not."

"She wears veiled hats, even indoors. There's always quite a bit of lace." Stroud wiggled his fingers in front of his face. "Lace is so alluring, don't you think?"

"Well, I should hope it's her character that matters," said the insurance salesman. "Her temperament and, er, good heart."

"She is kindness incarnate," crowed Stroud. "Why, she recently arranged to give my beloved hound to an orphanage, because she says the children have greater need of a pet than I do."

"She gave away your *dog*?" interrupted the passenger sitting across from Cordelia, a university student looking forward to a weekend on the town.

"She's not fond of animals," Stroud admitted. "But only because she's such a conscientious housekeeper."

And so it went. By the time they reached London, the other passengers were not-so-subtly suggesting that Stroud break off his engagement. Stroud stubbornly refused to understand any of these hints, no matter how pointed.

Cordelia disembarked and collected her luggage. She hailed a hackney and gave the driver her address. Before she could climb inside, Stroud captured her gloved hand and lifted it to his lips.

"*My* fiancé is a bit of a clown," Cordelia informed him, rather fondly.

Stroud winked. "It's a good thing that my fiancée is so extraordinarily patient."

Cordelia clucked, and Stroud laughed heartily as he tipped his hat and backed away.

CORDELIA WAS UNPACKING, trunks open and clothing in piles on her bed waiting to be sorted, when Ruby bumped open the door to the bedroom with her hip. She held a cup of tea in each hand and slow-walked toward Cordelia's desk, eyes on the rippling liquid, smiling gratefully when Cordelia approached with her arms outstretched. Cordelia took one cup, Ruby claimed the chair, and they settled in with a pair of matching sighs.

"I have had a *very* long day." Ruby silently sipped her tea. "Tell me about the wedding. How did everything go? Did the book you made on such short notice turn out well? Did Nell and Chilly make it to the altar?"

"The book turned out so well that I might try selling some of my other customers on the idea," Cordelia answered. "I, on the other hand, was glad have an excuse to spend most of the day in my room. But the ceremony was lovely."

"You're not mourning the loss of poor Nell's legal personhood?"

"Oh, that can wait for next week I think." Cordelia laughed wryly. "I've never seen such a beautiful ceremony. They're so in love, and so well-suited to one another. But it's true—whether you speak in jest or not—the injustice of our laws blights what ought to be a moment of pure hope."

"Speaking of blight: as of yesterday, Olympia is engaged to be married."

Cordelia groaned. "Oh *no*."

"She's thrilled of course."

Cordelia dropped heavily onto her bed, stricken. "Oh, but why? Poor Olympia. By the time she realizes she's made a mistake, it will be too late."

"Mr. Grant strikes me as selfish and flimsy—he'll be a bad husband but hopefully not a cruel one."

"What a thing to *hope* for," Cordelia murmured. "It's like Bonny and that awful Charles Gavin all over again. I *hate* watching my friends march headlong towards disaster. I can't stop them, I can't make them *see*."

"I called on her to offer my congratulations—or as close to congratulations as I could manage—and she described losing her virginity to Mr. Grant *at length*."

Cordelia gaped. "She didn't."

"She absolutely did. I'd give you a summary, but I'll buy all our sugar for the rest of the year if Olympia doesn't subject you to the same account the next time you see her. She was *quite* fixated."

"In all honesty, I won't object." Cordelia had no real under-standing of marital relations. Her mother had never been explicit on the subject, and Bonny, a married woman presumably equipped with all the information Cordelia lacked, had not been forthcoming. "Since I'll be getting married myself very soon."

Ruby dropped her teacup. She caught it before it shattered, but fragrant, milky tea spilled all over her lap. She cried out in pain, and Cordelia ran to fetch a towel.

Ruby limped after, stripping her sodden wrap and tossing it aside. "You're getting *married*? To—oh, I'm afraid to even say his *name* in case I'm wrong, but who else could it be?"

Taking note of the discarded wrap, Cordelia left the towel for later and went straight for their limited medical supplies. She fetched a small pot of salve and twisted the lid free while Ruby disappeared into her room to change. She re-emerged a moment later in fresh clothing.

"Sit down and let's see the burn." Cordelia brandished the salve. "That tea was piping hot."

Ruby hissed through her teeth as she lifted her skirts, revealing a splotch of scalded pink on her thighs. Cordelia made sympathetic noises as she cleaned the burn and rubbed the thick cream in.

"Better," Ruby said tightly. "Bring me a handkerchief, would you? Top drawer of my cabinet."

Cordelia obeyed, picking a simple square of linen and fetching it back to her flatmate.

Ruby tied the handkerchief around her thigh so the salve didn't smear once she let down her skirts. "I'll be fine by morning, I imagine." She narrowed her fine eyes at Cordelia. "So. His name? You're going to have to say it first."

"The Duke of Stroud."

"And you're sure he proposed *marriage*?"

"He phrased the question clearly, in the accustomed manner." Cordelia smiled wryly. "In front of witnesses!"

Ruby's burst of laughter faded into a wondering smile. "I wasn't sure what to think about Stroud, but now I've decided: I like him a very great deal. He has excellent taste."

Cordelia sat back on her heels. "I can't quite believe it's real. Perhaps he'll have second thoughts about marrying a penniless, outcast shrew. I'm not sure I'd blame him."

"Second thoughts? How? Don't tell me he wants a long engagement or some such nonsense? Because if so—"

"He said he'd obtain a special license. We'll likely be married in a week." Cordelia resealed the pot of salve and spun it idly, like an unwieldy top. "One of Nell's aunts and one of her cousins were out walking with us when he proposed, and he was more than pleased to inform them of our altered circumstances."

"And you accepted, obviously." Ruby tapped Cordelia's knee. "Any regrets?"

"It wasn't a difficult decision." Which sounded awfully bloodless, despite being true. "I think I'm in love with him, but if that were all, I might hesitate. And he's a duke—powerfully persuasive, but if that were all, I might hesitate. But to find the two together and still refuse… I try not to be a fool, Ruby. *Yes* was the only sane answer."

"Enough people already think you mad for having come to London on your own, then refusing to repent of it. No harm in living up to your reputation, if that would be your honest choice."

"Sometimes I feel like I'm the only person with any sense at all when the subject of marriage comes up… which supports the madwoman hypothesis, unfortunately." Cordelia sighed. "I'm not afraid to be alone. But I refuse to *remain* alone on principle, because I have something to *prove*."

"And that's why you're the best of us," Ruby soothed. "No one who knows you will be disappointed, Cordelia. I promise."

❦

OLYMPIA'S FIRST WORDS, BEFORE "HELLO" or "how do you do" or even "how lovely to see you on such a fine afternoon," were, "I don't want a lecture."

"I'm not here to deliver one," Cordelia replied.

Olympia narrowed her eyes. "I mean it. I won't listen. Start and I'll have you thrown out."

"If you want me to leave, say so." Cordelia straightened the cuffs on her coat. "Otherwise, invite me in and ask for my news."

Olympia hesitated—then she released a long breath, tension draining out of her posture as she beckoned Cordelia inside the house and into her arms. "I know you don't mean to be cruel, Cordelia, but you'll speak your mind, and I'll get angry about it, and that will be the end of our friendship. Do you understand? The *end*."

"Perfectly."

Olympia's arms tightened. "I do love you."

"And I love *you*." Cordelia patted her friend on the back. "That won't change."

Olympia pulled away. "Swear it."

"I swear that I am a true friend to you, Olympia. Through thick and thin," Cordelia said. And then, passionately, "Do you think I don't understand the meaning of friendship? I owe my life in London to you and to Bonny and to Ruby and to Tess. The four of you made it possible for me to choose my own way instead of being forced down the road to misery or ruin."

Olympia's voice wavered. "I know that you are grateful—but you only care about your principles and you can be so *uncompromising*—"

"What principle would cause me to abandon you?" Cordelia interrupted. "I firmly believe that women ought to be able to marry according to their own preferences. I gave you my honest opinion when you asked. You chose your own path and now, *principle* dictates I support you, whether or not I approve."

Olympia shut her eyes and took a deep breath. "Thank you." She regained her composure with visible effort, slipped an arm around Cordelia's waist, and tugged her toward the salon. "Let's have some tea and some cakes and exchange our news."

They ended up at a small table laid with porcelain and crystal, bathed in golden light streaming through a window framed in filmy curtains, the sort of glittery bower where Olympia felt most at home. Cordelia observed the change in her friend well before she broached the topic of her affair with Mr. Grant. It was obvious. Something both content and knowing had entered Olympia's expression while her posture, always languid, had shifted indefinably toward the sensual.

When Cordelia shared her big news, Olympia pointed a half-eaten cookie at Cordelia's nose. "I have some advice for you, so take heed. Sexual intercourse doesn't have to be unpleasant or painful or *anything* like you've been warned. On the contrary, it is *extremely enjoyable*. Do you understand?"

"Your meaning is clear."

"Take this to heart!" A few crumbs of shortbread shook loose from the cookie as Olympia shook it for emphasis. "I am frankly appalled that so many women are missing out on what is, unquestionably, the most pleasurable experience a body will ever have."

"This all sounds rather..." how to phrase it politely? "...extreme."

"You're dubious." Olympia leaned over her plate. "Has anyone explained the mechanics of the act to you? Shall I do it now?"

"I grew up in the country," Cordelia assured her.

"What does that have to do with anything?" Olympia wondered. "I thought country folk are meant to be innocent and naive and startled by city sophistication?"

"That is our reputation," Cordelia acknowledged. "But in the country we grow up around livestock. No one's yet explained to cows and sheep and ducks that they're meant to behave themselves in the presence of young ladies, so even as children we understand the *mechanics*. Some parents don't care to explain what's going on, but there's always a friend who's learned enough of the truth to pass it on."

"Oh *my*." Olympia appeared startled. "Well, do the cows and the sheep and the ducks enjoy themselves extravagantly?"

"Not that I've noticed."

"Then I'm glad we're having this conversation. You should know what to expect." Olympia nodded decisively. "Now that the important business is over with—have you picked a date? Stroud's never been one for pomp and circumstance—"

"Nor have I," Cordelia interrupted dryly.

"That's true." Olympia gestured for a waiting servant to clear away the plates and poured fresh cups of tea. "But he has rather a large family, and you'll have to meet them all eventually, so why not be efficient about it? You're a great proponent of efficiency."

"Stroud is set on a hasty wedding." He'd followed through on his promise so quickly she'd never had time to doubt. "He sent me a letter this morning asking if Saturday would suit."

"I hope you told him you'd rather take the time to plan something special."

"Oh, I agreed. I had no reason not to."

"So what's the matter?"

"Nothing at all." Cordelia tapped her knee, frustrated. "Nothing that makes sense anyhow."

"It's just wedding jitters. Perhaps you thought you'd be immune to such human emotions? Dear Cordelia, sometimes you are flesh and blood like the rest of us." Olympia confessed, hesitantly, "I've got them."

"Can I say something you won't like?"

"Be careful."

"I've arranged to speak with Stroud's solicitor tomorrow and I'll be arriving at the meeting with one I've engaged myself. I want to make sure that if things go badly, I'll be protected. As much as I can be." Cordelia took Olympia's hand. "Promise me you'll do the same."

"I love Martin." Olympia yanked her hand away. "I *trust* him."

"Marrying him is sufficient proof of that, I should think," said Cordelia. "Please, Olympia. A wee teaspoon of prudence won't do any harm."

"I'll think about it."

CHAPTER 18

A listair sifted through his mail. Since Fisk took care of everything that didn't require his direct attention, every letter that reached his desk was important. But he had an appointment coming up, so nothing too time consuming. He paused at an envelope bearing a familiar surname and began to read.

Your Grace,

My daughter informs me that you intend to marry this coming Saturday. As I have never met you and know nothing of your character, I cannot offer my blessing. Likewise, because I do know my daughter and her character, neither will I risk the consequences of an objection.

Rumor has it that you are frivolous and childish by nature. If so, I am baffled by your interest in my daughter. Nor can I imagine any decent reason for her to accept a proposal from a man such as you have been described to be.

But rumor and base speculation are a poor foundation for judgement, so I do greatly anticipate the opportunity to make my own observations and draw my own conclusions as a guest at your wedding.

My wife, also, will attend the ceremony and sends her kind regards.

Yours,

The Hon. Justice Aloysius Kelly

Alistair read it a second time, then a third. After his fourth pass he still didn't know what to think. He couldn't recall a single occasion when Coco had mentioned her family. Not a word about being close to them or estranged from them, missing them or loathing them. Now he'd had a letter from her father and—just the same—he couldn't decide if Justice Kelly's attitude was protective or callous, loving or contemptuous.

A knock interrupted his musing. He called, "Join us," and Fisk opened the door for his solicitor, Hubert Faber. Alistair gave Justice Kelly's letter one last look before flipping it face down and gesturing for Faber to enter.

"Your secretary tells me that we're here to discuss marriage contracts?" said Faber, sinking into the chair opposite Alistair's desk.

"That's right." Alistair nodded. "My fiancée will be here momentarily. I'll count on you to take the lead, following my guidance. We're going to agree to everything she asks—"

"Your Grace," interrupted Faber. "Of course one admires your generosity of spirit, but I cannot recommend such an unwise course."

"If she wants something that could damage the family's long-term interests, then consult me," Alistair conceded, though only because he didn't think the issue would come up. "Explain the matter in plain words, so I can understand, and I'll decide."

The solicitor went pale.

"She's sensible, I promise," Alistair soothed. "But I don't want to throw up unnecessary obstacles. She may react badly."

"Your Grace," cautioned the solicitor. "A fiancée who throws tantrums at the threat of sound financial limits to her spending will become a wife who does the same. Your means are significant, but they are not limitless. I hope you are prepared to exercise the oversight appropriate to the role of husband."

"I think you've misunderstood the situation."

"It's more likely that affection has skewed your perception," suggested the solicitor.

"Well, if you won't believe me, she'll be here in—"

The knock at the door couldn't have been better timed.

Mr. Faber startled when Fisk announced the name of Coco's lawyer. "You didn't tell me that Miss Kelly had retained *Henry Castell*," he hissed as they relocated to the table positioned at the center of the room, flanked by four empty chairs waiting for occupants.

"Who's Harry Castell?" Alistair asked.

"A barrister, a very *excellent* barrister." Faber sat, his eyes never straying from the door. "Prominent enough that I'm surprised to see him engaged in a matter so beneath his usual practice."

"Hmm." Alistair was only interested in Mr. Castell insofar as his presence could illuminate the puzzle posed by that odd letter. "Her father is a judge."

Faber froze in the act of arranging pen, paper, and ink around his seat. "A judge?"

"That's right." Alistair glanced at his desk. "Aloysius Kelly?"

"Her father is Justice *Aloysius Kelly*," Faber repeated.

"Yes?"

"He is… er." Faber didn't seem to know how to continue. "Also very well regarded."

"And?"

"He is brilliant. Uncompromising, principled, with a deep knowledge of the law." Faber flexed his hands nervously, blinking at the door. "Are you expecting him as well? Shouldn't he be directing these negotiations?"

"He won't be coming. If you want to know why not, you'll have to ask Miss Kelly." Alistair grinned. "Feel free. I'd be interested in her answer."

Another light knock preceded the entrance first of Coco, who'd arrived while Fisk was fetching Mr. Castell, and then the barrister. For all the day's surprises, Coco looked as she always did: dressed in drab gray, hair styled simply, back straight as a pike and eyes like sharpened graphite.

Mr. Faber made a soft, strangled noise as they rose to their feet.

"Mr. Faber?" Alistair asked, concerned.

"Miss Kelly resembles her father."

She offered him her cheek instead of her hand, cool and soft against Alistair's lips when he bent for a kiss.

Mr. Castell looked to be in his thirties. He had soft hands, narrow shoulders, a receding hairline, but he held himself with authority and looked Alistair straight in the eye. A Cit, and proud of it.

"Miss Kelly's goal is to secure her peace of mind against unrest within the marital bond," said Mr. Castell. "To this end, she requests stocks or property yielding a yearly revenue of fifteen hundred pounds be placed in trust for her lifetime use, without condition. Similarly, His Grace should designate a domicile—fully furnished and in good repair—as her lifetime estate, with the additional condition that His Grace will agree not to step foot on this property for so long as Miss Kelly is alive."

"Quite reasonable requests," Mr. Faber replied. "We can happily accommodate both. Now—"

"Wait," Alistair interrupted, looking only at Coco. "You want a place I can't even *visit*?"

Coco propped her elbows on the table and leaned over them, lacing her fingers together atop the polished wood. "I confess, Stroud, that the very night you proposed I sat down and asked myself how I would *most* like to indulge myself as a duchess. What luxury had been beyond my reach in the past which it would be within your power to provide? The answer is simply this: a place where I can be alone, from time to time."

The request almost sounded sensible coming from Coco's lips —but then *everything* she said sounded sensible. It was the inevitable effect of her posture and her tone and her bone-deep confidence. Strip all that away and she'd just told him, "What I most look forward to about marriage is neglecting my husband," which was definitely not a compliment.

But he knew what he wanted: Coco. And he trusted Coco to

know what *she* wanted. Which, apparently, was to marry him and to have a house he was forbidden to visit.

Better to keep these thoughts to himself, for now. If at all possible. "From time to time?"

"Wouldn't it be nice to know, with certainty, that every day I remain by your side it's because I've chosen to be there?"

Alistair snorted. "As though you'd tolerate anything less."

Coco stared at him expectantly.

"Oh," said Alistair, catching on at last. "I see."

Coco nodded.

"The cottage in Oxford ought to suit," Alistair told Mr. Faber.

"Oxford?" asked Mr. Castell.

"A fine cottage on the outskirts of town, with several acres of land," supplied Mr. Faber. "It's both convenient and comfortable."

"And the address?" prompted Mr. Castell. "I'll send someone to verify your information, of course, so we'll be grateful for an accurate description."

The two lawyers hammered out the details without much additional interference. At one point, while they dickered over the administration of funds held in trust for future children, Alistair leaned across the table and murmured, "Your father wrote me a letter."

"Did he?" Coco inched closer and answered, in the same low tone, "Don't humor him on my account."

"It sounds like he'll be at the wedding," Alistair replied. "It will be awkward if I don't humor him a *little*."

"Humor him exactly as much as it suits you to."

"Will the wedding reconcile you and your family?" Alistair asked. "Do you want it to?"

She went still, fingers laced together on the table and slowly going white as her grip tightened. "You told me once that you were a very bad duke. I think that I have been a very bad daughter."

"That's not true—" he assured her.

"It is true," she interrupted. "I do not think we will reconcile, Stroud. But I wish to do right by them. That is all."

Alistair had learned the hard way to notice when people were silent about their families. Whenever his memories were too dark to even contemplate, strangers inevitably filled the gaps with their own rosy assumptions. He let them, partly because it was easier for all involved and partly because, once he'd stopped being angry about it, he'd started to enjoy their charming little stories about the happy family he'd never had.

But now was not the time. "What were we discussing?"

"The provisions in place should any of your future children find themselves orphaned," said Mr. Castell.

And so it went. Coco had more patience for minutiae than Alistair, which surprised him not at all. She could maintain her concentration for longer—he found himself fidgeting toward the end, anxious to stand and move and most of all stop *talking*.

But at last the two lawyers had enough. Farewells were exchanged. Coco lingered in the doorway long enough for him to say, "I'll see you on Saturday."

She nodded, crisp. And then, to his surprise, "I'm looking forward to it."

THE WEDDING TOOK place at a small church in St. James, an old building built of red stone without many architectural flourishes. More convenient than memorable, but the vicar had been willing to accommodate them on short notice.

Cordelia had informed her parents of the wedding, specifying the date and location while not precisely *inviting* them. Mostly for her mother's sake. Mrs. Kelly had thought it her duty to find Cordelia a husband, and she'd done her best. She'd earned this moment of triumph, or tried to anyhow, and Cordelia wanted her to have it.

She'd received a note, two days before the wedding, notifying her of their arrival in London. They'd taken rooms at a hotel. Her father would be out visiting with colleagues, but would she agree to have dinner with her mother?

Yes, Cordelia had replied. Of course.

Her mother greeted her with an effusive hug that communicated, in a few short seconds, more affection than she'd displayed during the entirety of the last year they'd lived together. She had no interest in Cordelia's work, her causes, or her friends, but she wanted to know everything about her acquaintance with Stroud. Even when the details horrified her—she hid her face in her hands when Cordelia described meeting him alone at Kew, a public park —she soaked them up.

When Cordelia mentioned that she planned to wear a simple day dress to the wedding, her mother sprang into action. She'd packed all of Cordelia's belongings into trunks and brought them to London as a makeshift trousseau. She was able to locate one of the silk gowns that Cordelia would have worn, in the old days, to a holiday dinner or assembly.

"Let's make sure it fits," her mother suggested.

"I'll see a seamstress about it tomorrow," Cordelia promised, in order to avoid lingering so long that her father returned.

She couldn't avoid him at the wedding itself. He stopped her on the way through the church's porch, looking exactly as he always had: tall and elegant, forehead prominent in his long face, the pale hair and wintry eyes she'd inherited only slightly faded with age.

"I met your husband-to-be," he began, blunt.

"Oh?"

"He's an imbecile."

"I think he's brilliant." Cordelia kept her tone calm. He'd dismiss anything that sounded emotional, and a very small amount of emotion could qualify.

"He is an *imbecile*." Though the porch was small and private, he closed the distance between them and lowered his voice to a furious hiss. The rule about emotion did not apply to him. "We should never have taken you at your word, all those times you claimed to want a spouse who'd be *worthy*."

"Papa. Why are you here?"

Her father straightened. Mastered himself, or appeared to. "I wanted to take his measure."

"Why? What does it matter to you?"

"We're about to become family," her father answered.

"Family?" Cordelia laughed without humor. "No, you're not."

The air seemed to chill around her. Cordelia would have rubbed the gooseflesh off her arms if she could have managed it without denting her pride.

"Is this, then, your judgment on me?" he asked, in the voice he used on the bench: rich and resonant enough to almost mask the cutting harshness beneath. "A lifetime of care can't tip the scales weighed down by a single offense?"

"Are you sorry?"

He snorted. "No."

"I didn't think you would be. I didn't even hope for it." Cordelia shook her head, grieved by the truth of her own words. For most of her life, her father's approval had meant everything to her. She'd craved every glimpse she had of him in public, admired and respected by his peers. "I used to want so much to be like you. It was my greatest aspiration. And now it is much closer to being my greatest fear."

"I taught you everything you know," he said, with the tight control of a man who had been deeply, deeply offended.

"You did," Cordelia admitted. It was true. "Thank you. I'm grateful."

She continued into the chapel, looking for the vicar. She found Stroud instead, leaning against the wall, his amber eyes twinkling.

"Were you eavesdropping?" she demanded.

He nodded cheerfully.

"And?"

Stroud shrugged. "I'm the last person to insist on respect for one's father. Besides, I don't think he likes me very much."

"He is a brilliant man but, I have discovered, it is not enough to be brilliant."

Stroud touched her shawl. "It's strange to see you in fine clothes. You wore austere gray so well I had a hard time picturing you in anything else."

"I could change if you want."

"Coco, don't be silly. What if I said yes?"

"Then you'd tell the vicar to wait while I went home to change my clothes."

"You mean that," he said wonderingly.

"Why not? If that's how you've come to know me, it would be fitting."

"But this is the start of something new, isn't it?" Stroud smiled. "And a glimpse into your past—a side of you I'll only discover like this, from odd angles."

Cordelia blinked, oddly moved.

The vicar gestured, and in short order their small company assembled: Flea and Chilly on one side of the aisle, Cordelia's parents standing awkwardly apart from Tess, Ruby, and Olympia on the other. Bonny had written with her good wishes and to apologize for remaining at home, as she felt it would be unwise to travel at her stage of pregnancy.

Cordelia had never had much use for ceremonies, but she'd always wondered if her wedding would be different. In this specific case, a few words would change her name, her address, her finances, her rights, her responsibilities. Her whole future.

Most of the paths she might have taken with her life would meet a dead end when she reached the altar. She would never be an old spinster; she would never marry one of her father's legal protégés or one of the nice young men in New Quay, and for most of her life those had been the most likely options. The roads she'd seen unfurling ahead of her as a child, the futures that occupied her young imagination, would all vanish. Unrealized and unrealizable.

All the possibilities inherent in her existence would converge at this point and then branch out anew. She might rail against the customs and the laws that turned the map of a woman's life into an hourglass, forcing every grain of potential through the bottle-neck of a wedding, but such was the world she'd been born to. She might live long enough to see it change; she'd never escape it.

So she had wondered if the marriage ceremony might be different. If the ritual would move her, if the ring symbolizing her bond would settle against her knuckle and leave her feeling changed. Perhaps, she had thought. Just this once.

But no, she didn't feel changed. She felt like herself with a new piece of jewelry. Quite calm, considering that she'd done some-thing life-altering and, objectively speaking, fairly risky. She'd feared a thunderbolt of regret, a reverberating gong of sorrow, and felt neither. She'd made the right choice. She'd been right to marry Stroud. But the ceremony itself did not particularly move her.

The wedding breakfast took place at Stroud's townhouse. It had fallen to Lady Florence to arrange it, and she'd risen to the occasion without—to Cordelia's intense relief—going overboard. They ate a lavish meal in the house's dining room, an attenuated rectangle with a high ceiling and murals of a wooded glade painted on the wall, chandeliers of glass shaped into exotic flow-ers, a space so beautiful it needed little embellishment.

At the conclusion of the meal an enormous cake was wheeled in on a cart. Though only a single tier the cake was exceedingly tall, four or five layers at a guess, and coated in thick white icing. The twenty-odd guests at the table would struggle to eat a quarter of it.

"I think Rip should do the honors." Lady Florence gestured for the butler to pass the knife, a heavy, dull-edged silver thing polished to a mirror shine.

"What a beautiful cake." Stroud accepted the utensil and then paused, sweeping the room with a suspicious eye. "About the size of a hatbox, now that I think about it. Is that right, Flea? A hatbox?"

"Depends on the hat," replied Lady Florence.

"Maybe it's the hats that are cake-sized," called Mr. Old from his seat. "Have you ever thought about that, Rip?"

"Both are designed in relation to the size of a person's head." Stroud scratched along his jaw. "I think? Cakes *are* head-sized but maybe that's incidental. Maybe they're intended to fit in our stomachs. Or maybe they're not. Maybe they're made for our eyes. In fact—"

Lady Florence interrupted. "If you don't cut the cake, Rip, I'll do it for you."

"I'm cutting, I'm cutting." Stroud finally dug his knife into the icing, which promptly collapsed to reveal a cavity from which several panicked pigeons emerged.

They flapped their wings desperately, eager to escape the lightless container where they'd been trapped but struggling to gain height. One rose a few feet into the air and revealed a new curiosity: a bright ribbon dangled from the pigeon's foot.

Cordelia clapped a hand to her mouth to stop herself from shouting out her guess about what she was about to see and then, failing to resist, cried, "It's a hatbox after all, isn't it?"

"It most certainly is!" crowed Lady Florence.

A flat, wide-brimmed straw hat did finally emerge from the "cake," rising unevenly into the air and speckled with bird droppings, and causing much distress for the pigeons bearing it aloft. The pigeons had no training and no notion of flying in the same direction, let alone in formation.

Cordelia snatched the hat from the air; the pins fastening it to the ribbons fell away easily. The pigeons scattered as she cried out in triumph and planted it atop Stroud's head.

"You may not match the statue of Lord Nelson in height," she announced. "But given your rather extraordinary size, I'd say you're the next best thing."

Stroud fingered the hat—not a wise move—his eyes wide with wonder. Then, a smile breaking across his face, he snatched Cordelia's hand and raised it high. She couldn't help but remember the handshake they'd exchanged that day in Trafalgar

Square, perceiving but unable to articulate the direct line between it and the easy, natural way that Stroud guided her into a spin.

"Did you plan this?" Stroud demanded.

Cordelia shook her head.

"Flea and Chilly then," he concluded. "Go on, you two. Stand up and take a bow."

His sister and best friend, both seated at the same table, did rise. They shook hands and then bowed to the delighted cheering of Stroud's friends. Cordelia's father, for his part, looked like he'd bitten a lemon.

Cordelia had it in her power to pour a bit of sugar on the wound and, perhaps, make lemonade. She did not. He was among the first to leave, though the house emptied out well before dark.

When at last they were alone, Lady Florence having made herself scarce, Stroud suggested a tour.

"So you can get to know your new home," he explained.

"All right."

"All right!" he repeated brightly. "Well… you've seen the dining room now. We don't use it often. Flea doesn't like to host big parties, she says they're not worth it. You can do whatever you want, of course. You remember this salon, right? When you first came over? And my office, where we met with the lawyers… The library—*finally* someone will have a use for it—and last but not least we arrive at the bedrooms. This is yours"—Stroud opened the door and waved Cordelia inside—"and mine's next door."

Cordelia took in the half-dozen carpets layered over wood flooring, the huge windows, delicate nightstand, excessive lamps, overlarge vanity… the four-poster bed.

"Coco," Stroud's hand landed on her shoulder, so big and so *heavy*.

Cordelia steeled herself. Who knew? Maybe Olympia had been telling the truth. "Yes?"

He cupped her cheek. Gentle, gentle, gentle and yet each brush of his thumb along her lower lip made her tremble. She didn't know what to do, and she hated feeling boxed in, with only one direction to go and no way to see what was coming, alternately assured that she'd be miserable or thrilled by what awaited, no proper means to prepare.

Stroud's expression sharpened. "I think..." He hesitated over the words, feeling out the decision as he made it. "I think we'll take this slowly."

"Take what slowly?"

"Lovemaking." He shifted his grip and massaged her nape. "Not tonight, maybe not for a while. There's no rush."

Cordelia narrowed her eyes. "I'm not *afraid*—"

"I didn't say you were," Stroud interrupted.

"I've no wish to deprive you of the primary benefit of marriage." She'd made a vow. She intended to keep it.

"I don't suspect you of it," Stroud assured her.

"Well, then..." Cordelia had no idea how to finish that sentence. "Well."

"How about this: you can tell me when the mood strikes you." The words flowed smoothly now. Easy, confident, a little... a little something more. Dark. He leaned his shoulder against the door jamb, still massaging her neck. Cordelia was suddenly, intensely jealous of all the women she knew who'd married idiots. "Doesn't matter when. Any hour of the day. I'll be thrilled."

Because she wanted to remind herself of how nice it had been —and because she wanted to be brave—she tipped her chin up for a kiss. Surprise shattered Stroud's suave expression, but he dipped down obligingly and it was wonderful. Just the slow movement of his lips over hers, like he had all the time in the world. It came so naturally and felt so good and for some reason her legs didn't want to hold her up anymore.

Stroud laughed and slung a supportive arm around her waist.

"I must have spent more time on my feet today than I'd realized," Cordelia said nonsensically.

Stroud bit his lip. "That must be it." He eased her through the door. "Why don't I show you my room?"

Stroud's room was spacious, bright, and sized for a giant. His bed could have slept a family of ten if they huddled close enough, the mirror on the wall belonged in Versailles, her feet would surely dangle off the ground if she tried to sit in the well-stuffed chair by the fireplace, and yet she instantly felt at ease. A gorgeous knit blanket draped across the foot of the bed, a box full of individually wrapped sweets sat on a table by the chair, Stroud's puppy snoozed on a pillow by the hearth.

The room looked more like *Stroud* than any of the others she'd seen on the tour: comfortable and friendly and sweetly self-indulgent.

Cordelia couldn't hide her surprise. "It's wonderful."

"You like it?"

"I do." And then, because she knew it would please him, "I can see you in it."

A hint of pink stained his cheeks. "You should sleep here."

Cordelia blinked. Hadn't they just had a whole conversation about…?

"Just sleep," Stroud clarified. "Step one of my plan to take it slow."

Stroud and she apparently had different definitions of the word slow, but she wouldn't quibble over trifles. "Very well."

"Then I'll leave you to get settled. We've been getting deliveries all day, you must be anxious to see to your things. Though a word about Flea?"

"What about her?"

"Flea's run the house since my mother left. I talked to her yesterday." Stroud made a face. "*She* spoke to *me*, actually. She knew I wouldn't think of it myself. She expects you'll want to take over, and she's happy to assist or leave you to figure things out on your own, whichever you prefer."

"Very considerate of her," said Cordelia neutrally.

"She isn't the sort of person to make things difficult," Stroud returned, perceptive as ever. "But even if she were… This is her home, until she decides it's not anymore."

"Is that a promise you made her?" Cordelia asked.

Stroud nodded.

"And if I object?"

Stroud looked confused. "Why would you object?"

"Imagine I have a very good reason. Would it matter?"

"But you don't."

"Imagine that I do."

Stroud ventured, with an adorable squint-smile, "My imagination doesn't stretch that far."

"So I have a very bad reason to object. Now what?"

"You're never satisfied with bad reasons."

Cordelia laughed, delighted. "Of course she should stay as long as she wishes. I'm not trying to weaken your resolve. Only to measure it, and only because I remember what it was like to find out my own family's commitment to me did not meet my expectations."

Stroud grinned. "Satisfactory?"

"Only time will tell," Cordelia replied, unable to jest. "I'll have a chat with her and see to my things. Thank you for the tour."

"My pleasure," Stroud answered.

For some reason, this made Cordelia blush. She hurried her exit in order to mask it, and while the conversation remained fresh in her mind, she sought out Lady Florence. Stroud's sister had, she discovered, changed into a loose dressing gown and retreated to the sunroom with a book.

Lady Florence set the book down with a warm smile at Cordelia's arrival. "There you are…"

"Cordelia," Cordelia supplied. "Now we're family."

Lady Florence grinned. "Not Coco?"

"Oh, please don't," Cordelia said fervently. "It's almost tolerable from Stroud, but if the name caught on I'd…"

"Get revenge?" Lady Florence prompted.

"Put a stop to it *somehow*."

"Well, you should call me Flea." Lady Florence patted the spot beside her on the bench. "And sit, please. You don't need an invitation."

Cordelia sat. "Florence, perhaps?"

"I prefer Flea to Florence, believe it or not."

Cordelia hesitated. She wanted to be polite but something inside of her revolted against a request to refer to her charming new sister-in-law as a blood-sucking pest.

"I'll tolerate Florence *temporarily*. While you work your way up to Flea. Don't take too long at it, though. I've never liked the name Florence." Lady Florence grinned jauntily, confident and animated. "I take it you're eager to take charge?"

"Oh, no. That can wait until tomorrow. Preparing for the wedding exhausted me; I can only imagine what a state the staff must be in. Actually, I wanted to let you know I appreciate your position. You have a great deal of independence, and if I were you, I'd be reluctant to give it up. I'd be wary of anyone who might threaten my freedom. In other words—I'd be wary of *me*."

"I do believe you're putting words in my mouth, Cordelia."

"Then it's good you've cut me short," Cordelia returned calmly. "Why don't you tell me your concerns?"

Florence blinked, disconcerted.

Cordelia waited.

"I, um, I don't…" Florence flounced. "You started this conversation!"

"I want you to know your place here is secure," said Cordelia. "Every woman who has obtained—by whatever means, through birth or tragedy or both—a measure of independence and who values it enough to maintain it, and fight for it, is making the world a better place. I believe—"

Florence interrupted. "Is this your way of telling me I'm welcome to remain at home?"

"Remain a spinster for the whole of your life, if that is your wish. I will not complain. On the contrary, I will support you to the best of my ability."

"I'm not sure about the whole of my life but I do appreciate the sentiment. I'd rather be a drop in the bucket of my sister-in-law's crusade than a nuisance, and nuisance did always seem like the most likely possibility."

"I promise not to view you as a nuisance."

"Don't make any promises yet." Florence winked. "I am my brother's sister, after all."

"I *married* your brother," Cordelia pointed out.

"And you seemed like you had such fine judgment until then!" Florence laughed. "I'm joking. I'm glad Rip gave up waiting for a wife who'd overlook his flaws in favor of one smart enough to appreciate his strengths."

Cordelia gave Florence a hug, spontaneous but heartfelt. The young woman returned the gesture with full strength.

"Am I right that it's your father who convinced him he was lacking?"

Florence half-smiled. "Figured it out, did you?"

"It seemed a safe guess."

"If Rip had been born brainy, Papa would have told him he'd wanted a brawny son who played sport. If he'd been witty and fashionable, Papa would have harangued him about applying himself to his studies. He was that sort of man."

"And you?" Cordelia wondered. "Where did you fall short?"

"Where didn't I?" Florence sighed. "Luckily, as a girl, I was mostly beneath his notice. If my clothes were clean, I passed muster. If I spoke out of turn—if I spoke at all—he sacrificed a moment of his precious time to rebuke me. Awful as it was, I realized early on that I was the lucky one."

"My father badly wanted a son," Cordelia confessed. "Once, when I was much younger, I overheard him telling a friend that God could not be infallible, as the vicars claim, because He had clearly made a mistake by wasting such a good mind on me. In the world we live in... it helped me to see that he wasn't entirely wrong. So I set about changing the world. If I hadn't believed that he loved me as I am—as I did, once, but don't anymore—I'm sure I'd have taken a different path."

"You'd have turned to pranks in your despair?" Florence asked archly.

"Perhaps." Cordelia shrugged. "Perhaps something much worse."

IT TOOK MOST of the afternoon to unpack the trunks her mother had brought, reacquainting herself with possessions she'd never expected to see again. All the books she'd bound by hand and left behind, the high-quality binding tools she'd had to replace with cheaper wares and missed bitterly every day, all the jewelry—gifts and hand-me-downs—that she'd left behind, amber beads and pearl rings and a pair of little emerald earbobs set with pale gems the size of sesame seeds. She'd forgotten so much that it was like visiting a shop stocked entirely with things she liked.

Her mother had quietly slipped in a number of gifts, according to her bizarre taste: a gasogene for carbonating water, a hideous lace collar, a set of *pickle forks*... things Cordelia had no use for, which her expanded budget could certainly have afforded should she have wanted them, but which her magpie mother must have found very exciting.

Affection welled up in Cordelia's heart. Her mother could be silly and vain, and they'd never gotten along... but she had been true to her principles, misguided as they were, and loved Cordelia as best as she knew how. They hadn't had much of a relationship to ruin, and perhaps that was why Cordelia found it easier to renew.

She had been so close with her father. She had loved him so much, wished so profoundly to be *like* him. Yet seeing him had brought far more pain than pleasure. She recognized his presence at her wedding as an olive branch, however poorly expressed—he would not have made the journey to London if he didn't care, he loathed the city—but she had no desire to take it.

Relationships had their own logic, but it could be difficult to parse. She wondered if she ought to feel differently about her parents, but did not have the will to try. Now that she'd married, the painful spurs that might have compelled her had been ceremoniously removed.

Supper was light and brief, since everyone present had eaten their fill at the wedding breakfast. Lady Florence's maid helped Cordelia out of her gown and into her night things; she was efficient and skilled enough that Cordelia wondered if Florence would mind sharing. Cordelia had never had a lady's maid to herself and felt no urgent need for one. Perhaps she could find someone like Stroud's Fisk, who seemed to tackle any tasks that needed doing?

No doubt as she grew into her new role she'd acquire a whole staff. She didn't yet understand why she'd *need* a staff, but neither did it seem likely that she'd evolve into the only duchess in existence who managed just fine on her own.

She was still turning the question over in her head when she stepped into the doorway that connected her bedroom to Stroud's. He wore only a pair of thin drawstring pants—in the middle of the room! As though it were nothing!

His broad shoulders were bare—his chest—each of his thighs was thicker than her waist. *His* waist almost looked narrow by comparison, taut and gracefully elongated. Clothes could be such deceivers. Even men's clothes, tailored to skim the lines of the body, told terrible lies.

Clothes smoothed a body into straight lines when the reality was almost incomprehensibly different. Muscle curved from Stroud's neck to his collarbone and formed a crisp edge where the deltoid bunched. Muscle swelled across his chest—women would weep for a bosom as glorious as his swelling pectorals—and rounded his rear end.

"Oh, hullo," said Stroud, wielding a wick trimmer as he

fiddled with an oil lamp. "Don't mean to shock you, Coco, but I run a bit hot so I usually don't wear much to bed. Apparently—" He looked up and a slow smile spread across his face. "Look all you want. I don't mind."

Cordelia was speechless.

Stroud padded across the room, bringing all that bare flesh so much closer. Acres and acres of bare flesh. There was so much of him!

"Breathe," Stroud murmured.

"I'm breathing," Cordelia retorted, but it turned out she hadn't been. Not properly, anyhow, because she gasped like a hooked fish at the reminder.

Stroud started to laugh. He circled behind her and planted both palms at her hips. He pushed, and she advanced slowly to the bed.

"Climb in," he murmured, lips brushing soft at her ear. "And I'll join you."

Cordelia licked her lips. She wanted to say something witty— failing that, something scathing—but heat spread from Stroud's hands through the thin fabric of her nightgown to her own skin, sending shivers up to her lips and down to her toes.

She pulled back the sheets but before she could heave herself onto the mattress Stroud's grip tightened and he gave her a tiny lift. She stifled a cry of surprise—only just—and watched with wide eyes as he retreated to the freshly lit lamp and blew it out.

Had he lit it just to impress her? If so, the trick had worked. The afterimage of Stroud's sculpted silhouette lingered on her eyelids as she tracked his movements by the creaks of the floorboards, the groan of the mattress. And then... nothing.

"Stroud?" Cordelia asked finally.

"Mmhm?" he mumbled.

"Are you...?"

"Going to sleep," he affirmed.

"Oh."

"I told you," he said, slurring a little. "We'll sleep together. Didn't I tell you?"

"You were very clear."

A faint, pleased hum issued from the other side of the bed.

Cordelia snuggled into the sheets. She thought the bedding thin for spring—a single coverlet, not particularly thick, with a wool blanket on top. She'd used something similar at her flat, not because she found it adequate but because she couldn't afford better. For the last year, she'd bundled up on cold nights in two pairs of stockings and, occasionally, a coat.

She'd counted on Stroud outfitting his magnificent Mayfair home a bit better. But it was late in the day to make a fuss, so Cordelia huddled into a ball, shut her eyes, and tried to feel tired. Surely exhaustion would overtake her eventually, but she was *cold*, and there was a *man in the room*. Very nearby. Breathing audibly.

"Stop shivering," said Stroud, and an arm snaked out of the dark to hook around her middle and drag her across the neutral territory at the center of the bed, into the shelter of his body. "Now stay."

Cordelia stiffened, wondering what came next, but Stroud subsided. His breaths evened out. And he was so *warm*. Cordelia's muscles loosened of their own accord. She inched closer, soaking in more of her new husband's heat. Her toes unfroze; her legs uncurled from their tight, protective ball.

The last time she'd been this comfortable in bed had been months ago, early autumn before the weather turned bitter. Sleep closed in, but she fought it, savoring the delicious sensation of being cozy on a cold night. It would have taken mountains of coal —not to mention an attentive servant, sacrificing sleep to keep the stove burning hot through the night—to make her half as comfortable.

This, she thought as her consciousness began to drift, was luxury.

CHAPTER 19

The next morning, while drifting inexorably from sleep to wakefulness, Cordelia caught herself. Caught herself like a fisherman with a live one on the hook, only she was both the fisherman holding the line and the captured fish as well, working the reel and trying to thrash free.

She wanted to understand this moment. This *feeling*. Waking up in a man's arms. She'd never experienced anything like it.

She tended to freeze up when touched, to fret self-consciously about where to rest her arms in a friendly embrace and hold her breath for the duration. The closer she came to full consciousness, the more alien she found her current position, pressed up close to Stroud's hot skin, limbs tangled with his.

But so long as she held herself suspended between dream and reality, she remained completely at ease. Relaxed and comfortable, as though she were right where she belonged.

The arm Stroud had draped over her tensed slightly, the fingers of a previously limp hand toying at the sensitive skin along her ribs, teasing at the side of her breast. His lips brushed featherlight along her hairline.

It woke her, and she was sorry for it, but she reminded herself to be brave and turned into his embrace. He peppered kisses over her cheek, trailed his fingers down her side, pausing at her hip to ruck up the skirts of her nightrail. Their legs twined, and hesitant all the while, she reached out to touch the shoulders she'd so admired, hard muscle under hot skin, slightly damp.

It was such a wonder to see his body up close, *feel* it up close, smell musk overpowering the last traces of soap. His nipples didn't look like her nipples, his breaths didn't sound like her breaths. Everything about him was new and different.

She wanted to explore, to discover every detail. She wanted to know everything about him, actually. She wanted—

"Breakfast?" murmured Stroud. "I can hear the tray coming."

It took a moment to focus on the question. By then she, too, could hear the telltale clinking of utensils and crockery balanced on a tray.

Her voice came out raspy with sleep. "In bed?"

Stroud looked down at her, sweet and golden as honey toast. "Mmhm."

"What a ridiculous indulgence."

"Isn't it?" He tucked the sheets around her chest and heaved himself into a seated position as the door opened. "One of my favorites."

"We'll attract vermin." Cordelia propped herself up on her elbows. "Neither of us is ill."

"Are you casting aspersions on our cleaning staff?" Stroud asked. "Should I fear for the future of our poor housekeeper? She's a lovely woman, Coco, she deserves a chance—"

Cordelia groaned. "Don't be ridiculous."

"I'm always ridiculous." Stroud dropped a kiss on her nose. "By now, you should know better than to ask me to stop."

The food arrived as Cordelia ceded the point. In short order, she found herself reclining against a mountain of pillows, legs curled beside a massive silver tray crowded with a chocolate pot, a tea pot, several covered silver salvers, and a small crystal vase holding a single, perfect red rose.

Stroud paused with one hand hovering above the nearest salver. "Shall we lay wagers about what's underneath?"

"Perhaps some other time. I'm too hungry for it right now."

"If I do my job right, in future you'll be *hungrier*."

Cordelia blinked. "I will? Why is that?"

Stroud raised the lid. "Oh, bacon! Can I serve you?"

"Please do." Cordelia accepted a plate heaped with bacon strips and tiny red pepper soufflés and peeled orange segments soaked in orange flower water, mouth-watering and sweet.

"What are your plans for the day?"

As Cordelia began to answer, Stroud finished pouring tea into their cups. After a measuring look at the crowded tray, he leaned over to set the still mostly full pot on a marble-topped table just within reach of the bed. His whole body flexed with the motion: sides tense to stabilize him through the lean, biceps bulging as he held the pot aloft.

Her mouth went dry.

"Coco?" Stroud prompted, suddenly very cheerful. "Your plans?"

"Oh." Cordelia looked down at her plate and took her time spearing a bit of egg and bacon onto her fork, trying to compose herself. "I'll write to Tess this morning. I want to see her before Olympia's wedding."

"That's nice," he said. "Anything else?"

"I'll talk to Flea about taking charge of the household." Cordelia hummed. "There are so many possibilities, now that I won't be working. Perhaps I'll invite Miss Smith for tea. What about you?"

"Accounts, quarterly reports, family stipends…" Stroud grimaced. "All the boring things."

"Would you like help?"

He tucked a stray lock of hair behind her ear. "Don't you have more important things to do?"

She narrowed her eyes. Was he trying to put her down gently?

Had she discovered, too late, a hidden seam of disregard in her husband's character?

"Coco, if you want control of the books you can have it," Stroud said, suddenly wry. "If you want to help me, if you want to take over entirely—just say the word. I'll be delighted."

"Perhaps I do."

"All right."

"All right."

They stared at one another—Cordelia refused to back down or apologize, her fears were rational in *general*, even if not in particular—until Stroud picked an orange segment off her plate and held it out for her to take from his fingers. "Eat your breakfast, Coco."

She snapped the segment from his fingers with her teeth and, as she chewed, wondered at the flush creeping up her husband's neck.

PLEASANT WEATHER PERSUADED Cordelia to write to Tess about meeting for a walk. After sending a flurry of notes back and forth, they settled on Hyde Park in the early afternoon, just after lunch.

Tess arrived in a gown of deep aubergine that brought out the warmth in her dark skin, a heavy gray shawl snug around her slim shoulders. A bit of an optimistic choice, in Cordelia's opinion. Though evidence of spring was everywhere, bright blooms barely contained by their neatly maintained beds and a pair of swans paddling about the Serpentine, she wore a heavy coat against the bitter cold.

"You're looking lovely," Cordelia greeted her friend, exchanging a quick kiss on the cheek.

"And you!" Tess returned. "Is that coat new?"

"Old." Cordelia laughed. "My mother brought some of my things from home. I'll do a bit of shopping soon—it's been so long

I'm actually craving it—but until then my old things are an improvement."

They chatted idly for a while, Tess filling Cordelia in on society gossip and listening to Cordelia worry about the petition in exchange. Eventually the topic moved, inevitably, to Olympia.

"You know she wouldn't even speak to me at your wedding?"

"No!" Cordelia gasped. "I don't believe it."

"Not a word. I've collected all the things I used to store at her house and Ruby's keeping them now, in your old room."

"You've been the best of friends for how long? She owes so much to you—to your cleverness and your discretion and—"

"She'll hate me more once she realizes I was right all along," Tess interrupted, grim with certainty.

"I wish I didn't believe that." Cordelia sighed. "Could I offer you the use of my new home? It's open to you at any time, whether I'm present or not."

"The offer means a great deal to me. But, Cordelia, I'd appreciate it more if you'd tried harder to avert this catastrophe. You're so passionate about the pitfalls of marriage. I would have thought you'd want to save Olympia from the disaster she's running headlong toward."

"As a friend, that's exactly what I want," Cordelia agreed. "As a matter of principle, I think we must give women more freedom to chart their own course—telling women that we can only make our own decisions so long as we make the right ones isn't giving us any freedom to choose at all. We must be allowed to make mistakes."

"A mistake she'll spend the rest of her life paying for. You know she will."

"I do. I am afraid she will be very badly hurt. But if principle requires that I stand by while she makes a mistake then love requires that I stay close—and offer what help I can—as she learns to regret it."

"I'm not sure I like your version of friendship," Tess said sharply. "Imagine being in her place—what would you prefer? A friend who *stands by* while you fall or a friend who holds you back from ruination with all her strength?"

"I have *been* in her place. Any sensible friend would have stopped me from leaving home. By most people's reckoning, I could not have chosen a more foolish course or embarked upon it with less justification. Bonny sheltered me and gave me money. You and Olympia both helped me to settle here in London."

"Because we know you! You, Cordelia, are eminently capable of making your own decisions, of striving and struggling and overcoming."

"And Olympia isn't?"

Tess took a sharp breath and faced forward, damningly silent.

"Perhaps not." Cordelia laid a tentative hand on Tess's arm. "I know you would be there for her if she would let you. I know that."

Tess's breathing hitched and Cordelia, her heart breaking with sympathy, drew her friend into a tight hug.

Tess hid her face against Cordelia's neck. "I wish she would just *listen*."

"I know."

"She didn't invite me to the wedding."

"I'm so sorry."

"I wouldn't have gone, mind you."

"I wish it hadn't come to this."

"Me too. More than anything."

LATER THAT SAME DAY, Cordelia received her first guest as the new Duchess of Stroud. She found herself badly tempted to ask Florence for instructions about where to receive visitors, what sort of hospitality to offer. Even Stroud would have had good advice. But she had to make this place her own, and what better place to start than with a small, mostly familiar task? Stroud was out with his dog, so she made a circuit of the house alone, trying to really think of it as hers. A place she could alter to her taste, shape around her needs.

She wasn't entirely happy with her options. Which meant she had room to grow.

Miss Smith accepted the invitation to tea and Cordelia received her in the bright salon Florence favored. It was a friendly and welcoming space, but Cordelia remembered how intimidating she'd found it on her first visit, when she'd destroyed Homer the Roamer.

"Your circumstances have certainly changed for the better," noted Miss Smith, taking a seat. "When your husband approached me for a favor, I ought to have guessed which way the wind was blowing. But I only knew him by reputation, and I made the mistake of believing everything I'd heard."

"It *was* a lark," Cordelia assured her. "We'd only just met, and only very briefly. How do you take your tea?"

"Two lumps of sugar, please, and a squeeze of lemon." Miss Smith accepted her cup and breathed in the steam with obvious pleasure. "So you think he's earned his reputation? That surprises me. When I read about your marriage in the papers, I assumed the rumors had it all wrong."

"They do," Cordelia admitted, pouring for herself. The pot and cups had a bright floral pattern her mother would have adored; not to Cordelia's taste at all. Should she change them? Would that be extravagant? "He's cleverer and more far-thinking than hearsay would have it."

"Is he?" Miss Smith's eyebrows arched in surprise. "If so— you'll forgive me for being bold, it's an old habit I have no plans to change—but if so, you ought to ask yourself why he went to so much trouble for a woman he'd just met."

"What do you mean?"

"A clever and far-thinking man pursues a woman with a goal in mind." Miss Smith gestured broadly to the room. "And here you are."

"Oh, no. That's…" Cordelia trailed off. "Entirely possible."

"The thought really hadn't occurred to you?"

"Not at all."

"Then I'm glad to have given you something pleasant to contemplate." Miss Smith sipped her tea. "I don't know about you, but I certainly find myself in need of such reveries."

"But what about the speeches that Lord Lyndhurst has been delivering to the House of Lords? I've been reading summaries in the papers. He's arguing that women should have the right to petition for divorce on equal terms with men."

"Caroline Norton is behind those." Miss Smith's round, ruddy features settled into unfamiliar lines of disappointment. "They are remarkable speeches but, unfortunately, spell out the doom of our petition."

The name Caroline Norton inspired mixed emotions in Cordelia as well. "Mrs. Norton?"

"She's *close* with Lyndhurst."

"But what do Lord Lyndhurst's speeches have to do with the petition?"

"There has been a royal commission dedicated to the nation's divorce laws for some years now. Their primary focus has been judicial reform—and the elimination of the ecclesiastical courts—rather than the rights of women."

Cordelia nodded. "Much needed reform, at least according to my father."

"Much needed," said Miss Smith. "However, Lyndhurst's goal is to incorporate several measures guaranteeing legal and financial independence to separated or divorced women into this bill whilst leaving married women to struggle along as they have been, completely at their husband's mercy."

"Isn't that the history of progress?" Cordelia wondered. "We take one step at a time, first one small advance and then another—"

"Is it?" Miss Smith interrupted grimly. "If someone throws me crumbs I may eat them, but I will not call it a meal."

"I'm surprised to hear you so discouraged."

"Tomorrow—or the day after—I will pick myself up and start anew. But today, I can see that years of dedicated labor will end in a compromise that falls far, far short of a victory." Miss Smith sighed. "I am in mourning, or something like it."

"I see." Cordelia stared into the milky tea. "I have never devoted so much effort to a project where I had no control over the final execution."

"We can educate women until their knowledge equals a university graduate's, but can we make Oxford and Cambridge award them degrees? The nurses Mrs. Nightingale has been so effective at training do so much good, should we really be insisting that some ought to become doctors? Do we settle for the easier solution or exhaust ourselves in pursuit of the harder?" Miss Smith spread her hands. "We all answer this question in our own way. Your circulating library was valuable and effective, and it reached how many people?"

"Thirty, at its height."

"Our petition may lead to changes that affect the lives of millions of women… or it may lead to nothing and affect no one." Miss Smith raised her teacup in an ironic salute. "This is what comes of gambling."

"Yes," said Cordelia. "So I'm discovering."

CHAPTER 20

Cordelia spent the evening in her room, curled up with a roaring fire and a book. No stinting on the coal, no guilt because every moment she indulged in leisure could have been spent getting ahead on work, no debate between sleeping at a decent hour and cutting her reading short. So many of the concerns that had given order to her life, shaping and constraining it, had vanished in an instant.

She was staring into space, thinking about the odd turns life took, when Stroud stepped into the threshold.

"Come to bed," he suggested.

Cordelia shook her head. "I'm reading."

"Bring the book."

"I'd rather read alone," Cordelia protested. "When I read, I want to pay attention to my book. I don't like to be distracted or interrupted."

"Surely a little bit of distraction is all right?"

"You distract me more than a *little*." Cordelia laughed, charmed but not convinced. "I'll stay here, if that's all right."

"If you insist." Stroud paused in the connecting door and turned back round. "Wait. You're not embarrassed, are you?"

Cordelia kept a straight face. "Embarrassed of what?"

"Embarrassed about how reading makes you cry."

"I'm not crying."

"But that's why you only read when you're alone, isn't it? Because I already know, so you've nothing to be afraid of."

"You can take your cleverness somewhere else, thank you," said Cordelia.

"Does that mean I'm right?"

"If you're fishing for compliments, I suggest you change the subject."

"I think that means I'm right." He sounded rather smug about it too. "Coco, I don't care if you cry. It won't make me think any less of you. In fact—"

Cordelia glared as hard as she could.

"Well, another time," he conceded, retreating into his room. Though he left the connecting door open, so she could hear him shuffling about. His valet arrived, and they chatted in voices too low for eavesdropping. Eventually Stroud was alone again, and the creaking of the floorboards heralded a second approach.

He returned in his bedtime ensemble—which was to say, practically nude.

"Don't mind me." Stroud strolled over to her little vanity table. "I wouldn't want to break your concentration."

"Too late," Cordelia said dryly.

"A mind like yours must be marvelous at focusing." Stroud set a box of something that rattled like marbles on the vanity and lifted the top. "I won't bother you, and this way we'll at least be able to enjoy one another's company."

Cordelia sighed audibly and made a show of returning her attention to her book, though she could not stop her eyes from wandering away from the page and toward what seemed like acres of temptingly exposed skin.

Frustratingly, Stroud proved true to his word. He'd brought a small pot of black paint and a brush with him, and while she tried to read, he picked a milky-white marble from the box. He painted a black dot on the marble, blew gently on it, waited a bit, blew again.

"What are you doing?" Cordelia asked.

"Oh, sorry, was I making noise? I can try to be quieter."

"To the marble," Cordelia pressed. "What are you doing to the marble?"

"I'm making it look like an eyeball." He returned the painted marble to his tin and picked up a fresh one. "For a prank."

Cordelia waited for an explanation. It wasn't forthcoming. Lips pursed in concentration, Stroud painted a black dot onto the second marble and waited for it to dry.

"What kind of prank?"

"Nothing to do with you," he assured her, which did not answer the question at all. "Don't worry about it. Go on and read."

"It's hard to concentrate when you're so…" She waved vaguely in his direction.

A slow smile spread across his face. "When I'm so…?"

"Never mind." Cordelia forced herself to stare at her book, which deserved better attention than she was giving it.

"What are you reading?"

"*The Book of the City of Ladies* by Christine de Pizan," Cordelia answered.

"That's, um. Probably about a city full of ladies?"

"Mmhm."

"Sounds like something you'd like."

"It is."

"How was your meeting today?"

She slanted a glance up at her gloriously half-naked husband. "Discouraging."

"Oh? Why?"

"Miss Smith believes that another bill currently making its way through Parliament, one that reforms divorce laws, will likely incorporate a few of the petition's demands and—in the process—guarantee the failure of the rest."

"Really?"

Cordelia nodded. "Of course I'm new to this—and joined Miss Smith's efforts late—but it's a bitter disappointment."

"And what will you do next?" Stroud wondered.

"That's what I'm asking myself." Cordelia paused. "Olympia's wedding is tomorrow, and I'm dreading it."

"You really don't like Mr. Martin, do you?"

"It hardly matters if I like him. A man I dislike intensely might make an excellent husband for someone *else*. Who am I to say what would suit Olympia? But Mr. Martin is a clear mistake."

"You never gave him a chance."

"I gave him a chance."

Stroud picked up another marble and squinted very hard at it. "Maybe one chance isn't enough."

"Why would you—?" Cordelia cut herself short as realization dawned. "I hope you're not defending him because you think the two of you are in any way alike."

"I didn't say that."

Cordelia raised her eyebrows.

"You didn't like *me* when we first met," Stroud admitted.

"And you changed my mind. My opinion of Mr. Martin has worsened over time."

"What do you really know about him?"

"That he's content to base the most intimate relationship in his life—and Olympia's as well—on a series of lies."

Stroud grimaced.

"You showed me exactly who you were," Cordelia continued. "You never changed to pique my interest. For all your confidence, Stroud, you discount your good qualities. You have a great many of them."

Stroud abandoned his marble eyeballs, crossed the room in two quick steps and lifted her into his arms. She squirmed, startled to have her cheek pressed against the muscular expanse of his broad chest.

"Come to bed," he said, plain words at odds with the softness and warmth in his tone. "You can read in my room."

She did read. A bit. First Stroud asked if she wouldn't mind dispensing with her nightclothes. Cordelia reminded herself to be brave—it was easier each time, since Stroud never did anything she disliked—and obliged.

When she was naked, Stroud took a good long look and then said, "Hurry up and get in bed before you get cold," so she climbed between the sheets and, shivering, was delighted when Stroud joined her—removing his thin linen pants only after he'd slipped between the covers—and snugged her close.

Her heart beat faster as she wondered what would come next; what they might do, and what she had left to discover.

"Why don't you read aloud?" Stroud suggested.

"Read?" Cordelia repeated, confused.

"You wanted to read, didn't you?"

"I did," Cordelia acknowledged.

"So read aloud."

She'd left *The Book of the City of Ladies* on the bedside table, not really expecting to pick it up again. She reached for the tome and flipped it open. Stroud pulled her back against him but didn't otherwise interrupt, so she began to read. Aloud.

While she did, Stroud stroked and petted her. It distracted her at first, the way his hand drifted back and forth, cupping her breast one moment and tickling her belly button the next. She craned her neck around at one point, to see if her husband was paying attention, and he seemed peaceful but distracted, expression turned inward. When she fell silent, he coaxed her to resume, and so she did, until her voice had gone hoarse and the feel of his hand on her body was soothing rather than strange.

OLYMPIA HAD MANAGED, by undisclosed means which probably amounted to bribery, to have the ceremony held at St. George's on very short notice. The vicar who officiated administered the vows in a clipped, decidedly irritated tone.

Martin Grant preened from his position before the altar, Olympia glided down the aisle with the grace of a swan, and the wedding breakfast the couple hosted afterwards at Olympia's townhouse—until he spoke his vows, Martin Grant owned no property—was lavish on a scale that seemed absurd, even for Olympia.

"Was all this your idea?" Cordelia gestured for illustration, not at any one thing but the whole: silk ribbons fluttering gaily from every balustrade and finial, a four-foot-tall ice sculpture of a dancing maenad with gold-tipped fingers, lace-decked tables crowned with hothouse roses and wrapped gifts at every place setting. Engraved silver pocket watches for the men, matched pearl earrings for the women.

"Some of it!" Olympia beamed. After leaving the church, she'd set aside her veil and decked herself in a diamond parure that included bracelets, earrings, a necklace, and a delicate tiara. Anyone who looked directly at her risked being blinded. "Martin and I planned it all together. It was so fun! He never says no to me. I tell him one of my ideas and he answers, 'Lovely! Let's do that and, to make it even better, let's add to it.'"

"Ah," said Cordelia.

"You don't approve?" Olympia's chin notched up. She'd always been courageous, constantly but *cleverly* defiant, but it was harder and harder to have a conversation that didn't turn into an argument. "I thought your promises were worth a little more, Cordelia."

Cordelia weighed her next words carefully. She settled on something that felt true, and a good check to her own uncharitable thoughts. "There's no reason you shouldn't indulge yourself at your own wedding breakfast."

Olympia's eyes narrowed dangerously. "You think I don't hear the 'but' at the end of that sentence?"

"I'll tell you another day, perhaps."

"You will tell me *now*," Olympia snapped. "I'm not interested in false friends. Not when they'll abandon you at the first opportunity, for their own pride—"

"Is that what you think happened with Tess?" Cordelia interrupted. "Because I disagree, and if you choose to pursue this point, I will explain why."

Olympia hesitated.

"No?" Cordelia took a deep breath, calming herself. "Very well. I would only have observed—later, because while it's something I've been pondering, it's not appropriate to the moment—that perhaps there is a virtue in matching opposite yet complementary personality types, so that the strengths of one may bolster the weaknesses of another." Cordelia shrugged. "But perhaps I am engaged in an act of self-flattery."

Olympia's expression brightened. "So you're happy with Rip?"

"I think so."

"And what about our discussion the other day?" Olympia leered. "Have you taken it to heart?"

Cordelia shook her head minutely. "Olympia, not here."

"Has Rip disappointed you?" Olympia exclaimed, far less discreetly. "Should I have a word with him? Because—"

"You will do nothing of the sort," Cordelia hissed.

"So then what's the problem?"

"There's no problem!"

"Is it you?"

Cordelia felt her cheeks burn and hated it.

"For someone who gives advice with such conviction, you ought to learn to take a bit of it," Olympia chided. "And, since you're so thin-skinned all of a sudden, that's all I have to say on the subject."

Cordelia let Olympia have the last word—she could consider it an extra wedding present—and retreated to her husband's side.

"What was that about?" Stroud asked.

"Nothing."

"Nothing?" Stroud tipped his head to the side. "You're blushing about 'nothing'?"

"I'm not blushing."

"Your cheeks are very pink."

"Are they? I can't see them, obviously. Do you have a mirror?"

"Very tricky, Coco." Stroud dropped a kiss on her nose. "By the time I could fetch a mirror, you'd have stopped blushing."

A smile tugged at Cordelia's lips. Since when had she come to rely on Stroud, and his teasing, to put her at ease? She gave his arm an affectionate squeeze, silently promising to thank him properly later. "How did you find Fisk?"

"I advertised."

"Yes, but how did you know he was the right candidate for the job?" Cordelia pressed. "How could you look at a stranger and guess he possessed the competence and temperament to match your needs?"

Stroud made a face. "I know you like to imagine I'm brilliant, but I'm fairly sure my thoughts at the time were, 'he seems nice' and 'much smarter than me, at least.'"

Cordelia sighed. "Try to jog your memory. I'd like to find someone who's half as good, and I've no experience."

Stroud hooked an arm around her waist and dragged her close enough to plant a kiss on her temple. "Didn't we just have this conversation? You're an excellent judge of character. You picked me."

Cordelia let Stroud rest his chin atop her head. The weight settled her; she inched a little closer. They'd only been married a few days, but it already felt so natural to lean into his touch. "*You* picked *me*."

"I was trying to pay you a compliment," Stroud complained.

"Pity you didn't succeed, then," Cordelia returned, and found that she felt a bit better about everything.

The crowds thinned. Cordelia stayed until the end because she hadn't been to a great many weddings and—in her heart of hearts—she doubted she'd ever see Olympia quite so happy again.

In the end, her pessimism proved inadequate to the situation. With only a dozen people left, most of them lazily browsing the eternally overflowing trays of bonbons and drinking spring water imported from Switzerland, Olympia responded to some jest Mr. Grant made—Cordelia wasn't within hearing distance—by laughing uproariously and flinging her arms around his shoulders.

He shoved her away, hard, and while Olympia struggled to catch her balance, he strolled away to the next room.

Cordelia hurried to her friend's side, silent because she had no idea what to say. For months, Martin Grant had shown Olympia a false face. Everyone who saw them together could tell. Cordelia had hoped, for her friend's sake, that the truth would not be dire. Now he'd given the first sign that those hopes had been in vain.

But the vows had been sealed. Olympia would have to live with the truth, however grim.

Olympia accepted the steadying hand. "I can handle this, thank you," she murmured icily before straightening her shoulders and stalking after her new husband.

Suddenly Stroud stood at Cordelia's back, the tips of his fingers light on her waist. "Time to go home?"

"What if she needs me?"

"She just got married. She *needs* to be alone with her husband."

Cordelia shook her head. No. That couldn't be right.

"Do you want to set up camp right outside her bedroom?" Stroud waggled his eyebrows. "Press your ear to the door so you'll hear if she calls?"

"Don't be revolting."

"Why not?" Stroud grimaced. "There's nothing for you to do today. Let's go home, Coco."

She wanted to disagree but couldn't. So she bundled into her heavy outdoor gear, fur at her wrists and collar to ward against the deepening winter chill, and took one last look at Olympia's front hall on her way out.

The twin rows of marble statues stood on proper display for

once, no hats or necklaces or coats or scarves to obscure the elegant draping robes of these long-dead Romans. Cordelia had always thought Olympia's habit of dressing them vulgar on multiple levels, gaudy and disrespectful both. But, now that all the frippery had been removed, she hated to see the statues bare.

Hated it.

"Coco," murmured Stroud.

"I'm coming." She scurried through the spring chill to their waiting carriage, where she planted her feet against the hot bricks waiting on the floor and, when Stroud lifted an arm in invitation, snuggled into her husband's side. He provided more heat than the average furnace.

But the comfort of her surroundings nettled. She ought to be able to *do* something with all this good fortune. What had she accomplished thus far? She'd abandoned Olympia, disappointed Tess, stood by while the petition floundered.

Stroud knocked his knuckles on her forehead, and she startled.

"You haven't heard a single word I've just said, have you?"

"Not a one," she admitted.

"Hmm," he murmured.

"Tell me again? I'm listening now."

"Wasn't very interesting," he answered, which made her feel worse.

The carriage slowed to a halt. Stroud helped her down, escorted her inside, and paused on the landing of the stairs, head cocked as though he were about to say something. But he shook his head and left her to her own devices.

Full of nervous energy, she changed into more comfortable clothing and descended to his office, where she began sorting through his accounts. Someone—probably Fisk—kept everything in good order, so it didn't take long for her to find an anomaly. At the Copplestone estate, some four hundred acres of good land in Dorset, expenses were up, profits were down, and letters from the farm manager had a strange, ruffled tone.

It felt good to tackle the problem, taking notes, hunting down patterns within the figures. A clear picture had begun to emerge by the time Stroud wandered in, sleepy-eyed in a dressing gown with his sandy hair falling into his eyes.

"What are you doing *here*?" he wondered.

Cordelia straightened the ledgers, preparing to explain. "I found something strange at the Copplestone estate—"

"Oh, that." Stroud rounded the desk and leaned over her shoulder, sneaking an arm underneath hers and across her chest. "I've been ignoring it for years."

"I think I've figured out what's the matter—" She left off with a breathless little cough as Stroud's arm tightened, and he lifted her right out of the chair, catching her behind the knees to hold her aloft.

"Tell me tomorrow," he said.

"I wasn't done!" Cordelia exclaimed.

"I disagree," Stroud jogged her in his arms before heading toward the door. "I think you're done."

"Where are we going?" Cordelia waggled her legs. "Is it time for supper? I'm not hungry."

"Supper…" Stroud peppered kisses across her hairline "…was hours ago."

"What?"

"It's ten o'clock."

"No, it isn't."

"Here, we're about to pass by a clock." Stroud swiveled so she could read the face, which did indeed indicate that ten of the clock had come and gone. "See? Ten o'clock. I knew you were troubled and thought I ought to let you be. You should have told me you were looking for a distraction."

"Not a distraction," Cordelia countered. "I needed to make myself useful."

"In my office?" Stroud wondered, clearly baffled. He carried her up the stairs and down the short corridor to his bedroom, shouldering the open door wide enough to step through.

"You said I could."

"Of course you *can*." Stroud dropped her on the bed and stripped off his dressing gown, revealing his usual evening ensemble of bare chest and tissue-thin trousers. "I just don't know why you'd *want* to."

"If you'll let me explain about the Copplestone estate—" Cordelia began.

"Don't you dare." Stroud crawled across the bed to hover over her, arms braced to either side of her head. "I have better things to do."

"Better?" she scoffed, mostly to have the pleasure of Stroud silencing her with a kiss.

He responded predictably. She liked kissing so much. Her lips were exquisitely sensitive. With her fingertips, she could trace the ridges and hollows of Stroud's face. With a brush of her lips, she could discern so much more. She could, with eyes closed, tell the delicate texture of his cheek from the thicker, oilier skin of his brow. The knowledge was a pleasure. The pleasure was knowledge. She could smell him, candy on his breath and spiced cologne at his neck and musk at his armpits, and if she wanted *more* than smell, she had only to taste.

He clasped her wrists and brought her palms to his stomach, where his skin was smooth and hot. A thatch of coarse hair on his chest narrowed to a trail that disappeared beneath his linen drawstring pants. She pressed with her thumbs to feel muscle flex under skin as he untied the bow that held his thin trousers up.

He was very nearly as big as a horse, which surprised her even though she'd watched him strut about in nearly nothing for a week. He covered her hand with his own and guided it up and down his shaft in a pumping motion. "Squeeze as hard as you can," he advised. "Faster is more intense. Slower will draw it out."

She couldn't squeeze very hard at all from her current position and, without thinking much about it, pushed Stroud onto his back so she could climb him. He laughed but didn't protest, and it was oddly intoxicating to be perched atop a giant of a man, to feel him beneath her and at her mercy.

And yet when he threw his head back and whined high in his throat, reality seemed upside down. The rules she lived by flipped, common sense fled. And Cordelia, who could be contrary and defiant and cruel but always *tried* not to take any pleasure in it, let her grip go slack.

"Coco, don't stop, don't you dare—" Stroud bucked into her limp hand. "Just a little more, I'm so close—"

"Like this?" Cordelia tightened her hold a bare fraction.

"More," Stroud urged.

"But you said a *little*."

Stroud raised his head, panting and flushed a vivid pink. "You're *enjoying* this."

She bit back a smile. Poorly.

He let his head fall back to the mattress with a groan. "I thought you might but—"

"But?" Cordelia prompted, closing her fist around him as tightly as she could.

Stroud's eyes fluttered shut, and he fisted the bedsheets. "Nothing, that's amazing, you're perfect and can do no wrong, just keep doing that, exactly that—"

A shiver ran through her, settling hot between her legs. He hooked an arm around her waist, startling a yelp out of her as he pulled her down to lie flush against him.

"Sorry," he murmured against her cheek. The fingers of his other hand speared through her hair, holding her still so he could press his lips, wet and silky, hard against hers. "I should let you— Ah, don't stop, don't stop—"

Cordelia flexed her hand, which had begun to cramp, and Stroud whined so piteously that a sympathetic ache throbbed through her in turn. His kisses now were open-mouthed and lazy, synchronized with the movement of his hips. They melted her like honey, softened her excitement into something heavy and new.

Stroud buried his face in her shoulder, squeezing her impossibly closer as he pulsed in her hand. When he sucked in a deep, uneven breath and pulled away, looking at her with eyes gone soft as a fawn's, she blurted, "I've never felt like this before."

"Felt how?" He turned her, tucking her back against his front. She squirmed as he slid his hand up her legs, underneath her nightgown, but he only kissed the top of her head. "Felt how? Tell me."

A jumble of words came to mind: hot, cold, heavy, weightless, excited, *strange*. None of them really fit.

"Good or bad?"

"Good," she answered.

"Good," he repeated as he cupped between her legs. "Ah, Coco, I've been dreaming of this. Except that I always imagined you under me, and it never quite seemed real—I should have known you belonged on top."

While he spoke, he teased his fingers into the slick heart of her. She stretched her restless limbs, rolled her back deeper into the sheltering warmth of Stroud's chest, deeply satisfied by the press of his skin against her own.

"Let it happen—ah, what am I saying, you're not fighting it at all, are you? That's my Coco, you never hold back. You're never afraid. All right, I think— There, that's it, look how beautiful you are—"

Pleasure clapped like a thunderbolt, a sudden strike and an endless, rolling aftermath. It left her shaken, disoriented, changed in ways she wanted to examine. She didn't have even a fraction of the necessary mental capacity for it, though.

"It's just the beginning," Stroud promised. "There's so much more. You liked it, didn't you? I want you to. I want you to—"

Cordelia used up a great deal of her remaining strength by reaching up to plant her fingers across Stroud's lips.

He sucked one into his mouth and nibbled at the joint. She wriggled tiredly away, and he soothed her, nestled against his side.

CHAPTER 21

Cordelia felt she ought to say something the next morning— "Quite an interesting night we had," perhaps—but every time she tried, Stroud cut in with some new and unrelated topic. Apparently, he'd rather discuss the weather, the future of her petition, and even the Copplestone estate.

"What did you learn?"

"One of your relatives is living on the estate, is that right? A Mr. Nathaniel Chandos?"

"Washies," said her husband nonsensically.

"I beg your pardon?"

"Washies," Stroud repeated, his slow and careful pronunciation not helping matters at all. "Everyone calls him Washies."

"Washies," Cordelia repeated.

"He's got very skinny legs."

This did not clarify matters. "Mr. Nathaniel Chandos has—"

Stroud interrupted. "*Nobody* uses his name. Call him Washies."

"—converted a substantial portion of the estate's farmland to a vineyard."

Stroud paused with a bite of toast halfway to his mouth. "Really?"

"Apparently you told him, at some previous encounter, that he needed a hobby?"

Stroud nodded. "I did. And *he* did."

"He interpreted that instruction to mean you'd agreed to finance the acquisition of said hobby—hobbies, I suppose, since he adopted viticulture *and* oenology."

"Typical," muttered Stroud.

"The Copplestone estate has lost a great deal of money converting fields of barley and potatoes to grapes," Cordelia continued. "And profited not at all."

"It takes years to make wine," protested Stroud. "Maybe Washies deserves a chance."

"Dorset is not exactly known for its wines," Cordelia demurred. "Does Mr. Chandos—"

"Washies."

"Does Mr. Chandos have any experience at making wine?"

"He drinks a lot of it."

"You'd save a great deal of money by just giving him an entire bottle of Chateau d'Yquem every night with dinner."

"Oh, he drinks a lot more than that. Besides, then he'd need a new hobby."

"Has he tried painting?" Cordelia wondered. "Or collecting minerals?"

"How'd you figure this out, anyhow?"

"I read the accounts."

"So did I." Stroud paused. "More or less." Another pause. "Anyway, no one mentioned wine anywhere."

"The quarterly reports enumerate all expenses," Cordelia explained. "Including which varieties of seed the farm manager has purchased, and in what quantity."

"Oh, you read the charts." Stroud groaned. "I ignore the charts."

"I suspect that Mr. Chandos—"

"Washies."

"I'm not calling a grown man whom I've never met 'Washies,'" Cordelia insisted.

"It's fun, though." Stroud leaned close and whispered in her ear, "Washies."

Cordelia leaned away, but he mirrored her and whispered, "Washies," again, before tipping his chin down to nibble at her throat.

She tried to shove him back. "You'll upend the breakfast tray!"

"Oh, no." Stroud trailed kisses up to her ear. "Not the breakfast tray."

Cordelia squeaked.

"Say Washies," Stroud coaxed, tugging on her earlobe with his teeth. "Waaaaassshhh—"

Cordelia snarled her fingers in Stroud's hair, twisted them tight, and when he yelped, she rose up on her knees to steer him back to his place. This left her looming over him, feeling oddly pleased with herself, while Stroud panted and grinned like a maniac.

"Coco," Stroud crooned.

"No," said Cordelia.

Stroud laughed. "You don't know what I was going to ask."

"No to everything."

"A kiss," Stroud proposed.

"No."

"One kiss," he coaxed.

Cordelia closed the distance between them, until the tip of her nose brushed his. "And then what?"

Stroud swallowed audibly.

Cordelia pursed her lips in preparation for her next, "No," but before she could breathe the syllable into existence, Stroud's arm snaked around her waist, and he tugged. She flailed, her startled kick lifted the coverlet and, by unlucky chance, collapsed one leg of the breakfast tray. A pot of tea began to tip. A sliding platter of eggs interrupted its fall. Piping hot Darjeeling began to leak from the spout of the precariously perched pot; it pooled along the raised edge of the tray.

Cordelia twisted around to grab the tray. Stroud was faster, though he ended up on his side, carrying most of the weight of the tray with three fingers.

As quickly as she could, Cordelia straightened the leg she'd kicked. She donned her wrapper as she made her way to the door, flagging the nearest servant so she could explain, "We've had a bit of a spill. Could someone come collect the linens? I'm afraid they'll have to be laundered immediately."

Stroud thanked the three maids profusely as they trooped in, making them giggle, and hustled Cordelia downstairs to the breakfast room. Florence looked up from the fashion magazine spread out beside her plate as they walked in. "What brings you out so early?"

Cordelia raised an eyebrow at her husband. "I'll let him tell you."

"No, no, Cordelia, you can't leave Rip to answer," cut in Florence. "He's a dreadful liar."

"He is?"

"I am not," Stroud insisted.

"Oh? Then what brings you downstairs so early, brother?"

"I missed your sweet voice." Stroud filled a fresh plate from the buffet.

"You see?" Florence grinned at Cordelia. "He's a *dreadful* liar."

Cordelia settled herself across from Flea at the table, in the sunshine that almost felt warm streaming through the tall windows, and poured herself a cup of tea. "I guess you'll never know."

Flea clapped her hand to her bosom with a gasp. "Are you abetting his misdeeds? How the mighty have fallen."

"Some people call wives 'helpmeets' or 'angels of the hearth,'" observed Stroud, sitting between them and heaping his fork with pan-fried potatoes. "I prefer 'accomplice'."

"No one who's met you would be even the slightest bit

surprised to hear it," retorted Florence. "Cordelia, on the other hand. I thought you were going to keep my brother in line?"

"Whatever gave you that idea?" Cordelia shuddered. "Too many women are doomed to spend their lives curbing the excesses of husbands who refuse to learn any self-discipline. It's not a fate I'd ever choose for myself."

A surprised smile spread across Florence's face. "So you aren't going to try to stop Rip from pulling pranks?"

"His time is his own." They were both looking at her oddly now, and Cordelia found that she minded it. "Frivolity is not evil. I do perceive the difference."

"Oh, good." Florence smiled brightly. "Because I wanted to invite you to do something frivolous today. I thought we could go shopping together."

"For what?"

"Clothing, of course. You must need absolutely everything. Our tastes were always a bit alike, but now our budgets match as well. We might as well take advantage of it, don't you think?"

"That would be lovely, Florence," Cordelia answered. "I'd be delighted."

THE SHOPPING TRIP consumed the whole day. Florence knew all the best places, and she hadn't been wrong about the convergence of their tastes. Every haberdasher and cobbler and tailor they visited seemed to understand what Cordelia wanted better than she did herself. She had only to eye the stitching on a pair of boots or admire the color of a bolt of silk, for the assistant to pipe up with an obsequious, "Your Grace, if I might offer a suggestion?"

The suggestions were always better than anything Cordelia could have imagined herself. Interesting without being garish, flattering without making her feel like a peacock. By the time they returned home, they'd spent at least five hundred pounds between them. An astonishing sum, and while Cordelia might have felt ashamed—not so long ago she'd worked hard to earn one tenth that sum—instead it made her bold. After having her purchases sent to her room, she sat down and dashed off a letter to Mrs. Caroline Norton.

When duchesses reached out to prominent strangers, they didn't *impose*. They *condescended*, and people praised them for it.

Not only did Mrs. Norton accept the invitation to tea, Cordelia had her answer by the morning post. It brought home, again, the reality of her new position. Not only could she now reach out to strangers and assume her attention would be welcome, those strangers rushed to place themselves at Cordelia's disposal, instantly rearranging their schedules to suit her convenience.

The morning post also brought letters from Tess and Olympia. Tess accepted Cordelia's invitation, much to her relief. Olympia wrote that after arranging such an elaborate wedding breakfast, she'd "had enough of hostessing for a while," and offered to visit Cordelia instead. That seemed odd, since Olympia had never once tired of hostessing in all the time Cordelia had known her, but she replied with a date and a time and her sincere pleasure at being able to return the hospitality Olympia had so generously extended for so long.

Olympia arrived later that afternoon in an unfamiliar mood. She greeted Cordelia with a cry of welcome and a flood of questions ("How do you do?" "Tell me what's happening with your petition!" "Is that dress new?") and not a word about the joys of the bedroom, which Cordelia had rather *wanted* to discuss for once.

Even odder, Olympia wouldn't answer any of Cordelia's questions, no matter how innocuous. She had nothing to say about how she was enjoying married life, about her plans during the next few weeks, where she'd be summering, anything.

At last, and mostly out of desperation, Cordelia asked if Olympia had any advice about redecorating one of the rooms in the townhouse for her own use. "A place where I can work, store my bookbinding tools, perhaps have guests to tea?"

"That's entirely reasonable," Olympia assured her immediately. "Come on, let's choose one right now."

"Right now?"

"In fact, I have an idea." For a brief moment, Olympia was herself: vibrant, imperious, charging ahead without a backward glance, certain that any and all obstacles would be swept from her path before she could stumble.

"Here, this is what you want." Olympia strode into a large room with windows facing the street. It was on the first floor, where noise could be a nuisance, clean but disused.

The door had always been closed when Cordelia passed by, and Stroud hadn't stopped here on their tour. Now she understood why. It was a gentleman's retreat, with crystal decanters empty of liquor on a squat sideboard, several paintings of nude women on the wrong side of salacious, a card table surrounded by leather-upholstered chairs. The curtains and the carpet reeked of tobacco, smoky and sour.

"This must have been where Stroud's father spent his time," Cordelia guessed.

"And woe betide anyone who interrupted him," Olympia began, with relish. Then her voice went flat. "I once saw him slap the duchess so hard she bounced off the wall outside in the corridor, just for knocking."

"Ah."

"Well, he died before his time and I suppose it would be selfish to ask for more." Olympia smiled tightly. "I don't blame Rip and Flea for pretending the room doesn't exist, but it's a terrible waste. Clear everything out, change the decor so completely that no one who remembers the old duke will recognize it, and you'll have done everyone who knew him a favor."

"I suspect you're right."

"You suspect," Olympia pointed at Cordelia and then at herself. "I *know*. Unfortunately, I should be getting home. We'll see one another soon, won't we? Later this week, perhaps? I can't wait."

Before Cordelia knew it, Olympia was gone. Cordelia was sorry for the unusually short visit but glad that, at least, the door remained open for another. And then sorry, again, that she clung to such small signs of a friendship that had been so special and close.

She approached both Stroud and Florence about adopting their father's room for her own needs. Stroud said, "I'd forgotten it was there," perhaps a bit disingenuously, and "Do what you like with it." Florence was a bit more forthright: "What a marvelous idea! Have all the chairs chopped up for firewood, would you? Oh, I'm glad you're doing this while it's still cold. I can't wait to warm my feet on his old things."

She wasn't joking. As soon as the card table and its chairs were removed from the room, Florence sent one of the footmen to chop them into sticks, stacked beside the fireplace in the bright salon where she spent her evenings.

Meanwhile Cordelia unearthed a tea table, a rug, and a turn-of-the-century sofa in the Egyptian style in the attic, which she sent to be reupholstered. She ordered a new set of curtains, commissioned a joiner to build bookshelves all along one wall, and bought a solid table on which she organized all her bookbinding supplies into cunning little boxes while leaving ample workspace.

She'd have her hobby back. A pursuit for pleasure, rather than necessity.

She arranged a shelf containing her favorites of the books she'd bound herself, in her possession again thanks to the trunks her mother had packed for her wedding. The newspaper article about Miss Smith's petition that she'd clipped, describing how the petition had unrolled from one end of Parliament to the other, hung from a frame by her new desk.

When Mrs. Norton arrived, the room remained bare, mismatched, incomplete. But Cordelia felt at home in it. As a married woman, she had little formal power. Legally speaking, she had very nearly ceased to exist. But she could carve out a sphere of influence and, as a duchess, it could be substantial. She had to realize it for herself—see it for herself—assert her existence. She did not feel frivolous for spending so much time redecorating; she felt reassured. If she were lucky, she'd live long enough to make this place more than just a room of her own. It would become a hub of power whose reach was limited only by her imagination.

She greeted her guest in a fine new dress, beautifully cobbled leather slippers, a discreet jewelry set worth more than she'd paid in rent to Ruby over the whole of her time in London.

Mrs. Norton, a gentlewoman approaching the age of fifty, had separated acrimoniously from her husband. Ever since, she'd relied upon her own writing to support herself—when her husband didn't confiscate her earnings out of spite. She'd published books of poetry that ran through multiple printings and seen her own plays performed at Covent Garden. A renowned beauty and occasional artist's model, she'd edited many fashion magazines—including *La Belle Assemblée.*

She'd done all of this—and more—under the most agonizing of circumstances. She'd separated from her husband shortly after he'd sued Lord Melbourne for criminal conversation, accusing the then-prime-minister of having an affair with his wife and demanding compensatory damages (adultery with a wife being classed, by law, as harm to her husband's "property"). The action had failed, closing off any grounds for divorce and leaving Mrs. Norton at her husband's not-so-tender mercy.

He'd forbidden her from seeing her own children, a ban he'd only lifted when the youngest suffered a devastating horse-riding accident. The child had died before Mrs. Norton reached his side, and the tragedy had marked the beginning of her political career. Her work to grant mothers some legal rights over their own children had culminated in the passage into law of the Infant Custody Bill.

When Mrs. Norton tried to dip into a low curtsey, Cordelia stopped her.

"I have not yet earned your respect," Cordelia cautioned. "Please sit. I'll pour."

"I read about your marriage in the papers," Mrs. Norton said, once they'd settled. "A duke raising a gentlewoman reduced to trade up to the very pinnacle of the aristocracy? I'm sure I wasn't the only person to wonder if a bit of light fiction had been accidentally printed in the society news."

Cordelia smiled faintly. "And here I am, using my new position to demand your attention. I hope I haven't ruptured the fantasy with my forwardness."

"Not at all. I'm delighted to indulge my curiosity. Were you really—what was it? Sewing up bibles by candlelight?"

"Novels, mostly," Cordelia corrected. "And usually in the daytime, as candles were too dear."

"My *word*." Mrs. Norton laughed, her dark eyes sparkling. "How did you meet? I only know your husband by reputation, but I never took him for a *reader*."

"I don't think he is," Cordelia admitted. "We passed one another in the street—"

Mrs. Norton interrupted with a clap, laughing silently. "You passed one another in the street? He took one look at you and knew?"

"More or less."

Mrs. Norton relaxed into her seat with a deep sigh. "You know, sometimes I forget such stories exist—that Lady Luck can be kind and happiness real. It all begins to seem like a dream, but here you are."

"We haven't been married a month yet," Cordelia countered uncomfortably.

"And that's a month more of happiness than I ever had," Mrs. Norton said dryly. "Which you must know, if you've invited me. The story of my life has been splashed over so many papers I not infrequently meet people who imagine we're already friends. Or enemies, as the case may be."

"I would not presume so far," Cordelia said carefully. "Though

I was inspired, very early on, by your work on the Infant Custody Bill."

"Come now." Mrs. Norton's smile turned a bit cynical. "I won't be so indelicate as to guess your age, even indirectly, but you must have been a child when it was passed."

"I was seven," Cordelia admitted. "But my father is a judge, you see, and he likes to say that explaining legal problems to a child helped him refine his oratory. He's known for it, so it must be at least partially true."

"Extraordinary," murmured Mrs. Norton. "And you understood?"

"Oh, sometimes." Cordelia laughed. "Not very often."

"Then what concerns you now? Perhaps you are in need of help... or advice?"

"It is my understanding that you are the motive force behind Lord Lyndhurst's recent performance in Parliament. Is this true?"

"He's no dancing monkey, to perform at my command," demurred Mrs. Norton.

"So you had no influence over the speeches I've been reading about in the papers?"

"He is a dear friend, familiar—as even strangers are, yourself included—with my circumstances, and sympathetic to them. He is also a member of the House of Lords who takes his duties very seriously and never speaks without conviction."

Cordelia sighed. "I understand."

"You hoped for a different answer."

"I did," Cordelia admitted. "Have you been following the petition for the reform of married women's property law at all?"

"Of course." Mrs. Norton smiled faintly. "I didn't sign it, mind you."

"And may I ask why?"

"Because I wasn't invited." Mrs. Norton paused. "Miss Smith wanted to show that even good, respectable women earn money. A revolutionary notion, to be sure. I earn money—though I regret the necessity—but I am *not* respectable. Equally unfortunate, by the lights of Miss Smith and her set, I have never resented my place in God's grand design. I do not dream of equality for women."

"You weren't *invited.*" Cordelia could hardly believe it. But the rest followed easily. "And because you don't support the philosophy that anchors it, you didn't fight to have your signature included. It only makes sense that you'd be enthusiastic to see your good friend Lord Lyndhurst pushing for reforms that *do* speak to your specific needs and interests."

"Just so."

They continued to chat for a few minutes. When Mrs. Norton finally set aside her saucer and took up her gloves, she returned to the topic.

"I see that you are young and new to politics."

Cordelia nodded. Both were true, and she sensed no censure in Mrs. Norton's calm tone.

"You have been kind, and I will repay your kindness in a way I suspect you'll appreciate: by speaking frankly." Mrs. Norton tugged the fingers of her gloves into place. "I do not, in fact, object to Miss Smith's petition. Our disagreements are significant but I feel *deeply* for any married woman who cannot trust her husband to act in her or her children's best interest. I would lend my support to her efforts, if I thought they had any chance of success.

"They do not. The conservatives hold too much power right now. Lord Brougham is a formidable old warrior for the progressives. He's carried several important measures across the finish line. But for the most part, the causes he champions never reach further than the papers. They spark a bit of debate, burnish his reputation, and then disappear.

"Palmerston won't lift a finger to support a married woman's right to pocket her own earnings," Mrs. Norton continued. "But he wants the Divorce Bill, he wants the ecclesiastical courts done away with, and for the papers to stop covering the lurid details of divorce trials held before Parliament. It will pass—and I, personally, would rather support the bill that has a future than inscribe all my wishes onto a petition that does not."

"I see." The honesty stung. Cordelia felt like she'd been slapped.

"That is how I look at things," Mrs. Norton finished. "Miss Smith has written about the law. She has studied, she has talked to experts, she has distilled a grand and foolish vision into words. If that's how you wish to proceed, carry on. My plans are not so grand—but I have seen my demands become law and I think I'll live to see it happen again."

"You've given me a great deal to think about."

"I hope so." Mrs. Norton bowed. "I'll see myself out."

CORDELIA WAS STILL STARING GLUMLY at the two-tiered display of biscuits when Tess arrived.

"Did I come at a bad time?" Tess asked.

"You're always welcome," Cordelia demurred. "And I have news that I didn't want to put in a letter."

"That sounds ominous." Tess took a seat and poured herself a cup of tea. "Olympia?"

"Her husband *shoved* her at the wedding breakfast," Cordelia said. "I've been thinking about our conversation ever since, about how wrong I was. If I'd listened, if I'd tried harder—"

"Then, most likely, you would have lost Olympia's friendship as well," Tess cut in. "I've been thinking too. And I suspect we'd both be sitting here, wondering how she fared and unable to find out."

"Do you really think so?" Cordelia wondered, surprised.

"I think it's more likely than the alternative, where Olympia came to her senses and broke things off with a man who'd already taken her virginity." Tess paused. "Considering my low estimation of Mr. Grant's character, I doubt that would have been the end of it."

"No, probably not." Cordelia shuddered. "And yet the damage I can imagine a spurned Mr. Grant inflicting on Olympia pales in comparison to what he is capable of now, as her *husband*."

"Listen to me." Tess leaned close, her voice dropping urgently. "You chose this path and, whatever your regrets, here is how you will make the best of it: whatever happens, however odious Mr. Grant becomes, maintain your friendship with Olympia. Mr. Grant will have a very difficult time explaining why his wife shouldn't keep up an acquaintance with the new Duchess of Stroud."

Cordelia nodded. "You're right."

Florence popped her head in the door. "Cordelia? We were going to talk with the gardener about the summer planting. I could take care of it but you said you wanted to join us. What shall we do?"

"Go on." Tess waved Cordelia toward the door. "I have letters to write. You know how it is."

CHAPTER 22

Alistair arrived home at the tail end of an afternoon drunk, still too bleary to think straight. He shambled right into Coco's room, more interested in seeing her than his valet, and felt entirely vindicated when she looked up from her book and broke into a smile, quick and genuine and more than he'd expected.

He flopped on the bed, dragged himself across the mattress by the elbows, and buried his face in her lap. "I missed you."

"It's only been a few hours."

"It's been a whole day." He'd left early for a game of rugby with old school chums, then followed the game with a late lunch and the aforementioned drinking. "Long enough to miss you."

"If you say so." She still sounded skeptical but the fingers she ran through his hair were very gentle. She alternated little rubs and scratches until he purred into her lap.

Rolling onto his side, he settled his cheek comfortably in the cradle of Coco's thighs. "How was your day?"

Coco stared at the wall, looking rather bleak.

"Hey." He jostled her leg to catch her attention. "I've never seen you so glum. Tell me about it?"

"You're still in your outdoor clothes." She seized his cravat and tackled the complicated knot. "What happened to your valet?"

"He's a bore." Stroud stretched his neck to give her better access. "He's so *slow* and he does everything *carefully,* and it takes *forever*. I didn't want to wait."

"That's very sweet." Cordelia finished with the knot, slid the cravat free of his collar, and peeked at his feet. "Did you at least take off your shoes?"

It was so much easier with his valet's help. "Maybe."

"You put your shoes on my bed?"

Stroud said, "Nooooooooo," while shuffling his feet off the side of the bed, so that he wasn't lying. Exactly.

"You're filthy and a liar." Coco fumbled at the buttons on his coat. "That makes you a *filthy liar*."

"Are you trying to distract me?"

Coco kissed him on the forehead. "I think *you're* trying to distract *me*."

"But you tried to distract me first." He tackled his shoes, but they were almost impossible to remove without a shoehorn and some leverage; muscling through very nearly dislocated his ankle. "Ouch."

"Are you all right?"

"I am. Not sure about the boots." He dropped his head back into her lap. "Tell me about your awful day."

"I'd rather not."

"Please?" he coaxed.

"I invited Mrs. Caroline Norton for tea. Have you heard of her?"

"Um." Stroud scratched his stubbly cheek. "Is she the woman who had an affair with Melbourne?"

"That was never proven. But yes, that's Mrs. Norton. She's done a number of remarkable things, particularly to do with giving mothers a legal claim to their young children, but she's generated a fair bit of scandal as well."

"And you invited her to tea?"

"I was told that she's the motive force behind Lord Lynd-hurst's recent speeches," said Cordelia. "The two are close, rumored to be *indecently* close. She's formally separated from a husband she loathes, a man who retains a great deal of power over her and uses it to torment her. Naturally she is eager to be free of him."

"Naturally."

"If Lord Lyndhurst is successful, certain measures from Miss Smith's petition—ones that allow women to sue for divorce and to regain their legal personhood after a divorce—will be incorporated into the ongoing efforts of a Parliamentary committee dedicated to reforming divorce laws. The remainder would be jettisoned. That includes all reforms pertaining to the rights of *married* women, the vast majority of British women, which would be put off until who knows when."

Stroud followed perhaps one word in ten of that. The only thing that came through clearly was Coco's distress. "So what are you going to do now?"

"I wanted to understand Mrs. Norton's reasoning. If the terms of Miss Smith's petition were carried into law, Mrs. Norton would have everything she wishes and more—why settle for less?"

"More is better." That sounded safe enough.

"Mrs. Norton told me that Miss Smith had intentionally kept her from contributing to the petition. She wasn't even allowed to sign it!"

"And that's bad?"

"It's *troubling*." Coco sighed. "When Miss Smith explained how carefully they'd selected which women would sign, I followed her reasoning. The petition makes a point, and merely by asserting their existence, the signatories *prove* that point. Women earn incomes, women enter trade—and married women, *happily* married women, want the same rights as a married man."

"What's, um...?" Stroud still didn't understand. "What's troubling, exactly?"

"I never saw the insult inherent in Miss Smith's design, not

272

until it was pointed out to me." Coco paused. "Perhaps I'd approve, if the petition were poised to succeed. But the petition is doomed. Does that change how I feel about the compromises made along the way? Miss Smith drove away worthy women like Mrs. Norton for nothing. And I failed an important moral test without realizing that I had confronted one at all."

"So you prefer Mrs. Norton, then?" Stroud said. "As, er. A mentor?"

"Not at all." Her heart remained with Miss Smith, who saw farther and aimed higher. "Mrs. Norton achieves her goals because she fights for what is possible rather than what is best. It's a philosophy I dislike, though I can't deny she has proven its efficacy. And while she insisted she has no influence over Lord Lyndhurst, I don't believe it. I think she lied."

"So then why ask her advice?" Stroud wondered, baffled.

"I wanted to see the whole picture."

"And do you?" He certainly didn't. "See the whole picture?"

"I see more of it." She threaded her fingers through his hair again and resumed her scratching. "They say that the best is the enemy of the good, but I would rather fight for what I think is best. I do not wish to fight for the *leavings*—it is infuriating to dream of a fine dinner and battle for a crust."

Have the fine dinner, he wanted to say. But she was talking about passing laws, and he didn't have nearly enough power for that. He was a pariah among his peers. Coco might think he was smart, but nobody else did.

He'd never cared much about women's issues before. In all honesty, he still didn't. But everything Coco said stuck in his mind, thoughts and ideas he'd ordinarily disregard burrowing in like thirsty ticks. He wanted so badly to fix things, give her what she wanted, but all he knew how to do was pull pranks.

He carried Coco to bed. She leaned into him when he lifted her now, and traced her fingertips lightly across his chest, sweetly erotic. He'd handled this right, and somehow that made the ache in his heart even sharper. She was slow to change and formed opinions like a hen laid eggs, brooding over them grumpily until they hatched. But once she'd made up her mind, the transformation was complete.

If once he'd kissed her and hoped desperately for a spark, now he knew down to his bones she'd catch flame. She didn't hesitate or tire or daydream or blush. She'd been ready—more than ready —for days.

Maybe alcohol clouded his thoughts, spoiled his mood. But he'd barely followed her explanation. He couldn't do anything to help. It had been a long time since he felt so inadequate to a situation.

He wondered if she would rather have married someone else —or, worse, if she thought she *had* married someone else. She had such absurd ideas about him, hopes he could never live up to, expectations he was already falling short of. And the worst possibility of all: if she expected him to change to suit her needs, to become someone else. He'd tried that for his father, once upon a time, and it had never worked.

He admitted to himself—if not to Coco, who happily snuggled close and fell asleep—that *he* was the one with lead feet, because he didn't want to consummate a marriage that didn't quite feel real.

NEARLY THE FIRST article Cordelia read in the papers the next morning concerned the proposed Divorce Bill. It railed against Lord Lyndhurst's proposed amendments, lamented the proposed closure of the ecclesiastical courts—more out of respect for centuries-old institutions in general than the specific role of the ecclesiastical courts in contemporary Britain—and decried the death of tradition, which would surely usher in widespread moral decay.

What a fool. She would have liked to believe that the British public would recognize fearmongering for what it was and dismiss this man's misguided ravings as easily as she. Instead, she could all too easily imagine a sanctimonious footman ceremoniously whisking the crumbs of Miss Smith's petition off the metaphorical table and discarding them in the trash.

Another article discussing the Divorce Bill tightened the worry spooling in her gut. It argued that the bill wouldn't pass without Tory support, which it didn't have enough of, and that the Whigs ought to give up on it so they could direct their energies along more productive lines.

After rereading the article three times, she had the distinct impression that some ill-humored deity had decided to dispense with the usually lengthy gap between speaking words and being made to eat them. Apparently the time had come to battle for a crust.

She sent a quick note to Mrs. Norton, asking what she could do to help push the Divorce Bill across the finish line, and had an answer back within the hour. Mrs. Norton thanked Cordelia again for the invitation, acknowledged that the article she'd found so worrisome stated the situation accurately enough, and offered a list of names.

Cordelia had no idea what to do with a list of names.

Stroud wandered in just then, and poured himself a cup of tea. "You're staring at that letter like you want to burn a hole in it."

"Mrs. Norton sent me a list of the Tories she thinks could be persuaded to vote for the Divorce Bill."

"Hmm." Stroud sat down across from her. "Commons or Lords?"

"Lords. Since they'll vote on it this session."

"I know most of the Lords. At least by name and reputation. I do show up to vote occasionally."

"You should be present at every vote," Cordelia couldn't help but point out.

"They don't need me—"

"And also inform yourself about the issues at hand so you can judge for yourself when your vote is *needed*," she added.

Stroud groaned. "What if I let you tell me how to vote?"

"Wouldn't you rather have your own opinions?"

"If I would rather have my own opinions, would I have offered to let you tell me how to vote?"

Cordelia decided not to argue any further against the offer of a vote in the House of Lords. Instead, she pushed Mrs. Norton's letter to the other side of the table for him to read. "What do you make of these men?"

"Abbot, Wensum, Mandeville, Louth, Pye..." Alistair scratched his chin. "You'll have a hard time with Abbot. He's the sort of man who wouldn't trust a woman to tell him the time of day. No need to try his wife, either, for the same reason. Wensum is related to Gladstone, who's against, and has no mind of his own. I'd try..."

"Who?"

Stroud hesitated, and it wasn't hard to guess why. His quick analysis hadn't surprised her at all, but he was so reluctant to acknowledge his own acuity. "You've got good instincts about people," she insisted. "Much better than mine."

"You keep saying that, but..." He slanted a challenging glance at her. "What if I told you to go after Pye?"

"Lord Pye?" Cordelia couldn't hold back a brief, bitter laugh. The man had gone out of his way to harass her at Nell's wedding. "You're joking."

Stroud shook his head.

"*I'm* certainly not about to persuade Lord Pye of anything. But you know that, so I can only assume..." Cordelia eyed Stroud speculatively. "You want to try?"

"I have an idea," Stroud admitted.

That rang alarm bells. Stroud solved all his problems with pranks. "What kind of idea?"

Stroud fidgeted. "Well, you know my rule."

Cordelia combed her memories but couldn't think of any rules. "Remind me?"

"It was part of the instructions for Homer the Roamer." He

fussed with his tea, arduously squeezing every single drop of juice from a lemon wedge into his cup, and wouldn't meet her eyes. "If your first attempt doesn't succeed, try again—but by a new route every time."

"This isn't a prank," Cordelia said. "We're talking about laws that affect people's lives. We only get so many chances, and the petition's already failed."

Stroud stiffened but replied stubbornly, "It's a new route."

He was kind enough not to point out that she hadn't offered an alternative of her own, but she heard it anyway and forced herself to reconsider. She ought to hear him out, at least.

"I like your rule," she admitted. "What kind of prank are you thinking of?"

Stroud shrugged and began stirring a lump of sugar into his tea. "It depends on what I can talk him into."

Cordelia didn't like the idea of influencing the laws of a great country through pranks. She didn't think it ought to be possible and wasn't sure how she'd defend such an unorthodox method. If she'd failed a moral test by supporting Miss Smith's petition without ever asking herself who'd been left out, wouldn't this be worse?

"You don't think it will work?" Stroud asked.

"If you think it will work, it will work."

Stroud's spoon clanged in the teacup. He dropped it and looked up, stunned.

"I believe in you." She was surprised it needed to be said—hadn't she always? Her uncertainty rested within herself, desperation warring with principle. Should she hold firm or should she bend? Should she take the high road and fail or seize any chance for success?

She didn't entirely trust herself to answer those questions, but she wasn't alone. She had a partner, and she did trust *him*. "Do you think this is right? And fair?"

Stroud must have sensed the gravity of the question, because he didn't answer immediately. "I'm not going to trick him. He'll have a choice. Isn't that fair?"

It depended on how one defined fair. Fair to Pye? Fair by the lights of a good governance society? Fair to all the women who'd see progress pushed back another decade because Cordelia felt squeamish?

"Let me try," he said. "Let me approach Pye."

"All right." She nodded with far more confidence than she really felt. "Pye it is."

CHAPTER 23

A listair hated his father's club. He'd thought about letting his membership lapse, but it would have been more trouble than it was worth. Everyone had a club; if he'd left this one, he would have had to find a new one. It had been perfect for his father—and apparently his grandfather, who'd been the first to join—but Alistair had no friends at the place.

Which wasn't to say that he didn't know any of the members. He knew all of them by name or by sight and usually a bit better than that. The ones he hadn't grown up with he'd grown up *around*; they'd attended the entertainments his parents had once hosted, or he'd attended the ones they hosted.

Even if he didn't know these people deeply, he'd known them shallowly for a very long time and—it seemed to him—the two were roughly equivalent. A constant influx of superficial knowledge added up to something after a decade or so.

So he made an appearance in the early afternoon, finding the place as dim and gloomy as a coal cellar at midnight. He sat at a booth, ordered himself a drink, and pointedly did not look at the man he'd come to see.

Lord Pye had been, by all reports, quite the man about town in his prime. The life of every party, the bane of every happy marriage. Alistair distinctly remembered his horror when, while visiting Chilly while they were on holiday from Eton, he'd heard a pair of gray-haired matrons giggling to one another over Lord Pye's cocksmanship. He'd been appalled to discover that people didn't give up sex when their first gray hairs sprouted.

And when had that knowledge become a relief? Well, anyhow. A lifetime of dissipation had finally caught up to Pye. He looked awful these days, frail and watery-eyed, his deep unhappiness thinly masked by perpetual, petty dissatisfaction with his company and his surroundings.

Alistair downed a tumbler of gin punch before Pye wheezed his way across the room.

"Hullo, Rip," the old man said, levering himself into a seat across from Alistair. "Where've you been? I haven't seen you since the wedding."

"Here and there."

"Not *here*, actually," Pye countered. "Switched to another club?"

"What a thing to suggest," Alistair chided. "The Carlton is my one and only."

Pye snorted. "I know that line. Practicing for when you try it out on the wife?"

Alistair smiled blandly.

"Read about your wedding in the papers." Pye raised his glass mockingly. "I can't believe you married that shrew. I always thought your father had to be exaggerating about how stupid you'd turned out but you had one task—marry a woman with some money and some breeding, get a few heirs on her—and you whiffed."

"Completely," Alistair agreed cheerfully. "Do you know how it happened?"

Pye leered. "I can guess."

"Oh, I'm talking about something that happened years before I met my wife. The, er, the inciting incident might have been my mother's removal to Italy. That's the sort of thing that will put a young man in a contemplative mood. So I sat down and asked myself, 'How much money would a woman have to bring into the marriage in order to make up for a lifetime of unhappiness?' And I came up with a figure."

Lord Pye's marriage was extremely traditional. He'd married an heiress—Chilly's aunt Margaret—to provide his noble lineage with a much-needed cash infusion. Margaret then bore him four children, two of them sons, and looked the other way when he had affairs.

Pye twisted his mouth into an expression somewhere between a smile and a smirk. "How much?"

"I thought, oh, two or three hundred thousand pounds. That seems adequate, doesn't it?"

Pye burst out laughing. "Three hundred thousand pounds can buy a lot of happiness."

"So I made a list of all the young ladies I knew who'd bring that much." Alistair sipped from his gin punch. "It wasn't a very *long* list and I looked at it and I thought—no, no, I was wrong. I'd need least double. Maybe triple. *A million pounds.*"

Pye cackled.

"Since that's absurd I decided I'd marry whoever I wanted instead. And that's what I did."

"But why *her*?" Pye sipped from his own drink; there was no humor in his tone. "She's a harridan at *twenty*. Or whatever she is. You shouldn't need a clairvoyant to tell you she'll be a termagant by forty. She'll gain weight, lose all her humility, and you'll have a nightmare on your hands, boy. You and everyone else she meets."

"That's not a nice thing to say," Alistair chided.

"It's the truth." Pye snorted. "Someone should have told you before it was too late."

"*I* think she'll mellow with age. Like fine wine."

"She'll turn to vinegar, you poor idiot. You can't seriously believe that a woman, a *tradeswoman*, who was invited to mingle with her betters at a wedding party out of"—Pye spluttered—

"out of *pity* and then proceeded to pick a fight with every man in attendance is going to *mellow* with age?"

"That's not what happened," Alistair protested.

"It most certainly is," Pye insisted furiously. "Your new duchess is such an unnatural creature, so fanatical about her bizarre beliefs, she couldn't keep her mouth shut on an opinion if her life depended on it."

Alistair tried to contain his glee. "Do you want to bet?"

Pye hesitated. "What kind of bet?"

"About whether she can keep her mouth shut. For... say... an evening? The length of a dinner party?"

Pye narrowed his eyes. "What are you after?"

"A vote," Alistair admitted.

Pye began to laugh, rough and sharp like the grate of a saw on lumber. "She put you up to this, didn't she?"

Alistair tipped his head from side to side. "Not exaaaactly."

"Which vote?" Pye asked.

"In favor of the Divorce Bill."

Pye put his tongue to his teeth for a sharp, hissing *tsk*. "She sent you out to cadge votes for the law that would let her *divorce* you?"

Alistair shrugged. "I'm not worried about that."

"You know these reformers want to make it possible for wives to divorce their husbands on all the same grounds as men?" Pye lowered his voice. "For *adultery*?"

He hadn't, actually. "Are you worried?"

"Of course not." Pye snorted. "If you want my vote, then it stands to reason that if I win this little game, I can have yours?"

"Er..."

Pye's smile turned ugly. "Fair's fair, boy."

"But you don't care about the Divorce Bill."

"I don't," Pye agreed. "But I greatly dislike your wife."

"What are the terms? She remains silent for the duration, and you'll pledge your vote?"

Pye shook his head. "No, that's too obvious. Everyone will

figure out what's going on, and then they'll help or they'll aggravate her but either way, she'll dig in. I want her to attend a dinner party and—from the moment she removes her hat and gloves until the moment she puts them back on—she will converse as naturally as possible, without letting anyone guess at the bet, but not venture a single opinion."

"She can't even say she likes the soup?"

"That's not an opinion." Pye rolled his watery eyes, unamused. "That's a courtesy."

"So who's to judge if she offers an opinion or a courtesy?"

"How about..." Pye's lips pursed in a nasty little smile. "...you."

"What? I'll choose—"

"Fairly, isn't that your reputation? An honorable jester?" Pye laughed again. Unkindly. "I don't think she'll be able to keep her mouth shut. And I don't think you'll be able to lie about it. She'll eat you alive, and you'll deserve it."

Alistair swallowed, vaguely queasy. He was not as confident about the results as he would like to be. And Coco really would be furious if he had to vote against the Divorce Bill. "Eat you alive" might be an exaggeration but... perhaps only a slight one.

"Pleasure to see you, Rip." Pye drained his drink and slammed it on the table. "Expect an invitation in the mail."

"Wait, I thought—"

"You thought you'd be able to choose the guests?" Pye shook his head. "Oh, no. I'll take care of that."

After listening to her husband's explanation of the proposed scheme, Coco's first question was a slightly baffled, "Does he imagine this will be difficult for me?"

Stroud, who'd sat her down very seriously and explained the terms several times with slight variations in vocabulary, his brow deeply furrowed, seemed flummoxed by this response. "Won't it?"

"No." Because he appeared not to believe her she explained, "Stroud, all women learn how to be dull. It is the first thing we are taught. I'm no mistress of the art—which it can be, in the right hands—but I can manage for an *evening*."

"I think Pye means to invite a number of disagreeable people who will freely venture opinions that you dislike," he warned her.

"I'm sure that he will."

"Are you sure you won't…?" Stroud scratched his chin. "That is, what if you're rusty?"

Cordelia sighed.

"You see?" Stroud pointed. "That was an opinion! A strong one! I know exactly what you're thinking."

"What am I thinking?"

"You're thinking that I'm worrying over nothing," Stroud answered promptly. "But—and I want you to at least consider this possibility—what if you're wrong?"

Cordelia donned an expression of thoughtful uncertainty. Stroud looked encouraged until she asked, "Did you think I was considering the possibility?"

Stroud blinked.

"I wasn't," she told him. "Because I am quite certain."

THE PROMISED invitation arrived the next day, for a dinner taking place in a week's time, and while Cordelia felt quite at ease with the "challenge"—calling it a challenge credited Pye with more wit than he possessed—Stroud grew increasingly anxious.

"Why don't we play a game during the dinner?" she suggested finally.

"A game?" Stroud paced back and forth across the room. "Coco, you don't understand. If you venture any opinions during this dinner, I'll *have* to vote against the bill."

"But I won't venture any opinions. And a game might put you at ease?"

"What kind of game?" Stroud asked.

"I don't know." Cordelia waved vaguely in his direction. "You're the one who thinks of games."

"The game is that when you venture an opinion, I vote against the bill." Stroud resumed his pacing.

Cordelia sighed. "I will endeavor to think of a game."

"That was another opinion."

"I'm not sure whether I should be flattered or offended by your lack of faith in me." Cordelia pondered the matter. "A bit of both?"

Stroud snarled both hands in his hair and exclaimed, "You're supposed to take this seriously!" before storming out of the room.

Later that day, Tess dropped by to write a few letters. Cordelia rang for tea, and while they chatted, she explained the upcoming gamble for either Pye or Stroud's vote. "Stroud has been in an absolute panic for days," Cordelia complained. "I don't know what's possessed him."

"You ought to," Tess returned. "Remember what I told you, back when you didn't know who he was? Nobody thinks much of him. Nobody expects much of him. Nobody *counts on him.*"

"Ah," said Cordelia.

"You shared your troubles about a matter that gravely concerns you. He proposed a solution. Not only did you *agree* to his proposal—personally, I doubt he expected you to—you allowed him to carry it through in his own way. That means that if the gamble fails, he'll feel responsible. He'll have disappointed the only person who ever put much faith in him."

"But it will be *my* responsibility," Cordelia protested. "*I'm* the one who has to hold my tongue for an evening. *I'm* the one who will fail."

"But *he* set the terms," Tess insisted. "*He* accepted the wager and agreed to the forfeit. And if he has to deliver the final blow as well?"

"I'd never ask him to cheat."

"I'm sure he knows that. But he's very tender toward you, Cordelia. I think it will be quite hard for him to decide against you."

"Now you've worried *me*." Cordelia groaned. "I was confident before."

Tess smiled brightly. "I'm always happy to be of help."

"And I am ever so grateful," Cordelia teased back.

In truth, she planned to spend the evening imitating Bonny. They'd grown up together, been fast friends from such an early age, that Cordelia could imagine her friend's reactions to most situations and then copy them. Bonny was always listening to others, sharing their feelings and concerns, and almost never moved to express a contrary opinion. Cordelia couldn't radiate an aura of ineffable sweetness like her friend, but she didn't need to be perfect. Just passable.

It would be much easier if she had Stroud's good humor to bolster her. He was charming and optimistic; she always felt lighter around him, a little like she felt around Bonny. She'd need his good nature to steady her through a challenging evening. But, by the same token, if he floundered, she'd be more likely to stumble as well.

She had to invent a game. Stroud would do a better job of it, but the task had fallen to her. Sitting down with a blank page and an absurd task reminded her of when Stroud had challenged her to come up with a prank in order to win an introduction to Miss Smith.

Her life had changed quite a bit since then, hadn't it?

Unfortunately, this time she'd have to come up with something she could actually carry out. First, a title for her list.

Games to Maintain Good Cheer During an Aggravating Dinner Party

1. Make a silly face every time I say, "How interesting, please tell me more."

Too disruptive. He'd be mugging from soup to pudding.

2. I (discreetly) point at something in the room, and he must use the word in a sentence.

Entertaining, but she'd have no choice but to point at silverware a great deal, and that would lose its charm rather quickly.

3. Convince other guests to use a particular word or phrase, without ever using that word or phrase oneself.

Serviceable, but memorizing a list of words and phrases in advance, then keeping track of one's progress throughout the dinner, would prove difficult.

She needed something simple. Something diverting. Something that could be dropped and picked up again without any fuss. Wordplay would fit the bill best.

4. Rhyming game. The first word of a sentence one of us speaks must rhyme with the final word in the last sentence the other spoke.

That would serve. Just complex enough to keep Cordelia's mind off any attempts Pye and his companions made to bait her.

She went looking for Stroud and found him in the salon, on the floor with his dog—Peppermint, he'd let Florence name it—while chatting with Flea.

"I've come up with a game," she announced, joining Florence on the sofa.

"A game?" Florence wondered, right as Stroud jumped to his feet, eyes wide with what appeared to be panic. Peppermint copied him.

"Before you tell me to take this seriously," Cordelia said quickly, "I really think this will help."

"How could it possibly help?" Stroud flung his arms in the air. "I could end up voting against your bill!"

287

Florence burst into laughter. Not just a little chuckle, either—she laughed so hard she bent double, slapping the cushion of the sofa where she was sitting, eyes squeezed shut with mirth.

"What are you laughing about?" Cordelia wondered.

"It's like you've switched places," Florence cried, clapping a hand over her mouth to contain a new round of giggles. "*You* want to play games, and *Rip* is trying to be so serious and responsible!"

"Don't laugh," Stroud begged, to no benefit. "This isn't funny."

"When you're ready to hear about my game," Cordelia said finally, "you can find me. Until then—"

Stroud grabbed her by the wrist when she tried to leave and pulled as he sat down himself, roping her into his lap. "Don't be mad. I'll listen."

Florence gathered Peppermint into her lap, soothing the animal with gentle petting. "What kind of game?"

"A rhyming game," Cordelia explained. "We'll be seated opposite one another and won't often talk *to* one another, so this will require splitting our attention. Which is one of the primary advantages of the game. It's hard to be upset about a conversation you're not really paying attention to. The challenge will be to rhyme the last word in the other's sentence with the first word of your next. Like tennis, but with rhymes."

Stroud tipped his head to the side. "I'd need more *time* to find the rhyme. Forcing the first word will sound too *unnatural*."

"*Actually*, I think I could manage it," Cordelia countered. "But since you want to make it easier…"

Florence clapped. "Oh, someone fetch me a veil and some smelling salts, I must grieve the loss of my only brother. The poor man, struck down in his prime by his beloved wife, what a tragedy…"

"I'm just trying to be sensible," he complained.

Cordelia glanced at Florence, and this time they *both* erupted into gales of laughter.

CHAPTER 24

On the evening of the so-called challenge, Cordelia and
Stroud arrived at Pye's London residence exactly on time.
Pye greeted them politely—*too* politely, as when he bowed over
Cordelia's hand and said, "What a pleasure to see you again, and
in such improved circumstances!" she very nearly answered, "I
doubt that."

She caught herself just in time but couldn't contain the
shocked expression that flitted across her face.

Pye noticed. "I knew it." He chuckled. "You can't even take a
compliment. Well, make yourselves comfortable. The other guests
will be arriving shortly."

The other guests turned out to be three couples, each infuriating in their own way. The Melchiors weren't much older than
Cordelia and Alistair, Mr. Melchior heir to a nabob and Mrs.
Melchior the high-bred wife he'd chosen to secure his upward
mobility. Mrs. Melchior was a remarkably unpleasant woman,
both very pretty and very loud, with a tendency to frame everything she said as sage advice, hard won through experience.

"The trick is to knock your staff off balance early," she advised,
after learning that Cordelia did not have much experience in the
running of large households. "Dismiss someone over a small

infraction. Demote one of the downstairs favorites. They won't like it, but they'll settle down."

Cordelia desperately focused the whole of her attention on the conversation about horses that Mr. Melchior had engaged Stroud in. Her husband had just finished saying, "I don't ride very often. Every time I do I end up feeling sorry for the poor beast carrying me."

Working through the rhymes in her head helped her disguise her horror at Mrs. Melchior's advice. *Me* wasn't enough of a challenge and she found a pair for *beast* before *carrying*. "How do you *grease* the wheels? Surely if you employ a stick, you must also make use of a carrot?"

Stroud shot her a furious look before informing Mr. Melchior, who'd obligingly expressed sympathy for the unfortunate horses made to carry a man of Stroud's size, "I once knew a man who kept an African *parrot* in his stable, gave it a whole stall. After a while it started to whinny and neigh—it must have thought it was a horse too!"

Mr. Melchior appeared lost while Mrs. Melchior informed Cordelia that praise was a sufficient motivator, and Cordelia murmured, horrified, "A *few* kind words can really make a difference."

By the time they'd finished their champagne, Mr. and Mrs. Francis along with Lord and Lady Prisk had arrived. Mr. and Mrs. Francis were older, of Pye's generation, both very slow talkers who chortled indiscriminately. With both the Melchiors and the Francises, Cordelia surmised that Pye's goal was to provoke Cordelia into expressing an opinion out of irritation or—almost as likely—boredom.

Lord and Lady Prisk were a different matter entirely. As they were seated at table by rank, Lord Prisk escorted Cordelia into dinner and monopolized her conversation. Unlike the other guests, she was fairly certain he'd been told about the challenge and enlisted as support.

It could hardly be a coincidence that Lord Prisk opened the

evening by saying, *"Laborare pugnare parati sumus,"* and when Cordelia answered, "I beg your pardon?" Prisk replied, "Oh, Duchess, do you not speak Latin? Pye told me you were a blue-stocking sort. I assumed you'd been educated."

"I have not," Cordelia answered. (Across the table, Stroud: "You *bought* a new home recently, I heard?")

"And yet your area of particular interest is the law?" Lord Prisk tsked. "How do you manage without the necessary foundation?"

"Are you an *Oxford* or a Cambridge man?" Cordelia answered. "I'd love to hear more about your experiences." (Stroud, opposite: "Many *nuisances* arise from city life, it's true.")

Prisk was no fool. He refined his attacks as the evening went on. When needling her lack of education failed, he shifted to a new topic. "How can we influence the future more powerfully, more directly, than through parenthood?" he asked. When she answered only with, "What a striking observation," (Stroud was listening to a lengthy discourse on the subject of wallpapers) Prisk shifted again.

He ruthlessly chased the minute reactions she couldn't suppress. He cut very close to the bone with, "The movement to allow young ladies to choose their own spouses has been followed, almost immediately, by efforts to allow matrons to escape the marriages they've unwisely contracted. What ever happened to personal responsibility?"

Cordelia thought of Bonny, who had been pressured to choose a man whose grave sins were deliberately hidden from her, and of Olympia, who'd suffer for the rest of her life, and her whole body crackled with anger. He dismissed so much real tragedy. Women she knew—and all the women she'd never meet—thrown to the wolves and for what?

"Do you have any plans for the *summer?*" Stroud asked Mrs. Prisk, raising his voice almost to a shout. Mrs. Prisk startled. The other guests slid irritated, contemptuous glances his way.

Cordelia had never loved him more.

"A *number* of Parliamentarians have expressed similar views," she said slowly, carefully, and dully. "Including John George Phillimore of Leominster, I believe?"

"That's right," Lord Prisk acknowledged. "He said something very similar in the papers last week."

("The short *sleeves* on ladies' summer gowns do fill gentlemen with envy," Stroud announced, not precisely in reply to Lady Prisk's list of upcoming summer entertainments.)

Listening to her husband, game and silly to the end, quenched the molten rage—and left behind a core of tempered steel. Lord Prisk would not goad her. He would not beat her. She would thwart him, he would *fail*, and then Pye would owe Stroud his vote.

"You're lucky to have found a husband who likes being led around by the nose," Lord Prisk observed in one final, desperate gambit as Pye's footmen settled little golden cups of chocolate mousse in front of each guest.

He was running out of time.

("I like to go sea-bathing in August," said Stroud.)

"I *trust* you won't mind explaining?" Cordelia smiled sweetly. "I don't follow."

In the end, Stroud didn't have to render judgment. She hadn't even approached the line beyond which lay opinions, and Pye said so before either of them brought it up.

"I concede," he said, addressing Stroud in the foyer as Cordelia slipped into a light spring coat and straightened her gloves around her wrists. "I'll vote the Divorce Bill through."

"Better luck next time," Stroud answered with apparent sincerity.

Pye grunted.

She followed Stroud's example and searched for something gracious to say. "I enjoyed the evening." Surprisingly true. "It was clarifying."

"The only good thing about losing the bet was that I didn't

have to hear any of your atrocious opinions," Pye snapped. "Don't start now."

"Why speak to someone who won't listen?" Really, that had been Pye's first and greatest mistake: assuming she'd waste her breath. She had better things to do.

Things like passing the Divorce Bill.

As she let Stroud lead her to their waiting carriage, that once-distant goal seemed so much more attainable.

⁓

ALISTAIR'S HEAD swam dizzily as he stepped into the fresh air. He felt like he'd just pulled his best prank, gotten married all over again, and won a rugby match against Harrow *all at once*.

"You did it," he told Coco, whose serene expression didn't crack in the slightest. He'd thought Pye's parting shot would upset her, but if so, she hid it well.

At least, until they were safely inside the carriage, when she reached across the footwell and clasped both his hands in her own. "*We* did it," she corrected. "And the lion's share of the credit goes to you. *You* recognized Pye as a likely target. *You* lured him into a bet."

Alistair's cheeks warmed. "It didn't occur to me that I'd be sending you into a verbal boxing match with your hands tied behind your back," he apologized. "I thought it would be a fairly ordinary dinner, perhaps a bit dull without you to liven things up..."

"Pye hoped to increase his chances of success by deliberately provoking me," Cordelia replied, unruffled. "And it might have worked if not for the game. It kept me steady through a very trying evening."

Alistair squeezed the hands Coco had offered, taking a firm grip so he could tug her out of her bench seat and onto his lap. Both because he wanted her there and because, with Coco facing

ERIN SATIE

away from him, it was a safe position from which to ask, "Do you really mean it?"

"Mean what?"

"That I helped."

"Oh, Stroud." Apparently he hadn't been nearly as subtle as he thought because she twisted around and cupped both his cheeks in her palms, looking him straight in the eyes. "I am so lucky to have you by my side. You won his vote and you made it *fun*." Her lips curved in an impish little smile. "When you rhymed 'carrot' to 'parrot'!"

"You got them all so fast."

"I think we both performed admirably," she returned, and he couldn't help but kiss her again.

Whenever he caught a glimpse of himself through her eyes, the picture was so much different than what he saw in the mirror. As though he'd hired an especially flattering portraitist, someone who studied his features and then reproduced them on canvas with subtle yet profound improvements.

No wonder people paid so much for good portraits. The experience was intoxicating. *You're talking about me? Really?* he wanted to ask, and knew that Coco wouldn't have the patience for it.

She thought he'd done well. The dinner hadn't been a challenge for him. Nothing too different from the kind of pranks he'd organized in the past. Nothing he couldn't handle. She... knew him pretty well, actually. Knew him and thought well of him. Knew him and thought herself *lucky* for it.

The cloud of doubt lifted, and everything after that was so easy. Lifting Coco out of the carriage and throwing her over his shoulder, carrying her up to his room and throwing her on the bed.

She jumped right up to her knees, and when he hauled her in for a kiss, she grabbed him by the cock and steered him onto his back. A bold and clever move, very much within the realm of his expectations.

He quickly hooked an arm under her thigh and said, "Try something new?"

Her eyes widened, and she nodded.

Women tended to split between two extremes where his size was concerned. On the one hand, absolute horror. On the other, intense, vaguely unnerving delight. Coco didn't know enough to have an opinion, which left him to worry.

He thought about warning her that it would hurt and soon wished someone had been warning *him* instead. Once pain registered on her expression, his automatic response was to pick her up and set her down on the other side of the bed and never touch her again.

She batted his hands away before he could lift her. "Quit fussing."

He whined apologetically and kept very, very still. It was agony—a trial to test Hercules—and he was so addled and miserable about the whole thing that it took a while to realize that Coco was enjoying herself. He laid his palm between her breasts to feel the racing of her heart, swept the loose hair from her brow to reveal low-lidded and unseeing eyes.

Oh, he realized, startled. *She's getting lost in it.*

He rolled her onto her back and took over, slow and careful until he, too, got a little lost. Afterwards, she was so limp and incoherent he wanted to barricade the doors. No one else could ever see her like this, so sweet and vulnerable. He cuddled her close and peppered kisses over her hair until she fell asleep and felt a deep and irrevocable change creep over him.

"Forever," he promised her unhearing ears, as exhaustion claimed him as well. "Forever and ever and ever."

EPILOGUE

In late August 1857, Cordelia sat down to make a book. For pleasure, like she used to, and she was determined to enjoy every step of this process. She built the book block from ten signatures of thick, off-white paper with deckled edges. It had a pleasant width, substantial but not intimidating. She cut the spines from wafer-thin pine, chosen to be sturdy yet pleasantly pliable in the hand, and used fine cordovan leather for the binding, dyed the traditional red.

She had made more striking books, of colors and shapes more likely to catch the eye, but this one suited its purpose. Simple but beautiful and made to stand the test of time. On the inside cover she painted a portrait of herself and Alistair arm in arm, taking particular pleasure in adding characteristic humor to her husband's expression. She learned how to apply gilt, a delicate process involving a pair of fine tweezers, a very sharp knife, and tissue-thin sheets of pure beaten gold. The whole process was extravagant, but at the end of it she'd spelled out the words *Book of Love* in gold letters on the title page and surrounded them with colorful painted arabesques reminiscent of medieval manuscripts.

On the first page, she pasted an invitation to her wedding. On the second, a copy of the recently passed Divorce Bill. And then, after that, mementoes of all the votes they'd wrangled for the bill, through various means of persuasion: an invitation to Pye's dinner party faced a letter from Lady Mandeville, thanking Cordelia for the evenings of cards over which they'd discussed the matter, eventually leading Lady Mandeville to persuade her husband to vote in favor.

The bill had passed the Lords but run into great difficulty in the Commons. Opposition had been fierce, especially from religious conservatives. Cordelia and Alistair had secured at least ten votes in the Commons. One came from a blustery London MP who'd written to Stroud specifically to throw down the gauntlet. *I hear you're wagering on votes these days,* the letter read. *Well, I dare you to take mine.* They'd engaged in a drinking competition, of all things, and Alistair had walked away the victor. He had at least three stone on the poor MP, so it hadn't been a very fair fight, but the MP had insisted.

Cordelia had spearheaded a letter-writing campaign, had joined Mrs. Norton at various salons and soirees, and even written several articles for major newspapers. A duchess, it turned out, didn't have to ask anyone to publish her thoughts. The newspapers came with hats in hand to ask *her.* Clippings of the articles she'd written went into the book as well.

Palmerston had kept Parliament in session all through one of the longest, hottest summers on record for the sole purpose of pushing the bill through. Politics had been the talk of the town, though less for the bill that kept Parliament in session long after it should have recessed than for the awful stench rising from the Thames. Public attention turned to the subject of modern public works—notably, sewage—and by the time the Divorce Bill became law it had been weakened, amended, and diluted until the final document constituted a victory for the conservatives as much as the progressives.

Cordelia had battled for a crust and, in the end, received crumbs.

Still, the law had changed. Divorced, separated, and deserted women gained the right to own property. Wives were allowed to sue for divorce, though not on equal terms as their husbands. Adultery provided sufficient cause for a man to divorce his wife. A wife, on the other hand, required adultery along with an additional offense. Cruelty, for example. Or desertion.

Divorce trials were moved out of Parliament and into their own courts, though the price remained prohibitively high. The poor, effectively if not technically barred from obtaining divorces, could at least seek the relief of legal separation.

When she'd finished adding her mementoes, she'd filled perhaps ten percent of the pages. The rest remained blank. She wrapped the finished book in Japanese paper printed with a beautiful chrysanthemum pattern and presented it to Alistair on an evening when Flea had gone out.

According to Tess, Alistair was a popular subject of gossip. People said he'd finally matured into his position. Scandal sheets speculated that marriage had forced him to embrace a new stage of life, to let go of childish things. Cordelia, who'd spent half the day in shoes that pinched because he'd switched her favorite slippers out for an identical-but-slightly-smaller pair, knew he remained much the same as he'd been when they met.

But she wouldn't have it any other way.

She gave him the present after dinner, so they could linger over it with a glass of sherry. Alistair made flattering noises about the binding before finally opening the book.

"I forget that you paint," he said, finger hovering over the dual portrait. "Is this really how I look to you?"

Cordelia bent over the page. "It's as accurate as I could make it. I don't think I'd have a future as an artist—"

"No, no, it's just"—Alistair blushed—"you've made me very handsome."

Cordelia stared, confused. "You *are* very handsome."

Alistair snorted. "Moving along..." He flipped to the title page, where *Book of Love* glittered in gold, and paused for a long, long time.

"I love you so much," Cordelia confessed, her heart in her mouth. "Every day I am grateful to have you at my side. Every single day."

Stroud stopped her with a kiss. "I'm the lucky one. You'll never convince me otherwise."

He kept turning pages, marveling over each one. When he reached the first of the blank pages, he flipped quickly through the rest and said, "Wait a second…"

"Hmm?"

"Is this…?"

"Probably."

"It's a trick!" He shut the book. "This is your way of telling me you have a new project, isn't it? The bill's only just passed."

"It's the only way I can stomach what became of the bill," Cordelia admitted. "It must be the beginning of what we accomplish together, not the end."

"This is what comes of being taken seriously, isn't it?" Alistair slumped in his chair, mock-dejected. "People develop *expectations*. And then you have to…" He frowned at the paper. "*Accomplish* things."

"A fair summary."

Alistair whined, "It'll take *years*."

"That's the idea." Cordelia smiled. "Promise me we'll fill them all?"

"*You* will. No doubt of that." He sighed. "I might as well help."

AFTERWORD

Thank you so much for reading *Book of Love*. I hope you enjoyed it. If you have a chance to leave a rating or review, either at your favorite online bookstore or on Goodreads, I'd be thrilled. Reviews help readers find the books that will work for them and avoid the ones that won't, and that makes every single honest review invaluable to authors.

A word about the historical context. *The Petition for Reform of the Married Women's Property Law* is not a fictional document—every word of the petition I've included in my novel is taken directly from the real document, which was presented to Parliament on March 14, 1856. I've posted the complete text of the petition to my blog.

The characters and events related to the petition skew as closely to the real history as I was able to manage. Miss Smith, better known by her married name of Barbara Bodichon, organized the petition and Lord Henry Brougham sponsored it. Someone (though not Cordelia) really did stay up all night glueing the pages of the petition together, to allow for the dramatic unfurling.

As in the novel, the *Petition* ultimately failed. Caroline Norton —another real historical figure I've borrowed—ensured that certain provisions of the petition made it into the Matrimonial Causes Act of 1857, which (amongst many reforms) made it possible for women to sue successfully for divorce.

When I started writing, I assumed the passage of the 1857 Matrimonial Causes Act would be a triumph for early feminists. As I researched the progression of events, I was startled to realize that it was, instead, more like a consolation prize.

I was fascinated by the contrast between Bodichon and Norton. Bodichon was so far-thinking that most of the reforms she advocated for never happened in her lifetime. Norton had more limited ambitions but made several of them a reality.

The lesson is a bitter one, I think, and cuts the sweetness of my happily ever after. But that's also the thrill in writing about history; finding out what really happened and bringing it to life.

Any errors are, of course, my own. Though I've taken some liberties, I hope I've also thrown light on a little-known slice of history.

If this is your first book of mine, all of them mix romance with deep dives into the nooks and crannies of history. If you're interested in learning about my future work, sign up for my newsletter. Visit my webpage to get an overview of all my currently released books and to check out my blog, where I write about the books I'm reading and describe my research.

I'm always glad to hear from readers. Either send me an email at erin@erinsatie.com, pop by my blog, or look me up on Twitter at @erinsatie.

Or turn the page to try the first chapter of *Bed of Flowers*, the first book in the *Sweetness and Light* series. It's my take on Beauty and the Beast, featuring Cordelia's best friend Bonny.

BED OF FLOWERS

CHAPTER ONE

Bonny Reed walked the main street of New Quay with a heavy basket in her arms. Pearl-gray clouds massed on the horizon and a salt-scented breeze rattled the shutters on the shops. The storm wouldn't arrive for an hour or more, but Bonny quickened her steps all the same.

Her best friend and partner in the venture that they optimistically described as a circulating library—*optimistically* being her preferred word because optimism was good and lying bad—cast her an irritated look.

Cordelia, a tall woman with few curves to round out her slim frame, moved at an unhurried stroll no matter the occasion. Keeping pace with her meant slowing down or leaving her behind. Compromise was not an option.

Cordelia was the sort of girl people called stubborn.

Instead of slowing, Bonny nipped into the chandlery. A bell rang overhead, and Mr. Shaw, a retired seaman with salt-and-pepper hair and a leathery tan, rose from his desk behind the counter. The sweet scent of beeswax wafted up from the bundles of candles on the shelves, mixed with the bitter lye of soap.

"Miss Reed!" The stern expression stamped into Mr. Shaw's

wrinkles melted away, replaced by something soft and dreamy. "Seeing you is always the highlight of my day."

Bonny blushed. Her parents didn't care one way or another about the circulating library—"I'm glad you enjoy the project" was her mother's ringing endorsement—but they did insist that she always look her best.

That morning she'd put on a simple white gown so well-worn that it would have to be retired soon. But she'd tied a red silk sash around her waist and wrapped a fichu around her shoulders—she'd crocheted it herself—with the ends tucked into her décolletage.

"You're too kind," she replied. "Is Mrs. Shaw upstairs?"

"Here!" Mrs. Shaw brandished a book as she burst through the back door, pink-cheeked from exertion. "I saw you coming from the window and nipped upstairs to get last week's novel."

The slim volume boasted a pretty cover of flower-printed cotton that Cordelia had cut from one of her old gowns. Bonny's old clothes went to her sister; Cordelia's went to her books.

Bonny tucked it into her basket. "What did you think?"

"Mr. Dickens has a sharp wit about him, doesn't he?" Mrs. Shaw propped her hip against the counter, her shoulder just brushing her husband's. "I like his sense of humor."

"Me too." Bonny offered Mrs. Shaw a copy of *The Luck of Barry Lyndon*, sheathed in pink watered silk. "This is for you. I'll mark you down for a return visit in two weeks?"

Mrs. Shaw flipped the cover. Husband and wife bent their heads to examine the frontispiece, a watercolor of a sly young man in an ill-fitting officer's uniform.

"I can see *he's* up to no good." Mrs. Shaw traced the edges of the thick paper. "Is that Mrs. Henley's work?"

Bonny beamed. Mrs. Virginia Henley, the vicar's wife, had given Cordelia the pages and contributed the watercolor. She subscribed to *Fraser's Magazine*, where the novel had first appeared, and her gifts helped to keep their little library afloat.

"You've a good eye," said Bonny.

"Tell her that if the title weren't enough to make me want to read it, the picture would be."

"She'll be delighted."

"Thank you, dear." Mrs. Shaw beckoned Bonny close for a kiss on the cheek. "It's always such a pleasure to see you."

Bonny returned to the street, where Cordelia waited on the pavement. "Mrs. Shaw liked *The Pickwick Papers*."

Cordelia already had her little black book open to Mrs. Shaw's page, pencil at the ready. A neatly ruled grid listed the books Mrs. Shaw had borrowed, the dates given and returned, and a plus or a minus sign to indicate her opinion of it. *The Pickwick Papers* got a plus.

"And you gave her the Thackeray?" Cordelia asked.

"That's right."

Cordelia finished making her notes and tucked the book into the basket. They continued on to the salter's, where Mrs. Andrews exchanged an older Ainsworth for *The Pickwick Papers*. Mrs. Bailey at the Black Lion got *Jane Eyre*.

They visited fifteen homes on each delivery day and, by delivering two days a week—on Mondays and Thursdays—managed to cycle through all their members every fortnight.

They reached the elegant townhouse Cordelia called home, just before the rain arrived. "I'll see you on Thursday? You could come over a little bit early for tea."

Bonny bit her lip. The Kelly townhouse was beautiful and well kept, but she hated to accept invitations because she could rarely return the favor.

"With cakes," Cordelia added.

"You *know* how I feel about cakes," Bonny complained.

"I'll have Cook make the ones with raspberry filling and marzipan on top."

Bonny scowled. "Who taught you to be so cruel?"

Cordelia laughed and gave Bonny a one-armed hug. "I'll see you at eleven."

Rain began to fall as Bonny reached her own front door, only a few blocks down the same street as Cordelia's. The two houses were superficially very similar. Both built around the same time, from the same materials, with similar floor plans. Only the Kelly house was prosperous and well maintained while the Reed house was... not.

Mold blackened the mortar. The paint on the windowsills had begun to peel and the wood beneath to rot. Spots of rust mottled the brass lanterns bracketing the door.

Once Bonny stepped inside though, there was nowhere else she'd rather be. Several of her sister Margot's watercolors hung on the walls—mostly pictures of young people swooning tragically, plucked from the local theater productions her sister loved. Bonny, of a somewhat different temperament, had embroidered the runners and tablecloths in bright, cheerful patterns.

Fresh flowers filled the cheap glass vases scattered around the house—a few fine bouquets from Mr. Charles Gavin, Bonny's suitor, supplemented with simpler blooms collected during country rambles.

Margot darted into the foyer. At fifteen, she was tall and gawky, all legs and knuckles and nose. In a few years, she'd be elegant. As a matron, distinguished—like their mother. But she didn't have the temper to appreciate those reassurances, especially not from Bonny.

Probably because, for all their differences, they looked very much alike. They'd both inherited their mother's creamy skin, their father's mousy-brown hair and pale blue eyes.

"Bonny!" Margot whispered. "Bonny!"

Happy to play along, Bonny lowered her voice to a whisper too. "What is it?"

"Mr. Gavin is here."

"In secret?"

"No, silly! With Papa! They're alone!"

Bonny's heart skipped a beat.

Margot leaned so close that her breath fanned the loose strands of hair floating around Bonny's ear. "*He's proposing.*"

"Shush." Bonny grabbed her sister's shoulders and held her still, though it wasn't Margot who'd begun to tremble. "We don't know that."

She'd jumped to the wrong conclusion once before, two years ago. Her mother had been the one to whisper the news in the foyer: *Mr. Gavin is speaking with your father! Alone!* Bonny had been surprised, then delighted, then filled with a deep, glowing certainty. She'd been ready to become Mrs. Charles Gavin. She'd felt it down to her bones.

Then her father had emerged from his study with Mr. Gavin, and it quickly became clear that they'd been making plans for a hunting party. Nothing to do with marriage.

After that, Bonny had never quite regained her peace of mind. She had been ready. Ever since, she'd been *past* ready. If she'd seen any sign that Mr. Gavin's delight in bachelor life had begun to pall, she would have tried to bring him up to snuff. But he seemed content, so she tried not to get her hopes up anymore. It hurt too much to have them dashed.

But that was hard to explain to Margot.

"Margot, go to your room," said Mrs. Reed, bustling into the foyer. She had perfect posture and weary eyes, gray at her temples, and steady hands. Bonny admired her more than anyone else in the world.

"Bonny, why don't you come with me?" Mrs. Reed led the way. "We'll have some tea in the salon."

"In the salon?" That *did* sound serious. They reserved the salon for special occasions. With one exception, it didn't look much different from the rest of the house—a few pieces of simple furniture made locally. A few of Margot's paintings on the wall.

The exception was a large antique sofa. Made of heavy mahogany and upholstered with emerald-green silk brocade, a master woodworker had carved leaves and vines into the arms and legs.

It didn't belong in the room. It looked like exactly what it was:

an artifact of another life. A relic from the years when the Reeds had been wealthy and accustomed to luxury.

Those days were over—a devastating fire had brought them to an abrupt end—but before they'd sold all their fine things, everyone in the family had been allowed to choose one item to keep. Any item, though just one.

Bonny had chosen the painting that hung in her bedroom. Margot, who'd been five at the time, had decided on the sofa because she'd been convinced that fairies lived inside the carved foliage. Their father wanted the desk behind which three generations of Reeds had once helmed a thriving shipping concern. Their mother, exercising more sense than the rest of them combined, had safeguarded the house.

"You've been out all morning." Her mother gestured to the sofa. "Have a rest."

Bonny hesitated. Nobody ever *sat* on the sofa—they couldn't replace the silk, after all. Usually they maneuvered around it as though it were a sculpture in a museum.

Mrs. Reed gave Bonny's rear a gentle swat. "Don't be a goose."

The springs in the seat creaked as they sat, stiff from disuse. The family kept one servant, Emma, who handled the rough work, mostly cooking and cleaning. She wheeled in a rickety tea cart, and Bonny busied herself with measuring out the tea leaves, waiting for them to steep, and then pouring. She served her mother first.

Bonny's cup rattled in its saucer. She felt ridiculous and sick and terrified and tried for her most quelling tone. "It could be another hunting party."

Her mother smiled contentedly. "I put my ear to the door this time."

Bonny's breath caught in her throat.

"Breathe, dear," her mother prompted. "And drink your tea."

Bonny promptly scalded her tongue.

Mrs. Reed laughed. "Try again. By the time you've mastered the subtle art of sipping, I imagine we'll have company."

Just then the door to the salon opened. Her father and Charles Gavin entered. They made quite a contrast, standing side by side. Her father had heavy jowls and a shock of white hair, bright blue eyes and a deep, hearty voice. He'd been built stocky and thickened with age, his big barrel chest expanding in every direction while his legs remained stubby and short.

By contrast, Charles Gavin looked like he ought to be posing for a fashion plate. Tall, broad shouldered and trim waisted, he devastated the local tailors—each of whom longed for his patronage—by making periodic trips to London to outfit himself in the very latest fashions.

He'd been graced with fine features too, a high forehead and strong nose, a square jaw and perfectly straight teeth. He'd been the prize of New Quay since he was a boy: the handsomest, the best liked, and—since fortune had turned on the Loels—the richest.

He was everything a girl could want in a husband.

"Bonny dearest, Mr. Gavin would like to have a few words with you." Mr. Reed smiled at his wife. "Perhaps we should allow them a moment of privacy?"

"Just this once." Her mother stood and smoothed her skirt. She carefully positioned the door as she left, leaving it half-open. "We'll be in the next room."

"Miss Reed." Mr. Gavin strode to her. He took one of her hands and swallowed it in both his own. "How you dazzle me."

Bonny blushed. "You're too kind."

"You know that I've seen a bit of the world. I travel a great deal. I'm often in London." Mr. Gavin dropped down on one knee. "But I have never met another woman as beautiful as you."

"That can't be true."

"I assure you it is." Mr. Gavin squeezed her hand. "I confess, even a man who has everything feels the lure of a wife who will bring wealth or property to a marriage. It's not easy to turn away from the temptation. But I've given serious thought to the matter, and time after time, I reach the same conclusion. A woman who's beautiful *and* kind *and* rich will, quite rightly, set her sights on a man of higher rank than I. Though my family is good, my income excellent… I must sacrifice."

Bonny blinked. Was he admitting that, during the years when she'd patiently waited for his proposal, he'd been considering other options?

While down on one knee?

"I don't mean to be vulgar," Mr. Gavin continued, "but the fact of the matter is that I can make money without any help from a wife. Whereas I cannot make a woman more beautiful or teach her the exquisite feminine manners you display on every occasion."

"It's wonderful that you're so thoughtful and cautious," said Bonny, trying to believe her own words. "It's wise to consider all your options."

"Just so." Mr. Gavin smiled gently. "I want you to understand my thinking. It's important that we're of like minds. After all, we're talking about the rest of my life—or, should I say, the rest of *our* lives?"

Bonny pressed her fingers to her lips to stifle a startled, joyous cry. She blinked moisture away from her eyes, though the tears spilled over anyhow. Finally. *Finally.*

"Miss Reed, will you make me the happiest man in the world?" Mr. Gavin pressed his lips to the back of her hand. "Will you marry me and be the mother of my children?"

"Oh yes." Bonny threw her arms around Mr. Gavin's broad shoulders. "A thousand times, *yes.*"

Want to keep reading? Check your favorite online bookstore for *Bed of Flowers* by Erin Satie or click this link to buy it right now.

Made in the USA
Las Vegas, NV
26 March 2021

20245502R00184